THE DIDO DECRYPT

Charles Owen

Books by Charles Owen

Novellas:

FIAMMA

CRY CASSANDRA!

Telling Tales:

Vol. 1: A CRACK IN THE GLASS

Vol. 2: THE MARK OF THE BEAST

Vol. 3: MAN OVERBOARD

Vol. 4: ESCAPADE

Published by Charles B. Owen.
Copyright © Charles Owen 2017
Front cover photograph by:
Michael Rosskothen (Tank) www.shutterstock.com.
Paul Atkinson (Hunter) www.shutterstock.com
Back cover photograph by Andrzej Grygiel: Epa/Rex/Shutterstock.
Photograph of author by: Ed North. Alamy.
Cover Design by Tracey Winwood.
Map by Helen Stirling

Paperback ISBN: 978-0-9931552-4-6
Ebook mobi ISBN: 978-0-9931552-5-3

For

PIERRE

'I have a rendezvous with Death
At some disputed barricade . . .'

Alan Seeger

CONTENTS

MAP

PROLOGUE

5 a.m. Central European Time, 4 November 1956
The Legation of the United States of America,
Szabadság Square, Budapest, Hungary

Warren Rokeby shook the telephone receiver as if he were throttling a poisonous snake. 'Secretary of State, I do not need reminding that this is an open line but it's the only line we have and we may lose it any moment. Did you hear what I said? Four, possibly five thousand tanks crossed the Hungarian border early this morning. Ten, maybe fifteen Red Army divisions. The tanks will be in Parliament Square within the hour. We are expecting artillery shelling at first light. Then they will send the MiGs.'

'Where is the Minister?'

'Destroying sensitive documents, Secretary of State.'

'What is your rank?'

'I command the Marine Guard. My colleagues have their hands full trying to get American nationals to safety. We cannot wait while—'

'Hang on, Warren, the Security Council will be in emergency session in a few hours.'

'*In an hour, Secretary of State, we may all be dead.*' In his fury Rokeby thrust the receiver at the radio and turned up the volume. 'Listen to this!'

'*Help . . . help . . . SOS . . . we cannot hold out . . . tell the world we have almost no weapons . . . our young people are fighting in the streets . . . children are running up to tanks with petrol bombs . . . do not abandon us . . . for God's sake help us . . .* '

'Secretary of State! A nation is dying out there!'

'The West is trying—'

'*Damn the West!* The United States cannot just stand by and watch this happen.'

A shout from the compound in front of the Legation. A man was struggling with the marine on the gate. Behind him were a woman and a small boy. Warren Rokeby was still shaking with rage. He thrust open the windows and leaned over the balcony. '*Marine! What the hell's going on! Who are those people?*'

'I don't know, sir. Probably Hungarians. They may be criminals.'

The woman turned and pointed down the street. A desperate cry burst from her lips. Several heavily built men in long leather coats were coming round the corner. Now they were running. Falling to her knees, she stretched out her arms towards the figure on the balcony. The man at her side grabbed her by the shoulder and dragged her to her feet. He raised his arm as if to hit her and then let it fall despairingly.

The boy did not plead like his mother. Gripping the bars of the gate that separated them from sanctuary, he stared up at the face of the man who held their fate in his hands as if locking those features in his brain to the last vestigial detail. Now his eyes shifted to the woman who had joined her husband. The boy's face was frozen, carved out of ice. In the light from the street lamp, his hair glittered like frost.

Warren turned away. They were not his responsibility. Looters for all he knew. The woman shrieked as the police ran up to them and seized them, prising the boy's fingers from the gate. The man got his arms free for a moment and shook his fists at Warren as if he would bring the building tottering down about his head. '*MEGÁTKOZLAK TE, AMERIKAI!*' he howled. '*Be cursed, you Americans! You and your wife and all your family! From this day may you never know an hour free from fear! As long as I live and those who come after me live, we shall never forget! Be sure of it – we shall be avenged!*'

There was an appalled silence as if the listening darkness had heard the birth cry of something monstrous, something that would be working its purpose long after the terrors of that night were forgotten. The rattle of a diesel broke in upon the stillness and a van drew up in a screech of brakes. There was a slam of doors. The sound of the departing vehicle was lost in the renewed crackle of gunfire.

1

MAINE, USA

A YEAR EARLY IN THE NEW MILLENNIUM

Something told Mary Seton that it was going to be a bad day. She had slept restlessly, the foghorns droning like souls lost in the white miasma beyond the windows. Fog always made Warren jumpy. He hated the time of year, the biting cold, the dull March light. Up on the balcony with his binoculars, day after day, scouring the pink rocks that stretched like a granite bulwark along the seaboard. Scanning the low range of hills behind them, then the woods that ran down to the shores of the lake. Always on the look out.

She had lit the fire for him in the sitting room and left him in the big chair crouched beside the powerful short-wave radio, his eyes motionless, his head canted like a dog at the mouth of a rabbit hole, his fingers turning the knobs by minute gradations like an accomplished safe-breaker. Just a hobby, he told the handful of people who asked. Something to keep an old man occupied. After all, he had retired years ago, packed it in when the Cold War ended, shaken the snow of Moscow, Warsaw, Prague and the rest off his shoes. Come home.

She had been his housekeeper since the day he retired but she felt that she knew him no better than the day he engaged her. She had tried to be a mother to his son for years before that. Scott was barely two years old when his mother was killed.

Scott had come back to the US to do his schooling, sometimes staying with her during the holidays rather than return. It was not surprising. Sharing the beleaguered, claustrophobic life of a diplomat was no substitute for family life. Warren cannot have been an easy father. Difficult to get close to. He never got over his wife's death and it turned him into a lonely man.

Scott was not far short of forty. He had his father's square jaw but the dark eyes and the Slav cheekbones were his mother's. He kept an apartment in New York but he was rarely there. Occasionally he visited for a day's fishing or sailing. He had never really settled anywhere. Never put down proper roots. She used to think that it was just a question of him meeting the right girl. Now she wasn't so sure.

At eleven that morning she bustled into Warren's study with a cup of coffee.

He almost knocked her over in the doorway. 'Sorry, Mary, no time for that. I have to go to Europe. I must leave at once.'

'How long—'

'Under a week, God willing.'

He went upstairs to pack. She poured away the coffee and then returned to the study to tidy up. A newspaper was missing. One of the foreign ones. She went over to the fireplace. A few charred fragments had settled on the logs.

Warren pulled out the hunting rifle from under the bed, stowed it in a steel locker and took the key. On the bedside table there was a photograph of Erika, his wife, in the garden of their apartment in Prague. It was the last one taken of her.

He packed quickly, snapped the suitcase shut, and threw it on the bed. Closing the bedroom door, he picked up the telephone and called Railton Ross. He wanted to speak to Scott.

'I'm afraid he is in a meeting at this time—'

'Then you must interrupt that meeting.

'Very well, Mr Rokeby. I will see what I can do.'

'Have him call me back. Five minutes – no more.'

His eyes travelled round the room. Whitewashed walls, a chair, a table, a wooden crucifix above the narrow bed. More like a monk's cell

13

than a bedroom. He was not a religious man, not a man given to unreasoning fears. He believed in good and in evil. In evil incarnate. Most assuredly did he believe in that.

On the table lay the Zeiss binoculars, his second pair of eyes. There were two framed photographs. One of him in Korea in 1950 where he had taken a bullet in the thigh. The wound flared up again and in 1954 he went into hospital for treatment.

John F. Kennedy was there, convalescing from an operation for a spinal injury. The other photograph had been taken in the garden, the two of them, each with a glass in their hand, the most important friendship in Warren's life. Kennedy smiling at one of the nurses. He never could resist a pretty face – or the rest of the goods in the store.

In 1950 Warren had joined the marines. In Korea, he won rapid promotion to sergeant and was commissioned in the field at the Battle of the Chosin Reservoir. In 1956 he was a captain in command of the Marine Guard at the US Legation in Budapest during the Hungarian uprising. He resigned from the army in 1960 after seven years with the Marines and three in Military Intelligence.

He was twenty-seven, fluent in German and with a smattering of Hungarian, Russian and Polish. He joined the State Department. The Iron Curtain splitting Europe in half was the new front line and they wanted him there. The cemeteries with their acres of white crosses, the ships rusting in their ocean graveyards, the burnt-out hulks of tanks and warplanes with their relics of what had once been human – unless all that suffering and sacrifice was to go for nothing, men of his stamp were needed to go back. Warren became a cold warrior.

In 1965 he was posted to the US Embassy in Prague, Czechoslovakia, as military attaché. He married Erika, a Czech national, that same year. The State Department raised objections to his marriage to a foreign national of an iron curtain country and threatened to withdraw him. His ambassador did not want to lose him, intervened on his behalf and the marriage went ahead.

The following year, their son, Scott, was born. In 1968 the Czechs rose up against their Soviet oppressors. Erika's brother, one of the freedom fighters, was arrested by the secret police. Warren had locked his wife in her bedroom but she had got out of a window, climbed down a drainpipe and rushed out of the house into the darkness to search for her brother. Neither of them was seen alive again.

Warren's hand fell on the phone. 'Scott?'

'Sorry to keep you, Warren.' He mouthed an apology to his visitor, the vice-president of a large New York banking corporation.

'Do you fancy another trip to Europe?'

'Not now. I just got here.'

'I was only asking. Sorry to trouble you.'

'No trouble. Where are you going?'

'Paris for a start. I should be back inside a week. Got some loose ends to tidy up.'

'So long, Warren.'

'So long, Scott. Come up to the lake one weekend and we'll frighten a few fish. I don't see enough of you.'

'I would like that.' Scott never spoke to his father again.

2

THE PENTAGON, WASHINGTON D.C.

Mike Saxon, Secretary of State, prowled round the small room. 'The Pentagon has got four million square feet of offices,' he grumbled. 'Here we are in a top-level meeting and they shove us in the john.'

Sam Coaker, Secretary of Defense, bit off the end of his cigar. 'You asked for a small room, Mike. No aides, no calls, no bugs. Just the three of us. That's what you got.' He flicked through the report on his desk. 'I take it you've all read this crap. Because that's what it is. Canton, a CIA case officer in Geneva got lonely. Felt like writing home.'

'There's more to it than that. The guy – let's call him Pedlar – who sent the audio-tape is not just scared – he's bloody terrified. He's running around with our property and he wants to do a deal. While he's still breathing.'

'OK, Mike. But Canton couldn't identify him. The voice was disguised. There were no fingerprints. It worried him. He had to get it off his chest. So he told the Chief of Station. And the Chief of Station wanted to cover his ass so he sent it to Evaluation. That should have been the end of it.'

Saxon smiled thinly. 'But it wasn't. Someone slipped a note under my door.'

'And you just happened to pick it up.' Coaker levelled his cigar at Bradley Vaughan, Secretary of the Treasury. 'Brad—'

'Is that thing loaded, Sam?' Bradley asked. He was not wholly in jest.

'I wish it was, Brad. I surely wish it was.'

16

Saxon stopped by the window and straightened the blind. He was tall with strong angular features, and his shoulders drooped with weariness. 'It's no good sniping at each other. I don't share Sam's confidence. That officer is on to something. What do we tell the President?'

'Nothing,' Coaker rasped. 'This is between us three. Let's keep it that way. If the shit hits the fan he'll know soon enough.' He thrust out his huge jaw. He had boxed for the army. Never been put on the floor. And he didn't like changing his habits.

Vaughan took a handkerchief from his pocket and mopped his forehead. The room was cool but he was perspiring freely. 'I agree.'

Coaker smiled nastily. 'Sure. I would in your position.'

'That's not fair,' Vaughan protested. He tugged at his shirt collar.

'*Not fair!* Fifty million dollars walked out of the Fed more than forty years ago and the Treasury just looked the other way. And that dough is still out there!' He thumped the table with his great fist. 'By rights they should give you a job in the back office bagging dime pieces.'

Saxon took a chair. 'Now gentlemen, let's try to stay calm. Let's think back. The Cold War was at its height. The Berlin Wall had gone up. Concrete walls fifteen feet high dividing the city in half. Barbed wire and mines from the Baltic to the Black Sea, cutting Europe down the middle. The countries of the Warsaw Pact – Hungary, Czechoslovakia, Poland and the others – were no more than vassal states, their peoples enslaved. In Cuba, the Russians were building missile sites for weapons to be trained at American cities.'

'Kennedy had their measure.' said Vaughan.

'You had better believe it,' Saxon concurred. 'And Kennedy never forgot what happened to Hungary. Why? Because Warren Rokeby never let him forget. Rokeby was in the Legation in Budapest in fifty-six. In command of the Marine Guard. Up the sharp end. A few days of freedom – that's all the Russians gave the people. Then they came back and crushed them. The nearest GI was miles away with his head on a pillow.

Kennedy took that personally. What rankled with him was the double-dealing. Even the Russians knew that we wouldn't intervene. Ike told them. Hungary was a bad setback.'

'It was a disgrace, Mike. A national humiliation,' Coaker retorted. 'And it was something worse. It was a sham. Dulles's speeches about the liberation of Eastern Europe were being beamed to Hungarian radios. CIA and MI6 agents were in the forests outside Budapest training the Resistance.

'The Hungarians were led to expect that they would get support. Those who crossed the border during the uprising expected to find NATO armies in the field. We had plenty of muscle. We should have used it. A tactical nuclear strike would have pinned the Soviet Army back to its borders. A limited conflict in Europe might have lasted a week or two. What happened instead? Eastern Europe was turned into a prison camp and we got thirty years of Cold War.'

Saxon shook his head. 'Direct intervention would have meant a hot war. The critics say that what the French did at Suez gave Russia a free hand but that's rubbish. The Soviets had that already. The lines on the map were drawn at Yalta in 1945. What the Communists did on their side of the street was their business. That's what it amounted to. Anyway, Congress would never have allowed us to go in.'

'But when Kennedy became president he was determined to be in the driving seat. That meant having funds under his direct control.' Coaker scowled at Vaughan. 'Isn't that right, Brad?'

'All governments have slush funds,' Vaughan muttered. 'Politicians don't like admitting it – nor do central bankers. But it's a fact.'

Saxon pushed his chair back sharply. 'So Kennedy could have by-passed Congress. Set up a secret account somewhere, maybe in Central Europe, to support the next uprising against the Soviets. The Commies might suspect that we provided the finance but they couldn't prove it.'

Coaker screwed his cigar into the bottom of the ashtray. 'I can see you guys didn't major in armed insurrection. *Look!*' He numbered off on his stubby fingers. '*Fact* – a revolution is fucking chaos. Mobs charging round the streets, turning over buses, throwing paving stones, torching cars, using telephone boxes for arms dumps. Hotheads standing on ammunition boxes at street corners making inflammatory speeches.

'*Fact*. Effective power – control of the news channels, the police, the army, the airports is changing from hour to hour. A dozen splinter groups each claiming that they are running the show. How do you find your leader out of that lot? And if you find him how do you know he isn't going to piss off with your money? And even if he is the right guy, how do you know he is going to be alive an hour later?'

Coaker glared at the other two men but he was not interrupted. '*Fact* – you can have cheque books, secret accounts, you can have a mountain in dollar bills but they won't stop a T54 with a shell up the spout. Revolutions need arms and they need ammunition. And they can't wait for the banks to open. The Russian Ground Forces don't telephone for an appointment. They just turn up.'

Vaughan reached into the briefcase beside his chair and pulled out a single sheet of buff paper. He pushed it across the table.

Coaker stared at it suspiciously. 'What the hell is that?'

'It's money. It comes in a dozen different forms. This is a bearer bond.'

'So what?' Coaker snorted. 'I'm still no wiser.'

'It's as good as the cash that backs it. It could be scrap paper – or worth millions.'

'But it still isn't cash, Brad,' Saxon protested. 'How do you turn it into cash? How does the revolution get the money to buy its arms? Forget the banks – they could be a heap of smoking rubble.'

'What Mike is saying,' snarled Coaker,' is that your revolutionary chief has a Russian airborne division up his backside and all you've sent him is a few scraps of paper to wipe his ass.'

'That may be all he needs. A scrap of paper with a few numbers that he can text with a mobile phone. The funds could be transferred to arms dealers in seconds. They could be making air drops within the hour.'

Coaker groaned. 'Does the news get any worse?' He leaned forward. 'Don't fart around, Brad. Give it to us in one hit.'

Vaughan spoke quietly. 'I can't tell you if that fund is in bearer bonds or what sort of system JFK set up but over the years it must have been upgraded. My guess is it's protected by security codes – encryption keys, if you want to be technical.'

'And if the bond was stolen?' Saxon shook a cigarette into his hands and lit up.

'Whoever stole it could use it. All they need are the codes.'

'*Jesus Christ!*' Coaker's fingers drummed a tattoo on the table. 'What if a terrorist organisation got hold of that sort of dough?'

Saxon drew deeply on the cigarette. 'They could get more mileage for each million dollars than at any time in half a century. Fortress America has pulled up the drawbridge. Our people won't tolerate any more military adventures. Forget the Brits and the French. Iraq and Afghanistan have bled them white.' He squared the papers in front of him. 'Have either of you guys heard of DIDO?'

Vaughan shifted in his chair. 'I didn't hear that, Mike. *Nobody* has heard of DIDO. The President is stone deaf in that ear.'

'Well, pin your ears back. Rokeby has heard of DIDO. He has a short-wave radio. The traffic is heavily encrypted. NSA has been trying to break into it for years. Yesterday they managed to decode a couple of words. DIDO ALERT. Rokeby was on a plane the same day.'

Coaker left his chair and went to the window. 'That fits. First Pedlar. Now Rokeby,' he muttered.

Saxon gave Coaker a long steady look. 'I know the way your mind is working, Sam.'

'Tell me, Mike. I would like to know myself.'

'Find out what Rokeby knows. Sweat it out of him if need be. Then go after Pedlar. Send an undercover team to Geneva. Lift up a few stones, see what's underneath – and don't put them back too gently.'

Coaker raised his eyes to the ceiling. 'I won't pretend it hadn't occurred to me.'

Saxon spoke slowly, weighing his words. 'Forget it, Sam. Keep your gorillas caged up. I'll send round a bunch of bananas. Lift the latch and the President will have a report of this meeting within the hour.'

'Is that a threat, Mike?' Coaker raised his fists like a prize fighter waiting for the bell.

'It's a promise.'

Coaker's huge fist crashed down on the table. *'So what do we do for Chrissake?* Fart around filing intelligence reports? Watch the fuse burn all the way to the powder keg? We used to have something called a foreign policy.'

'We used to have something called a defence policy,' Saxon snapped back. 'What about your supergun? That was a game-changer – but it never left the drawing board.'

'It was too heavy. It would need a regiment to move it. But as an infantry weapon, there would be nothing to touch it. We'll get there one day.'

'Well, pray that our enemies don't get there before we do. Greed we can live with. Theft we can cope with. But fanaticism is something else. Bonds and codes translated into cash. Cash turned into a superweapon in the hands of violent, rootless nihilists whose sole ambition is to wreak destruction on a scale that will make the San Francisco earthquake look like a few slabs of misplaced concrete. Is that what we have now? *A waking nightmare?'*

'What do you propose?'

'Warren Rokeby has flown to France. We trace him and we put a tail on him. As for Pedlar, Canton must winkle him out of hiding. If Pedlar has those bonds, we have to get to him first.'

21

Vaughan gathered up the files and put them in the shredder. The three men, their faces taut with strain, made for the door. What remained of the old certainties had gone. The ground was shifting under their feet.

3

NEW YORK

Mary Seton telephoned Scott at his office. 'I didn't want to bother you, Scott, but I'm worried. Warren has been gone two days.'

'Warren is a bit of a lone wolf, Mary. You must know that after all these years. And you know how he hates anyone fussing about him.'

'Sure I know, but he has his rules and he sticks to them. He goes to Europe March and September, regular as clockwork. Never says where he is going – just that he has got to keep an eye on things.'

Scott laughed. 'That sounds like him. He's always been pretty close about his affairs. All the same—'

'Hear me out, Scott. This is his third trip in the past three months.'

'I wouldn't worry too much about that.'

'*Well, worry about this*. He always telephones me at six in the evening, Maine time. He's never missed.'

Scott was listening now. The alarm bells were ringing. They should have sounded sooner. Warren had wanted him on this trip. He had never done that before. 'When he checks in, Mary, what does he say?'

'He asks if there are any messages. Urgent messages.'

The old man retires, drops his former acquaintances, buries himself in the middle of nowhere, lives like a hermit and calls in for his urgent messages. 'And are there ever any urgent messages?'

'No.'

'You don't think he's . . . ill?'

'*Off his head?* Is that what you mean?' Mary Seton was very direct.

'He's getting old, Mary. His mind may not be as good as it was.'

'There's nothing wrong with his mind,' she retorted.

'Did he seem worried at all these last few days?'

'When *doesn't* he seem worried? Poring over those foreign newspapers, glued to that radio of his, pacing up and down that balcony.'

Scott flicked over a page in his diary. Scribbled a note. 'Let's give it another day, Mary. He'll call in tomorrow. You'll see.'

Mary Seton sat at the window, watching the snow flurries gusting round the eaves. Did Warren have any enemies? Those hours up on the balcony with the binoculars day after day. Questioning her when she got back after shopping whether she had seen any strangers in town. That loaded rifle he kept under his bed. Was there something in his past that made him afraid?

After all these years, she still knew so little about him. Only once had the veil been partly drawn aside. One winter, he had gone down with double pneumonia. She had sat up with him a whole night while he fought the fever, raving or rambling by turns, the sweat running from him like a stream. At the height of the delirium he had half-risen from the bed and grabbed hold of her, his eyes dilated in horror, saliva trickling from the corners of his mouth. He had babbled of a woman who had gone down on her knees to him, a man who had cursed him, cursed him horribly. A boy with the face of an avenging angel, with hair that glittered like frost, with eyes that burned into your very soul.

She sighed. It was gibberish. Wild, fantastic talk. But when Warren recovered, he had questioned her closely. In his fever, had he said anything? She had reassured him. After all, what did it amount to but the incoherent gabbling of a sick man.

She did a tour of the house. When she came to Warren's bedroom she picked up the binoculars. It was a comfort somehow to hold them in her hands. She went to the window. The light was failing but on the far side of the lake she could make out a car parked under the trees. There were two men inside, their heads turned towards her, their faces partly obscured. Were they using binoculars? She tugged the curtains across the window. Why didn't folk mind their own business instead of prying into other people's lives? She put down the glasses. Pull yourself together, Mary Seton, she told herself. Stop behaving like a jittery old maid. Why should anyone be watching the house?

She would be round later to check the security lighting. Warren liked to be able to see the whole garden at night right up to the eight foot wire fence. She opened the door of his study and drew the curtains tightly together. For a moment she stood looking down at the cheerless grate, the unlit lamp beside the deep leather armchair and the radio set with its myriad voices muted. She couldn't help herself thinking of one voice that she might never hear again.

Scott yawned and stretched. Rising from his desk in a corner of the sitting room, he dropped his files into his briefcase. It had been a long day and there had been several hours' work when he got back to his apartment preparing for the next morning's board meeting.

It was under a week since he got back to New York but he was already restless. He had seen all eight companies in the group and put out feelers towards acquiring another two. Five countries in ten days. You had to be a bit of a maverick to enjoy the life. For eight months a year home was a plane or a train or a hotel bedroom. A typical evening was talking business with his colleagues over a bottle of the local panther piss.

The apartment on the tenth floor was a perch like the mast of a ship for a bird in mid-passage. On the desk was a framed photograph of his parents taken on honeymoon. He couldn't remember his mother. His father was still almost a stranger, even after all these years. On the mantelpiece was a college photo and a few silver cups he had won at polo.

He took his polo seriously, flying down to the club in Palm Beach, Florida, most weekends during the season. His handicap had reached a level where sponsors looking for high-goal players were prepared to bankroll him. For the last two seasons Joel Montford had met the bills. Montford had oil money and plenty of it but he was close to pulling out. 'Find another backer, Scott,' he had said, 'unless you can spend more time in the saddle and less warming a seat for the airline companies.'

Occasionally he went up to Maine for a weekend but that was no holiday. The old man was as jumpy as a marlin with a hook in its gullet and always relieved to see him go.

He was in bed and asleep when the phone rang. Cursing, he fumbled for the light switch. It was Jeff Turcan, Railton's chief executive.

'Scott? Are you asleep?'

'I was.' He checked his watch. 'It's only three o'clock in the morning. I can't think what came over me.'

'I'm sorry but I just got a call from our embassy in Paris.'

'Lou Vyner?'

'Yeah. He's just got hold of an advance copy of a privatisation list. It's red hot.'

'Which country?'

'It's your territory – that's all he would tell me. He's got a line to a minister there. If anyone knew he had tipped us off he'd be in trouble.'

'Who else has he told?'

'Fraser Outram.'

'That fits.' The company was their closest rival. Jeff's father had started it, built it up with the help of his sons and made a pile when it went public. Jeff and his father had never got on and eventually they had parted, Jeff to start Railton, while his brother Todd took over running Fraser Outram when his father retired. 'Lou has made some good contacts with eastern European companies looking for a tie-up with a US outfit. It's his pension plan. The day he retires he'll be knocking on our door asking for a consultancy.'

'Meanwhile he's trying to do us a favour. I wouldn't want Todd to steal a march on us.'

'Fraser Outram doesn't operate in Europe.'

'Not yet. But this could be just the break they're looking for.'

What was the point of telling Jeff that he didn't target companies that had been run by communist apparatchiks for half a century? That it took too long to change the culture, that the politicians would steal most of the privatisation shares, that they could have them for all he cared. Lou Vyner had sent the silver dollar spinning into the air and Jeff wanted to beat his brother to the draw.

'I'll fly to London tomorrow night after the board meeting, make a few calls and go on to Paris. Meanwhile I would like to get some sleep.'

Railton Ross occupied the tenth floor of a glass and steel tower close to Wall Street. The boardroom was furnished with an oval table, some greenery in the corners and abstract paintings on the walls. The meeting was almost over. Jeff Turcan looked pleased, as well he might. Profits in the companies in which Railton had a controlling interest were sharply up. The documentation was being prepared for an initial public offering. Within the week, a detailed registration statement would be filed with the Securities Exchange Commission. All going well, the company would have a listing on the American Stock Exchange inside a couple of months.

Jeff Turcan poured himself another cup of coffee. He was overweight and balding. Walking up a flight of steps was enough to leave him out of breath. He looked at the agenda in front of him. 'Any other business?'

Mal Hain nodded. 'I've been checking out a company making self-diagnosis kits which might fit into our operation. Small potatoes at the moment but it's got a hell of a future. Press a button and you can check out your blood sugar level, cholesterol, alcohol – you name it.'

'*You name it, Mal*,' said Scott. The others laughed. Mal's reluctance to divulge the identity of a target company before he had all the credits under his name was well known.

Hain's eyelids came down like shop blinds at closing time. 'I shall report to the board when I'm good and ready,' he said sullenly.

Ben Gowan had a point on staffing. 'Most of us round this table were trained in law or accountancy. We have sector analysts, experts on taxation, corporate finance and so on. But we need more scientists.'

'Ben's right.' Liz Usborne took a deep breath, inflating her white silk blouse for the benefit of the audience. 'Railton has come up fast on the back of a reputation for rewarding investors quickly. We pick high-tech companies with a protected position in the market place and grow them fast. But product assessment is everything and we lack the expertise in-house. Going outside for it costs us time – and money.'

Turcan's eyes panned round the table. 'We all know there's a problem. In pharmaceuticals and biotech we are light on scientists, but if we employed what we need we would double our overheads. It's not on.'

'Pick the best companies and put in first-rate management. Leave it to them to get their products right,' said Bill Marquand. For the benefit of Liz Usborne, he tucked a lock of dark hair behind his ear. In his candy-striped shirt he looked like an advertising executive. He was the weakest member of the board and sprinkled his sentences with adjectives like 'high quality', 'first rate' and 'top class' as if their repeated incantation would provide a counterweight for his vestigial management skills.

Scott let the debate wash over him. The companies he had brought to Railton employed 20 per cent of the group capital but they had kicked in with almost 80 per cent of the profits – this despite the handicap of operating in an undeveloped market and under governments by no means converted to the capitalist system. It was a good performance, but at Railton Ross success was taken for granted. If things went wrong he wasn't sure how far he could count on his colleagues' support. There were those who would take him on one side at the end of a contentious board meeting and tell him they would go to the stake with him over some point of principle – but when he climbed on to the woodpile he had an uneasy feeling he would find them helping to unwrap the firelighters.

Jeff Turcan tapped on the table. 'A few thoughts on privatisation in Eastern Europe before we wind up.'

Jeff knew as much about Eastern Europe as one can learn from a comfortable armchair in Warsaw's Marriott Hotel. What he knew about privatisation could be written on the back of a postage stamp but he liked to encroach on areas of expertise his colleagues considered their own. It was one of the boardroom games that people played. As Scott listened wearily he wondered whether there was a more specific reason. The meeting was scheduled to end at eleven and Jeff would talk out the remaining time rather than have him raise the issue of the share allocation in the initial public offering.

Jeff Turcan and Mal Hain controlled Railton with 60 per cent of the voting shares, split forty-five to fifteen. There was an institutional holding of 20 per cent. The remaining 20 per cent was split equally between Gowan, Marquand, Usborne and himself. Each of the four was responsible for a profit centre. Gowan had pharmaceuticals, Marquand biotech, Liz Usborne healthcare computer services and Scott Eastern Europe.

To give Jeff Turcan his credit, he had bought a business that was going nowhere, put in some money, borrowed more, restructured it and given it a sharp focus. Bringing in Hain as an administrator was an astute move. Hain was Jeff's creature. If it came to a vote, his 15 per cent share would follow his master.

Jeff and Scott had met in Frankfurt. Scott was working in the corporate finance side of one of the big banks. The Germans had put a mountain of money into Eastern Europe. Scott was spending three weeks in every four there.

Over a glass of Löwenbräu at the airport, Scott had spelt out the opportunities. Good profits could be made if you could manage the risks. Corruption was rife. A venal government official or a crooked employee could put a company out of a business overnight but the problems had a big upside – they frightened off the amateurs.

Scott was competent in the languages, he knew the area and he had the training. Jeff made him an offer. He would have an equity stake. This was a chance for him to make some capital for the first time. They considered Russia and rejected it. Scott had spent nine months in Moscow and St Petersburg and he didn't like what he saw. A country where the local Mafia had a stranglehold on the newly privatised corporations. A country with ten thousand private security firms, a high proportion of them with criminal connections. A country where it cost two hundred dollars to get a man killed and a businessman could spend three times that on a bodyguard and still waste his money. Others could have it and welcome.

They settled on five countries – Hungary, Poland, the Czech Republic, Croatia and Ukraine. The first three were medium risk, the last two were for punters who liked a shot of adrenaline with their company reports. That was way back. His 5 per cent stake had been a fair offer at the time but things had changed.

Scott had crossed swords with Jeff over the shareholding at the previous board meeting. He had no beef with the compensation package. It was the 5 per cent stake that stuck in his throat. 'It's hardly more than a token interest. Railton Europe is producing the bulk of the profits.'

'I set up the company, Scott,' Jeff countered. 'It needed a major turn-around. That was a big risk and I took it. Without me there wouldn't be a business to argue about.'

'Without me your business wouldn't have the profit level you need for a SE listing.'

Jeff had smiled nastily. 'Has it ever occurred to you that you might have taught us how to run the European side without you?'

Scott had laughed to disguise his anger. 'It's bandit country, Jeff. You need more than a MBA and set of risk assessment reports to make money there.'

Jeff's neck had flushed a dusky red. 'In Railton Ross, you are as good as your last set of figures,' he had said belligerently. 'Try to remember that.' His eyes went to the door as if to say that if Scott wasn't happy he could put on his coat, leave his car keys on the desk and get his ass out of there.

Today the meeting broke up with Jeff announcing that he had been given a tip-off by a top diplomat. Lou Vyner would have hardly recognised himself. Scott would be flying back to Europe later that day to follow it up.

He shook his hand. 'I'm sorry we haven't seen more of you on this trip, Scott.' *Like hell he was.* Scott went to his office. He needed to call his father's travel agency.

The manager didn't know that Warren had flown to Europe. 'Mr Rokeby usually books through us but not this time.'

'Can you pull a few strings? Find out what flight he took?'

'Is it important?'

'It could be.' A pause. *This is where he puts the bite on me.*

'We would like to handle some of your firm's business, Mr Rokeby.'

'I'll see what I can do.'

'That's good to hear. One last thing. Would your father have travelled under his own name?'

Why not? His father didn't go in for amateur theatricals. Within the hour he had his answer. Warren had flown to JFK and taken an Air France flight to Paris.

Scott checked his luggage. The compact leather case held a zip-down laptop and an overnight grip. He slotted a recent photograph of Warren into a fold in his wallet. He would fly to London and call at the embassy in the morning. In the afternoon he would try to see Greg Luppitt, a retired diplomat and a friend of his father. The next day he would go to Paris.

It was growing dark when the Boeing lifted off and in a few minutes the last glimmer on the corrugated surface of the Atlantic had faded. He unfastened his seat-belt, settled back into the seat and tried to stretch his legs. There was never enough room in these darned things. He closed his eyes, running over the last hours. There had been just time for a call to Mary Seton.

'I'll keep in touch,' he told her. 'Don't contact Railton or we'll get our wires crossed.'

'Is there hope?'

'Of course there is. I can think of half a dozen things that could have gone wrong.' He had been bracing. He didn't believe a word of what he was saying. Nor, he supposed, did she. Warren was missing. A cold wind was blowing through their lives.

4

LONDON

Dawn was breaking as the Boeing touched down at Heathrow airport. The clouds were low and rainwater stood in shallow pools on the runway. Within half an hour, he was through customs and a taxi was taking him to the Travellers Club.

It drew up in front of an elegant period building in the heart of London's clubland. Stepping through the doors was to return to an earlier and more gracious age of open fires and leather armchairs, oil paintings on the walls and silver entrée dishes on the sideboard. The British did not so much live in the past as live off it, puffing along in pursuit of the present in the cheerful expectation that they would never quite catch up.

He washed and shaved in his room and had a quick breakfast. At ten o'clock he was walking up the steps of the American Embassy. Colin Filner was the Minister for Commercial Affairs. He was brisk and impatient, his dark eyes returning every few seconds to the crowded diary in front of him. The guy had problems. Obsessions. The situation in Russia with crime and corruption at the highest levels, much of the country's wealth in the hands of a few obscenely rich individuals.

Germany was united in name only. Democracy had never taken root. The Neo-Nazi movement was growing in strength and confidence with every day that passed. As for Britain – Britain was an irrelevance. Uncertain whether she was in Europe or out of it. But her civil servants still went on writing reports, briefing ministers for roles for which a hundred years of national decline disqualified them.

They talked for some minutes about the levels of World Bank lending in Eastern Europe and the development of the financial markets. 'There's a good paper on investment opportunities in Eastern Europe in the Department of Trade and Industry,' the Minister told him. 'I'll put a call through. They can have a copy waiting for you at reception.' Before he left, Scott mentioned casually that his father was in Europe and asked whether he'd been in touch. One of Filner's colleagues recognised the name but that was from years back.

He took a taxi to Victoria Street, collected the papers at the desk and lingered for a moment. The girl on reception was lovely, her blonde hair tight against her head, a wide smile, a pert little nose, long eyelashes, youth and ripeness pushing at the crisp, white blouse.

He turned sharply at the sound of an altercation behind him. A young woman in an anorak and jeans was struggling with two burly security guards. Business men in dark suits demonstrating the British genius for ignoring uncomfortable situations quickened pace as they made for the revolving doors.

'*Let me go you . . . you apes!*' she cried. '*You have no right . . .* ' She twisted and turned in their arms, the guards staggering from side to side in their efforts to control her.

'We have our orders . . . Miss . . . not to let you in.' The two men started to drag her towards the door.

Scott crossed the hall in rapid strides and caught one of the guards by the elbow. 'I'm sure this isn't necessary. Why not ask her politely?'

'We've tried that, sir.' A red, perspiring face jerked round. 'And I'll thank you to mind your own business.' He gave a cry of pain. '*You little bitch!*' He dropped his hands, doubling up to nurse himself. But the girl had won only a moment's respite. They tightened their grip on her and with a final shove spun her out of the doors with such force that she floundered, splay-legged like a new-born foal in a desperate effort to keep her balance.

Scott plunged after her, snatching at her arm in an attempt to stop her falling. Shaking him off, she turned a flushed, infuriated face on him. *'Why can't you sod off and stop interfering?'* Tears of rage and frustration streamed down her cheeks.

Scott stepped back, raising his hands in surrender. 'Sorry, I thought you needed help.'

'Well, I don't! Anyway, much help you were.' She unzipped her jacket and examined the small camera hanging from her neck. 'If those two thugs have damaged this, I'll serve a writ on the minister himself.'

'In person.' His lips twitched.

'Yes!' She shouted at him. *'In person!* And stop grinning at me! What do you find so funny?' She pushed a hand through a tangle of dark hair. 'God knows what I look like.'

'You look a mess.'

She smiled. It lit up her whole face. 'If you had said something nice I would have chucked something at you. I'm not in the mood for compliments.'

'I'm not handing out any but if you promise to find a comb, I'll buy you a cup of coffee.'

They found a café and perched on tall stools by the window. She took a paper napkin and dabbed at the smudges of blood on her hands. Her fingers were still trembling.

Scott held a lump of sugar over her cup. 'How many?'

'Ten.'

'I'll make it two and I'll stir. You are shaking so much you'll have the coffee in your lap. Or mine.'

She sipped noisily through gritted teeth. 'I wish my hands were shaking round the necks of those brutes.'

'Why wouldn't they let you in?'

'Orders.' She stared morosely through the grimy window. Outside it was cold and grey. Passers-by had their hands in their pockets, collars turned up.

'Whose orders?'

'Forget it,' she said quietly. 'It's my problem.'

They drank up in silence. Scott picked up his briefcase. 'I'm taking a taxi. Can I drop you off somewhere?'

'I've got a flat in Fulham. I ought to go back and tidy up. Is it out of your way?'

'Not far.' He flagged down a taxi.

He introduced himself.

She nodded. 'Julie Dixon. I'm a journalist when I get paid, which isn't as often as I'd like.' She relapsed into silence. Once she turned and stole a glance through the rear window. The closer they got the edgier she became, moving to the tip-up seat opposite and staring over the driver's shoulder.

She tapped urgently on the glass. 'This will do.'

'It's another hundred yards, Miss—'

'I know. But please stop here.' She was out of the door before the taxi had come to a stop.

'I thought you was goin' on, guv . . . ' The driver kept the meter running.

'I thought so too.' Scott pushed a note into the man's hand and caught Julie up. He pointed across the road to where a small crowd was standing outside a red-brick house, one of a terrace of identical buildings. 'Do you live there?'

'Yes, worse luck. In the basement.'

Heads turned and there was a little stir of excitement as they pushed through and went down the steps. The iron bars over the window had been wrenched apart and the window forced. Small flakes of paintwork speckled the ground.

The door was open. As they entered, a woman police constable rose from her chair at the table and switched off the television.

'Anything good on?' Julie enquired with heavy sarcasm.

'I can't do any more here until the officer comes from Fingerprints,' the WPC replied sourly.

The bed-sitting room was a scene of utter confusion. The bedding had been stripped and piled in a corner, drawers had been opened and overturned, flower pots emptied and their contents strewn across the carpet. The screen of the word processor was smashed and the computer casing crumpled out of shape.

The WPC pulled out her notebook. 'You will be Miss Dixon?'

'Nobody's told me different.'

The woman pursed her lips and made a note. 'Where were you last night?'

Julie glowered at her. 'I was staying with a friend.' She flung a hand at the chaos about her.

'Surely *someone* must have *heard* something? *Seen something? The place has been trashed.*'

'We've interviewed most of the flat-owners.' The policewoman sounded resentful. 'The couple on the ground floor did hear a disturbance, but they didn't investigate.'

'Prudence seems to have got the better of community spirit.' Scott righted an upturned lamp. 'It happens in New York too.'

The WPC gave him a frosty look. 'They would have done better to call us. We weren't alerted until seven this morning when the milkman was doing his rounds.' She turned to Julie.

'Is this gentleman with you?'

Julie shrugged. 'I never got -round to asking.' She went over to the window. 'How did they get through the bars?'

The policewoman shook her head. They both looked at Scott.

'The burglar – or burglars – used a car jack. You can see the marks. If you get the right model, they're very effective.'

'Is that so?' The WPC turned a page of her notebook. 'And what line are you in, sir?' From her tone she might as well have asked him what branch of felonious activity kept him busy.

'I'm a businessman,' Scott told her flatly.

An hour of questions, answers and note-taking followed and it was another hour before the fingerprint officer had finished and they had the place to themselves.

Julie shouted up the steps, 'The show's over for today, folks! *You can all bugger off home.*' There was a babble of indignation and then the sound of retreating footsteps.

She went to a cupboard in the kitchen, pulled out a bottle of Johnny Walker and poured out two stiff glasses. 'Sorry. No ice. You didn't tell me you were coming.' She took a long gulp. 'Where did they find that policewoman? Did you see the way she asked the fingerprint man to start in the kitchen so that she could make herself a cup of tea?'

'But the policeman wasn't dumb. You could see he was puzzled. Why smash up the computer? Why leave the video and the TV? Are you sure there isn't any jewellery missing?'

'*Jewellery!*' she snorted. 'Do I look like the sort of person who has jewellery?' She glanced down at the bedside table and gave a little moan of distress. The photograph of her with her brother had been taken. She shot a glance at Scott but he had the clock to his ear.

'When did you last sleep here, Julie?'

She buried her nose in her glass. 'Three nights ago.'

'Why?'

'Why not? ' She met his eyes, then dropped them. 'Because I was frightened, if you must know.'

The telephone rang. She placed a hand on his arm. The colour left her face. There was a click from the answering machine as it took over the call.

'This is a message for Julie Dixon . . . '

'*Quiet!*' she mouthed at Scott, her fingers digging into his arm like dogs' teeth.

'There is no need for alarm, Julie,' the voice continued. 'It is a friend calling. We know that you have been making some investigations and we have some information which will be of great value to you. Come to the Peace Pagoda at midnight tonight. Battersea Park will be closed but you will find the gate at the end of Albert Bridge is open. Keep this to yourself and come alone.' The message ended.

Scott stared at her. 'Who the hell was that?'

'I haven't the remotest idea.' She turned away, the blood returning to her cheeks.

He laughed scornfully. 'Of course it's a trap. A child could see that.'

'How can you be so sure?'

'I'm sure – but run it again.'

A man's voice, a foreign accent, an undercurrent of menace. Dark, echoing vowels.

'It's probably a recording, Julie. He's trying to disguise it. Don't tell me you're going to show up?'

'I must. Some of my best leads have been from people who don't want publicity. Anyway taking risks is part of my job.'

Scott shrugged. 'It's your neck. But I think you're crazy.' He looked round the room. 'I don't like leaving you with all this mess.'

Julie crouched down and started scooping earth off the carpet and back into the flower pots. 'You've made your little speech,' she said quietly, 'and as you can see I have a few things to do. So it would help if you just cleared off.'

'I'm going. But take my advice. Change your friends.'

'I've had advice . . . ' she swept the edge of her hand across her throat, 'up to here.'

'Then take some more. The police pick up girls like you every morning crammed into bin liners with their heads the wrong way round.'

'How come you know so much about it?' Her chin went up a defiant notch but her face was grey.

'It wouldn't interest you.'

'You're right. It doesn't.'

But he hesitated at the door. 'Suppose we make a deal, Julie? You tell me what's going on. I'll come along tonight and stay out of the way unless you get into trouble. Isn't that fair?'

A long moment of reflection and then she nodded. 'All right. But keep clear unless there's trouble – and I mean real trouble. If this bloke just wants to horse around, leave him to me. I can be very discouraging when I'm pissed off.'

'I've noticed. Now tell me why—'

'Why would someone want to break in here and trash the place?' She unzipped the inside pocket of her anorak and dropped a disk on the table. 'That's what the fuss is about. This disk holds the locations of every private airfield that I've managed to track down.'

'Where?'

'The UK, France, Germany, Belgium and Holland. Some are no more than strips of grazing land. At least that's what people are meant to think. Farmhouses with their barns and grain silos are wonderful cover. So is horse racing. There are specialist companies in the business of flying owners, trainers, jockeys and bloodstock all over the world but often that's just a front.'

'Front for what?'

'Moving drugs or arms or illegal immigrants or dirty money.'

'How can one—'

'Girl?' The chin went up again.

He smiled. 'How can one person cover all that?'

'I'm concentrating on the night movements. The Civil Aviation Authority couldn't help so I switched to the Department of Trade. I tried telephoning. I tried writing. The only answer was to kick in a few doors.'

'But you made yourself such a pain in the ass, they won't have you in the building.'

Julie picked up a drawer and shoved it back into place. 'I give as good as I get. One of those guards will have his dick in a splint when he reports for work tomorrow morning.'

'Do you behave any better on the continent?'

'Paris, Frankfurt, Brussels – you name it – I run into the same brick wall, the same excuses. I have to get my information under the counter. Air shows. Flying clubs. It's amazing what a girl can pick up in the bars when the beer has done a few rounds.'

'With dinner thrown in and a bed for the night.'

Julie tossed her head. 'I'm not ashamed of it. I didn't invent the system. You've got to use what you've got or pack it in and run a children's creche.'

Scott smiled. 'I'll let that go. Who else do you tap up?'

'Insurance brokers . . . air charter executives . . . anyone who will buy me a drink and run off at the mouth.'

Scott turned over the disk in his hands. 'Is this really what they were after?'

'Yes. All they found was the disk I was working on. Mercifully it had very little on it.' She drained her glass. 'Someone out there is worried. That means I'm getting close.'

'And so are the guys who turned over this place.' He looked at the poky sitting room with its Sin City comic book posters on the walls, its battered sofa, the tiny galley kitchen. 'Travel in Europe doesn't come cheap. This research must be costing plenty.'

Julie laughed ruefully. 'I can tell what you're thinking. How do I live? There's nothing here that a junk shop would give more than a tenner for. My paper pays me a low basic and expenses, but if I get the story I want I get well paid for it.'

'A story? Is that what drives you? A few column inches in some rag. You strike me as being the crusading type.'

'Well, I'm not.' She straightened a picture on the wall, avoiding his eye. 'I owe a couple of month's rent and it isn't going to get paid by chattering to you.' She looked at her watch. 'The Peace Pagoda at midnight.'

'I'll be there. But you leave that disk behind. Better still – put it in the bank.'

'OK. I'll do that. But remember, I don't want to see you or hear you unless thing's get nasty.'

'Don't worry. They will.'

5

THE PEACE PAGODA

Julie tucked her hair under her beret and hunched down into her raincoat. It was blowing hard and the rain was driving in from the west. She could feel the water trickling down her neck. Her socks were damp from stepping into puddles. It's easier to be brave when you're warm and dry. She was wet and cold and it chipped away at her courage.

As she walked across Albert Bridge, curtains of rain swept over her, blotting out the comforting lights from the embankment, spattering the roadway, hissing into the river. She paused at the gate and listened. No human sounds. Only the threshing of the trees in the wind and the swish of car tyres on the wet road. She turned over the padlock. The hasp had been forced and fell open in her hands. Easy. Much too easy. She pushed through the gate.

She remembered the riverside walk overhung with lights strung between the trees but it was late and there were not even the dim pools cast by the lamps to comfort her. She walked towards the Pagoda, keeping close to the low wall that ran along the bank. The water swirling in the darkness smelled sour and oily. A distant barge hooted mournfully.

Now she could see the outline of the Pagoda, incongruous against the grubby orange of a London sky. The dark shapes of the trees swaying in the wind were unnerving, the patter of raindrops from the branches like quick, light footsteps following her.

She walked slowly round the high wall of the Pagoda and then climbed the steps to the circular platform. At the top she paused to listen, trying to filter out the chime of a church bell tolling the hour, breathing a silent prayer to the golden Buddha gazing impassively down.

An explosion of sound! *A blinding light in her eyes!* The motor cycle was coming full tilt at her, using the guttering inside the balusters.

She ran . . . not a chance of outrunning it . . . *must get down* . . . a shout . . . but in that delirium of noise impossible to guess whose . . . reached the next flight . . . a second bike soaring up at her . . . the dazzle so intense . . . *had she been hit!* . . . was this the last moment of consciousness! . . . 'Scott!' . . . she screamed . . . '*Scott!*' but how could he hear her in this bedlam . . . she vaulted the parapet . . . she was in the air when she saw it . . . a beam beyond the embankment wall . . . shining straight up into the night . . . *had she lost her wits* . . . there was only the river . . . landed badly . . . the bike right behind her . . . lost the beam in its headlights . . . the din of the engine . . . snarling like a savage animal . . . *must reach the wall* . . . ten yards . . . five . . . the wheel catching her, sending her windmilling . . . grabbing the rail . . . sprawling over . . . a hand clutching at her ankle . . . kicking free . . . a steel edge like a blunt knife scraping the length of her shin . . . no pain . . . falling . . . her knee catching a ledge . . . a glimpse of a figure in the stern of a boat . . . fingers snatching at her wrist . . . the shock of the water . . . numbingly cold . . . a sudden turbulence . . . propellers scything the dark water . . . death was down here . . . life a pale nimbus in the murk above . . . as if the moon had fallen in . . . the water clinging . . . enfolding her in its shrouds . . . struggling free . . . stretching towards the light . . . reaching up . . . a hand grabbing her . . . hauling her aboard as they shot away from the bank.

She lay wheezing and gasping in the bottom of the launch.

'Try not to make such a racket,' Scott hissed at her.

'*I'm trying to breathe, damn you!*'

'Then breathe quietly.'

He cut the engine, judging that the boat had enough way on her to ride the swell to the other side. Masking the torch with his fingers, he stooped down to look at her. 'Just a graze or two. Nothing to worry about. It may bleed a bit when it warms up.'

'What a comfort you are.' She raised herself and peered over the side. They were nosing in among the small craft tied up to a line of half-submerged barges used as moorings.

Scott pointed upstream. 'There are your two sweethearts.'

Julie swallowed the taunt. The bikers were cruising over the bridge, their engines put-putting softly, the lights picking up the sheen on their black leathers.

'Do you think they spotted us?'

'We'll soon know.' He cursed under his breath. The two had stopped and were leaning over the bridge, looking their way.

Julie shook her head to clear the water trickling into her eyes. Her teeth were chattering uncontrollably. 'I'm cold. I must get out of these clothes.'

'Be my guest. We'll invite those guys along and have a floor show.' His eyes followed the bikers' headlights along the embankment and he waved her down below the gunwale. They were only partially hidden by a line of moored boats between them and the embankment.

'They've stopped.'

'They know we're here.' They watched the two dark shapes slither down the steps to the short jetty that ran out to the moorings. In their black leathers they moved slowly, silently like giant slugs, easing themselves round the metal framework that supported the overhead awning. They worked the first line of boats together, using their flashlights in rapid blinks.

They were close now. Julie could hear the wooden planking creak under their feet. Three more boats to search and then they would turn and come back down the second line. Why hadn't Scott made a move? There had to be better places than this . . . the men were turning . . . starting back . . .

Scott signalled to her to hold on and pressed the starter button. A sputter from the engine. The men were running. No whoops or cries. Just the padding of their feet, moving surprisingly fast for such big men.

He grabbed the boathook and threw it to her. 'Quick! *Shove us clear!*' He tried the starter again.

Julie put all her weight on the wooden prong . . . the muscles in her arms and shoulders burning as they strained . . . the tide was against her . . . the boat too heavy . . . a foot of clear water . . . a yard . . . still not enough . . . the current too strong . . . the men were almost on to them . . . their arms coming forward like grapples . . . their eyes lifting . . . their stride shortening . . .

The engine fired. Scott flung out a hand as the first man jumped, catching him under the chin. He seemed to hang in limbo like a giant cartoon cat before splashing down into the river. They could hear him thrashing in the water behind them as they sped under the bridge.

Scott pointed to the hatch. 'Have a dig in there. You will find a pair of overalls – and a towel. I'll give you a rub down.'

'*No, you won't!*' She turned her back on Scott, stripped and towelled herself. The rocking and bucking motion of the launch made it difficult to keep her balance. Then a tail end of spray caught her. She gasped, her naked body corkscrewing with the shock of it. 'You're enjoying this, aren't you?' she yelled at him.

'Loving it,' he shouted back. 'I've seen enough to make me sorry I'm not spending a couple of days in London.'

Julie bent down to turn up the bottoms of the overalls. 'You better memorise it because the show closes tonight.'

'What a waste of a nice body. You'll regret it one day. When you're old and wrinkled . . . '

'It's men like you who make us old and wrinkled.'

They wheeled into the marina and tied up. Scott pointed to the hire company's office on the quay. 'You can come and retrieve my deposit in the morning. Put it in your piggy bank.'

'Do you mean that?'

'Yes.'

'No strings?'

He looked at her and shook his head. 'The girls I go for take a bit more trouble with their appearance.' He ducked as she hurled a bundle of sodden clothing at him.

'Are you spending the night in London?'

'Not much of it. I have to be in Paris early in the morning. So I shan't be here to hold your hand – or whatever. Mind you stay clear of that flat for a day or two. Better still, move in with a friend.'

Julie nodded. They ran along the quay. A taxi was pulling up in front of a large hotel. Scott kissed her lightly on the lips. 'You've had a warning, Julie. Sometimes one is all you get. And I don't buy that fairytale you told me. At least, not all of it. But let that pass. I don't want to pick up the paper one morning and read about you.' He gave her his mobile number. 'If things get too tough you can always call me.' He grinned. 'So I'll know where to send the flowers.'

He handed the taxi driver a ten pound note. The driver was an old man with a wrinkled face under a cloth cap. He watched gloomily as Julie deposited a pile of dripping garments on the floor of the cab and climbed in after it. 'If the lady wants to throw herself in the Thames, she should dress up for it,' he grumbled. 'I remember the time when the river police used to fish women out of the river. Wearing ball-gowns some of them were and their best jewellery.'

Scott watched the taillights until they disappeared round the curve in the road. She didn't turn her head.

6

PARIS

As the Airbus touched down at Charles de Gaulle airport the sun was sliding up into a new day. Scott was four days behind his father. The trip to London had produced no leads. Warren's old friend had been charming but of no assistance. There had been no contact between them for years.

He showed his passport at the kiosk. There was a fractional pause before it was returned to him. One of the officers picked up the telephone. He would have missed it if he hadn't been looking for it.

He had a wash and shave and then found a bar and bought himself a coffee and a baguette. The airport was coming to life, the boutiques opening, the newsstands crowded with people buying the morning papers, checking yesterday's share prices or skimming through the girlie magazines. Two CRS policemen were patrolling with automatic weapons. A young man with a guitar was still asleep slumped against a pillar. A vagrant waved a wine bottle in an unsteady salute to another day.

Had the trail gone cold? This was where it began – or ended. In his blunt, take-it-or-leave-it way Warren had been asking for help. If only he had laid it on the line. But that wasn't his style. He had flown overnight. He would have been tired. Had he spent the first day in Paris? Where was he heading? Why had the old man been so darned close about his affairs?

At nine, the manager of the Tourist Information Office arrived to open up. Scott showed him a photograph of Warren. His eyes blinked his impatience through his spectacles. No, he couldn't remember seeing him. He saw hundreds of people every day. Now, if Monsieur would excuse him . . .

His assistant came through the door, a young woman in a blue coat and skirt, her dark hair tied back in a bun. She looked curiously at Scott.

'May I?' she took the photograph and moved to the window, holding it up to the light. She turned and Scott watched her head tilt back as she tried to remember. Then she nodded slowly. 'I cannot be sure . . . but I think so . . . yes, I am almost certain.'

She pushed the print back to the manager. 'Don't you remember, Bernard? An American gentleman . . .grey hair . . . distinguished looking. He walked with a slight limp. He wanted the name of a hotel near the Gare de L'est. I showed him the list and he chose the Hotel du Commerce. It has only two stars. I was surprised at the choice.'

Scott smiled. 'We Americans don't always stay at the George V.'

'I don't remember him.' The manager rustled his papers. 'Now, Sabine, we have things to do.'

The woman returned the photograph. 'The gentleman is a relative?'

'My father.' He thanked them. They could have asked a lot of tiresome questions, referred him to the Missing Persons Bureau or the police or the casualty departments of the hospitals.

He took the Metro to the Gare de L'Est. From there it was only a short walk to the hotel. It was cold but clear, the sun low in the sky making the pavements shine. He found himself in a long narrow street. A black Citroën passed him, the driver in a dark suit or uniform, his passenger in a white military style raincoat. It was being driven slowly as though they were looking for somewhere to pull in but the cars on either side were parked nose to tail. They went to the top of the street and stopped on the corner. Thirty yards ahead he found the hotel. It was a drab grey stone building but the shutters and the carved window surrounds gave it an air of shabby elegance.

At the reception desk the manageress greeted him warily and took the photograph from him. 'You are an American, I think. You speak good French but with a slight accent. Are you a policeman?'

He shook his head. 'I believe my father stayed here a few days ago. He has not called home and I am anxious about him.'

'I don't like to talk about our guests. Have you some identification on you?'

She flicked open the passport and concern showed in her dark eyes. 'What a worry for you. Of course I recognise the photograph of your father. There is a strong family likeness.'

She turned to the register, stooping as she ran her fingers down the names. 'My husband says I ought to wear glasses but that I am too vain.' The dress was tight over her body and her hair which must once have been black was almost entirely grey. 'He used to complain that I was putting on too much weight. Now he doesn't bother.'

Scott smiled. 'Perhaps your husband is the one who needs glasses.'

Her eyes glittered with amusement. 'Perhaps there is someone else he does not know about. A younger man who doesn't need glasses. Someone who enjoys what the old man has lost the taste for. Ah . . . I have it . . . a Monsieur Rokeby. He stayed for a few hours only.'

'Did he seem quite . . . normal?'

'You are worried that he may have been taken ill?'

'Or suffering from loss of memory.'

She raised her eyes, casting her mind back. 'He arrived late in the evening. He was carrying a small leather suitcase and I remember that he had some newspapers under his arm. He seemed tired and rather preoccupied. He checked out about eleven o'clock the next morning.'

'Did he tell you anything about his plans for the day?'

'Very little. He wanted the address of a car hire firm. There are three local companies that we recommend.' She pulled two leaflets and a business card from the rack at her side and passed them to Scott.

He thanked her. She agreed to look after his grip and came with him to the door. 'If your father had been involved in an accident, you would have heard. I trust you have good news of him soon.'

He pulled up his collar, shoving his hands deep into his pockets. The air in his nostrils was like splinters of glass. An icy puddle crackled underfoot. Somewhere over a high wall, he could hear schoolchildren playing. At the end of the day, they would go home to mothers and fathers. Homework, supper round the table, perhaps a bedtime story. Family life. It was like a far-off country of which he had heard only rumours.

The Citroën was still there but the driver was alone. As he approached, it pulled smoothly away from the kerb and disappeared down a narrow side street.

He phoned the first two names. They checked their books. No, they had no record of a Mr Rokeby. Autos Collines was no more than a few minutes away and he walked there. He had his hand on the glass-fronted door when he caught the reflection of a grey BMW coming slowly down the street behind him. The passenger door opened and a man slipped out and into a doorway. He had the impression that the guy might have been wearing a black leather top but he could have been mistaken. The car turned the corner and disappeared.

At the counter, a young woman was dealing with customers, checking driving licences, tapping details on to her screen, making out contracts. A blackboard behind her listed the cars out on hire. Three had been marked as overdue but, of these, two had had the hire period extended. Against the third, a Peugeot 407, the name Rokeby had been scrawled in chalk, only partially erased and the words *Refer M. Duclos* substituted.

He tore a sheet from his pocket diary, wrote 'DUCLOS' and waved it over the heads of the waiting customers.

He was ignored for some moments and then the girl's eyes flicked up from the screen.

'Monsieur Duclos is busy,' she said curtly.

'So am I,' he snapped. Heads turned to look at him.

'If Monsieur wishes to hire a car he will have to wait his turn.'

'I don't. I wish to see the manager on a private matter.'

'Your name, Monsieur?'

'I said it was a private matter.'

Her mouth turned down. She stabbed at a button. 'Monsieur Duclos? You have a visitor.' She pointed to a glazed door at the end of the room and returned to her screen.

The manager still had the receiver in his hand as Scott entered the office. The office was warm and airless. A length of frayed cord snaked across the floor to an electric fire. The desk was cluttered with files. He half rose and stretched out his hand. He had a swarthy complexion and oily black hair which curled over the back of his collar. 'Paris in winter is not so good. You should come in the summer.' He gestured to a chair.

'One day, maybe. We can talk about the weather then.' He wrinkled his nose. The smell of stale cigarette smoke was almost overpowering. 'Meanwhile I am enquiring about a Mr Warren Rokeby who hired a Peugeot 407 four days ago. He is my father. I have heard nothing from him. He seems to have disappeared.'

The man's eyes cut to the door and then back to his visitor. No, he didn't recall the name. 'Are you sure that your father hired a car from us?' He opened a file on his desk and made a show of digging through a sheaf of papers.

Scott pulled his chair close to the desk and leaned forward. 'Listen carefully, Monsieur Duclos. Warren Rokeby is an American citizen of some standing in my country and he has influential friends.'

Duclos shrugged his shoulders. 'No doubt he has, Monsieur, but I fail to see what this has to do with me.'

'I haven't time to play games, Duclos. At the moment, this is between the two of us but one call to the American Embassy and things could get very busy around here.'

Duclos shook a cigarette into his hand from a packet of Gitanes. He went to the door, opened it, looked behind it and closed it once more. He picked up the phone. 'No calls,' he growled. He returned to his chair and sat down heavily. 'You could make a lot of trouble for me, Mr Rokeby. I am asking you not to. This problem is not of my making.' He pulled nervously at his cigarette, his black eyes darting at Scott.'

'I cannot promise anything. Tell me what happened to my father.'

'I don't know. And that's the truth.'

'*You don't know!*'

'I do . . . not . . . know.' Duclos repeated emphatically. 'I had a visit yesterday from a government official . . . for that is how he introduced himself. He gave me cash for the full value of the car against a signed receipt.'

'Did you insist that the man identify himself?'

'The man made a call from this office. He put me through to a senior official in a government department. It could have been the Ministry of the Interior. In France that ministry is a law unto itself. He knew all about the company, reeled off the business corporation number, tax and social security references. The lot.'

'Do you have a copy of the contract that my father signed?'

He hesitated. 'Yes . . . but the official may make trouble. He insisted that—'

'Don't worry about the official. Worry about me. I can make so much trouble that you will be lucky to get a job out the back washing cars.'

Duclos tugged viciously at his collar. Perspiration was trickling down his neck. He took a key from his pocket, opened a drawer, extracted a document and put it on the table between them.

Scott skimmed through it. Warren had hired the car for three days. A white Peugeot 407. Unlimited mileage. Itinerary left blank. 'Did my father say where he was going?'

'No.'

'Did he plan to travel outside France?'

'I have no idea.'

'Do you know where the car is now, Monsieur Duclos?'

'No. I assume that it is being held by the authorities. Naturally, I asked the same question but I was told that the matter was no longer any concern of mine.'

'There must have been some paperwork.'

'I signed a form disposing of my company's interest in the vehicle and an undertaking to make no enquiries about it. It is my turn to ask you something, Mr Rokeby. Why should the authorities be so interested in a car being driven by your father? Is it possible' . . . he tapped the end of his nose, 'that he was involved in activities that had come to their notice . . . undesirable activities?'

'My father was not that sort of man.'

Duclos pursed his lips. 'To me it stinks of the DST – Directorate of Territorial Surveillance. You won't get any answers from them. They are also a law unto themselves.'

Scott stood up. Before he left he wanted a copy of the contract. He tucked it into an inside pocket. 'Is there anything more that you can tell me?'

'I regret there is nothing.' He held the door open. 'May I enquire where are you going now?'

'Where would you be going?'

Duclos spread his hands despairingly. 'Who can say? I would not know where to start. You will not find the Ministry or the DST helpful. If you go banging on their doors you could find yourself on the way to the airport with a police escort and a deportation order.'

Scott took a taxi to the American Embassy in the Avenue Gabriel. He waited a few minutes and was shown into Lou Vyner's office. It was exactly midday. Vyner left his desk and shook hands. 'You used to see my old chief, Chuck Holman, I believe. He's retired.'

'So I heard.'

'Lucky sonofabitch has gone to Florida. He's got all the golf and fishing he can handle, and that's plenty.'

Vyner had a florid complexion and a belly that strained at the confines of his trouser belt. He was the sort of man to be found on a golf course at weekends and rarely very far from the club house. He gestured Scott to a comfortable leather chair. Returning to his desk he unlocked the top drawer and withdrew a buff envelope. 'I would rather you didn't open it here.'

'Can you make it exclusive to us? It would give us a few days start.' He didn't care one way or the other but Turcan was sure to ask.

Vyner went to a small fridge in the corner of the room and came back with a couple of bottles of beer. 'I'll be up front with you, Scott. I try to be even-handed between your outfit and Fraser Outram. I spoke to Jeff Turcan a few minutes after I telephoned Todd. If Todd sends one of his guys to see me, I can't very well refuse to let him have a copy.'

'I understand.' He did, only too well. 'May I ask how you came by the list?'

Vyner grinned. 'You may but I won't tell you. Someone did us a favour; that's all I can say.'

'That someone will want a kickback.'

Vyner shrugged. 'Let me take care of that.' He took an easy chair facing Scott and poured out the glasses. 'How's Warren? Somehow I can't picture the old war horse turned out to grass.'

'Did you know him?' Scott tried to keep his voice casual.

'I never met him but I heard plenty. He was a legend in his time. The Russians had Gromyko. We had Warren Rokeby. Icebergs both of them.'

'He was out there for too long.'

'People say that he changed when his wife—'

'When my mother was killed. Maybe. I can't judge.'

Vyner shifted in his chair, discomfited by the harshness in Scott's voice. 'That was a bad business,' he muttered. 'A very bad business.'

Warren had been offered a home posting but he had stayed put, like a dog lying across his master's grave, refusing to move. The whisper was that he had gone a little mad, buried himself out there, deep down in the permafrost.

His father had flown to Paris a few days earlier, Scott told Vyner. He hadn't been in touch since he left. Naturally he was rather anxious.

'The son of a gun is probably having a ball. Making up for lost time.' His eyes drifted back to his desk.

Scott got to his feet. 'If he makes contact you can get me on my mobile phone.' He gave Vyner his business card. 'Meanwhile . . . ' he tapped his pocket. 'Do you want any feedback on that list?'

Vyner shook his head. 'It's off the record. This time next year when I'm drawing my pension, I may look you up and remind you that I did you a favour.' He gave a broad wink. 'It would be nicer still not to have to remind you.' As the lift doors slid open, he thrust out a hand. 'So long, Scott. Drop by the next time you are passing. As for Warren, I think you are worrying unnecessarily. He will show up in a day or two. His breed is indestructible.'

Scott found a café on the boulevard and sat at a small table under the awning. Was Vyner levelling with him? Something about that performance didn't ring quite true. The waiter came out, swatted a napkin at the tabletop and took his order. A ham omelette and a Kronenbourg to wash it down. It was nice to see the foaming lager arrive in a tall glass. Some of the places he went to, you bought your liquor in sealed bottles unless you wanted to wake up a few hours later with the top of your head lifting like the lid of a pressure cooker and your pockets turned out.

A black Citroën went past swishing through the puddles. The driver was talking on his car phone. Scott caught the man's eyes on him in the wing mirror and made a note of the number plate.

Tearing open the envelope, he ran his eyes down the list. These companies were not for him. It was a high-risk country. Government officials and their cronies would have creamed off anything worth having.

After years of corruption and mismanagement, the infrastructure was crumbling. He would tell Jeff Turcan to steer clear. And Todd wasn't dumb. He would go for it with all the enthusiasm of a cat invited to the opening of a new fur shop.

Across the road, a silver BMW had stopped. The traffic was one way and the stream of cars glided smoothly round it. A sandy haired man in a black leather tank top was leaning forward talking to the driver. The driver adjusted the angle of his mirror. Scott had a feeling that the two men were discussing him.

It was absurd, he told himself, paranoid, but it was beginning to get to him. Fifty yards along the boulevard, there was a set of traffic lights and, as far away again, a cinema. He glanced at the bill and slipped a note under his glass. Walking quickly, he reached the lights and crossed the road. To his right, there was a blare from a car horn. The BMW had pulled out into the road.

As he reached the pavement, he quickened pace. The road narrowed here. For a driver not prepared to risk a fanfare of protest from the motorists behind him there was nowhere to stop. If the men in the BMW were following him they had some quick thinking to do.

The cinema was showing four films. He didn't look at the titles. He wanted Studio Two. The grey-haired crone in the kiosk pushed a ticket at him. A muttered '*Salaud!*' followed him as he turned away. It was as if he had dropped his pants but this wasn't the moment for an argument.

An usherette met him at the top of a flight of steps covered in a grubby red threadbare carpet. She held out her hand for a tip and left him to find his way through the haze of cigarette smoke drifting in the glare from the projector. The audience consisted entirely of men occupying the first few rows.

The screen showed a naked woman emerging from a swimming pool, her long dark hair running down her back to waist height where it tapered to a fine point. She climbed to the top of a flight of steps and grasping a pair of hand rails to support herself leaned forward and spread a pair of shapely legs. A well-built young negro, climbed the steps behind her and grabbed her. Their gasps and moans mingled with the sighs of the rapt little audience.

In the far corner of the auditorium there was a sign marked *Toilettes*. He stood in the darkness under the archway and looked back. A door opened. A man was silhouetted in the lozenge of yellow light. He beckoned to the usherette.

Scott darted down the corridor, contracting his nostrils against the acrid smell of stale urine. A shove on the push bar and he was in a narrow street. From his right came the *slap-slap* of running feet.

He dodged round the corner and into a street market, jinking in and out of barrows laden with fruit and vegetables, through an arcade lined with boutiques and back on to the main boulevard. A man in a denim jacket was lounging up against the outside of the cinema engrossed in his newspaper while sandy hair was taking the exercise. *Where the hell was the BMW?* It took him a few anxious moments before he found it at the top of a ramp leading to an underground car park.

He tried the doors. The boot. All locked. A red Volvo estate came off the street and stopped behind him. The driver had hair that matched the paintwork but a better body. 'I won't be a moment,' she cried breathlessly. 'I'm just picking up my dry cleaning. Be an angel and keep an eye on my car.' She skittered away, her high heels click-clacking on the pavement.

In the boot of her car, he found a tyre wrench and an oilskin bag to deaden the sound. A sharp tap on the side window of the BMW and he had the door open and was sweeping the glass fragments from the seat into the floor well.

Nothing in the glove compartment. He tried the pockets inside the doors . . . zero . . . under the driver's seat . . . something there . . . just out of reach . . . his fingers nipping the edge of it . . . wedged under the metal seat frame . . . a plastic wallet.

Two photographs inside. His father walking up the steps of the Hotel du Commerce. Blurred, probably taken through a car window. It gave him a strange feeling. As if he were looking at a ghost. Perhaps this was the last image of his father alive.

He turned quickly to the other. A Peugeot 407, a snapshot taken from the rear. Warren's hire car at a filling station. No name on the canopy. No sign of the driver. Beyond the forecourt, there was a lorry park with a Total petrol tanker sideways on. He memorised the number. Something else. A photograph of him going down the steps to Julie's flat. It sent a chill through him.

He pushed the wallet back under the seat and jumped out just as the redhead bustled round the corner with most of her wardrobe in her arms.

'How kind of you,' she gasped. 'I do hope I haven't delayed you. Parking in this city! *It's sheer persecution!*' He was still holding her wrench. He hadn't even had the wit to hide it behind his back. He dropped it into a refuse bin. She didn't look like the sort of person who changed her own tyres.

He took several taxis in quick succession, getting the driver to leave him at the wrong end of a one-way street and then walking against the oncoming traffic. It was very amateurish but it was all he could think of.

A bar produced a badly needed cup of coffee. He telephoned Total and asked to speak to their transport manager. He resented the necessity to lie but he had no choice. He told the man that he worked on the claims side of an insurance company. 'One of our clients has had a car stolen off a garage forecourt. The idiot left his keys in it when he went to pay.'

'It happens all the time. Why don't you leave it to the police? It's their job.'

'It's our money. Who do you think is going to try harder?'

The manager laughed. 'The police don't bother to get out of their cars unless they find someone with his throat cut. But why call me?'

'Because one of your tankers was in the lorry park at the time.' He gave him the number on the cab. 'I wondered if your driver saw anything?'

'I doubt it. He was probably too busy with his *moules et frites* or peering down the front of the waitress's dress.' There was a pause. 'I hate these frigging screens,' he grumbled. 'Hang on a moment . . . Jacques Vannes was the driver. He was on the St Die to Colmar run. It's a slow stretch. At sixteen-thirty he delivered to Autos Brumes.'

Scott thanked him, adding that he hoped it wouldn't be necessary to trouble Jacques. He called Autos Brumes and asked for directions. It was just east of Nancy. So Warren was heading for Colmar on the German border. Into the Vosges mountains. It would be getting dark. Was he being followed or lying trussed up in the boot of the car? In either case, why take a photograph? Why abduct Warren? He wasn't rich. He wouldn't make the short list of wealthy American tourists. Or any list, for that matter. *Why, a thousand times why, hadn't his father confided in him? Trusted him?*

As he left the bar the rain was streaming down. In the east of the country, snow was forecast. He hailed a taxi. He would pick up his grip and take the train to Colmar.

7

LONDON'S EAST END

There was a bleep from his mobile. Kolar reached into the pocket of his denim jacket. Pieter Rohr. That bloke really spooked him. The man was everywhere and nowhere. He tensed for what was coming.

'That fuck-up in Battersea Park, Kolar . . . I expected better of you.'

'I'm sorry, Pieter, I was really gutted. Give me twenty-four hours and I swear—'

'No. I will handle it from here. Did you sort out those two clowns?'

'They won't make the same mistake again.'

'I can't afford people who make mistakes.'

Kolar shivered. He didn't scare easily but he could feel the hairs rising on the nape of his neck.

The two men exchanged a few more words before Kolar turned with a sigh of relief to watch the taillights of the container lorry fade into the murk of a foggy London morning. Another consignment of top-of-the-market cars on its way to Dover. Within hours of being lifted off the streets, the cars were out of the workshops with new registration plates, engine and chassis numbers and documentation. A new identity. Only fools said it was easy money. It was a rough business. A dangerous business.

He banged his hands together to restore some warmth to them. This was the front line. The workshops under the railway arches with their steel reinforced doors, the yard with its potholes brimming with pools of oily water, the gut-rotting worry that the cops were on to him every time a passing car slowed or a man walked his dog across the litter-strewn wasteland.

A train rumbled over the viaduct, the grubby panels of yellow light snaking away into the gloom. He wrapped his arms round his body. It wasn't good to spend too long in this line of work. People started to look like creatures that lived beneath the ground, like the rats that crawled out of the drains with their suspicious eyes, sharp predatory features and the smell of the dank underworld they inhabited.

Another year or two and he would have enough money to buy himself a big house with a pool. He would put in a bar and a snooker table, a kingsize bed and a woman who knew her way round it. Spend the winters in the sun. Become a middleman, a fixer. He could live very comfortably on a few good scams a year. Leave the donkey work to the donkeys.

He rubbed his jaw. Two days stubble was like sandpaper against the palm of his hands. Leave the Dixon girl alone Rohr had told him. 'She won't trouble us much longer.'

'You have something special in mind?'

Rohr gave a throaty chuckle. 'Special? I like that. Yes, something rather special is going to happen to her.'

Kolar felt no pity for her. She had no idea what she was getting into. She must pay the price. As for him, he was a tiny cog in a very large operation. He already knew too much about it. Enough to kill him if he was foolish enough to talk.

Some years earlier, he had taken a lorry-load of cars to Kiev. Low grade stuff, packed in a container. He was just starting out in business and could not afford the heavy winches that he used now. So, a Maserati parked in Chelsea Square at two o'clock in the morning stayed where it was. In Chelsea Square.

In Ukraine, he had to use the back roads. The surface was terrible and it was winter. He broke an axle. It was perishingly cold, dark and coming on to snow. A mile walk, cursing his luck every yard. Then he saw the lights of a farm house at the end of a muddy track. He didn't have to knock on the door. The owner came out with a shotgun in his hands.

He was called Maisk. Pavlo Maisk. He must once have been a great ox of a man but his chest was sunken and his skin was grey. Using a mixture of German, Russian and a bit of Czech, they had little difficulty in understanding each other.

'Where are you from, Kolar?'

'Stratford. East London.'

Maisk laughed. 'That wasn't what I asked, but let it pass.' He led the way to barn and pulled back the big doors. He walked with a bad limp and his breathing was harsh and uneven. He started up his truck and they drove to the lorry. 'You would rather not answer any questions about your load,' he grunted, sizing up the situation immediately. 'Don't worry. Very few cars come this way. As for the police,' he turned and spat on the ground, 'they have more sense than to come nosing round here.'

'Can you put me up for the night?' asked Kolar. The wind was freshening, the snow was drifting across the road and visibility was down to a few yards.

The man gave him a long, searching look before answering. 'You can sleep on the couch in the sitting room. I live alone.'

'Alone? In this isolated place? No wife? No children?'

'I had a wife. Nadiya. She visited me once in the camp . . . and that was to tell me that she was divorcing me. I don't blame her. I was hell to live with. *Come!* We will make up the fire, have supper and a few drinks.'

'What about the repair?'

Maisk pulled a torch from his pocket, crouched down and directed the beam underneath the vehicle. He straightened with a grimace of pain. 'I have a shed where I repair tractors, farm implements and so on. In the morning, I will cobble something together. It will get you as far as Kiev but you had better get it fixed properly.'

'I'm grateful. How much will it cost?'

'Not much. I won't rob you.'

Thirty minutes later they were sitting at a table in the kitchen. Maisk had produced a tureen of borscht, followed by a large, greasy pork chop and a big helping of cabbage and potatoes, washed down with a bottle of Georgian red wine.

Maisk pushed back his chair and rolled himself a cigarette. He pointed to a cupboard in the corner of the room. 'You will find another bottle there. Your legs are in better shape than mine.'

Kolar crossed the room and opened the cupboard door. He grasped a bottle and was pulling it out when his eye was caught by something nailed to the inside of the door. It was as leathery and wrinkled as a old parchment and on it a crude portrait of Stalin had been tattooed. Kolar was so startled that he nearly dropped the bottle.

Maisk blew a cloud of smoke at the blackened ceiling and started laughing. He slapped his thighs with his huge, brawny hands and the tears ran down his cheeks. 'I'm sorry, Kolar, I have got so used to it that I don't see it any longer.

'It looks like human skin.'

'It *is* human skin. Are you not curious about how it got there or are you too busy worrying about whether I will cut your throat in the night, flay you and eat you for breakfast?' This sally brought on another roar of laughter which ended in a violent fit of coughing. 'Come, Kolar,' the man gasped, 'fill our glasses and I will tell you a story. I swear on my parents' grave, you will not be bored.

'My grandparents were kulaks. Prosperous farmers. They had good land near Lvov in the west of the country. In 1932 their house was taken from them, their livestock sold and their grain exported to pay for one of Stalin's crazy schemes. They starved. Tens of thousands were dying every day. In desperation, parents smothered their children or cut their throats.

'My father was ten years old at the time. He only survived because he ran away. He lived off roots and berries but winter was coming and he was just a bag of bones when he was found and taken in by some peasants. When the police came looking for him, they lowered him in a bucket and hid him in the well.

'Later on, he got a job in Kiev with a firm of printers. He married my mother and I was born in 1950. My father was never at home. He had his day job. At night, he used the presses to print anti-Soviet leaflets. He was caught and given a twenty-year sentence in a forced labour camp as an "enemy of the people".'

'My mother and I – we belonged to the family of an "enemy of the people", so we were sent to the same camp. It was Kraikus 5, one of the Perm group, near the Urals. I was six. The first thing I noticed was the colour of the prisoners' skin. It was grey from lack of air. We slept on bed boards. The air in the huts was foul with the smoke of cheap tobacco and kerosene lamps and the stench of mildewed clothing.

'At night there was shouting and fights breaking out and people sobbing. My father had had a trade. So he was picked on as *an intellectual* and forced to sleep in the lower bunks. If the cell leader was in a bad mood, he would wake him up and pour the slops and filth over him.

'There were armed guards in watchtowers and savage dogs attached by a chain to a wire that circled the camp. The food was dreadful. Soup made of entrails and rotten cabbage. But we ate like wolves. We were hungry all the time.

'My father was sent out into the forest to haul logs. If you did not fulfil your quota, your rations were cut. You became weaker. Your output fell. You were put on punishment rations. They harnessed him to a sledge. His arms and legs were like sticks. They worked him to death. Soon after that, my mother got typhus. She was dead within a week.'
Maisk threw a log on the fire and refilled their glasses.

'In the next hut, there was a very rough crowd. Murderers, sadists, thieves, sexual deviants, extortioners, lunatics driven mad by hunger. It turned the children into savages. Cruel, vengeful, dangerous creatures. Their bodies didn't belong to them until they were big enough to defend themselves. They were bought and sold, used as wagers and won or lost in gambling sessions. Sometimes, having lost everything, they staked their own lives.

'One of them, I shall never forget. We called him Kraik and the name stuck. He was nine years old when I first came across him. Nine, going on ninety. He had been in the camp for three years. The others left him alone. He was as cold as a block of ice. His skin was like ivory. His hair was white. He never raised his voice. He hissed like a snake. He never lost his temper . . . but he never forgave. Cross him and something bad happened to you. An accident in the forest or a beating from a guard or a dog got loose and tore your throat out.'

'Did he have a family?' asked Kolar.

'Janos was his father's name. He was a clever man. Brilliant even. He had been condemned to death but Moscow gave him a life sentence instead. They needed his brains.'

'What had he done wrong?'

Maisk chuckled. 'Nobody knows. There were rumours that he downed a couple of Soviet MiGs.'

'*Downed them!*'

'In November 1956 the Soviet Army's tanks were moving in to Budapest to crush the revolution. At first light, the MiGs were over the city strafing the centres of resistance. Two of them collided. Their instruments had been scrambled. The circuitry was fried. Janos was up on the roof of one of the office buildings with a generator and an antenna. It wasn't any ordinary generator. It sent out a powerful, short-lived, electromagnetic pulse. Those two MIGs flew into an electronic minefield.'

'How was he caught?'

'He was betrayed to the AVO, the State Security Police. Some of the equipment he had made himself. Other components had been stolen. When he came to the camp, he was sent to work in a research establishment in the town. He worked under a German, a rocket scientist who had been captured by the Red Army in 1945. Janos was always escorted by an armed guard and searched when he came back. One day, they caught him trying to smuggle scientific drawings into his hut. That finished him.'

'He was killed?'

'Of course. Round the perimeter of the camp there was a strip of ground that prisoners were not allowed to cross. In the summer, the earth was raked. In the winter, the snow was left untouched. A footprint would always be spotted and alert the guards in the watchtowers that there had been an escape attempt.

'Janos was put in a punishment cell for the night. The next morning, we were paraded in the square for roll-call. It was still dark. Bitterly cold. Forty degrees of frost. Janos was brought out. He saw his son. He was looking for his wife. A searchlight from one of the watchtowers moved across the snow. His wife was the other side of the strip. She was tied to a stake. She was naked. I knew what was going to happen. Janos was told to cross the strip and bring her back before she froze to death. He must have known it was the end. I heard his boots crunching through the snow. Then the rattle of a machine gun as it opened fire.'

'So Kraik watched his mother and his father die.'

Maisk nodded. 'But his father had managed to copy the most important of the drawings and smuggle them to him. Kraik concealed them and took them with him when he escaped.'

'*He got away from there?*'

'He was with a working party ordered to bury bodies. It was the depth of winter. There was a terrible storm. Visibility was down to nothing. He grabbed the guard and killed him. He took an accomplice, a man called Vyaz. Vyaz was a thief. He had been condemned to death for stealing food. They were going to shoot him but Kraik saved his life. He got a tattooist in the camp to put a picture of Stalin on the man's chest. Nobody dared fire bullets into that. Vyaz was given a terrible beating, but he lived.'

'Why did Kraik take him with him?'

'He needed him. Vyaz knew the area. Their clothes were little better than rags. Their shoes were made out of sacking and bits of automobile tyres. They had no papers. No money. The temperatures were well below freezing. There were few villages. They were tracked by dogs and bounty hunters. Had they been caught they would have been shot or beaten and brought back to the camp.'

Kolar's eyes were drawn irresistibly to the cupboard door with its grisly relic. 'How did Vyaz die?'

'Kraik killed him when he had served his purpose. There were rumours that he lived off the man's body to keep himself from starving.'

'And the tattoo?'

'It would have linked Kraik to that camp. He wasn't going to let that happen.'

'Surely he didn't flay Vyaz alive!'

' Let us hope that the man was dead.'

'But why keep the skin?'

'He found a use for it. When I got out of the camp, a man called Pieter Rohr, one of Kraik's henchmen, tracked me down. I thought he was going to kill me. But he let me off with a warning.'

'And with the tattoo?'

'Yes. To remind people like me . . . and you, Kolar . . . to keep our mouths shut.' Maisk rose to his feet and stretched. 'I am a solitary creature and not used to company. I blame it on the red wine. I have already talked too much.'

8

THE BALTIC

As the bows carved into the onrushing line of white-crested breakers, a cascade of green water slammed against the reinforced glass of the bridge. The MV *Ludmilla* was butting through heavy seas to Tallinn having discharged its cargo in Felixstowe. A consignment of machine pistols concealed in the false bottom of a container packed with tractor parts was already on its way to a dealer in Ilford.

The skipper took the call in the radio room, his feet planted wide astride, his heavy torso swaying with the roll of the ship.

'Werner? Are you having a good trip?'

Pieter Rohr. He would know that voice anywhere. 'If you call riding a roller-coaster with half a hurricane up your backside fun, then yes.'

'I wasn't talking about the weather.'

Werner laughed. 'The customs officer gave us no trouble. They should issue him with a white stick.'

'I told you Kolar would fix it. What about the other business? Did your man enjoy the swim?'

'Someone must have spotted him in the water and reported it. The police picked him up as soon as he got ashore. He spent a night in hospital. Hypothermia.'

'I hope he remembered his lines.'

'Nadym is a good bloke. He won't let you down.'

'I'll remember that. *Gute reise*, my friend.' Rohr was in a good humour. The trap was in place. Now it would be baited – *and sprung*.

9

WHITEHALL, LONDON

Julie left the offices of the trade association at eleven o'clock. As she came out of the doors into Whitehall she heard her name called. It was Detective Sergeant Robert Calvert. He came up to her and stared at the plate outside the building. 'What are you up to?'

'Minding my own business. Try it and let me know how you get on.'

'I want to talk to you, Julie.'

'It had better be important.'

'It is. We can have a quick jar and a natter.'

'I haven't time to natter.'

'You'll feel better after a drink.'

There was a large public house a few minutes' walk from New Scotland Yard. While Calvert went to the bar for the drinks, Julie found a small round table at the rear of the saloon and looked round her. Bogus panelling, fake antique mirrors and the sour reek of unwashed beer glasses. No wonder people drank. She took a phone from her shoulder bag and checked her diary. The table jolted and she turned her head.

'I don't think I have seen you here before, sweetie.'

Stained trousers and a gaping zip at eye level. It didn't get much better higher up. She followed the whisky fumes to the crumpled bow-tie, the rheumy eyes and purple-veined features. 'It's my first visit,' she said. 'Something tells me that it's going to be my last.'

'This is not my favourite watering hole but it has the advantage of propinquity.' His face contorted in a grotesque wink. 'I have a pad near here where we could beguile an hour or two very agreeably. Permit me to offer you a little refreshment and then I will tell you some of the amazing things we could do together.'

'I'm busy,' she snapped. 'Amaze someone else.' She bent over her diary.

He waggled a reproachful finger at her and shambled off in search of easier game.

'Made some new friends?' Calvert deposited two glasses of foaming lager on the table.

'I had a date with a sex maniac before you came along and spoiled everything.'

Calvert threw his raincoat over the back of a chair and sat down. 'That dust-up in the Department of Trade . . . I was told to have a word in your ear.'

Julie stiffened. 'And the word?'

'Stop trying to do our job for us.'

'You aren't doing your job.' She chewed on her lip, her temper rising. 'The people I'm after are into every sort of scam. Drugs, illegal immigrants, counterfeiting. Those landing strips are usually tucked away in remote areas but they are the key to these operations.'

'We haven't the money or the manpower to go after all of them. We have to concentrate on the big boys. My advice to you is leave them to us. There are some major villains out there and they play rough. One dark night someone will take you up to five thousand feet and let you find your own way down.'

'My editor would enjoy that. Duggie Bains hasn't seen much for his money so far. Give him a little notice and he would send along a photographer.'

'Have you told him about your brother?' The raised eyebrows put it another way. Or are you still telling porkies?'

'*How can I?* Bains would take me off the assignment. Probably fire me.'

71

'When David disappeared, didn't the *Courier* cover the story?'

'Of course. All the nationals did. It was a seven-day wonder.' Her laugh had a bitter ring to it.

'And your boss never suspected that you were David's sister?'

'Why should he? The telephone directory has pages of people called Dixon.'

Calvert tapped a cigarette into his hand. 'What sort of work was he doing at Fleetwood Institute?'

'Haven't you read the file?'

'It's not my case.' Calvert leaned back and watched a thin plume of smoke drift up to the ceiling.

'That wasn't what I asked you.'

'I know that he was a research fellow at Fleetwood and it's no secret that he was working on a new capacitor.'

'The bulk has been the problem in the past. This one would have an enormous power-to-weight ratio. He was very excited about it. He said that it would make solid state batteries look like something out of the Stone Age.'

'You were very close to him, weren't you?'

'He's all I've got. My father was a sheep farmer in Cornwall. He died two years ago.'

'An accident?'

'Some sort of toxic poisoning. The doctors said he might have picked it up from the chemicals they use in the dip. My mother died of cancer when I was seven.'

Calvert shook his head. 'I'm sorry. I didn't know.'

Julie shrugged. 'Now that you know, let's get back to my brother. When David disappeared I had a visit from some moron who—'

'From Inspector Morris.' Calvert cut in quickly.

'That's the man. Morris the midget. Five foot nothing and not enough brains to make them plural. That was nearly three months ago.'

'Be fair, Julie. Morris might have made more progress if you had been frank with him.'

Julie raised her chin mutinously. 'Who says I wasn't?'

'Were you?'

'His first brainwave was that David had had some sort of a nervous breakdown. David's doctor disposed of that. His next inspiration was that he had run off with the college spoons, despite the fact that the bursar confirmed that nothing was missing. *Pig ignorant, he was.* How can you trust someone like that with the truth?'

'So what didn't you tell him?'

'Off the record?'

'I thought we were friends.'

'I can't afford friends. At least with my enemies I know where I am.'

'Then we are just having a drink together but there's no need to be so damn prickly.'

'I'm sorry, Bob . . . ' she began and for a moment couldn't go on. The long months of searching, the loneliness, the fear, sometimes they piled up and almost overwhelmed her. She drove her teeth into her lip, using the pain to steady herself. 'David telephoned me when he finished work on the Friday night,' she whispered. 'It was . . . ' her voice struggled in her throat like a small animal caught in a snare. 'It was the last time we spoke together. He told me he had an important meeting over the weekend. Something that could change his life. He was really fired up about it.'

'Did he say where he was going?'

'Only that he planned to be out of England for two days. Just a short hop to the continent and back.'

'Were those his words?'

'Yes.'

'If Inspector Morris had known that—'

'He would have used it against David. He had it in for him from the start.'

'He'll find out anyway . . . and probably charge you with obstruction.'

'So what?' Julie retorted angrily. 'So he gets me a few hours' community service, watering some pensioner's window box. That would be a fine boast to make after months of pissing around.'

Calvert screwed his cigarette into the ashtray. 'Do you think you're being fair to your editor?'

'What's it to you?' She glowered at him. 'If Duggie sticks with me he'll get his money's worth.' She drained her glass and shouldered her bag. 'Now, if that's all—'

'It's not all.' Calvert waved her back into her chair. 'Inspector Morris went to Fleetwood Institute yesterday.'

'So what else is new? If he spends any more time there they'll have to give him a cap and gown.'

'He had a meeting with Sir Lucas Micklem.' Calvert hesitated. *This wasn't going to be easy.*

'Go on,' Julie pleaded. 'I'm not a thought reader.' Calvert was stretching her on the rack.

'I'm afraid it's bad news. The file on your brother has been sent to the Serious Fraud Office.'

'Fraud! David! Of all people! Do you really believe that he would chuck away his career for a few lousy quid! *Of all the crass, imbecilic—'*

'Keep your voice down!' Calvert hissed. 'What your brother had in his head was worth mega money. Fleetwood was paying peanuts. Try to be realistic, Julie. It must have been very tempting for someone like David.'

'Someone like David?' She shook her head violently. 'I don't have to listen to this.' She pushed her chair back and ran to the door.

Calvert hurried after her and caught her arm. 'Where the hell do you think you're going?'

'Where do you think? To see Micklem.'

'You can't just go barging in on the Vice-Chancellor.'

'*Can't I?*' She shook herself loose and slammed the door behind her. '*Just watch me!*' she mouthed furiously through the glass that separated them.

'*Shit!*' Calvert delivered a vicious kick to the brass doorplate and headed back to the bar. He needed a Scotch. A double.

10

FLEETWOOD INSTITUTE OF ADVANCED TECHNOLOGY

George Fleetwood made his fortune out of a chain of chemist's shops in the Midlands and retired to a large mansion overlooking the Thames about twenty miles west of London. On his death, he left a considerable sum of money to establish Fleetwood Park as a centre for engineering studies.

A modern hall of residence was built together with lecture rooms and laboratories. Research fellowships were awarded to outstanding post-graduates drawn from all over the country, but over the years the facilities became out-dated and it was only able to attract top scientists because it gave them more freedom to pursue their own interests than they could find elsewhere.

It was half-past two in the afternoon. Sir Lucas Micklem, the Vice-Chancellor, was entertaining heads of department to lunch. Seated round the polished oval mahogany table were Gilbert Tench from Particle Physics, Wystan Luff from Metallurgy, Roger Buckden from Kinetic Science and Edmund Maffey from Automotive Engineering.

Sir Lucas was a tall, spare, ascetic-looking man with a high forehead and sparse white hair grown rather long. He watched with impatience as the decanter circulated again. He disliked conviviality and the obligation to consort with intellects that he judged to be inferior to his own. Traditionally, however, the gathering took place once a year and Sir Lucas was nothing if not a traditionalist.

As he let the conversation eddy round him, his eyes glanced up to the portrait of the founder over the carved marble mantelpiece. Florid of face and heavy jowelled, the founder looked as if he had enjoyed the good things in life.

Sir Lucas sighed. He envied entrepreneurs like George Fleetwood, just as he envied the rising generation of scientists. They weren't going to be fobbed off with academic honours. They were too smart to fall for that nonsense. They weren't going to end up like him with an alphabet of letters after his name, living in some dingy coastal town, eking out a pension giving remedial lessons to dim students. They were going to team up with venture capitalists, float their companies and retire rich.

This Dixon affair had distressed him greatly. The man had a brilliant mind and had pulled off a starred double first at one of the older universities. As a post-graduate, he had worked for CERN in Switzerland during the construction of the Hadron Collider. Sir Lucas took considerable pride in having persuaded him to come to Fleetwood. He had been quite open with him, warning him that his research work would be underfunded and that it might take a little longer to develop the capacitor to the stage of field trials.

But what were a few years in the life of a young man? He would virtually have a free hand. All that Fleetwood asked in return was that when recognition and honours came his way he shared the credit with the university. But Dixon couldn't wait to cash in. He had betrayed him, betrayed them all. It was unforgivable.

There came a knock on the door. It was Sneath, the butler in a state of some agitation.

Julie had pushed the Fiat Panda hard. She swung off the road and under the stone archway without braking, scattering gravel like grapeshot over the immaculately tended lawn. In her mirror she could see the college porter running out of his lodge, waving his arms like a tic-tac man at a race meeting. She ignored him just as she ignored the curious stares of the students on their bicycles who turned their heads to follow her.

The signs for the various faculties swept past her in a blur. At a notice marked *Private* she dived down a long avenue of leafless limes leading to a red-brick building with pillars and high chimneys. Whizzing round the driveway, she came to a skidding halt in front of the stone portico.

Jumping out of the car, she ran to the door, pressed the bell and banged the knocker for good measure. The shiny brass plate beside her read *Vice-Chancellor's Lodge*. Some lodge. She could hear the sound of footsteps approaching.

The door was opened by a lady in an elegant blue cashmere dress. Her auburn hair was in a chignon and round her neck hung two ropes of pearls. She stared at Julie and frowned. Sir Lucas disapproved of women. Especially modern young women in shiny black zip-up jackets, skin-tight trousers and ankle boots. 'The Vice-Chancellor has a faculty luncheon,' she said frostily. 'Have you an appointment?'

'No, but it is very important that I see him. So if you don't mind—' She ducked under the woman's arm and ran into the hall, her heels click-clacking on the polished parquet flooring.

'Come back! *At once!* This is quite outrageous!' the woman shouted after her as she set off in pursuit.

Where, where, *where* was the dining room? Without slackening speed, Julie cast her eyes about her . . . a large open hearth . . . a stairway leading to an upstairs gallery . . . portraits of gowned academics. Dodging down a passageway to her left, she passed a large reception room . . . a glimpse of lawns running down to the river. Behind her the cries of protest grew ever more shrill. The impassive figure of a college servant in a black jacket and pin-stripe trousers loomed up in front of her.

'I must see Sir Lucas,' she gasped, putting her hand on his arm and rocking the silver tray with its box of Havana cigars. 'It's terribly important.' She looked up into the man's sallow face.

The butler's pendulous lower lip trembled with consternation. 'This is most irregular, young lady. You cannot interrupt the Vice—'

'*Please!* Give him a message. Tell him that Julie Dixon *must* speak to him. It's about her brother.'

'You are Mr Dixon's sister?'

'Yes. Now *please* hurry!'

The butler tapped on the door and went into the dining room, closing it firmly behind him. Julie pressed her ear to the door. The footsteps of her pursuer grew louder.

'A Miss Dixon? *Here? To see me?* About her *brother*?' A thin piping voice on an ascending scale of indignation. 'It is quite impossible! Tell her that the matter is out of our—'

Julie had heard enough. Blue cashmere was bearing down on her. She thrust open the door. Faces turned to stare at her, eyes glassy with food and wine, exclamations of protest mingled with deprecatory mutterings as she swept into the room. 'Which of you is the Vice-Chancellor?' she demanded.

Sir Lucas rose from the table. Wiping his lips carefully, he dismissed the butler with an imperious wave of his napkin. 'I have that honour.'

Julie faced her circle of enemies like a duellist, her head and shoulders lined up on them, her eyes like rapier points. 'So, you are the ones whom my brother called friends and colleagues, the ones who have made these horrible accusations.'

'*Miss Dixon!*' Sir Lucas expostulated,' I cannot permit—'

'And you,' Julie exclaimed, 'you are the slanderer-in-chief! Not content with ruining my brother's career, you are now trying to hound him into prison.'

'*Miss Dixon!*' Sir Lucas protested. He held up his hand, his face averted as if to escape the full force of the blast. 'This is a working lunch and one of the few opportunities I have to get together with my esteemed colleagues.'

'I will not be denied a fair hearing, Sir Lucas. You would have to go far to find a man as loyal and honest as my brother. It is inconceivable that he has done anything shameful. He may have been abducted, he may even be dead, while you and your cronies sit here drowning in port.'

'*Miss Dixon! This is intolerable!* My colleagues and I are not prepared to be abused in this manner.' Sir Lucas stooped under the table and pressed a bell. 'If you do not go at once I shall have no alternative but to ask the college servants to have you removed.'

Julie strode to the far end of the room and stood with her back to the window. 'If anyone lays a finger on me,' she said quietly, 'I shall sue for assault. All I am asking is the right to be heard. I have friends in the press. We can keep this between ourselves. Or, if you prefer, you can read all about it in tomorrow's newspapers.'

The Vice-Chancellor took out a handkerchief and mopped his forehead. 'This is all most unseemly. I can give you five minutes of my time, Miss Dixon and not a moment longer. I suggest that we repair to the library.' He turned to his colleagues who had risen from the table.

'Gentlemen, excuse us, please.'

The lady in the cashmere dress was hovering nervously in the passage and shrank against the wall to let them pass. 'We shall talk about this later,' Sir Lucas told her in a ferocious whisper.

The library was a large gloomy room with marble busts in the dimly lit alcoves either side of the fireplace and tall shelves lined with leather-bound books. A faint smell of wood smoke hung in the air.

Sir Lucas did not offer Julie a chair. He stood with his back to the fire, his thumbs thrust into the waistcoat pockets of his brown tweed suit. 'It would be helpful,' he began in his high, reedy voice, 'if we could conduct the remainder of this discussion in a civilised manner. Let us consider the facts. Most of them are undisputed.'

'*I dispute them.*' Julie tossed her head angrily.

'Hear me out, young lady.' He extracted a pipe from the pocket of his jacket, filled it from a leather pouch and lit up. 'Your brother was working on a new, compact, immensely powerful capacitor. The potential was so enormous, not least in the field of weapons development, that in the interest of national security we had to delay publishing his results. It is impossible to exaggerate the importance of what he was doing. We had the highest hopes.' He sucked on the pipe until it was drawing freely. 'Then, three months ago, David disappeared without warning taking with him everything—'

'*David wouldn't steal!*'

'Let us say that he took what he needed in order to negotiate the most advantageous deal.'

'*Not for himself!*'

'For whom, then? For whom? He made no attempt to contact us and despite the best endeavours of the police they have been unable to trace him.'

Julie could not remain still while she listened to this. She paced up and down the room her lips pressed tight together, her face very pale save for two livid spots high up on her cheeks. Now she stopped and swung on her heel to confront the Vice-Chancellor.

'Sir Lucas, you didn't know David as I did. He may have been a little naïve but he was as true a friend as anyone could have. His work here, his research was his whole life. He believed that his invention would transform the world we live in. A new source of energy would revolutionise the transport industries. It would eliminate the dependence on oil and bring relief to millions whose lives are blighted by inhaling carcinogenic fumes. That was what motivated him – *inspired him*. If he had one anxiety it was that the completion of his work might be delayed by shortage of money.'

Sir Lucas smiled sardonically, 'Ah . . . shortage of money . . . there you have put your finger on it.'

Julie stamped her foot. '*I will not have my words twisted, Sir Lucas!* David was worried about the conditions at Fleetwood. He said that it was impossible to do first-class work with second-rate facilities.'

Sir Lucas snorted. 'I have yet to meet a scientist who is satisfied with his equipment or the level of funding he receives. We looked after David. We cherished him. No, Miss Dixon your faith in your brother does you credit but the truth is that he had hit on something that big industrial companies would pay a fortune for. His days of toiling in the groves of academe were over. These organisations are quite ruthless. Temptations . . . inducements . . . would have been placed in his way—'

'So, you've decided he was bribed? That he is nothing but a crook?'

Sir Lucas spread his hands resignedly. 'We have to live in the real world, uncomfortable though that sometimes is.'

'Thanks to you, David is now a suspected criminal.'

The Vice-Chancellor raised his shoulders in a little shrug. 'Your brother is the author of his misfortunes. The papers are with the Serious Fraud Office.'

Tears of rage pricked at her eyes. She blinked them away impatiently. 'I intend to find my brother, Sir Lucas, and clear his name. When the truth comes out, which it will, I shall consider what further action to take. Meanwhile, I hope you and your colleagues can live with yourselves.'

'I anticipate that we shall be able to do so,' said Sir Lucas complacently. He emptied his pipe into an ashtray with the satisfaction of a man who has adroitly disposed of a tiresome problem. 'Now, Miss Dixon, on your assurance that the manner of your leave-taking will be more decorous than that of your arrival, I shall accompany you to the front door.'

'*Oh, go to hell!*' Julie snapped. She ran blindly out of the room and down the long passage to the hall.

11

GENEVA

It was fifteen minutes to three on a dull afternoon in Geneva when Marc Canton left his office. Rain was falling in a thin drizzle, making the pavements shine. He was expecting a call from Leah Stein, Sam Coaker's PA. He reached the Place de Cornavin in front of the main railway terminus and waited in the bus shelter until the telephone kiosk became vacant. He checked his watch as he stepped inside. Just under four minutes to go.

Canton was born in New Orleans of mixed parentage. His mother was a professional dancer of French origin and his father a long-distance truck driver from Denver. The marriage of this strangely assorted couple was a happy one. They had made considerable sacrifices to put their son through college and university and it was the proudest day of their lives when he secured a job with the US Treasury department.

Over the next few years he showed a modest talent for investigative work and in due course became a full-time Treasury agent, one of a team put together to counter large-scale money laundering by international criminals.

After five years in Washington, with a failed marriage behind him, he was posted to Switzerland. He became a liaison officer between the Treasury and the Swiss National Bank who were setting up a system to monitor transfers of funds from Eastern Europe.

It was frustrating work. Swiss banking law set a high price on confidentiality. The banks were secretive, their management autocratic and resistant to change. He was in his mid-thirties and seemed to be getting nowhere. A chance meeting in a bar led to a surveillance job with the CIA. He didn't flatter himself that the Agency was the force it had been. There had been budget cutbacks and morale had suffered. Taxpayers were weary of foreign adventures in far off countries.

His new job was to investigate and report on the activities of rich businessmen from Eastern Europe making regular visits to Switzerland. It was no secret that many of them owed their wealth to the unregulated sale of state property.

The CIA set him up with a small office. To all appearances he worked for an advisory committee on hydro-electric power, an organisation with connections to the World Bank. He was not a man whom people remembered easily. Of medium build, with wavy brown hair and a soft-spoken manner, he merged into the crowd.

At exactly three o'clock the telephone rang.

'Canton?'

'Yes, ma'am.' He had never met Leah Stein, only seen her in photographs. A bottle blonde with a reputation for having a very sharp brain under the hair-do.

'Skip the courtesies. We haven't much time. You received an approach from someone with product to sell. Code name Pedlar. Has he made contact again?'

'No.'

'Do you think he will?'

'Yes. He must be frightened. He will try to do a deal with us first.'

'Why?'

'Others may offer more but their money comes with a health warning.'

'Have you tried to trace him?'

'All I had was that audio-tape.'

'We have examined the tape. The voice has obviously been disguised. There are no fingerprints. You must trace him and meet him. It is urgent.'

'What about the money?'

'Tell him there won't be a problem.'

'I shall need written authorisation.'

'You can't have it. We are out on a limb on this.'

'Who do I take my orders from?'

'This comes from the top.'

'I'm worried. Supposing there's trouble—'

'There's always trouble. It's what we're paid for.' She rang off.

12

TRAIN TO COLMAR

Scott had hoped to have the compartment to himself but two passengers got in at the last moment. The older man was leaning on a stick and burdened by a heavy suitcase. He paused in the door to catch his breath.

'May I?' Scott took the case from him and slung it up on the rack.

The old man inclined his head and thanked him. 'I am not so young as I was and this cold weather gets into my bones.'

Scott turned to look at the next arrival. An army officer out of uniform was his guess. The upright bearing, the beaky nose, the neat, clipped moustache, the red ribbon in the lapel of the dark suit. The two men settled themselves in opposite corners leaving him to his newspaper.

Tensions in Germany dominated the front pages. The euro had exposed the old rustbelt industries in the east of the country to merciless competition. Unemployment was rising rapidly, giving birth to a new underclass bitterly resentful of the failure of unification to transform their lives.

Disaffected young Germans had no need to search for a new creed, merely to exhume an old one from its shallow grave. Groups akin to the notorious Hitler Youth held secret meetings in cellars and attended rallies in disused drill halls draped with Nazi flags. They flouted the laws banning the wearing of proscribed uniforms or insignia, often with police connivance. They lacked one thing only – a voice, a leader through whom to channel the pent-up anger and bitterness of years. Now they had found him.

Wolfgang Muhlder was the leader of the Extreme Right Party. Aged thirty-nine, shaven-headed and powerfully built, he was an 'Osti' from the former German Democratic Republic and had served in the National Peoples' Army. He was a man of great physical magnetism, a mob-orator who could orchestrate the emotions of his audience like a Wagnerian conductor.

The paper carried a report of his latest rally, held in a stadium on the outskirts of Aachen. Muhlder had stepped up to the podium to rapturous acclamation from the huge crowd and it was some time before the marshals could restore order.

He began quietly, as if speaking to friends gathered round his fireside. 'The British will leave the European Union. London will become a back number. Frankfurt will soon be the financial centre of the Continent and Germany will be the leading power this side of the Atlantic.' He leaned forward over the dais, his forehead glistening under the powerful arc lights.

'*Kameraden*, believe me. The resurgence of our great nation after the devastation of war did not happen by itself.' The voice grew harsher like the sound of an orchestra as the brass instruments come in. 'It was built, brick upon brick, by the grinding labour of two generations. This granary full of golden grain is the product of privation and sacrifice.' The pitch of the voice carried higher. 'It belongs to you and me, whose forebears made it possible. It belongs to those who have brought in the harvest. Not to every pigeon that flies down to gorge itself at our table.'

This last sally drew a full-throated roar from the multitude, but to the clamour was added a menacing base note. At first no more than a low muttering, '*Aus-länd-er-frei, Aus-länd-er-frei.*' 'Foreigners out. Foreigners out.' Then taking on a rhythm like the feet of marching soldiers,

'*Aus-länd-er-frei! Aus-länd-er-frei! Aus-länd-er-frei!*'

The sun was setting, making a bonfire of the old day. Torches were being lit throughout the arena. Muhlder's words swirled around

87

them like a great wind, his powerful hands slicing and chopping as he increased the tempo.

'*Kameraden!* So long as we cringe and crawl, so long as we apologise for our very existence, the German people will be denied the greatness that is their birthright.'

The crowd showed signs of restlessness as the voice rose to a crescendo, stirring them, goading them. The chanting rose and swelled like a line of incoming breakers gathering strength with every yard. '*Aus-länd-er-frei! Aus-länd-er-frei! Aus-länd-er-frei!*'

Muhlder's delivery was clipped now, the phrases barked out like a drill sergeant. 'What is Germany's destiny? *To ask or to demand?*'

'*To demand, mein Führer!*' the crowd roared.

A forest of arms swung up in the forbidden salute. It was the signal everyone had been waiting for. A ripple went through the crowd like adrenaline in a muscle primed for violence.

There was a surge towards the exit. The umber light from the torches flickered on headbands bearing the skull and crossbones, on brawny forearms emblazoned with emblems of hate or the crude, unenigmatic *Hass* framed by the SS runes. As they broke into a run, the chant was taken up once again in time with the menacing jog-jog of their feet. A woman peeping fearfully from behind her curtains described the sound as being like stones pattering down a mountainside, first small ones, then larger. The precursor of an avalanche.

The police, never more than a token presence, melted away as the clamour grew louder, the baying more insistent. Then came the clash of breaking glass as the windows of foreign cars were stoved in. Shops selling foreign goods were next. Metal rubbish bins were lifted off the streets and hurled through the plate glass. Obedient to some self-imposed code, stocks were not looted except to provide ammunition with which to inflict further damage.

Then came the fires. A Lada was overturned and torched. The spare wheel of a Cherokee Jeep was torn from its mountings, set alight and sent bowling down the street. An American fast- food restaurant was hosed down with petrol and set ablaze. A Turkish immigrant was chased, cornered in a building site, stoned and left crippled for life. The destruction was ruthless but selective. German property remained almost unscathed.

There were soothing words from the German Foreign Minister. Germany had no military or territorial ambitions. That benighted era was over, finished for ever. Elections were due to be held within a few days. The extremists would be consigned to the lunatic fringe. Everybody would see that democracy was in strong hands, safe hands.

Scott put down his paper. 'My father fought the Germans,' the old man was saying. 'He was killed at Verdun. We never really recovered from that battle. It was the charnel house of the French army. As for me, I was luckier.' He tapped his knee. 'Just a piece of shrapnel at Caen in forty-four.'

'You were with the Free French?'

'I was with Leclerc when we marched back into Paris.' He shrugged. 'I don't know why I am telling you all this. You must think I am a silly old buffer . . . ' His voice tailed off.

'Of course not, Monsieur,' His companion stifled the yawn and smiled encouragement.

The old man sighed. 'That's what I should have thought at your age. I should have polished the buttons on my uniform and worried about nothing besides making a fine figure for the ladies. But the nation asks more than that of its soldiers when the shooting starts.'

'So you think that there is going to be trouble with Germany?'

He spread his hands. 'It is inevitable. But not the sort of trouble that you are thinking about. Your eyes are fixed on the conjuror but you see only what he intends you to see.'

'I don't understand,' said the younger man frowning.

'Huge amounts of arms are being smuggled into Germany and hidden deep in the countryside. In cellars, in barns, in forests, in caves deep in the mountains.'

'*You astonish me!* What are the weapons for? And who is behind this? What is he planning?'

'Many people would like to know that.' The train rattled over the points, picking up speed. The older man turned his face to the window, his eyes as bleak as the failing light.

At Mulhouse, Scott had to change trains. He called his office and asked for Jeff Turcan, but the girl put him through to Mal Hain.

'What's happened to Jeff? Has he got a sore throat?'

'He's in a meeting but he asked me to give you a message. Forget about the privatisation list.'

'I already have. If Fraser Outram want to waste time on it, they're welcome. What's new?'

Problems. Chiropan had missed out on a big hospital contract. The trials on Anadrol had been extended by three months. The timing couldn't be worse. They were on the point of putting in an application for a listing on the New York Stock Exchange.

'Hudson Caird aren't going to be happy, Mal. We hyped Anadrol to hell and back.'

'Anadrol will come good but we needed that fast-track certification.'

'You know my views on borrowing short term to buy these companies. Any slippage and the bank has got us by the short hairs.'

'It's the business we're in, Scott. Buy right, gear up, put in strong management and keep the cream for ourselves. Don't bring in more institutional money than you need or you'll be living off skimmed milk.'

'We are undercapitalised, Mal. That worries me. If we lose a big contract or our licences get delayed, our profit projections aren't worth the paper they are written on.'

'Jeff reckons there's more to it than bad luck. He thinks someone put the skids under us.'

'Jeff's fantasising.'

'Don't bet on it. The whisper is that it's the French. That company in Lille were underbidders for Pharmazin. Those guys are bad losers.'

'Who isn't?'

'You went to the embassy. Didn't you get a whiff of anything?'

'No.'

'Then you're going to have to dig around until you do. If it isn't Paris, go to Brussels.'

'Or Amsterdam or The Hague. Do you want me to piss around the whole of Europe?'

'It's your territory, Scott. Just come up with some answers – *and quick!*' He hung up.

The cold hit him as soon as he stepped on to the platform and he hunched down into his coat. Why did bad news have to come on a raw March night in a strange town? He found a taxi. He wanted a hotel in the centre. 'I don't want to buy the place. I just want a room for the night and a bottle of Jack Daniels.' The driver chuckled. He knew just the place. But they always said that.

'Why do people come to Colmar?' Scott asked, watching the sleet drifting into the yellow beam of the headlights. 'If they do, that is.'

'It's a beautiful town, Monsieur,' the driver replied reproachfully. 'We get many tourists in the summer.'

The hotel was old-fashioned but comfortable, the bedroom fitted with heavy provincial furniture and a big bed with a shiny white duvet. He went to the window. On the rooftops, the snow glistened like icing sugar. In the gloom he could make out the shape of the cathedral spire.

The houses across the narrow cobbled street with their gables and mullioned windows looked hunched and misshapen like old men on crutches. In New York it would be early afternoon. The teeming life of the markets, the glass and steel of the towering office blocks, the knife-edge geometry of the streets. It could be on another planet.

He showered and changed, gave the maid his laundry and went out. He was ready for a large steak and a bottle of red wine. *What in hell's name had Warren gotten into*? He had some hard thinking to do.

13

THE CHALET HIRSCH, LAKE ZURICH

The man looking over the wide expanse of lawn to the smooth surface of the lake gave a little shiver. The water looked so cold and grey and lifeless. Like the face of a corpse. '*Schock!*' He called sharply to his dog. He must put these morbid thoughts out of his head. The most dangerous part was behind him. A few days ago, Franz Strauben had been just another manager of Zoltán Zaros, a small private bank, the course of his life dictated by the foibles of an autocratic old man. Now the sky was the limit. All that was needed was a steady nerve.

The audio-tape had been inspired. He would give anything to have seen the faces at the CIA when they played it over. *Talk about putting the cat among the pigeons!* But there was nothing they could do except sweat until he made contact again.

His faithful Doberman padded after him as he climbed the stairs to the bathroom. Removing the panel on the side of the bath, he inserted a key in the small cylindrical safe sunk into the floor. Lifting the lid and reaching inside he pulled out the tightly furled documents and returned to his dressing room. He went to the table and tried to spread them out but they curled up shyly as if their secrets were not to be wrested from them so easily. Chuckling to himself, he weighted the corners with small objects to hold them down.

The dog brushed against his leg and he bent down to smooth the wrinkled frown from its forehead. 'You may well look puzzled, Schock,' he murmured. 'If you only knew what your master has in his possession.

But how could you know?' How could anyone even dream of it? It was beyond imagination.

He never tired of poring over the bonds, even exciting the curiosity of his wife who normally took little interest in his business affairs. He had lied to her, telling her that it was a legal opinion on his employment contract.

'I hope the lawyers advise you to sue. For a few days I thought you were going to have a breakdown. Zaros treated you abominably.'

He was amused and touched by her indignation. 'The old man is very ill, my dear. He doesn't know what he is doing any more. Provided he does not repeat his accusations, it might be better to let matters rest.'

'But what are we going to live on, Franz?' she had asked anxiously. 'Our son is still at university and this big house is not cheap to run. It is all so worrying.'

He had taken her in his arms and kissed her. 'Don't worry, Gabi. We shall manage. Believe me, I have plans, great plans.'

Great plans indeed. *What was beyond the reach of a man who had secured such a prize?* Five bonds with a face value of fifty million dollars! When it had first hit him, he had felt like running into the street and shouting the news at the top of his voice. He had to lock himself in his office until he was sufficiently master of himself.

After the scene with Zoltán Zaros, he had driven home. He had not dared go into the house until he had made certain that the police were not there before him. Then, when he discovered that without the missing codes the bonds might be worthless, he thought he would go mad. To plunge from euphoria to despondency in the space of a few minutes would try any man's reason.

For several days he had been in despair, pacing up and down his room hour after hour, refusing to come down to meals, cursing Gabi when she tried to remonstrate with him. But his professional training had come to his rescue. It was inconceivable that a man as astute and resourceful as Franz Strauben could not make something remarkable of this. He had retreated to his study and examined the bonds in the smallest detail.

The paper was cream coloured and stiff like parchment. Apart from the serial numbers in the top corner, they were identical. The nominal value of each bond was shown as ten million dollars. In the centre there was a fine engraving of the White House. Across this, in heavy raised gold lettering were the words:

Directorate Insurgency Deployment Operations (DIDO):

Established on the authority of

The President of the United States of America

The lower half of the bond was taken up with a map of Europe. The Soviet Union and its vassal states were in vivid red. Hovering over it with its spread wings, fierce eyes, distended claws and sickle beak was the American eagle, looking as if it was about to swoop down on to a slab of raw meat.

At the foot of the documents appeared the signature of President John F. Kennedy. All the bonds carried a stamp. The wording, in bold lettering using magenta-coloured ink, read:

Access to the funds can only be gained by logging in, using the serial numbers of the bonds in combination with the encrypted codes.

There was no issuing bank. Tracking down the missing codes was beyond him but surely the documents were gold dust in themselves. *Insurgency operations!* While hiding behind the DIDO smokescreen, was Kennedy planning to finance revolution in the enslaved satellites of the USSR?

The bonds would be political dynamite! And Russia was striving to rebuild its empire. They would regard the threat the fund posed as dangerous as it was fifty years earlier. What would the US government pay to prevent the bonds from falling into the hands of the Russians – or pariah states like Iran – or terrorists! Ten per cent of the face value would not be exorbitant. The US Treasury might go to twice that.

He rolled up the bonds and returned them to the safe. As he turned, he caught sight of himself in the mirror. The features that stared back at him, the high forehead, the glossy black hair brushed straight back, the thin, sinuous lips would soon become familiar in the international resorts frequented by the rich and famous. For a man with a fortune in ready money the world was full of possibilities. He would get another message to Canton in Geneva. Arrange to meet. Set up the deal. But he must tread carefully. Suddenly the world had become a very dangerous place.

14

IMMIGRATION DETENTION CENTRE, ESSEX

Julie eased back on the pedal. The speedometer had been hovering on ninety. She was still seething from her confrontation with Sir Lucas Micklem. *The arrogance of the man!* The phone bleeped. Duggie Bains.

'Drop what you're doing tomorrow, Julie. I've got a job for you. Do you remember that feature you did on asylum seekers?'

'About twelve months ago.' She had visited an immigrant detention centre near Heathrow.

'A seaman jumped ship last night, a mile off Felixstowe, and swam ashore.'

'Name?'

'Kiril Nadym. The ship was coming from Tallinn in Estonia. He was carted off to hospital for the night, suffering from hypothermia. Today he applied for asylum. He's being held in an ID centre near Colchester while his application is being processed.'

'It isn't much of a story. Surely the local papers—'

'He refuses to talk to them. He insists on seeing you.'

'Why me?'

'You've got a tongue in your head. Ask him.'

'Does he speak any English?'

'How the hell should I know? Speak to my secretary. She'll fill in the details.'

Carol came on the line. She had found an interpreter. 'She's a student called Kristina. She speaks Estonian and Russian. She'll be waiting for you at the entrance to South Kensington underground station

97

at seven tomorrow morning. Give two taps on the horn and she'll come to your car. Your appointment is at eleven sharp. Don't be late – and Julie, *try* to get into the office in the afternoon.' Girls like Julie irritated her. They were completely undisciplined but they seemed to get all the fun. It was very unfair.

Kristina was waiting for Julie by the newsstand. She was a slim girl with dark hair almost concealed by a grey woollen shawl. Her shapeless black overcoat nearly reached her ankles.

An accident on the motorway held them up and they arrived with no more than a few minutes in hand. The detention centre was an old army camp, a scattering of brick buildings and concrete pathways surrounded by a high chain-link fence. The security guard emerged from a wooden hut, glanced at his clipboard and waved them through.

They checked in at reception. The uniformed officer looked at the list. 'I only have one name here, a Miss Dixon. Journalist.' He sniffed.

'Kristina is here as an interpreter.'

'Then we should have been given notice that she would be coming.'

'I'm sorry. We were very rushed.'

'It's always the same,' he muttered. 'Rush, rush, rush . . . ' Laboriously he took down Kristina's full name and address.

'And you have come to see? '

Julie took a deep breath. 'Mr Kiril Nadym.'

They were escorted down a long corridor with interview rooms on either side. Through the glass partitioning they got a look at some of the recent arrivals. Hollow-eyed with exhaustion, dishevelled, unshaven, their gaunt cheeks telling of days holed up in the backs of lorries, they made a striking contrast with the officials in their uniforms or business suits.

They were taken to an interview room and a few minutes later Nadym arrived accompanied by an escort officer, who left them together.

He was a short, balding, sturdily built man with a barrel chest that filled his seaman's sweater. His black eyes shifted from one to the other as they introduced themselves.

'You still work for newspaper?' he asked Julie.

'For the *Courier*.' She took a copy from her briefcase and passed it to him. She gestured at her companion. 'Kristina is from your country. She has agreed to interpret for us.' She waited while the girl translated.

Nadym smiled, showing teeth stained with nicotine. 'I know this paper.' From the recesses of a back pocket, he produced a tobacco pouch and extracted a crumpled newspaper clipping. Unfolding it carefully, he placed it on the table between them.

Julie glanced at it. It was her article. 'How did you get hold of this?'

'Some friends in Tallinn gave it to me. They help people like me, people who have problems. They told me that when I arrive in England I must try to contact the person who wrote this.' His voice had a wheedling tone which Kristina mimicked in translation.

'Why do you want to stay in England?'

'Because I am worried.'

'Worried about what?'

He spread his hands. 'I am a Russian. Things are very difficult for us since Estonia became independent. There is discrimination. Many of us have been thrown out of our apartments to make way for nationals. When we can get work it is only the dirty jobs.'

'It is not true what he says,' Kristina broke in fiercely. 'We all have problems finding good jobs and somewhere decent to live.'

Julie raised her hand and frowned her into silence. She asked some more questions and looked through her notes. How could she make anything of such dreary material? Then Nadym refused to be photographed. That put the lid on it. He would be lucky to get half a column on an inside page. She shook her head. 'I'm sorry. I can't see how

I can help. I'm a journalist. What you need is a lawyer. Someone who specialises in cases like this.'

Nadym jumped up from the table. '*Talk, talk, talk!* That is all lawyers do. Talk and take our money!' He slapped the paper down on the table top. '*Sometimes we are beaten and thrown into prison!*' he shouted. 'You tell your readers how bad things are! Newspapers have power. People take notice!'

The officer tapped against the glass and Nadym subsided into his chair.

Kristina glowered at him. 'It makes me furious to hear the way he talks. My country is not a police state. I don't believe his story.'

Julie put a hand on the girl's arm to calm her. The situation was getting out of control. She would speak to her editor, she told Nadym, but she was not optimistic. She dropped her notebook in her briefcase.

Down the corridor there came the sound of a commotion. She opened the door and looked outside. A burly, middle-aged man with several days' growth of beard was directing a torrent of what had to be abuse in any language at the hapless official assigned to him.

Nadym moved closer until he could look over her shoulder. A piece of paper was pushed into her hand. The officer stepped back into the room. 'All right, Mr Nadym, time's up. Let's be having you.' Nadym gave a little shrug. He appeared to have given up. He held out a limp hand, but in the dark eyes that held hers there was a message.

Kristina turned away to button up her coat, her expression glacial. On the way back she said nothing until Julie dropped her off at Liverpool Street station, thanked her and paid her. 'I hope you British throw him back in the sea like a fish that isn't worth catching.'

Julie unravelled the crumpled ball of paper, ironing it with her fist until the pencilled scrawl was legible. From the uneven spacing between the words it seemed probable that he had broken off several times to get help over a sentence. She skimmed through it and then read it slowly, puzzling over the alterations.

'It not possible to say this when we meet. I leave that ship because I am frightened. Owner of *Ludmilla* is very bad man. He smuggles guns. I know too much. It is dangerous for me. He also owns *Galinna.* Ship unloads weapons in Hamburg docks at midnight. Tonight. Go alone. Take camera. Get proof of what I say. Then print in paper. Help me to stay in England. Do not show this note to anyone until I am safe.'

She bought a copy of *Lloyd's List* and found the MV *Galinna*. Nadym's story checked. She telephoned Carol. She had to see Duggie at once.

'I'm afraid Mr Bains is tied up in meetings all day.'

She ground her teeth. Obstructive cow. 'Come on, Carol,' she pleaded, 'I only need five minutes. Be an angel and fix it.' She swung the car out into the traffic.

15

NEW YORK

Hudson Caird was a fast-growing investment house in New York, young and aggressive, with a reputation for getting top dollar for the companies they brought to the market. Ken Northop, the CEO, had already had two top-level meetings that morning and was going into a third. He put in a quick call to Railton Ross. He wanted to see Jeff Turcan and he was in a hurry.

'Your place or mine?' Turcan joked when the call was put through. Northop's manner had unsettled him.

'Off campus.' Northop grunted. He named a hotel on Lexington Avenue. 'I'll meet you in an hour.'

'Can you tell me what it's about?'

'It will have to keep till I see you.'

'I would like to bring Mal Hain.'

'Come by yourself.'

Hell. That was no way to talk to a client, but Turcan didn't argue. There was something in Northop's tone.

They met over two large glasses of Perrier in a dimly lit corner of the opulently appointed hotel lounge.

Northop was slim, dark and sharp-eyed with a restless habit of tapping his pencil against his teeth. It was like listening to the remorseless ticking of a clock. 'Good of you to see me at short notice, Jeff.' Tap . . . tap . . . tap. 'I was sorry to hear about the Chiropan contract.' Tap . . . tap . . . tap . . .

Turcan shrugged. 'You can't win them all. We had hoped to sell Meducain on the back of that contract but we're bringing forward the sale of Ribodox.'

'A bit early isn't it? Ribodox is a turn-around. You need a minimum of three years' good profits. You only have one.' Tap . . . tap . . . tap . . .

'We will still double our money. That should put us back on target for our SEC application.'

'Have you had any offers?'

'Two.'

'What sort of money?'

Turcan told him. 'And we can squeeze them higher.'

Northop shook his head. 'I doubt it. Not in the time frame.' He levelled the pencil with its needle-fine point at Turcan. 'And I don't think the market would be very impressed by the sale, anyway. It smells of a frantic last-minute attempt to meet your projections.'

'That's bull, Ken, and you know it! The issue will be a breeze. Investors will get knocked down in the rush. They don't get a chance to buy into a company of our quality every day.'

'Don't get me wrong, Jeff. I like the company. Especially the pharmaceuticals division.'

'So you should. We have a formula that works. Why bust our ass developing new drugs? Leave that to the majors. Wait till the brand names are out of patent, clone them and cut the prices.'

'Yeah, the results have been good,' he conceded.

'You better believe it. We have a tried and tested product in months – not years – and at a fraction of the cost. Result? Good profits for us and a huge saving in the US health care bill. No wonder the politicians love us.'

Northop smiled humourlessly. 'Who says they do?'

'*I say so*. Railton has unrivalled connections – a profile with key Congressmen that a multi-national would kill for. I think of the Hill as an extension of my office.'

'Connections are like a rope bridge, Jeff. Overload them and they start to fray.'

'Our bridge is holding, Ken, though I admit it's stretched as tight as a banjo string.'

'Someone has taken an axe to it, Jeff. It's hanging down like a donkey's dick.'

Turcan sat very still. So it was true. The calls that had not been returned, the rulings from the Food and Drug Administration postponing the granting of licences, problems that should have taken thirty seconds to sort out on the telephone bogged down in paper and bureaucracy.

He rallied and went on the offensive. 'This issue is going to go like a rocket, Ken. We are days from blast-off. *If you haven't got the balls to push the button, get off the launch pad!* There are firms lined up all around the block crying out for a piece of the action.'

Northop leaned forward keeping his voice low. 'You are talking about yesterday, Jeff. Yesterday I would have agreed with you.'

Turcan stared at him stony-faced. 'So, what's new?'

'Rick Wraxby called me at home this morning. Early. It was still dark.'

'Wraxby retired years ago. He's history.'

'He retired from the SEC last year. He still works for them as a consultant.'

'So . . . ?' Turcan's cheeks were as yellow as dried apricots.

'Rick wants you to postpone your application.'

'*Postpone it!*' Turcan shot out of his chair. '*Why, for Chrissake!*' He stole a glance round the room. Heads had turned their way. 'What's Wraxby talking about?' he hissed through gritted teeth. 'And why should we give a shit? He has no official standing with the SEC.'

'It's a request, Jeff. Informal. Off the record. But don't ignore it.'

Turcan gaped at him. 'What do I tell my board? What do I tell the bank? What reason did Wraxby give?'

'The SEC are worried about your European operation.'

'Then someone should tell them to get their heads out of their asses. The Eastern Europe companies are going like a train. In the last quarter—'

'I have read the draft prospectus, Jeff,' Northop reminded him quietly.

'*Well, read it again!*' Turcan snorted. 'Those babes are doing great.'

'That could change very fast.' Tap . . . tap . . . 'How closely is Scott Rokeby involved in that operation?'

'It *is* his operation. He identified the companies, took a chainsaw to the old management. His name is all over it.'

Northop jerked his head in the direction of the lobby and they walked out into the street together. He thrust out his hand. 'I don't know what the problem is, Jeff, but take my advice, find out and find out fast. And don't put your application in to the SEC until you've come up with an answer.'

Turcan waved down a taxi. The acid was pooling in the pit of his stomach. This was trouble and trouble of the worst sort. Rokeby had fouled up and it had backed right up the drain. Railton Europe had always worried him. It was too far from base and the natives played by their own rules. Why go looking for problems when there was a huge market on your own doorstep? And he'd always had reservations about Rokeby. That upbringing in the Commie block, the mixed blood, the polo. What sort of a candy-assed sport was that? Why didn't he go to the ball game like the rest of them?

'Can't you get some more speed out of this thing?' he snarled at the driver. 'They sell toy cars that go faster than this.' Railton needed cash and they needed time. Both were running out.

16

THE VOSGES, EASTERN FRANCE

Scott had an early breakfast in the hotel before returning to his room and spreading the map on the table. Until he found his father's car he hadn't got to first base. He rang down to the hotel porter. He wanted copies of the local newspapers sent up to him, back editions as well. No, he didn't mind what condition they were in. He skimmed through them quickly. Nothing in the news sections.

On one of the back pages there was an interview with the manager of a vehicle recovery firm with a photograph of him standing beside his pick-up truck. He looked cheerful. Business was brisk. Winter was his busiest time. The narrow, twisting roads, snow and fog and icy surfaces.

Of course, he didn't like to profit from people's misfortune but no, he wasn't complaining. He found the number in the directory. The guy was out on a job but he got him on his mobile, explained that he was doing a survey for a large insurance company. 'They are worried about the high incidence of claims in this area.'

'Here am I up to my waist in mud . . . and you want to talk statistics.'

'No. All I want is an overview. How does this month compare with the average?' Warm him up, Scott told himself, get the guy to talk and see where it led.

'I haven't got time. I've got a BMW upended with a tree growing through the roof.' He rang off and went down the list. On the tenth call he struck lucky. Bernard Maron ran a small family-owned garage on the outskirts of the town. He was having his mid-morning coffee and was happy to talk for a few minutes. 'High claims? It's not surprising. It's difficult driving round here and if you get bad weather you get trouble. There's steady business in the winter. Our main gripe is that we don't get our fair share of it. The insurance companies have their favourites. A small outfit like mine can't afford the kickbacks.'

'Do you get any work from the police?'

'Don't talk to me about the police,' he snorted. 'They cost me the best part of a day last week. A Peugeot 407 came off the road and I was—'

'Are you sure it was a 407?'

'I said so, didn't I? A white Peugeot 407. Anyway . . . ' He paused, suddenly suspicious. 'What difference does it make?'

'I was surprised, that's all. They usually hold the road fairly well.'

'If the road is there, they do, but some of these maniacs must have taken their test in a hovercraft.' He added that one of the forest rangers had been out early looking at a new plantation and had tipped him off.

'Was the car badly damaged?' Scott tried to keep his voice casual.

'What do you think? It was a hell of a drop. All the way down to down to the stream bed.'

'Where did it go over?'

'Do you know the mountain roads?'

'Enough.' With his finger he traced the line of the road on the map while the man was speaking.

'It's very narrow there. There's a series of S-bends and only light metal rails at the edge of the road. They wouldn't stop anything heavier than a bicycle.'

Scott took a deep breath. 'How did the ambulance get there?'

'A standard vehicle would never have made it. They used a Mercedes G-Wagon. Reinforced suspension. But there was no hurry. Nobody could have gone over there and lived. There was just one passenger. An elderly man. By the time I got there, the police were all over the place. They were just finishing sheeting the car. I've never seen that done before. Don't go telling anyone you got this from me. My wife tells me I talk too much. It will get me into trouble one day, she says. Now, if you don't mind, I have a living to make.'

It took him an hour to track down a Range Rover, three years old, dark green and with sixty thousand kilometres on the meter. His next visit was to a store selling camping equipment, where he got a rugged weatherproof jacket and trousers, a pair of sturdy boots, a good flashlight and the largest-scale map he could find.

The police pound was on the edge of town close to an industrial estate. He drove slowly past, feeling the muscles in his stomach tighten as he saw what he was up against. A high chain-link fence with a double steel gate at the front. A two-storey brick-built block. Probably offices on the first floor and a workshop underneath. Security lights at each corner. A CCTV camera mounted high up under the eaves. He counted a dozen cars and a pick-up truck. No sign of the white Peugeot. He would be back after dark.

An hour later, he was in the Vosges, on small roads, twisting and turning, climbing all the time. Below him lay dense pine forests, above him low clouds that hung about a barren hillside furnished only with tussocks of grass and outcrops of rock.

He glanced in the mirror. A biker in black helmet and leathers was about three hundred yards behind, keeping pace with him. How long had he been there? But the road was snaking this way and that and he lost sight of him.

He turned off down a narrow track. It was early afternoon but here it seemed to be perpetual dusk. He followed it downhill, his ears popping as the pressure changed, the vehicle riding smoothly over pine needles or lurching into half-frozen ruts where tractors had hauled timber into clearings to await loading.

The track levelled out and started to rise again. He stopped, wound down the window and listened. Rain drops falling from overhanging branches tapped like ghostly fingers on the roof. The air was raw on his cheeks. In his nostrils the smell of the pines was sweet and cloying. To his left, a narrow firebreak seemed to channel the rippling sound of a river.

He took the steep gradient carefully. Small branches, their foliage still green had been churned into the mud by heavy vehicles. It was hardly more than a stream gurgling between boulders and smaller rocks. Beyond it there was some fifty yards of barren ground to a rocky cliff that rose almost sheer to the road above.

Along the bank there were tyre tracks. Rounding a bend where the trees came down close to the water he saw it at once. Journey's end. Where the car had come to rest, the area had been staked out like an old mining claim. The posts were still there but only a few shreds of white tape clung to them to show that the site had been cordoned off. Scott left the car and using the rocks as stepping stones forded the river and searched the area yard by yard.

Slivers of glass like miniature daggers glinted among the stones. He picked up a chip off a mirror, a flake of paintwork, a shred from a tyre. On the air there was a faint smell of oil and here and there black stains where it had soaked into the scree.

He moved slowly, tracking the tell-tale depressions in the ground where the car had landed, bounced and skidded. Could his father have been conscious in those last moments as the car plunged into that grave-pit darkness? The final spasm of the heart, the lungs snatching their last shallow breath – and then . . . oblivion. These were the images that would haunt him. Evil had done its work unhindered. Its monument was here.

His eyes travelled up the face of the cliff. There was a ledge about a third of the way from the top where the car had gouged a wide furrow. A thorn tree stripped of its bark was leaning out at a crazy angle.

He crossed the river and drove back up the track and stopped again. His ears picked up another sound, muffled by the trees. A bike engine, throttled down, snuffing like a hunting dog that had caught the scent of game. Further along there were signs of felling and the trees were thinning out. He left the track, the Range Rover pushing through clumps of bramble and brown sodden bracken, his heart missing a beat every time they bounced across a half-hidden ditch or lurched over a concealed tree stump.

It was impossible to take any bearings. He must have driven in a semi-circle for there was the track again no more than fifty yards away. The only cover, a pile of neatly stacked timber. He switched off the engine, cruised in behind it and slipped out of the car.

The put-put of the bike was very close. In sight now, the rider paddling along to bring it into the clearing. His feet surprisingly small. Black helmet, gauntlets, leathers and boots. Even the machine was black. A pair of hands going to the strap under the chin, raising the helmet. The movements precise, economical, almost robotic.

A woman! Why had he assumed it was a man? Her hair was dark hair and cut short. Her face chalky white, devoid of expression. Her eyes panned slowly across the clearing, narrowing as they came to rest on the woodpile. She raised herself off the saddle.

Somewhere a jay screeched. A flock of pigeons burst from the trees. The head jerked round. The helmet came down. Gunning the engine, she raced back up the track leaving a cloud of blue smoke that hung in the air until the noise of the engine had faded.

Scott waited a full ten minutes, the perspiration drying on his skin, before he turned the ignition key. It took him almost an hour along a winding circuitous route before he got back to the metal road.

He knew he was close to where the car had gone over when the track seemed to double back on itself. It skirted the head of the valley and went into a series of tight bends. Round the next corner he pulled in hard against the side of the hill and walked across the road. A crude metal barrier ran along the edge. The police had run strips of warning tape across a missing section. Crouching down, he examined the verge. Tyre marks were clearly visible where the car had left the road. He would have given a lot to look at that missing length of fencing.

There was something else. A footprint, one of many in the soft ground but this one was about twelve inches away from the off-side tyre marks. About eighteen inches behind it there was a deep indentation, almost certainly made by the toe of a shoe or a boot. He looked for similar marks on the near side. And found them. If two men, one each side of the car, had pushed the car off the road to the verge and then over the cliff, the marks tallied.

As he straightened and turned back to the car, his eye caught a spark of reflected sunshine high up on the top of the hill. There could be a house up there. Perhaps whoever lived there had seen or heard something. He slammed the car into gear and took a lane to the left, climbing steeply between high banks.

Over the crest, he was surprised to find his progress blocked by a stone archway too narrow to permit a vehicle to pass. Through it, he could see figures in long robes walking along a row of colonnades which formed three sides of a square of lawn. A monastery of all places. To his left, a gravelled path led to a door in a high stone wall. Pushing through it he found himself in a bleak heathland with wind-torn trees and views to the forested hills across the valley. Below him, just visible over the curve of the hill, was the road that he had travelled a few moments earlier.

He turned at the sound of a door creaking behind him. An old man in the brown robes of a Franciscan monk was approaching.

'I am Père Joseph.' He introduced himself with a grave inclination of the head. 'Is there some way in which I can be of help?'

Scott explained that he was making some inquiries about an accident. He pointed to the road below. A car had gone into the ravine. 'Does anyone know what happened?'

Père Joseph shook his head. 'One of our brethren was awakened by a noise in the early hours of the morning. It came from down the hill but he assumed it was a rockfall. They are not uncommon in this valley.'

'Did the police come here?'

'They asked a lot of questions but we could tell them very little.'

They walked back together to the car. Père Joseph turned towards his visitor, concern showing in his pale grey eyes. 'I trust that you will visit us again one day when this trouble is behind you.'

'Trouble?' Scott smiled to cover his astonishment. 'Is it so obvious?'

'That you have not been completely frank with me?' Père Joseph's smile was rueful. 'In my line of work I have to make a little of the truth go a long way.' He held out his hand. 'Secrets can be a heavy burden to bear. They are not for the young who still have far to go. They are for old men who are close to the end of their journey.'

As Scott drove away, Père Joseph raised his hand in what might have been a blessing or a gesture of farewell and stood watching him until the road dipped and hid him from view. Warren was dead, harried to the very end. There seemed to be forces at work as malign as they were unfathomable. Would they rest now like predators sated after a kill? He sensed that they were casting round, trying to pick up the track of their next prey. Why hadn't Warren confided in him? Told him what he was up against?

The sky was darkening. As the car left the shelter of the high banks, the wind drove a flurry of snow against the windscreen with extraordinary violence.

17

THE *COURIER*

The *Courier* occupied three floors of a one of London's new landmarks, a steel and glass obelisk towering over the old docklands. Where once there were ships and cranes and a cloth-capped army making a living from the mercantile trade passing through the Port of London there were now high-tech offices, modern warehouses, yacht marinas and upmarket residential estates.

It was half-past four in the afternoon. The sub-editors daily meeting had broken up. News just in on the wire service reporting a sharp rise in the opinion polls for Wolfgang Muhlder's party was being moved to the front page. The pundits were saying that the Extreme Right could hold the balance of power in Germany's forthcoming general election.

Through the windows came a glimmer of late afternoon sunshine. Security was tight. The queue stretched across the marble floor of the hall and it was some minutes before Julie could show her pass at the counter and take the lift.

She was weaving her way across the newsroom when Wal Pittard grabbed her arm. '*Where the hell do you think you're going to*?' He had made his name in telephone sales and was one of nature's bullies.

She shook him off. His short spiky hair reminded her of pigs' bristles and he had the black button eyes to go with it. 'Duggie wants to see me,' she told him with a toss of her head.

'*So do* I,' he snarled. 'I'm your departmental editor, in case you've forgotten. I never see any work from you. I never know where the hell you are or what the hell you're doing.'

'Duggie knows what I'm doing.'

'Well, he can pay you. I can't afford you on my budget.'

'*Then tell him so yourself.*' She gave him a prod in the bulging waistband of his trousers. 'But get rid of that beer gut first or he'll send you out door-stepping to shed some of that lard.' She pushed past him, her eyes on the door at the far side of the room.

'And one more thing,' he shouted after her. 'You borrowed about a thousand quid's worth of photographic equipment. That was six weeks ago. We want it back.'

John Miller was hovering, hoping to catch her eye. He was tall and gangly, with a habit of twisting his legs round each other that made him look like a pipe cleaner.

She gave him an impatient smile. 'No time to talk, John, but can you do me a favour?'

'Of course, Julie. Anytime.' He trotted behind her like a faithful dog.

'Get me on a flight to Hamburg tonight. I have to be there by eleven. I'll pick up the ticket at the check-in desk.'

'Of course, Julie, but . . . but whose authority shall I give?'

'Bains.'

'Straight up?'

'Straight up. I'm going in to see him now.' She tapped on Carol's door and pushed it open.

Bains' secretary pushed her glasses up over her forehead. 'I thought I told you that Mr Bains was in meetings all afternoon. He can't see you. You're wasting your time and mine.' She frowned angrily at the screen. She had a deep tan which disappeared under the cream blouse. Carol's private life was a mystery. Whatever secrets she had, she shared only with her sunlamp.

In the next office, there was a sound of chairs being pushed back. Julie pointed at door panel behind which the shadows were moving. 'Look, Carol. Duggie's finished. Surely he can spare me a few minutes?'

'No, he can't. He's going to a press briefing in Westminster.' She tapped the diary in front of her. 'And he's late already.'

As the door started to open Julie held it wider, smiling at the dark-suited men who emerged.

The secretary stood up, 'Mr Bains, I told Julie you were too busy to see her now.'

'It's all right, Carol. I'll have a word with her on my way out.' The editor swept his papers into the briefcase, snatched his coat from the back of a chair and they crossed the newsroom floor together. Julie gave Pittard a mischievous wink as she passed his desk and received a venomous scowl in return.

Bains checked his watch as they crossed the hall. 'We can take a couple of minutes in the car. It will never do to be on time for Sir William. He's insufferably conceited as it is.' Bains had grown up in a tough working-class area of Glasgow. With his deep chest and rolling gait he had something of the prize-fighter about him.

As they climbed into the back of the Jaguar saloon, he slid the partition shut. He listened in silence until Julie had finished. 'Let me see this note that Nadym gave you.' The bushy grey eyebrows contracted as he studied it. 'Do you trust the man?'

'No. But he's telling the truth about the *Galinna*. She's due in Hamburg tonight.'

'It will be dark and the port area is huge.'

'I have done my homework. I have a map of the dock area and I know exactly where she is berthing. As for the cargo, it's common knowledge that Russian weapons are being smuggled in via the Baltic ports.'

Bains groaned. 'We can't run with that, Julie. It's got as much flavour left in it as last week's chewing gum.'

'Maybe. But there's an election coming up. If the extremists—'

'That's a side-show, Julie. Muhlder makes a lot of noise. The Neo-Nazis break a few heads. But it's no worse than Clydeside on a Saturday night after the pubs close.'

'If they are bringing in arms, they could be planning a coup.'

'*A coup!* They haven't got that sort of muscle!'

'Maybe they're working for an organisation that has. Nobody has photographic proof of these shipments. I can get it. Back me on this, Duggie,' she pleaded. 'We may not get another chance.'

He swivelled in his seat to look at her. 'I've given you a lot of rope these past months, Julie, and got bugger all for it. Now you want more.'

'You won't regret it. I promise.' She widened her eyes at him. He ran his hand through his sparse hair. 'It worries me. Isn't this a job for a man?'

'*No! It bloody well isn't!* It's my story and I'm damned if I'm—'

'Calm down, Julie.' He patted her knee. 'It's your safety I'm worried about. How good is your German?'

'Good enough. If I get into trouble, I can talk my way out of it. A woman has . . . certain advantages.'

'Don't think I haven't noticed.' He grinned and pushed open the door. 'Then go, and good luck. But be careful!' He tapped on the glass in front of him. The car pulled smoothly away from the kerb.

At Blackfriars Bridge, he telephoned his secretary. 'If anyone calls for Julie just say that she's doing a job up north. I don't want—'

'I'm sorry, Mr Bains, but Pittard had a man on the line asking for her a few minutes ago. He said that it was important.'

'What did he tell him?'

'He put the call through to me. Julie's expenses slip was on your desk for approval. I said she was flying to Hamburg. I hope I didn't—'

'Did you get the man's name?'

'No. He rang off.'

'See if you can get her on her mobile.' Knowing her, she would have switched it off. He massaged his jaw, his eyes troubled. He wished that he could have the last few minutes over again. He tried to push it out of his mind but it gnawed away at him.

In the newspaper business, you develop antennae very quickly or you're out with your last payslip in your hand, an ulcer chewing at your gut and a broken marriage to come home to. There was a blip on his personal radar screen and it was coming in very fast. He didn't like the look of it. He didn't like the look of it at all.

18

HAMBURG

The grime-streaked houses along the terrace were boarded up, their windows broken, their paintwork peeling. Behind them lay a wasteland of tangled wire and rubble, shards of glass and rusting cans. They would soon be pulled down to make way for another row of featureless warehouses. The road with its jagged potholes where water stood, winter and summer, would be replaced by another broad ribbon of concrete. Few people came this way anymore.

The fog had been bad all week, lingering in alleyways and hanging about the wharves, muffling the sounds from the harbour. To a casual observer, the last house in the terrace looked little different from its neighbours. The same gap-toothed railings, the same short flight of crumbling steps leading down from the street, but there the similarity ended. At the foot of the steps, there was a steel-reinforced door. Behind it a passage lined on each side by Nazi posters.

At the end of the passage, life-size cardboard cut-outs of soldiers in the uniform of the Waffen-SS stood guard. The door opened into a large windowless room lit by naked light bulbs hanging by cords from the ceiling. The walls were draped with Nazi flags. A huge blown-up photograph showed the Führer in his staff car driving down the Champs-Élysèes at the head of his stormtroopers.

In the corner stood a tripod of regimental standards surmounted by the Imperial eagle. On a bench against the wall there was a transistor, CDs of army marching songs, booklets on guerrilla warfare, a dog-eared pamphlet on the manufacture of explosives, a US-army training manual and a photograph of a group of para-militaries training in Nebraska.

A pile of crudely printed leaflets rubbed shoulders with a book on Nordic lore. At the end of the room a heavy punchbag hung from a beam. Lifting weights and chest expanders were stacked in a corner. A metal ladder led to a wooden trap-door in the ceiling.

The two powerfully-built men at the black oak table were in brown shirts, federal army trousers and paratroopers' boots. Tattooed on their forearms they had identical dagger designs. One wore a black headband with the SS skull and crossbones motif. The hair of the other was clipped round his head in a crude helmet cut.

At the sound of heavy booted feet approaching down the corridor, the two men sprang up. Buhl ran to the door. 'That will be Wulf.'

Rodach held up his hand. 'Not so fast. It is always best to be certain.'

The code was tapped out. The door swung open. They snapped to attention and gave the stiff arm salute.

Wulf raised his hand in acknowledgement and unbuttoned his long black leather coat. He strolled across the room with the languid arrogance of one used to giving the orders and gestured to the chairs. 'Rest while you can. We have a busy night ahead of us.'

Rodach grabbed a chair back and sat astride it. 'So you have you heard from Pieter Rohr?'

Wulf nodded. 'The *Galinna* is on time. The contractors have a rush job at the next wharf. Lots of coming and going. Plenty of noise.'

Rodach drummed his feet on the floor. 'Excellent. What is she carrying?'

'Nothing for us. It's a dummy run.'

'*Nothing!*' Buhl thumped the table with a fist like a mallet head. 'How long is Rohr going to jerk us around? It took two years to raise that money.'

'Then we can wait another week,' said Wulf coolly. 'Let's see if the she gets through. Let's see if Rohr is as smart as they say he is. If there's trouble we can try further up the coast.'

Rodach nodded. 'It might be safer. She can stand off Warnemünde and we'll take the stuff ashore by launch. A dark night, a couple of hours before dawn when everything's quiet.'

'Maybe too quiet,' Buhl cut in. 'We would stand out like pimps at a prayer meeting and those coast guard launches are no slouches.'

'How do we know we can trust Rohr? He's been paid. What's to stop him pissing off with the money?' Rodach's chair rocked under him like a restive horse.

'Because Pieter Rohr is a business man,' Wulf retorted. 'Swindling us would be bad business.'

Buhl paced up the room, slashing at the punchbag with the edge of his hand as he passed. 'OK, but when are we going to stop farting about and see some action.'

'You will get your action,' said Wulf quietly. 'But not till I say so. Not till we are ready. Rohr told me that an English reporter, name of Julie Dixon, has been giving him some problems, poking her nose into things that don't concern her.'

'A woman!' Buhl's hands went to his groin. 'Wait while I tell my best friend.'

Wulf's lip curled disdainfully. 'Our job is to find out how much she knows. She's booked on a Lufthansa flight. She will probably hide up on the wharf, wait for the *Galinna* to dock and try to get some photographs.'

Rodach scratched his head. 'So a sack of potatoes comes up in the hoist. Where does that get her?'

Wulf slid a knife from its sheath and pared his nails carefully. 'She doesn't know that. She's expecting an arms shipment.'

'*The bitch!*' Buhl locked his hands together and jerked them apart. 'I'll tear her in two!'

120

Rodach chuckled. 'But not until I have had my fun with her. Then we will take her to look at the harbour . . . close up . . . see how she likes the view.'

'What if she brings the police?' Buhl waggled a stubby finger at Wulf.

'It's not her style. But if she does, the *Galinna* is clean. They won't find anything.'

The two men stood at attention to receive their orders.

'Rodach. You fit up the van. It must look right. Drills, discs, grinders. All the usual gear. And you'll need tape, cord and bin liners. Buhl, put the battery on high charge for a couple of hours. We don't want any problems with starting.'

Rodach frowned. 'We'll be checked on the way in.'

'When the shift changes there will be a line of trucks waiting to come through. Tag on at the end. Remember, it will be late, everybody will be in a hurry and the man on the gate will be tired. Getting out won't be a problem. Just make sure you keep the girl quiet.'

'I don't want her quiet.' Rodach fingered his belt. 'I want to hear her sing. When I get to work she is going to make more noise than a cathedral choir.'

19

THE POLICE POUND

It was dark when Scott got back to his hotel and a long time since he had eaten. He had some sandwiches sent to his room, showered and deliberated his next move. The sensible course was to go to the police and confront them with what he had discovered. Threaten to contact the US Embassy and create mayhem unless they told him what had happened to Warren.

But supposing, as seemed almost certain, the American and French authorities were involved in a joint cover-up. The police would make a telephone call to the Department of the Interior, have him declared an undesirable and packed back to the US on the first flight.

The telephone rang on the table beside him. It was Turcan. He came straight out with it.

'The application to the SEC has had to be postponed. Hudson Caird say we won't get it through.'

'What reason did they give?'

'I thought you might be able to tell me that,' Turcan replied nastily.

'Why me? Chiropan has problems. That's your territory, not mine. When Mal suggested I go bird-dogging round Europe asking where we went wrong I thought he had gone off his head.'

'Well, think again. I'm backing Mal. This has got your name all over it. I'm not having Railton turned into a basket case because your end of things screwed up.'

'I'm not taking that from you, Jeff, or any of your buddies. There's nothing wrong with our operation here. We're on song. Profits are heading for a thirty per cent hike.'

'Then send some back to us. We're licking the paint off the walls.'

'Won't the bank help?'

'The bank was bitching before they heard the news about the SEC. Now they're going ape. We need cash, Scott, and we need it now.'

'I can't raid those companies, Jeff. We're in the middle of a big modernisation programme. Some of the equipment belongs in a science museum. If we're going to meet our targets we need every dime.'

'Scott, we're leaking cash like a sieve.'

'Sell Ribodox. You should at least cover your costs.'

'Don't you think I haven't tried? I had two offers on the table. Both on the low side. They were withdrawn today.'

'They're trying to starve us out.'

'You don't need an MBA to figure that out.'

'I don't suppose your brother is shedding too many tears.'

'Keep Todd out of this. Fraser Outram aren't pulling the wires.'

'What about your shares? You and Mal have a big stake in this group. Too big.'

'There's no point in going into all that now. Anyway, most of them are pledged to the bank.'

'Then raise money on the rest.'

'If we offload shares now we're dead. The news would be round the market in ten minutes.'

'It's better than going belly up.'

'Find out who's gunning for us and we won't go belly up. What are you doing in Colmar? When I heard where you were I thought you'd lost a slate.'

'I'm on to something, but I need more time.'

'A few days, pal – that's all we can give you. If we aren't back in the loop by then we shall have to find some other way out.'

'Meaning?'

'You'll find out soon enough.' He rang off.

It was close to midnight when Scott left the hotel. He was glad to get out of the place. Moping in his room with an empty bottle of bourbon for company had few attractions. Anger and worry were eating into his guts making it hard to think straight.

He drove out to the edge of the industrial estate, parked in a quiet service road and changed. He put on thick leather gloves and Nike trainers and stuffed a flashlight into his pocket. There was nobody about. Everything seemed quiet, but that meant nothing. There were bound to be regular patrols. The night was starless and the clouds full of snow. Tall concrete lamp-posts sited at the corners of the pound shed a dim orange haze. He hooked his fingers into the steel mesh, the links biting into them as they took the weight of his body.

He straddled the top. A dazzling white glare straight in his eyes! *The demented clangour of an alarm bell!* He threw himself over, landed hard and ran through the line of cars to the building. Ground floor windows barred, sills too high to give him a hand hold. Bending low he scurried along the wall to a large roll-down metal door. Secured by a stout padlock to a ring in the concrete ramp. Forget it.

He felt his way round the corner of the building. A steel door. The only way in. Could it be forced? He was so ill prepared, he almost burst out laughing. What the hell was he of all people doing there? You needed practise for this. The noise made coherent thought impossible. He felt light-headed, almost giddy. It was like the onset of madness.

He hared back down the line of the cars, trying the boots. All locked – then along the fence, checking for anything that could be used to prise open that door. Nothing. Another sound in that bedlam – the two-tone wail of a police siren. He could see the flashing lights along the far side of an area of open ground. A saloon travelling fast. It had to negotiate three sides of a square. Say five hundred yards down each side. It must be doing at least seventy. How long did that give him? A minute? Less. He couldn't do the calculation. Common sense said run. This crazy stunt wouldn't bring his father back.

Too late! The car rounded the last corner. He looked wildly about the yard. In the shadow cast by the angle of the building he could make out a tractor unit. He ran to it. Tried the doors to the cab. All locked. Crawling underneath, he crouched down in the shadow of the axles.

The alarm went dead. The tormented air adjusted to new sounds. A squawk from the patrol vehicle. The slam of a car door. In the amber haze of the headlights, Scott could see the patrolman in sharp profile, his breath like steam in the crisp night air. The beam of his flashlight on the gates. The clink of a chain. The jangle of keys. The clatter as the gates opened and closed again.

'Need any help, Marcel?'

'Not for the moment. But you had better report in. We may be here for some time.' He unbuttoned the flap of his holster and walked to the parked cars, checked doors and windows, flashed the light round the interiors, then underneath. He moved to the building. Checked the main door, then the windows.

He turned back. Scott shrank into his hiding place, burying his head in his jacket, welding his body to the metal. Boot studs ringing on the tarmac, scraping on the steps as the man climbed up to the cab. The rattle of a door handle. Boots descending. His shadow telescoping to a toad-like hump as he squatted, the flashlight sweeping the pools of shadow before it. With a grunt he straightened and moved to the other side of the vehicle. Up on the step again. A cursory inspection this time.

He walked to the side door of the block. A bleep from the alarm system. A moment later the lights came on in the windows.

Scott rolled clear and scuttled crab-like to the rear of the building. He inched round the corner, his face grazing the brickwork, his breath hot on his cheeks. A silent curse. He should have checked the sight lines. But the side door was wide open, covering him.

He could hear Marcel going upstairs to the offices. He slipped through the door and into the workshop. Four saloons, a pick-up truck and a Mercedes sports car up on a ramp. A line of inspection bays, two trolleys with electronic test equipment, a rolling road for brake testing and a weigh bridge. A few gas cylinders and cutting rods stacked against a workbench. On the walls, metal posters with vehicle data.

In the far corner, another vehicle under a nylon sheet, the cords hanging loose. Stooping below the level of the windows he crossed the floor and lifted the cover. It was Warren's car.

Until that moment, in defiance of all logic, a faint hope had stayed with him like a shallow imprint on the sand that the tide has not yet washed away. Now that had gone. The roof of the Peugeot was buckled and crushed down on to the headrests. A door was missing, torn off its hinges. The dashboard was caked with congealed blood as thick in places as if it had been daubed on with a palette knife. Tiny shreds of cloth and what might have been flesh were impaled on the jagged glass in the windscreen frame. The door to the glove compartment dangled by a single screw. He reached inside. Only a motoring guide. He tucked it into his trouser pocket. A forlorn gesture.

There was nothing under the seats. He flashed the torch into the back. The crumpled lid of a first-aid box. A blood stain on the seat where a man's head might have lain.

'*Marcel!* What are you doing up there? Are you going to keep us here all night.' The other man was at the foot of the stairs.

An excited shout. Scott's stomach knotted. Marcel was running the video recorder.

'Anything on the tape?'

'Yes. *Plenty!* Stay by the door, Claude. You and I are going to search this place from top to bottom.'

Scott came out from behind the car and walked into the middle of the floor.

Claude's hand dropped to his pistol butt. He backed against the door. '*Marcel!*' he shouted, 'Come and see what I've got here!'

As the patrol car headed back to the station it started to snow, the flakes floating down like white moths and settling where they fell. An invisible flock of geese went honking over their heads. Scott sat handcuffed in the back.

Marcel asked the questions. 'Let's start with your name.'

'You will find it in my passport.' Scott sighed and closed his eyes. This couldn't be for real. Arrest, indictment, sentencing, jail, disgrace, ruin. They ran through his head like ticker tape.

Claude flicked through the pages. 'Scott Rokeby. American citizen.'

Marcel raised his eyes to the driving mirror. 'What were you doing breaking into police property?'

'I shall save that for your inspector. I may have a few questions for him myself.'

'How long have you been in Colmar?'

'Since yesterday.'

'Where are you staying?'

He told them. They laughed. 'You won't find our accommodation quite so agreeable.'

At the police station his belongings were removed. The duty sergeant took the passport, opened it and frowned. Reluctant to abandon their prize, the patrolmen waited. The sergeant gestured to the door. 'I can handle this. You two get back on the job.'

As they pushed open the door, a gust of icy wind blew in a flurry of snow. The flakes melted slowly on the stone floor.

Scott spent the night in the cells, lying cold and cramped on a concrete bed under a single blanket. A dim bulb in the ceiling stayed on all night. A barred window reinforced with wire mesh was the only evidence of the existence of a world outside. His mind turned to his father as sometimes it did at times of great loneliness. Loneliness was something they both understood. It was the bridge between them that somehow they never quite managed to cross.

He should have tried to see more of the old man instead of going on punishing him. Warren couldn't help what he had become. Something had snapped inside him that night when Erika was killed. He saw that now, saw also that deep down the anger and resentment, the desolation of those childhood years were still there. Still unexorcised. His jealousy of other children who belonged to that unattainable paradise of being part of normal families. The hurt of seeing the anguish in his father's eyes and knowing that unwittingly he had stirred some memory painfully laid to rest. Of what use was maturity unless it brought with it a little generosity, a little understanding?

And now it was too late. For a moment the guilt and remorse, the sense of what was lost beyond recall, beyond any hope of remedying, almost overwhelmed him. At last he slept, slipping in and out of troubled dreams until the sky paled with the coming of the new day.

20

HAMBURG DOCKS

Julie had cut it very fine. Collecting her ticket at the check-in desk, she dashed through passport control just as the final call was being made. The plane swept down the runway and pulled up into the clouds. Rain drops spattered against the windows. She ordered a brandy and ginger, sipping it slowly, letting it warm her before the splinter of ice returned to the pit of her stomach.

Why couldn't she behave like other people? Get herself a steady job and a cosy little life and be happy with that? But she had never listened to good advice. As a teenager she was just the same. Let someone try telling her that a cliff was too dangerous to climb or the sea too rough for sailing and the challenge to prove that person wrong was irresistible.

There was that crazy weekend when she had flown up to Scotland for a couple of days' skiing. Her boyfriend Alan had only just got his pilot's licence and the plane looked as if it were held together with sticky tape. It was snowing when they left and north of the border they ran into a white-out. They had put down in the Cairngorms and against all the odds got out in one piece.

At eighteen, Hugo had been the man in her life. He was on a short-term commission with the army. He was tall, nothing special to look at and with a conversational range that could be flatteringly described as monosyllabic. Something he almost said about modern women must have irritated her and she decided to shake him up a bit, turning up in the middle of a night exercise on Salisbury Plain and hitching a ride on his tank.

Blackmail got her aboard – she had threatened to tell the brigadier that she was there by invitation. The brandy bottle did the rest. She bumped each of the crew out of their places in turn and finished up in the driver's seat. Hugo had complained that his teeth had been loose in his head ever since.

She checked over her equipment. The Nikon F3 was at least ten years old and looked well used but it had been recently serviced. She loaded it with a roll of Ilford HP5, checked that the 58mm F/1.2 lens was clean and replaced the lens cap. After a glance at the Nikkor 180mm F/2.8 she put it back in its soft pouch. With a little luck she might be able to use it to get photos of a few faces when the *Galinna* started unloading.

Her thoughts turned to her brother. Months of search had yielded nothing. Looking for clues was like pulling threads out of a tangled ball of cotton hoping that one might come free and lead somewhere.

It was a relief to have the captain's voice break in. There had been fog in Hamburg all day but a window in the weather had appeared and they were cleared for landing. As the aircraft began its approach the engine sounded a deeper, huskier note. Outside there was nothing to be seen but swirling cloud. Seat-belts were being fastened, tables folded away, the passengers suddenly silent until with a light bump they were down and skimming past the spectral shapes of hangars and warehouses.

She took a taxi into the city. Wartime bombing had destroyed so much. Only the part round the Alster lakes had retained some of the charm of an older, more elegant age. But Julie felt an odd affection for the place, for the port with its rain-swept wharves and miles of winding railway track, its tankers with their hefty shoulders and bullying ways, and the gaunt steel skeletons of cranes and gantries.

At little after eleven o'clock she was in the port area. The driver was curious. They didn't get many tourists asking for that part of the city, especially at night. Too much crime. The docks covered a vast area. The customs and police could only do so much.

She explained that she worked for a magazine. 'They want some photographs. Something with a bit of atmosphere.' Her German was a little rusty but it was coming back quickly.

His shrug as he took her money spoke for him. 'Rather you than me.'

She walked the last few hundred yards, stopping twice to check with her map. The shadowy warehouses loomed out of the vapour as if drawn to the gaunt, gibbet-like lamp-posts with their orange sodium lights. Lorries rumbled slowly past her. She could hear the hum of plant running, the screech of a tracked vehicle, the staccato hammering of a pneumatic drill. Fifty yards ahead a builders' truck had turned in and stopped, the driver leaning out to speak to the man on the barrier.

A mobile hot-dog stand overtook her and pulled in just short of the entrance. The driver switched on the light and checked his watch. She tapped on the window. He had a plump, rosy face and long sideburns. Obviously one of the local characters. 'Any chance of a frankfurter and cup of coffee?' she asked.

He pushed the door ajar. 'You're in luck. I'm just going to open up.' The contractors were working through the night, he told her. 'I'll be going down to the wharf when the shift changes over.' He looked at her quizzically. 'What's an attractive young woman like you doing in the docks at this time of night? It can be a rough area after dark.'

She patted her bag. 'I'm after some photos for a magazine feature.'

He chuckled. 'Wait until I have finished work and I'll show you the sights. We'll start with the Reeperbahn – they call it the Mile of Sin.' He threw the sausages in a pan. 'We can have a few beers, get to know each other.'

'I'm afraid this is a working trip.' She laughed to cover her irritation.

He slapped his thigh delightedly. 'And you thought I was making a pass! Don't worry, Fräulein. It was only old Stefan having a bit of fun.'

While she munched on the sausage she explained that she wanted to get some shots of the harbour. 'Ships, cranes, the lights in the water. If the fog lifts a little it could make a great picture.'

He shook his head. 'They won't let you through. Only the workmen are allowed in.'

'But they are letting you through,' she insisted.

'Yes – but everyone knows old Stefan. Besides, the men are cold and hungry.'

Julie took a note from her wallet. 'Will you take me with you, Stefan?' she pleaded. 'If the man on the gate spots me you can say that you have a new assistant.'

He scratched his head for a moment and then stuffed the note into his pocket. He would take her with him but she must find her own way back.

'Thanks. It's a deal.'

He made another cup of coffee. 'Give this to Klaus on the gate as we go through.' They drove the few yards to the entrance. Klaus came out of the hut stamping his feet and banging his hands together. He took the steaming cup from her with a grin. 'Aren't you rather young to be going out with that old crock?'

She laughed and Stefan answered for her. 'These young chicks can't resist me.' He pointed to his cheeks. 'It must be my curly whiskers.'

As they drove on to the quay they could see men working in the glare of the arc lights, a shower of golden sparks running from a cutting disc, a mechanical digger nosing among a pile of rubble like an anteater foraging in a termite heap.

Stefan glanced in his wing mirror. Klaus was talking to a man in the truck behind. 'Nip out quickly. If anybody spots you, don't blame me.'

'I'll say I arrived by parachute.' She squeezed his hand.

'That's only my hand you've got,' he complained. A wheezy chuckle followed her as she slid out, closing the door gently.

The fog was thinning slowly, swirling round in wide, lazy spirals. To her left, a long low warehouse ran the length of a wharf that offered no cover except for a stack of wooden pallets and three cranes that leaned over the edge like giraffes at a waterhole. At the far end was a huge slab side of a grain silo. Behind her some vans were on the move. She checked her watch. Eleven-thirty. The shift was changing over.

She ran over to the centre crane and looked up, suppressing a shudder at the sight of the shiny hook on the chain hanging from the derrick. She climbed the steep metal ladder and tried the door to the cabin. Locked. She would have to lie on the platform and aim her camera like a sniper's rifle.

From across the harbour came the rumble of containers being shifted, the rattle of a train over points, the mournful note of a foghorn. Another sound. The steady chug-chug of a marine diesel. The mist was rolling back, exposing an ever-widening expanse of oily black water. The engines were louder now as the blunt bow of a cargo vessel, showing only riding lights, nosed out of the white vapour.

Julie flattened herself against the cold metal plating of the platform. Peering through the 58mm lens there was more light than she had expected. The fast black and white film would allow her an aperture of F/5.6 with the camera selecting a shutter speed of 1/60th. For the close-up shots with the 180mm lens she would be able to rest her hand against a steel rail to avoid camera shake.

Something else was moving at the edge of her vision. A van showing sidelights was rounding the corner of the warehouse. It stopped. Two men in dark clothing got out. They moved quickly, their flashlights chasing the shadows from their hiding places. She shifted backwards, breathing a little prayer as flakes of rust dropped to the quay below.

They checked round the pallets, one of them swarming up to the top, as agile as a monkey. They were coming her way, conferring in low voices. Her heart began to thump like a rabbit's foot warning of danger.

'Nothing so far, Rodach.'

'The girl will be here somewhere, Buhl. We'll start with the cranes at the end and meet in the middle.'

It was a trap! A set-up! For a moment she lay there too shocked to move. *How could she have been so dumb!* But there was no time for self-recrimination. Rodach was already climbing. She crept down the ladder. Her bag slipped and clunked against the railing. She froze, counting the passing seconds, waiting for the shout that meant discovery but the engines were louder now and it never came.

There was a capstan on the edge of the wharf, nine or ten yards away, a coil of rope at the base. It was like exchanging Goliath for a midget but she dare not stay where she was. She flitted to it like a shadow and crouched behind it. Buhl was off the ladder and padding like a big cat towards the crane she had left. Rodach had moved into the open where he had a clear view of the whole length of the wharf. Nowhere to go but over the edge. Lower herself into the water and swim for it. She tested the rope, slithered to the edge and rolled over.

A change in the note of the engines, a frothy white turbulence in the water as they went into reverse and the slap-slap of the swell against the side of the wharf. She went down, hand over hand . . . looked behind . . . no use trying to swim . . . the *Galinna* was too close . . . the throb of her engines beating in her ears . . . something below her . . . the top of a big tractor tyre . . . her toes stretched down . . . found a foothold . . . she relaxed her grip on the rope . . . too soon . . . her feet sliding on the greasy rubber . . . her knees catching the top of the tyre . . . the rope scorching her palms as she broke her descent.

Footsteps overhead . . . the two men must be right above her . . . her feet in the bottom rim . . . she hugged the sides of the tyre . . . let the rope go . . . it snaked past her . . . a shout from the ship . . . her heart stopped . . . but it was only a crewman calling for a line.

She wriggled inside the rubber womb, curling herself up like a foetus, breathing in the reek of oil, seaweed and slime. The rope went hissing over her head. The *Galinna* was moving towards her like a steel mountain. The walls of the tyre that had looked so huge a few moments ago now felt puny. Someone shouted something. A spotlight above the bridge was switched on and swivelled. A white brilliance poured into her hiding place. A triumphant cry from one of the crew was quickly silenced. The mountain leaned over her squeezing out the light.

'I wouldn't be caught inside one of those things when a big ship was berthing.' It was one of the men above her. 'They flatten to the thickness of a bicycle tyre. Your spine would snap like a matchstick.'

The mountain brushed against the tyre. '*Let me up, you bastards!*' she screamed. '*Get me out of here!*' The beam of the vessel rolled against the next tyre, crushing it to a third of its width.

'Wulf wants to question her,' Rodach grunted. 'Better bring her up.' He lowered a rope. 'Hold on tight! *Schlampe!*'

'*Who are you calling a slut!*' she yelled with more bravado than she felt.

She was raised to within a few inches of the top. Buhl reached down and gripped the sides of her head. He grinned at her, his face close to hers, his breath hot and rank like an animal's. 'Look what I've caught, Rodach.' He furled his tongue and agitated it between his lips.

Rodach pushed him aside. 'You can play games later.' He ran the tape across her mouth. 'Up with her. Roll her on to her front. I'll take her bag.'

Buhl pulled the shoulder bag over her head. 'Let's take a look inside, Rodach. See what toys she's brought us.'

'We haven't time. Tie her hands behind her back. Hold the little bitch still. Now her ankles. Pass the loop round her neck. If she struggles, she will choke. Go and get the van.'

She was bundled into the back and lay still, trying to quiet her breathing. What were they going to do with her? *The police pick up girls like you every morning, crammed into bin liners with their heads turned the wrong way round.* Where are you, Scott, now that I need you?

The van slowed at the gate but only for a moment and then they swung right and picked up speed. A heavy object rolled against her. Stretching out her fingers she touched it. Curved, metallic, a gas cylinder. They made a series of turns. Left, left again, right, left, right again . . . she gave up trying to keep track. Slowing now. Stopping. Ice on a puddle cracking under the wheel. The back doors creaking open.

'Anybody about?'

'No.'

'Then give me a hand.'

'Shouldn't we leave the van round the back? Wulf doesn't like it left here.'

'We'll need it again soon. She's booked in for swimming lessons.'

Two pairs of arms seized her, pulled her along the metal ribs of the floor.

'Sling her over my shoulder.'

The loop was pulling tight about the neck, slowly choking her.

'Gurgles like a baby, doesn't she?'

'Baby is going to grow up fast when I get to work on her.'

Down the steps. A key scratching on metal. The door opening, snapping shut.

'She gives me the hots the way she moans and jerks about like a ferret in a sack.'

'Cut that cord, Buhl. And take the bags off her. We don't want her passing out on us.'

Julie snuffed at the dank air, blinking the corridor into focus. A second door. A code tapped out. 'Bring her in,' a voice called from inside. The door creaked open. 'Frisk her.'

'Passport, air ticket, money. The bag—'

'Leave the bag. Cut her hands free. Put her in a chair.'

She gasped the air into her lungs, trying to clear her brain, hammering away at the same message. Stick to her original story. And if they knocked her off that perch, find another. She pushed her hair away from her eyes, looking for the man who was giving the orders.

'Forget the beauty treatment, Fräulein. It's wasted on us.'

She started. The voice had come from behind her. 'Before I take the tape off your mouth, Fräulein Dixon, I want you to listen very carefully. This building is empty. So are the others in the street. You are in a concrete bunker under the ground. You can howl your head off but no one will hear you. So make things easier for yourself and answer my questions.' He wrenched the tape off her mouth, leaving the skin red and raw.

She tried to turn round but his hands clamped down on her shoulders. 'I demand to know why—'

'You are in no position to make demands. We know who you are and who you work for. Now tell us what you find so interesting about the *Galinna*.'

'The *Galinna*?' She frowned. 'I don't understand.'

'The ship that docked tonight. Buhl tells me that he could hardly keep the two of you apart.'

She shook her head. She knew nothing about the ship. She needed some photos of the port for her paper. That was all. 'Now, you will please return my property and let me go.'

'*Let you go! What an astonishing suggestion!* I received a report that you were coming here to spy on us. My men investigated and discovered you hiding over the side of the wharf.'

'I was trying for a difficult angle. I got too close to the edge.'

'And slipped over.' Wulf clapped his hands together softly. 'Very ingenious. So why didn't you shout for help?'

'I did shout.'

His fingers skewered into the joints of her shoulders. 'No more games. I want the truth, Fräulein.'

'If I came here to spy . . . ' she writhed, trying to escape from the pain, 'my paper would know exactly where I was going. When I don't report in—'

'The whole of the city police force will turn out to look for you.' Wulf laughed mockingly. 'And even if they do, they won't find you here. I give you your last chance. Tell me what you were doing on the wharf.'

'I have told you everything . . . everything.'

'Very well.' He went to the door. 'My comrades have other ways of obtaining information. I shall leave you to them. I shall be surprised if I do not find you in a very different frame of mind when I return.'

'Why don't you stay and watch?' she taunted. Anything to keep him there. Anything rather than being left alone with those animals.

Wulf turned and gave her a blank stare. His mind was somewhere else. For him she had ceased to exist. She was already lying in the silt at the bottom of the harbour, nudged this way and that by the tide. 'Because I haven't the time,' he said curtly.

'Because you haven't got the guts!' She spat the words at him. 'You march up and down with your sham uniforms, your pantomime salutes . . . '

'Shut her up!' Wulf yelled. Buhl caught her across the mouth with the back of his hand.

A trickle of blood ran from the corner of her mouth. 'That was brave work,' she whispered through clenched teeth.

Wulf tugged the door open. 'Do what you like with her,' he snarled, 'but find out what she knows.' The door slammed behind him.

The two men moved towards her, their eyes running over her body, their fingers twitching, their imagination already claiming her.

They dragged her to her feet and stripped her, hauling her over the table, catching at her hands as she tried to cover her breasts, tugging at her ankles as she doubled up, rolling her this way and that, kneading her flesh with their huge hands, glorying in their power over her.

Buhl made a grab at her, dragging her to the edge of the table. He bent low over her, jerking his hips. 'You don't know what it's like to have a real stud between those pretty legs,' he taunted, 'after those little boy's pea-shooters you're used to.' As he brought his face down to hers she raked his cheeks with her nails.

'*Little hellcat!*' he screamed, jerking back. His hands left his face and he stared with disbelief at the blood on his fingers. Drawing his knife he drove the blade into the table top leaving it quivering inches from her eyes. '*Rodach!*' he bawled, 'Help me turn her over and tie her up.'

They roped her wrists and ankles to the table legs spreading her out like a starfish. Rodach ran a finger along her lip where the skin had broken, licking the film of blood from it.

Fear trickled into the pit of her stomach. He was unbuckling his thick leather belt, doubling it, running it through his great fist. 'The slut can talk and she can scratch. Let us see if she can sing.' He slipped the tongue through the buckle.

Buhl chortled. 'Can you sing? *Schlampe!* Rodach is an artist with the belt. You will find yourself hitting notes that you did not believe possible.'

'*You perverts!*' Julie fought at her bonds, careless of the cords sawing into her flesh. 'You . . . you deformities . . . masquerading as soldiers!'

They laughed, throwing off their jackets and shirts, parading their brawny arms and massive chests, one of them tweaking at the oily black hair curling over the top of his vest. She could smell the heat in them, the lust, the excitement.

Buhl moved behind her. With the tip of his finger he traced the length of her spine from the nape of her neck to the cleavage between her buttocks. 'You have lovely skin, slut, It will mark very dramatically. Don't you agree, Rodach?'

Rodach dropped the belt on the table and went to one of the benches that ran along the wall. Returning with a pot of red paint and a brush he prised off the lid. 'You have given me an idea, Buhl.'

Buhl had pulled off his boots. 'Get on with it, then. This pissing about is driving me crazy.' His taurine neck flushed a dusky red, his voice was hoarse with frustration.

'Be patient, my friend,' hissed Rodach. With the brush he daubed a broad crimson circle on the girl's back and picked up the belt once more.

Buhl frowned. His eyes darted from the paintwork to Rodach. 'What are you doing?'

'I am going to make her a party member.'

'But you have no more paint.'

Rodach ran the belt through his hand. 'What do I want with paint? The slut has brought her own with her.'

Buhl's eyes screwed up in perplexity and then his face cleared and he bent double to slap a huge thigh. 'That is magnificent, Rodach, but should it not be black?'

Rodach's fingers tightened round the belt. 'Nature will soon see to that.'

Little tremors ran over her. She cursed her limbs for their weakness but she couldn't stop the shivering. The warm blood seemed to be fleeing the surfaces of her body in search of somewhere to hide.

Rodach planted his feet astride. He balanced himself, his eyes running from the point of his shoulder to the intended mark. Julie's eyes, dilated with fear, rolled up to follow the upraised arm. She braced herself, her fists clenched, her fingernails digging into the palms of her hands as the belt whistled down. There was an explosion in her head as if a gun had gone off in the brainpan. Then came the pain. Searing pain, a branding iron clamped against her flesh, tearing the cry from her.

Buhl watched in fascination as the insignia took shape, the welts deepening and filling before his eyes, becoming livid bands as the blood flowed to the contusions and the skin began to lift.

As he drove each blow home, Rodach gave a hoarse, grunt of satisfaction, his ears drinking in the cries that echoed about the room. He paused for a moment to strip off his vest and mop his forehead. His shoulders and chest were shiny with perspiration. He grinned at Buhl. 'Hot work, eh? Now, let's see if she's ready to tell us what she's up to.'

From the far end of the corridor came a clang of steel on steel. Rodach grabbed his jacket. '*Someone's using a sledge on the door!*' Grabbing a flashlight from the bench he ran to the ladder.

Buhl hadn't moved. His feet might have been nailed to the floor. He stared after Rodach, his livid face puckered like a child's with baffled rage. '*What about me!*' he bawled, 'I can't quit now!'

'*Leave her, you dickhead!*' From outside came the crash of splintering metal. The front door had given way. Rodach heaved up the trapdoor. Lumps of earth and rubble pattered down on to the floor.

Buhl could hear men running up the passage, their studs ringing on the concrete floor. He ransacked the pockets of Julie's jacket. The door shook under the thump of the sledge. *Scheisse!* No time for the camera. Hitching up his trousers he scrambled towards the ladder.

21

PREFECTURE DE POLICE

Scott awoke to find his vest damp with sweat despite the cold, his throat raw as if he had been shouting. Throwing the blanket aside, he swung his legs off the bed, rubbing his feet and calves to restore the circulation.

At six o'clock a warder opened the door and produced a razor, a sliver of soap and a soiled towel. 'Don't cut your throat,' he joked, 'or you will get us all into trouble.'

The basin was cracked, the plug missing and the water icy. He regretted having to wear his clothes of the previous evening. The cat burglar's outfit was unlikely to enhance his standing with the inspector. A baguette with a sprinkling of grated cheese arrived, accompanied by a metal mug without a handle. The coffee was good. Whatever else the French got wrong it was rarely that.

At seven, he was taken to the office of Inspector Daniel Ferreux. The inspector was a short, stocky man with prominent ears and grey hair cut close to his head. He nodded to the gendarme to leave them, gestured to a chair and pushed a packet of Gauloises across the desk.

Scott returned them. 'I try not to.'

'*Moi aussi*. I try to go straight but soon I offend again.' He lit up and blew a cloud of smoke at the ceiling. 'I'm sorry if you had an uncomfortable night, Monsieur Rokeby, but we have our duties.'

'You might consider widening them to include the provision of a second blanket.'

The inspector pursed his lips. 'Am I to understand that you are planning to extend your stay with us?'

'I intend to remain in France until I find out what happened to my father.'

'Your father is dead, Monsieur Rokeby. Please accept my sincere regrets.'

'I think he was murdered.'

The inspector studied his nails. 'Have you any evidence to support that statement?'

'I have seen where the car went off the road. He was up in the mountains. I don't believe it was an accident.'

'Monsieur Rokeby! If every driver killed on our roads ended up in homicide statistics, the Commissioner would soon have me back on traffic duty.'

'My father would not have taken that road voluntarily. I think he was followed and abducted . . . perhaps tortured . . . before the car was pushed over.'

'Why should anyone want to torture your father, let alone kill him?' Inspector Ferreux stared at him under untidy eyebrows.

'I don't know. That is what I came to France to find out.'

'And have you learned anything from your visit?'

'I have learned that information about my father's death is being withheld. A prominent American citizen has died in suspicious circumstances. It is the duty of the police—'

'Monsieur Rokeby,' the inspector crushed his half-smoked cigarette into the ashtray, 'you would do well not to lecture us on our duties. You are in a foreign country. You have committed a serious offence. If I chose to press charges, and I am minded to do so, you would be convicted and sent to jail.' He flicked open Scott's passport. 'I see that you give your occupation as a company director. It is difficult to believe that a sentence for a felony followed by a term in a French prison would advance your business career.'

A court case could be very damaging, Scott conceded. 'But if it's the only way to bring the facts out into the open, I must take the risk.'

'I must warn you that if you are committed for trial, the court will not allow you to use the proceedings for your own purposes.'

'It may be difficult for you to stop me,' Scott replied hotly. 'The press might be very interested in what I have to say.'

The inspector shrugged. 'Making unsubstantiated accusations against the police would only prejudice your position.'

'I'm a bad loser, Inspector. If I find myself in trouble, I shall see to it that I have company.'

Ferreux plucked at a fold of loose skin under his chin. 'It might be simpler to put you on a plane back to the US. The charges against you would be held over. If you made trouble for us we could reinstate them.'

'I might prefer to take my chances at a trial. Where would you be then?'

'I might be out of a job but it wouldn't bring your father back.' The inspector spread his hands. 'Come, Monsieur Rokeby, let us have done with this sparring. Each of us can make things very difficult for the other.'

'Tell me how my father died. I don't believe—'

'The police deal in facts. Not speculation. Such facts as we have in our possession point to your father's death being accidental.'

'What facts are you talking about?'

'The pathologist made a very careful examination of your father's body.' He paused and lowered his eyes. 'I'm sorry. I realise that this is distressing for you.'

Scott wrapped his arms about himself. 'Go on, Inspector. At least it makes a change from the conspiracy of silence that I have been battling with until now.'

'I have seen the preliminary report. Your father's neck was broken. He was not wearing a seat-belt.'

'He always wore a seat-belt.'

'Not on this occasion. The fracture was consistent with the injury that he would have sustained on impact after the car went into the ravine.'

'Was there much bleeding?'

'Lacerations, yes. All that glass and metal. Bleeding – no.'

'He was a careful driver.'

'Darkness. A route that he did not know. Black ice on the road.'

Scott stood up and went over to the window and stared out over a yard. Two crows were squabbling over some small casualty of the hours of darkness, their sickle-sharp beaks slicing into the carcass. Tearing. Pulling. He turned away.

Perhaps something showed in his face for the inspector went on, 'Death would have come very quickly. Your father would have known nothing about it.'

Scott remained standing, his back pressed to the wall. 'If you believe it was an accident, why then did you bring the car back to your workshops?'

Ferreux shifted in his chair. 'Because we wished to make a thorough investigation.'

'Because you weren't convinced it was an accident. You had reservations.'

'A good policeman always has reservations.'

'I found the car concealed under a sheet. Is that standard practice?'

The inspector rose to his feet. He shook his head impatiently. 'This conversation is getting us nowhere.'

'On the contrary. I have found it very instructive. What about the inquest? Let me guess. You cannot give me a date because it has been held over indefinitely.'

Ferreux spread his hands. 'It is not my fault that it has been delayed.'

'In short, Inspector, you are not running this case. Your superiors have instructed you to dissemble and to prevaricate. *Why?*'

The inspector pushed the blade of a paper knife under the flap of an envelope and with a savage thrust sliced through it. 'My instructions arrived from the Minister of the Interior in Paris by courier. I am not permitted to discuss them with you. I don't know what your father was involved in but his activities have come to the notice of officials at the highest level.'

'You speak about him as if he were a criminal,' Scott exclaimed furiously. 'What evidence have you that—'

The inspector held up his hand to cut him short. 'Monsieur Rokeby, please remember where you are and try to control yourself. Do you know where your father was going or what he was doing in France? It would assist us a great deal if you could tell us.'

Scott shook his head. 'I don't know. If I did, I wouldn't be wasting my time here.'

Ferreux ignored the taunt. 'Can you tell me who his associates were?'

'So far as I know he had no . . . "associates" . . . as you put it. He was a retired diplomat. He had spent his working life away from his country at great cost to himself. He had few friends.'

Ferreux tapped the thick file in front of him. 'Your father was virtually a recluse.'

Scott stared at the file. 'The resources of the authorities must be limitless. You have a file on the habits of an old man living a quiet life on the other side of the Atlantic?'

'I am not prepared to comment on that.'

'Then comment on this. My father had a housekeeper, a woman who was devoted to him and was like a mother to me. What do you expect me to tell her?'

Ferreux rapped the desk with his knuckles. 'Tell her that he was killed in a motor accident. Tell her that the police have not completed their investigation. Tell her that an inquest will be held in due course. There is nothing more that you can tell her.'

He spun the paper knife between them. 'I have a question for you, Monsieur Rokeby, and I should like you to reflect carefully before you answer.' He stopped the knife with its blade pointing directly at Scott and leaned forward over the desk. 'Have you any reason to believe that others have taken an interest in your movements since you arrived in France?'

'Why do you ask?'

'Why don't you answer?'

There was silence between them. The inspector nodded slowly. 'So. You are being watched.'

'I did not say that.'

'Not in so many words, perhaps.' Ferreux leaned back in his chair and tapped another cigarette out of the packet. 'A competent policeman gets to know his district. He gets to knows what's going on and who's up to no good, even if he cannot always get them into court and make the charges stick.

'In this area we have our petty criminals and our share of the larger villains and we feel reasonably comfortable with that. Without them we wouldn't have a job.' He lowered his voice. 'But in the past week my officers have reported seeing some new faces. Faces we don't know. Faces we don't want to know. These individuals have a different stamp to them.'

'Isn't it the job of your men to check them out?'

'The men on my force are no different from other human beings. They would like to collect their pensions, tend their gardens, win a few prizes in the summer at the village shows and in due course die in their beds.'

'So?'

'So we would like to see these new faces move on and go somewhere else.'

'You have no idea who they are? Or what they are doing here?'

'No.' Ferreux tapped the end of his nose with a finger. 'And my instincts tell me that I shall live longer if I restrain my curiosity.'

Scott walked back to the desk. He rested his hands on the worn leather top and stared into the inspector's eyes. 'I want to bring my father home, Inspector. How long before you quit stalling?'

Daniel Ferreux gave a deep sigh. 'I could give you a date just to see the back of you. I could tell you that the inquest will be held as soon as our inquiries are complete.'

'The truth, Inspector.'

'The simple truth is that I do not know. The matter is out of my hands. Meanwhile, I regret that it is necessary for you to make a formal identification of your father's body. I warn you that the duty is a disagreeable one. And there are some documents to complete.' He flicked a switch in front of him. 'Ask Doussard to come in.'

The inspector rose to his feet. 'We shall hold over the charges, Monsieur Rokeby. Take my advice. Stay out of France and keep what you have heard in this office to yourself. If you don't make trouble for us, you will hear no more about last night.'

'Will you do what you can?'

'We shall complete our investigations and do all that is possible to expedite the return of your father's body to the US.' He held out his hand. 'Go home, Monsieur Rokeby, and try to put this behind you. Have a good life, a long life . . . and die in your bed.'

Doussard was young and fresh complexioned and could not have been long in the force. He exchanged a few words with his superior before leading Scott to another office. He seemed a little overwhelmed. 'A sad business, Monsieur,' he said, 'and so many formalities to be dealt with.'

'Then let us deal with them quickly.' Scott was conscious from the look of reproach that he had been put down as a hard-nosed, unfeeling American but he hadn't time to soft-pedal anyone's feelings, even his own.

There were many forms involved. A letter to write requesting the shipment of Warren's body to the USA. A notarised certificate for the US port of entry. An export licence, a doctor's certificate and there were others.

There were his father's personal effects to check through. The travel documents and credit cards told Scott nothing that he didn't already know. He was carrying euros and Swiss francs. Everything was put in an envelope and sealed in front of him. The police would need to retain them, he was told. There was also Warren's half Hunter, an antique gold watch, which he always kept in his trouser pocket secured by a chain to his belt.

Scott asked whether he might keep it. 'It has great sentimental value. My father was never without it.'

Doussard frowned. 'It is rather irregular.'

'The request or the watch?'

The policeman laughed. Perhaps the American was human after all. 'I think I can stretch a point. But don't say I gave it to you.'

He turned it over in his hands. It gave him a strange feeling for his father had never let him touch it. The old man was odd in that way.

Scott would never forget that visit to the morgue. The echoing corridors, the central chamber with its shiny green walls glistening like an ice cavern. Or that pervasive smell. A sweet cloying odour like the last exhalation of the dead. A brisk, impatient man in a white tunic slid open a drawer with the indifference of a shop assistant pulling out a shoebox and drew back the sheet.

Scott hurried away, his eyes seeking the arcs overhead, flooding his brain with their dazzle, exposing the negative to the brightness of day as if he could ever hope to blot it out, obliterate that grotesque memorial to what had once been human.

The policeman pursued him across the room, 'I'm sorry . . . but I have to ask . . . there's no doubt in your mind?'

'None.'

He was driven back to the police station where he recovered his car keys and belongings, checked and signed for them. Doussard walked with him to the Range Rover, which was parked in the yard at the back of the building. 'Which way will you be going, sir?' he asked.

'Is that an official question?'

'I have a report to complete,' he replied rather diffidently. Something told him to go carefully. The American had a strained look about the eyes.

Scott shrugged. 'Wherever it takes.' He tossed his grip into the back seat and took the wheel.

'Then, take my advice, sir, and leave the police work to us. Otherwise . . . ' He left the sentence unfinished.

'Otherwise is for another day.' Scott turned the key in the ignition. Doussard raised his hand to the peak of his cap. The car moved off and disappeared from view.

22

NEW YORK

In the offices of Railton Ross, the meeting had started at seven. It should have been over by eleven. It was close to midday.

Jeff Turcan looked at the sombre faces round the table. 'We have been talking for five hours and nothing has been resolved. You have heard the options. Doing nothing isn't one of them. It's decision time.'

'Why has all this happened so suddenly?' exclaimed Bill Marquand in an aggrieved tone. A lock of hair had fallen over his forehead and for once he hadn't thought to stroke it back into place. 'We were doing great. Making good profits.' It was the first time he had been in a crisis. It was frightening. The world outside was threatening to intrude in an alarming way. It was like an ogre pulling horrid faces at them through the window. His instinct was to ignore it and hope that when he looked again it would have disappeared.

Turcan reached into his pocket and palmed a pill into his mouth. The acid in his stomach was eating him up. 'For the benefit of the financially illiterate, profit isn't cash. We need cash. The bank has put a gun to our heads. We have got to get our borrowing down by thirty per cent. The question is simply – *how the fuck do we do it*? We can't float the company because the SEC will throw out our application. We can't sell Ribodox because the offers have been withdrawn. We can't trade out of trouble inside the time frame. We have got to cut back. So what do we chop out?'

Mal Hain squared off the files in front of him. 'If we downsize here, we can kiss good-bye to a public issue for two years minimum.

Maybe for keeps. Anyway the problem isn't here. It's in Europe. Rokeby's operation is a tumour in a healthy body. I say that's where we cut. We cut fast and we cut deep.'

Liz Usborne stared at him open-mouthed. 'How can you say that companies like Pharmazin and Biomocem are a tumour? They are producing a better return on capital than all our other—'

'Liz!' Turcan cut her short. 'We are not criticising the trading record of those companies. We have got ourselves a political problem and believe me they are the worst. My sources tell me that Scott is a liability. Those sources are reliable. I trust them.'

'OK,' Gowan burst out, 'but let's be fair. Scott needs more time. He's got to get round the companies, the embassies, the government departments and give it to them straight. He's got to say, "Look, you guys, what the hell's going on?"'

'But what has he done?' Hain countered, 'He's still holed up in Colmar. I ask myself whether he has had some sort of breakdown.'

Turcan banged the table. 'We can't spend any more time on this. Whatever the problem is, we have caught the backwash. If we don't act now it will be up over our heads. Mal and I have talked this through. There is only one solution. We find a buyer for Railton Europe and use the funds to repay the bank.'

'Of course!' Bill Marquand clapped his hands like a child at a birthday party. It only went to prove that if you trod water long enough a wave would come along and carry you right up to the beach.

Turcan stared at him contemptuously. 'It's hardly a moment for celebration. The cash realised by selling our shares will go to the bank to reduce borrowing. Years of work and a big investment are straight down the pan.'

Liz Usborne's mouth was working silently as she rehearsed her little speech. She had to support Scott. It wouldn't change anything but it would be nice to be able to tell him she had tried to help. People of very moderate ability could go a long way in business by not making enemies unnecessarily. She raked her fingers through her hair, bringing herself to the boil. 'Are we really going to take this decision with Scott out of the country? Shouldn't he be given a chance to fight his corner? Those companies are not just his livelihood – growing them has taken a big chunk of his life. The people who work in them are not just names on a payroll, many of them are his friends. In a way they are his family.'

'Scott gets too emotional about these things,' said Hain brutally. 'Sentiment has no place in business. It's dangerous. It clouds the judgement. Someone's playing dirty pool. Scott ran the saloon. We gave him a chance to clean it up and he blew it. Now we are closing him down.'

'If it's the only way out . . . ' Gowan began tentatively.

'It is. We're talking about survival.' Turcan opened his briefcase and dropped his papers inside. 'We want a single purchaser, preferably a large investment company with a stake in Europe already. We can't afford to horse around with guys who have to get out a map every time we mention a place east of Paris.'

'And it has to be done quietly.' Hain was nailing down the coffin lid. 'The market is already a rumour mill. If this gets round, we're dead.' His dark eyes travelled from Marquand to Gowan and settled on Liz.

The woman stared back at him defiantly. 'And Scott? What is he to be told?'

Turcan stood up. 'Nothing. There is no need to trouble Scott with this until we have a buyer and a contract. You must see that, Liz. The next few days are going to be critical. We mustn't rock the boat.' He snapped his briefcase shut. 'This must not go beyond the five of us. Anyone who breathes a word of it will have to answer to me.' He picked up the telephone and asked for his messages.

23

GENEVA

Marc Canton hunched into his heavy overcoat and set off along the damp cobbled streets that led from the old quarter to the heart of the city. It was half-past seven in the morning and traffic was already building up. The bankers would soon be at their desks checking through their list of appointments. Another day making the rich richer. Another day buttressing their defences against a world growing ever more intrusive.

He crossed the river by the Pont des Bergues. The buildings with their awnings over the windows reminded him of the stolid, expressionless faces of poker players, eyes heavy-lidded with fatigue after a long night at the table.

He preferred Geneva in the summer when the steamers plied to and fro across the sparkling surface of the lake, the fountain spurted its plume of white water hundreds of feet into the air, and in the distance the snow glinted on sunlit mountain tops.

There was a café in the Rue Rousseau where he had taken to having breakfast. Latterly, he had become a creature of habit, his movements as predictable as the station clock in the Place du Cornavin. It went against his training.

On the street corner, the daily papers were stacked in crude metal boxes. Where else but Switzerland would the citizens be trusted not to take them without paying? He put a coin in the slot, swung open the door and picked up the *Tribune de Genève*.

As he seated himself at a table by the window, the waiter bustled over to him. 'The same as usual for Monsieur?'

'Of course.'

When the croissants arrived they were warm and so light they crumbled in his fingers. He stirred a lump of sugar into the steaming cup of creamy coffee. A clock was chiming the three-quarters.

Canton led a simple life. Occasionally he lunched out. More often he would have a sandwich in his office in the Rue de Chantepoulet and go through the international editions. In the evenings, he sometimes went to a restaurant in the Rue du Mont Blanc. The fondue was excellent, small pieces of tender fillet steak cooked at the table, served with french fries and a green salad.

He never thought to ask himself whether he was lonely. He was by nature a solitary individual. He had no children. His wife had refused to leave the United States and they had divorced. He turned to the business section. A postcard had been inserted, a picture of the Botanical Gardens. Some letters had been cut from a magazine and pasted on the back to form a message. *Twelve Noon Today. Bring This Newspaper. Come Alone.* Pedlar had made contact again.

It gave him an eerie feeling. Pedlar must have watched him, waited until he approached the newspaper stand and then taken a paper and slipped his card into the one underneath. Tucking the card into his wallet, he paid his bill and walked quickly to his office.

Inside the heavy brass front door was a row of mail boxes. One morning he had opened his box and found the cassette. 'I shall make contact again,' it concluded. 'Come alone but, be warned, do not try to follow me.'

He had taken the tape to Brett Vernham, his chief. Vernham had laughed. 'Secret bearer bonds, encrypted, signed by JFK himself! Trash it, Marc. It's garbage! Dreamed up by some screwball! We get dozens of them. You're the new kid on the block. When you've been with us a bit longer you won't even bother to call me.'

'But it could be genuine,' he had insisted. 'We dare not ignore it.'

His chief had been irritated. 'Oh, very well. Give the guy a code name and send it to Evaluation.' They will bury it, his expression had said, as clearly as if he spoken the words.

It was humiliating. Like a child being palmed off with a candy to keep him quiet. Instinct told him that this was the real thing. Riled, he had sent a confidential report to the Secretary of State at his private address. It might have cost him his job. Saxon hadn't replied. He had spent some nail-biting days. Then he got that call from Sam Coaker's PA. Pedlar was being taken seriously. His judgement had been vindicated.

At ten minutes to twelve, he left his office, tucking the *Tribune* under his arm. It was a few minutes short of noon when he reached the end of the Quai Wilson and followed the main path through the gardens. There was a teasing wind from the lake nudging at the mist which hung about the trees.

The gardens were almost empty. An old man leaning on a stick was stooping down to look at the label on one of the shrubs. A uniformed nurse was walking briskly, pushing a pram in front of her. Two elegantly dressed women were strolling arm in arm engaged in earnest conversation. A clock was tolling the hour.

As the last chime faded, a miniature train in a bright buttercup yellow trundled round a bend in the path. He stood on the verge to watch it pass. The first carriage was packed with school children in the charge of a harassed-looking teacher. A woman with her teenage son was sitting at the front of the second. Right at the back was a man in a grey nailhead overcoat with a homburg pulled down over his eyes. On a leash beside him, was a full-grown black and tan Doberman.

A bell tinkled and the train slowed to a halt some twenty paces beyond him. The woman and her son alighted. The man in the homburg got to his feet and came to the doorway. He hesitated for a moment, looking about him before descending the two steps to the ground.

The dog leaped down ahead of him and then stopped, its eyes fixed on some movement in the mist-shrouded bushes. It strained at the leash, its nose pointing like an arrowhead, a low rumbling coming from its throat, its muscular body quivering with pent-up energy. The man spoke sharply to it. Ignoring its yelp of protest, he gave it a violent tug and returned to his seat.

The train started off once more. Canton cursed to himself. Something had happened to alarm the man. Perhaps he suspected he was being followed. But he had seen him. Pedlar now had a face. He must report to Leah Stein. At once.

24

KK KEMIKAL, THE ARDENNES

The video conference was over. The panels round the walls of the boardroom went dark. The features of the vice-presidents, beamed in from six continents, faded from the screens. All but one had been congratulated on the latest management figures. That unfortunate individual had been given two minutes to explain why his services should not be dispensed with.

Ashen-faced, he stumbled over his words, locking his fingers together to stop their trembling. Assurances that his group would meet its target and make up the shortfall within three months were heard in sceptical silence. At the end he bowed his head, his voice breaking. He had had problems at home. His family had been under great strain. He begged to be given another chance.

The chairman wrote a few words on a slip of paper and passed it to his colleague. The managing director announced the board's decision. The executive's contract was terminated forthwith. He had ten minutes to return his car and leave company premises. He would receive generous severance pay and a month's paid holiday for himself and his family. Within ten days he would be dead, drowned while scuba diving off St Lucia.

Kraik closed the file in front of him. 'So much for industrial chemicals. Let us turn to IAC. Your report, Pieter.'

Rohr's great bulk shifted in the chair. He was a soldier, not a number cruncher, a man who carried seventeen stone and not an ounce of overweight. He had been a paratrooper in the South African Army but the life had been too tame and he had joined the Afghans as a mercenary in 1985 at the age of twenty. International Arms Consortium were supplying Stinger missiles to the jihadists and the Soviets were looking for a way out.

A shrapnel wound received in action in the Farakh province against the crack Soviet Spetsnaz units had left him with a slight limp. Consultancy posts had followed in Libya and then in the Yemen. He had been in Sri Lanka as a military adviser with the Tamil Tigers when Kraik had recruited him to IAC to head up the sales team.

'Our final quarter was a very difficult trading period,' Rohr began. 'Profits showed only a small increase. The problem—'

'I have seen the accounts,' Kraik cut in. 'I do not employ people to tell me that there are problems. Their job is to solve them.'

Rohr flushed red under his ginger stubble, but he was not to be browbeaten. 'Facts are facts, nevertheless. Defence budgets are being slashed. The market is flooded with surplus equipment. There is too much competition. Where once we had the Americans, Russians, British and French there are many new players. China, Brazil, Israel, North Korea and others. It is an unregulated market. Rates are being cut to the point where we would make more money selling water pistols.'

Kraik's fingers drummed impatiently on the table top. 'But market outlets have increased, Pieter. There are scores of dissident organisations. There can be no excuse for not making up the lost revenue. We are running a business, not a home for inadequates.'

Rohr flinched under Kraik's viperish tongue. 'My contacts in these groups are the best there are. That is—'

Kraik cut him short. 'That is why you work for me.'

Rohr wiped the sweat from his forehead. 'Good men are hard to find and expensive to train. We have lost three top operators in the past twelve weeks.'

'I know that.'

'All on sales missions,' Rohr persisted. 'In Pakistan. In Chechnya. Tulloch disappeared in Iran.'

'Disappeared?' Kraik whispered. 'Nobody in my company disappears. Unless it is six feet underground. Find him.'

'And if he is alive?'

The tongue flickered between the thin lips. 'Dispose of him. An arms salesman is like a fighting bull. There is only one way he can be allowed to leave the ring. As hoof and hide. He knows too much.'

Kraik rose to his feet and walked with short, quick strides to the window. He looked out over the tall radio masts of the antenna field, the huge white domes housing the satellite monitoring dishes, the airfield with its rows of hangars, the complex of buildings for the research laboratories and the pilot manufacturing plant. His eyes ran down the long lines of electrified fencing with their watchtowers and lifted to the tops of the trees beyond which the forest ran to the horizon.

'We have a good situation here,' he said softly, the syllables slipping from his lips like the rustle of a snake through dry grass. 'We straddle the border between countries where the authorities let businessmen get on with making money. We have a chemical brokerage business that is highly profitable. We pay large sums in taxes. We make donations to political parties and other groups in order to be allowed to operate without interference.'

Deep in thought, he walked slowly back to the boardroom table. 'Suddenly we have an opportunity which comes only once—' He checked himself abruptly. 'But these are not matters for discussion.' Seating himself once more, he turned to Snoeck. 'Let us have your report on Detonard, Ulrich.'

Ulrich Snoeck was still under thirty, Belgian born, a top-class scientist and a former high flyer at the UK Defence Evaluation Research Agency. His career at DERA had ended in disgrace when officers from Special Branch had raided his home after an anonymous tip-off and discovered classified documents. Within an hour of his dismissal, Kraik had offered him the job of director of research at double the salary.

Detonard was a recent acquisition. It was a company that had gone bankrupt attempting to develop a new missile launcher. There had been initial opposition to a sale from the French government but after transfers had been made into the off-shore accounts of certain highly placed individuals these had been resolved to everyone's satisfaction.

Snoeck removed his heavy black-rimmed spectacles and folded them into his top pocket. 'A man-portable, shoulder-fired weapon incorporating a sophisticated control and guidance system and capable of firing a projectile with a velocity in excess of Mach 10 could be described as the Holy Grail of military weaponry.

'Billions of dollars have been poured into attempts to overcome two seemingly insoluble problems. How to dissipate the frictional heat created by the high muzzle velocity and how to generate the colossal amount of launch current required.'

Kraik glanced at Rohr, amused to see the contempt on his face. Rohr had no time for this boffin with his sallow features, his slight frame and lank hair that curled over the collar of his white coat.

'What we needed—'

'Was a submarine or a battleship to launch it,' cut in Rohr.

'We needed neither,' continued Snoeck smoothly. 'Detonard developed a new alloy capable of dissipating the heat but it ruined them. We have taken over their patents and their manufacturing facilities. As for the launch current, Dixon's capacitor produces an intense electrical pulse in one ten-billionth of a second. We have the new muzzle and we have the power without any sacrifice in portability. The chairman supplied—'

Kraik gestured to Snoeck to be silent. 'Using drawings in my possession, we have developed a new projectile. It is a kinetic energy round and requires neither explosives nor propellants. The weapon will be known as the KRG.'

Rohr pushed his chair back with a screech. 'An infantry weapon that would vaporise a tank. Or an airliner. And could devastate whole cities. In the hands of some fanatic high on coke. *You cannot let that loose on the world!*' His face was grey.

'You do your job and leave me to do mine,' said Kraik sharply. 'A scale model will be tested in the pilot plant after this meeting. Field trials will be completed within the week.' Turning back to Snoeck, he asked, 'How much does Dixon know?'

'Nothing. Not yet.'

'*Not yet!* Have you followed my orders?'

'I have. He has been told that we are developing a powerful battery for a range of electric cars that will make the petrol engine obsolete. His technical work is first class but he is too easily distracted.'

'Say what you mean,' Kraik hissed.

'He asks too many questions.'

'What questions?'

'He has been badgering the laboratory assistants.'

'Dixon's work is finished. He can help to convert the nerve gas into powder while we decide what to do with him. The prototype of KRG will be demonstrated at Sharpshooter. Leave us now and return to your duties.' With a click of his bony fingers he dismissed him.

Snoeck gathered up his papers and hurried from the boardroom, leaving the two men alone.

Kraik pressed a button and a large-scale map of Germany came up on the wall. 'Let me have your report on the Combat Units.'

'We have recruited from the pick of the Direct Action groups. They needed discipline and a purpose in life beyond breaking a few heads as they came out of the bierkellers. We now have complete coverage from the Danish border in the north to Munich in the south. They are tough, well trained and they are all volunteers. The weapons caches are in place but only the commanders have been given the locations. My worry is that they are growing restless.'

'They must be patient. Their time will come.'

'There is another problem. The army is holding one of my men. Ludger Buhl. He is a deserter. He knows a great deal about the organisation. A great deal that Generalmajor Herman Stier would like to know. If they sweat him, he may talk.'

'We know a few things about Stier. Things that the Generalmajor would rather remained hidden from view.' Kraik picked up a file in front of him. 'What do you know about Zoltán Zaros, Pieter?'

'Very little beyond the fact that Zaros is a private bank in Zurich.'

'Then you do not know that Warren Rokeby used to visit the bank. He came several times a year and more often during periods of international tension. He always arrived after closing time. He and Zoltán were together for about an hour on each occasion. I was intrigued. What, I asked myself was the connection?

'Zoltán is old and in failing health. I made an offer for the bank but he refuses to sell. It is not a question of price. He is governed by a sense of loyalty. Many of his depositors are elderly immigrants, refugees from Central Europe like himself. He insists that they depend on him to look after their affairs.'

Kraik slid the file across the table. 'Zoltán appointed a manager, Franz Strauben. I contacted Strauben and put certain proposals to him. He seemed receptive. Then, suddenly he went cold. My sources inform me that he no longer works for the bank. The contents of a safe deposit box have gone missing. Zoltán accused Strauben. There was a quarrel. The old man had a stroke and Strauben left in a hurry.'

'He only had to wait and he would probably have stepped into the old man's shoes. Why risk everything by acting too soon?'

'That,' Kraik murmured, 'is what I intend to find out. Strauben has a house on the edge of Lake Zürich. He has a large dog, a Doberman, and he has recently installed CCTV and new security lighting.'

'It's a job for Ulla Cranz.'

Kraik sniffed. 'Is a woman up to the assignment?'

'Ulla is a professional.'

'So, no doubt, were the men you picked for that London job.'

'The men failed. They have been punished.'

'In Hamburg it was no better.'

'The Dixon girl has had a sharp lesson. You won't have any more trouble with her.'

'As for Warren Rokeby, my express orders were that he was to be brought here. What went wrong?' A film seemed to come down over his eyes as he waited for an answer.

Rohr shuddered. It reminded him of an encounter with a king cobra in the Sri Lankan jungle. This pathological hatred of the Rokeby family. There was no reasoning with Kraik on the subject. 'Ulla did her part. She staged an accident with her motorbike. She was lying in the road. Rokeby stopped to help. Skoko and Vlak were following. Vlak slugged Rokeby but he hit him too hard. They tried to revive him but he was dead. They were scared.'

'They had every reason to be scared.'

'They put him back in the car and pushed it off the road into the ravine.'

'So they told you that he had had an accident?'

'Yes. Ulla told me what really happened. I will deal with—'

'Leave them to me.'

'We can pick up his son.'

'When I am ready. I am planning something rather special for Scott Rokeby.'

'And Strauben?'

'Brief the Cranz woman and return the file to me. Take no copies.'

25

HAMBURG HOSPITAL

Julie's head was still muzzy from the sedatives and her back burned like the bed of an old fire. She tried to shift on to her side and groaned. Her arm was tender where they had inoculated her. Her legs were so stiff they felt as if it would take a winch to move them. She wrinkled her nostrils, sniffing at the sharp tang of antiseptic, the smell of polished linoleum.

Raising her arm gingerly she felt for the light cord above her head. White walls, a side table, a basin, venetian blinds over the windows. Manoeuvring herself into a sitting position, she pushed back the bedclothes.

Her eyes went to the cupboard in the corner. Money. Camera. Mobile phone. The passport had gone. She tottered across the floor, screwing up her face as the lacerations flamed into life. The door opened and she stared up at a severe-looking woman with iron-grey hair wearing a crisp uniform.

'What are you doing out of bed? Get back there at once. The night nurse will change your dressing before she goes off duty. Inspector Horst will be here at seven to ask you some questions. At eight you will be discharged. We need this room for our patients.' With a sharp nod she left the room.

Julie gave a vicious tug to the blind cord. Outside it was still dark. An ambulance was backing up to the hospital entrance. The rain was beating on its roof and pooling on the ground.

The night nurse came in and deposited Julie's clothes on a chair. 'These have been laundered. They were in a terrible state.' Julie had to stuff a corner of the pillow into her mouth to stop herself crying out as the nurse stripped away the surgical tape and removed the dressing. 'This may sting a little,' she said briskly as she picked up a can.

Julie gritted her teeth as the iodine spray was applied. It felt as if an army of soldier ants was foraging on the lacerated skin. The nurse busied herself with lint and tissue. 'We see a lot of foreign girls who come to Hamburg and get themselves into trouble. They hear about the easy money to be earned in the bars and the clubs. They think that all they have to do is take off their clothes and do a few twirls but it isn't so easy. The men running those places are vicious. We see girls with broken bones, others mutilated. I have even seen girls who have been—'

'*I don't want to know!*' Julie cried. 'Whatever you may have heard about me isn't true!'

'All I am trying to do is warn you.'

'*Well, stop trying!*' Her voice broke and she found that the tears were streaming down her face for no reason at all. She thumped the pillow with her small fists in an access of rage and misery.

'I'm not going to give you any more advice,' the nurse said quietly, 'but if I were you I would go back home to my family.' She pressed the dressing into place and straightened. 'There, that's the best I can do. Change it once a day, keep the back clean and dry and it should heal all right.' She left her with a packet of strong painkillers.

Julie had wiped her eyes and was sitting up when an orderly arrived with a breakfast tray. Two bread rolls, apricot jam, slices of ham and cheese, an apple and a cup of coffee. She was hungry, devouring everything but the apple which she dropped into her jacket pocket. She gulped down a pill with the last of the coffee and slowly, laboriously washed and got her clothes on.

At precisely seven, the matron escorted her to the waiting room and shut the door firmly behind her. The inspector was sitting at the table reading a file. Without raising his head he gestured to a chair. Her eyes flicked over the stack of tattered magazines, medical notices on the walls and the assortment of cheap plastic toys in the corner and returned to the inspector. His face was lightly tanned and had she been in a better mood she might have credited him with passable looks and even complimented him on his well-cut tweed jacket.

With infuriating deliberation he turned another page of the file. Julie's impatience boiled over. 'Inspector, you wanted this meeting. Please ask your questions so that I can start work. I have a lot to do today.'

'Forget about making plans,' he replied curtly, 'until you know what plans we have for you.' He spoke in English but the accent gave his tone a harsh, uncompromising edge.

Julie seethed in silence until he closed the file and leaned forward over the table. 'I am Inspector Erich Horst. When you came into casualty early this morning, you gave your name as Julie Dixon.'

'I try to use my real name whenever possible. It's less confusing.'

The inspector gave her a wintry smile. 'What were you doing soliciting in the dock area last night?'

'I was doing no such thing. I'm a journalist. I was doing a feature for my paper.'

Horst sighed wearily. 'Hamburg by Night. If I could impose a fine every time I heard that story, I could retire.'

Julie struggled to control her temper. Her head was throbbing, she was short of sleep, she had been duped, robbed and beaten. She pointed to her shoulder bag. 'Take a look. My camera is inside.'

The policeman shrugged. 'That proves nothing. We find all sorts of things on girls we pull in. We have heard most of the fairy tales by now.'

'Do you really believe that I was strutting my stuff on that wharf on a cold, foggy night? You might credit me with more sense.'

Horst jabbed a finger at her. 'I credit you with very little. You were lucky last night. If the driver of that hotdog stand hadn't kept an eye out for you . . .'

She shook her head wordlessly.

'He saw the van being driven away and phoned through the registration number. But for that you might be lying at the bottom of the harbour with a car battery tied round your ankles.'

Julie swallowed. It wasn't good to be reminded. She returned to the attack. 'Why don't you catch those thugs instead of pestering me?'

'We caught one of them. Ludger Buhl. He is a deserter and the army want to talk to him.'

'I hope they lock him up and throw away the key. Now, if that is all, Inspector . . . '

' It is not all. Did you get any photographs?'

She shook her head. 'There wasn't time.'

He stood up. 'My advice to you, Fräulein, is to leave police work to the professionals. We are not blind. We have had our eyes on the *Galinna* for some time. We will move but not till we are ready.'

She picked up her gear and hobbled to the door. He offered his hand. He was sorry that she had had a bad experience in his city. 'Germany has many problems at the moment. Come back when the elections are over. I can promise you things will be different.'

She called her paper to check when Bains would be in. She dreaded having to tell him that all she had to show for a night's work was a back that felt like a cat's scratching post. He would order her straight home. He might even fire her. Carol was already there. She never seemed to go to bed. 'Where are you, Julie?'

'In Hamburg.'

'It's a good thing you called in. You have got to go to Berlin for a Ministry of Defence press briefing at midday. Skip the buffet lunch afterwards. You are booked to Zurich for a big conference this evening.'

'I thought the paper had a man there. What's happened to him?'

'He's broken a leg.'

'Too much German gin. The way he poured the stuff into him it's a wonder he ever managed to stand upright. I shall need passes and money.'

'It will all be waiting for you at the check-in desk.'

'Carol, I must have a temporary passport.'

'What happened to yours?'

'I think I must have dropped it in the Reeperbahn. This old man in a dirty mac came towards me and before I could stop him he—'

'Stop fooling, Julie. What do you expect me to do?'

'Call our consulate in Berlin. Get someone to meet me off the plane.'

'Julie, do you know what you're asking? There will be forms to fill out, photographs . . . '

'I will get some photos done at the airport.'

'I'll try but—'

'Carol, you're a star.'

26

MINISTRY OF DEFENCE, BERLIN

The room was crowded with journalists from the world's press. The overhead lights were strong and cameras flashing every few seconds. Generalmajor Herman Stier was seated at the table on the platform flanked by his aides.

The Director General of Weapons (Army) was a tall, handsome man in his late forties. The fierce blue eyes, the beaked nose, the clipped moustache and the immaculate cut of his uniform gave him the air of a man who knew what he wanted from life and took it. In his day he had been a fine race rider with a reputation for driving his mounts hard. His sons by his first marriage had followed him into the army.

He tapped his watch. 'We have overrun our schedule. I will take two more questions.' His eyes widened at an attractive, dark-haired girl in a jacket that looked as if it had been dragged through a farmyard. She scowled back at him. *Impudent creature!* From the *Courier*. He couldn't read the name on her badge. What wouldn't he give to have fifteen minutes alone with her after work. He would soon teach her some respect for her elders and betters.

Renata Dziak, foreign correspondent of the most influential of the Polish papers, was trying to catch his eye. She had golden ringlets like a princess out of a fairy story. Idly he wondered whether they were long enough to plait and tie to the bedpost. She stood up, moistening her lips a little before putting her question. 'Director General, the election is almost upon us and Exhibition Sharpshooter is a few days away. The armed forces are under pressure from certain quarters to go for a big increase in defence spending. Can you confirm that the pressure will be resisted?'

Stier blew out his cheeks angrily. 'That question has been raised in half a dozen different forms already. The defence budget is subject to tight political control. Sharpshooter is a showcase for the whole defence industry. Germany is merely a participant.'

Jean-Michel Jamyn raised his hand. He was Moscow Bureau Chief for a French broadsheet with a big following on the left. 'There have been disturbing reports that many young and middle-ranking officers have established close links with Muhlder's Extreme Right Party. It is also rumoured that self-styled combat groups have been assembling stockpiles of concealed weapons. What conclusions should we draw?'

Stier rapped the table. 'Combat groups, mostly drawn from the Extreme Right, and their stocks of concealed weapons are a growing problem. These thugs have no place in a modern democracy. The police are overstretched and they can count on my help in ensuring that these groups are hunted down and their members prosecuted. Those found guilty can expect lengthy sentences. As to the other part of your question, I can assure you that these so-called reports are sheer fabrication. The quickest way for an officer to find himself out of uniform is to involve himself in politics.'

He swept up his papers and rose to his feet. 'Ladies and gentlemen of the press corps, I will not deny that we face difficulties at home and a volatile situation globally. I look to you to use your influence responsibly.' His aides would be circulating a press release. There was a buffet lunch for those who felt in need of refreshment. Regrettably he had a busy schedule and they must excuse him. The meeting was over.

Stier returned to his office, a large panelled room with portraits of Clausewitz and Bismarck on the walls. He was in excellent humour.

Ingrid Berger, his confidential secretary, brought him a cup of coffee and his diary.

'You work me too hard, Ingrid,' he complained. It was a fiction he liked to foster. In reality much of the work was handled in Bonn and Koblenz but it was unthinkable that a man of his standing should live anywhere but in Berlin, at the hub of things.

'The Director General enjoys his work.'

'Some of it more than others.' He smiled at her, showing his strong white teeth.

She knew the signs. He would work late that evening and spend the night in the top-floor apartment provided for the use of high-ranking officers. It had recently been refurbished and he had taken more than a casual interest in the details. A gas log fire had been installed in the sitting room, a dining area added, the kitchen re-equipped and the bathroom fitted with a jacuzzi. A commodious bed had been purchased to replace the austere object that had done service before it.

He ran his finger down the page. 'Meetings, more meetings, mountains of paper work.' He sighed cheerfully. 'I shall be burning the midnight oil, Ingrid.'

'I will see that everything is in order, Herr Direktor. Will you be going out for supper or staying in?'

'I shall stay in, tonight, Ingrid. I enjoy sampling my own cooking from time to time. Please arrange to have a couple of nice fillet steaks sent up.'

'Leave it to me. Perhaps some caviar to start with and a good French cheese for dessert?'

'Excellent, Ingrid. And be so good as to ask the orderly to put a bottle of Krug on ice.'

She returned to her desk to make the arrangements. Stier had enjoyed a number of romantic liaisons since the breakdown of his second marriage but he had never involved a member of his staff until now. Sonja Peetsch should never have been employed in a government department. The green eyes, the full red lips, the long black hair that fell below her shoulders, the body squeezed into a dress that showed every flaunting line of her, the young woman had the sort of looks that made men careless of their duty.

Ingrid had reminded him that Peetsch had a low grade security clearance but he had laughed and told her she was fussing unnecessarily. He had, however, agreed to restrict her to the social side, typing invitations to receptions and helping with official entertaining.

Earlier that morning, Ingrid had walked the length of the typing department, handing out copies of a memorandum. Tucked under Sonja's desk she had seen what she expected to see. A shopping bag from one of the top department stores, large enough to contain a négligée, a sponge bag and any other accessories required for a night's adventure.

Stier had a lunch appointment and would not be back before three. She arranged an early lunch with Annette, the personnel manager, a pleasant, competent woman in her late thirties. They often went to the vegetarian restaurant, choosing a time when it was half empty and they could talk without the risk of being overheard.

They ordered a herb omelette and chatted about general matters before Annette broached the subject that was on their minds. 'I'm as worried as you are, Ingrid, but I can't interfere. It's more than my job is worth.'

'Surely you can find some way of getting the Peetsch woman transferred to another ministry?'

'How? What reason could I give? Nominally she is a member of the typing pool but in fact she is working under the director.' Her cheeks crimsoned as the words echoed in her head.

Ingrid grimaced. 'I couldn't have put it better myself.' She lowered her voice. 'You could go to Security . . . on the quiet.'

'And do you think it would stay quiet? These things always leak out. He would get his wrist slapped for being a naughty boy. I might find myself black-listed. I might never work again and I have a sick mother to support.'

'Are you saying that we just ignore the situation?' She ran a finger feverishly down the wine list.

'What else can we do?' Annette stared across the table. She was quite shocked. In all the years she had known Ingrid she had never known her to touch alcohol at lunchtime.

27

KK KEMIKAL, LABORATORY

David Dixon bent over the scales as he measured out a white powdery substance. The reading swam in and out of focus. He sometimes wondered if his mind was going. His work at KKK was finished. Why wouldn't they let him go home? He stooped down to rub his ankle where the metal tag was rubbing it raw.

'*Leave that alone!*' the guard bellowed at him. He came over and checked that the tag was still in place before resuming his patrol.

Dixon waited while a technician checked his work. He had been made to help with converting a new gas into powder and storing it in cylinders. Almost everything he did was checked. Every instruction he gave had to be confirmed by Snoeck. A laboratory used to be home to him, the tubes and slides and glass retorts the furniture of his life. This was a prison.

A thousand times he had cursed himself for a fool. Only a naïve, idealistic fool would have fallen for that story, would have believed that these people were prepared to put millions into his research and demand nothing in return. Even now he wanted to believe that Snoeck was different from the others because he was a scientist and that he could be won over, made to understand that his discovery belonged to humanity, not to gangsters who wanted to patent it and gouge the last cent out of it.

But Snoeck wasn't interested in ethics. 'Keep that sentimental preaching to yourself,' he had said. 'What matters is that the new capacitor must be worth hundreds of millions.'

He tried to persuade himself that the substance he was working on was for a new anaesthetic. The problem, he discovered, was that it was inherently unstable, potentially lethal. He had protested to Snoeck. Doctors would be mad to use it.

'Who said anything about doctors?' Snoeck had taunted.

'*You devil, Snoeck*! When I get out of here—'

'You cannot get out, Dixon. You cannot even leave the building without us knowing. The fence is electrified, the watchtowers are manned day and night. When the lights come on at dusk, the dogs are let loose. Escape is impossible.'

Rohr had come into the laboratory demanding to know what the row was about.

'Dixon is threatening to go on strike,' Snoeck told him.

'Is he?' Rohr hadn't raised his voice. He walked over to where Dixon was standing and hooking his fingers into the collar of his white overall hoisted him off the ground. As Dixon choked and squirmed, he put his face up very close. 'We know where your sister is,' he whispered. 'If we get any trouble from you we shall bring her here and try out the new formula on her. She will be – how do you say it in English? – our first guinea pig.' Opening his huge hand he dropped him. 'Now get back to work.'

28

ZURICH

Scott crossed the Rhine and stopped at a lay-by close to the motorway junction. France was behind him. Germany was one way. Switzerland another. What should he do? Toss a coin? He might as well. A movement in the rear mirror caught his eye. A hundred yards behind him a dark blue Alfa had stopped. The driver's face was hidden by the sun flap. Scott took out his father's watch and wound it up. To his surprise it was still working. He put it in his pocket with the chain attached to his belt.

What else had he got to show for a night in a French jail? He leafed through the motoring guide he had found in the Peugeot. It was old and dog-eared and there was no name inside. The cover had been dusted for prints and the powder came off on his hands. He skimmed through it. Driving regulations in the various European countries. A list of hotels and garages. Plans of the channel ports. At the back there were street maps of the larger cities. Paris, Lille, Lyons, Amsterdam, The Hague, Brussels, Luxembourg. No notes or markings of any kind.

Berlin, Hamburg, Bonn, Frankfurt. Nothing. Basel, Bern, Geneva, Lausanne. Nothing. Zurich. *Hang on!* A faint pencil mark on a small street close to the National Bank. He screwed up his eyes. Z? No, it was ZZ. He should get himself some glasses, acknowledge the passing of one more milestone on the journey to the grave. He checked the mirror. The Alfa was still there. As he moved off, it pulled away smoothly, keeping its distance.

It stayed with him halfway to Zurich before turning off. A white Audi took its place. He yawned. He was short of sleep. Starting to imagine things. He stopped at a gas station, filled up, bought a ham roll and used the WC to change his clothes. Outside Basel, a container lorry had jack-knifed and there was a long tailback. It was close to midday before the twin towers of Grossmünster church came into view. He knew the city well. Clean and efficient, a good place to eat if you had money and the digestive system to go with it. The food was like everything else. Rich.

He parked the car near the Münsterhof and walked. People passed him with their heads down, huddled into their overcoats against the biting wind. Where was ZZ? He found his answer in a side street near the Paradeplatz. The building had such a narrow frontage he almost missed it. A polished brass plaque on the wall read 'Zoltán Zaros, Private Bankers'. Above it, tucked under a stone ledge was a security camera. He was surprised to see the heavy mahogany door open and a man in a business suit emerge. Why was the bank working on a Sunday? He walked past and crossed the street.

He had to find a hotel. The agency in the station wasn't optimistic. Hadn't he heard that there was a big international conference in town? The hotels had been booked up for months. Eventually they tracked down a pension in a back street. There was one room left. No credit cards. Payment in advance. They would hold it for an hour. He took it.

From the street came the wail of police sirens. Two vans packed with police in riot gear raced past. He went to a newsstand and bought a local paper. Wolfgang Muhlder was addressing a meeting in the city that evening.

'Listen!' the woman behind the counter was saying. 'You can hear them boarding up the windows. Muhlder's bully boys are on their way.' She flung her hands in the air. 'We don't want their kind here! Why don't the authorities keep them out? I would stop them at the border and take their boots off them. Tell them to walk home.'

He got a cup of coffee and called Mary Seton. She would have to be told about Warren.

'A part of me went on hoping, Scott. The house is so quiet without him. I don't think I shall ever get used to the silence. I still find myself listening for the sound of his footsteps on the balcony.'

He searched for the words to comfort her but they weren't there. Only the guilt, the anger and a resolve that he didn't trust himself to put into words.

She wanted to stay and look after the house until Warren came home, as she put it. There was something else. Someone had got in while she was out shopping. 'There was no sign of a break-in but the lock on the kitchen window isn't very good. And those jars of herbs that I keep on the ledge had been moved.'

'Is anything missing?'

'Some newspapers. The foreign ones. They were beside the radio.'

'Are you sure you didn't use them to light the fire?'

'Of course not,' she replied indignantly. 'I had strict orders not to touch them.' And Warren's old attaché case had gone. 'I'm sure it was empty.'

'What about the drawers in his desk?'

'They are still locked.'

'Do you know where he kept the key?' She wouldn't admit it but she knew all the old man's habits.

'Of course not. Warren never confided in me.'

'On the wall in his bedroom there's a small barometer in a brass case. It's taped to the back.' He asked her to go through his father's desk and let him know if she found any documents or letters that might be important.

'What are you looking for?'

'I don't know.'

He called Zoltán Zaros and was put through to Fräulein Heideck.

'Does Mr Zaros know you?' The wary courtesy of the experienced private secretary.

'My name is Rokeby.'

'Not Mr Warren Rokeby, surely? I know his voice.'

'Scott Rokeby. I'm Warren's son.' He was in Zurich, he told her. A few minutes' walk away.

'I cannot talk freely,' she whispered. 'Things here are very difficult. Have you heard that Mr. Zaros has had a stroke? He is very ill and in hospital. We have been expecting your father's visit for several days.'

'My father has had an accident.'

'A . . . bad accident?'

'As bad as it could be.'

There was a moment of silence before she spoke again. '*That is terrible!* When he did not arrive I feared that something awful had happened.'

'Could you not call him at home.'

'*Certainly not!*' She sounded shocked.' I had my instructions. Under no circumstances was I to attempt to communicate with him.'

'Fräulein Heideck, we must meet. There is so much that I need to know.'

She was going to visit Mr Zaros in hospital later that afternoon. They could meet there. 'Come to the waiting room on the fifth floor. Come alone and don't mention this to anyone.'

29

ZURICH – EARLY EVENING

The conference was over. The amber beams of the headlights pushed through the sleet, the wipers sweeping the slush into the slipstream. The convoy of official cars escorted by police outriders was heading for the airport. The Secretaries of State and Defense had to be in Washington the next morning.

'I don't know why they called it *Towards a Safer World*,' Saxon grumbled. 'Our frontiers are as riddled with holes as a Swiss cheese and the same goes for our European partners. Slamming the door shut to keep out undesirables is what we should be talking about.'

Coaker pointed down a side street. Armoured cars equipped with water cannon were standing by. Police in riot gear were piling out of vans. 'That says more about what's going on than a dozen speeches.'

'Switzerland doesn't need any lessons in xenophobia but Muhlder's thugs are going to give them one just the same.' He slid the glass screen home. 'Have you heard from Canton?'

'Only a bit of gossip. I didn't want to bother you with it.'

Saxon swivelled in his seat. 'I want to be bothered with it, Sam.' He spoke with quiet menace. 'I want a little warning before I have to go to the Oval Office and tell the President he's got fifty million fire crackers stuck up his pants.'

Coaker tugged a cigar from his top pocket and crackled the leaf between his fingers.

'Canton had a meeting set up but Pedlar chickened out. He got a look at him, that's all.'

'Didn't he follow him?'

'He couldn't take the risk. Pedlar has the ball. We play by his rules or not at all.'

'I don't like it.'

'Do you think I like it?' Coaker growled. 'A few good men could nail that sonofabitch within hours!'

'I said no and it's still no. Pedlar carries insurance. Scare him and a photo of those bonds will be spread over every front page from here to Honolulu.'

'He would spend the rest of his life in jail.'

'That wouldn't help the President – or us.'

Coaker bit the end off his cigar and jammed it into his mouth. 'Mind if I ask you a question, Mike?'

'Shoot – but that doesn't mean I'll answer it.'

'Who put Warren Rokeby on ice – and I mean on ice?'

Saxon massaged the back of his neck. He was tired. It had been a long day. 'I'm no happier about it, Sam, than you are.'

'Don't fence with me, Mike,' Coaker snapped. 'Rokeby was an ex-diplomat, one of the home team, a man with a distinguished career in public service. The least he is entitled to is a few cubic feet of good American earth.'

'My spread runs from Alaska to the Rio Grande. That has priority.'

'How long does he stay in the freezer with the French sitting on the lid?'

'For as long as it takes. The DST picked up the trail of two men in Paris and put a tail on them. They discovered the guys were shadowing Warren. That threw them. Who the hell was Warren Rokeby and why was he being followed? They contacted the CIA.'

'Who checked with you?'

'Right. I pulled every wire I could to get them to play it my way, to keep their distance and see where it led.'

'Why didn't you tell me?'

'Because I don't trust you to work your side of the street and stay out of mine. And I was right. Was it one of your men who got into Rokeby's house and turned it over?'

Coaker grinned like a schoolboy caught with his fingers in the jam jar. 'I heard that you could use some help.'

'You're a ruthless bugger, Sam. Always cutting corners. One day you'll meet something coming the other way and it will flatten you.'

Coaker wound down the window and blew a jet of smoke through the opening. 'The DST fucked up. If they'd done their job, Warren might still be alive.'

'And his son would still have a business. Railton Ross has close connections with Congress. Much too close. Scott Rokeby doesn't know what he's getting into.'

'He may end up on a slab like his father.'

'The Hill dare not get caught in the fall-out. I had no choice. I had to cut the wires.'

The two men completed their journey in silence, each sealed in with his own anxieties. Coaker had not told Saxon about his meeting with a senior official from the Swiss Department of Foreign Affairs, based in Bern.

The man had button-holed him during the coffee break. 'May we talk off the record?'

'Certainly.'

'Very well. I will be quick. The US has no Embassy in Tehran. Am I right?'

'Correct. We closed it in 1979 after the Iran hostage crisis.'

'As you know, we have a US Interests Section there that looks after American affairs in the country. Yesterday, a man called Tulloch turned up begging for asylum. He had been badly beaten. He had been negotiating an arms deal with dissident groups in the country. He seemed to be as scared of his own employers as he was of the Iranian security forces.'

'Did you find out who he worked for?'

'KK Kemikal. That's all we were able to discover. Do you know them?'

'I know KKK by name. Will you allow one of our men to question him?'

'No chance of that. Tulloch died early this morning.'

30

ZURICH HOSPITAL

Scott came out of the lift doors to find Fräulein Heideck in the waiting room across the corridor. She was a tall, spare woman with grey hair tied back in a bun. He estimated that she was in her late forties, but the strain of the past days showed in her eyes and she could have been younger.

She took his hand between hers. 'It has been a great shock. First Mr Zaros has a stroke and now your father has gone. Please accept my deepest sympathy.'

They sat together at the table. He explained that he could tell her very little about the accident. His father had been driving through the Vosges when his car left the road. The police were still making inquiries.

Did he know anything about his father's connection with the bank, she asked him.

'No. He never talked about it. He didn't even tell me that he was going to Zurich. I had hoped that Mr Zaros might be able to make things a little clearer.'

She shook her head despondently. 'He is unable to speak. The doctor is with him now. The ward sister will tell us if he is well enough to see you.'

'Have you worked for Mr Zaros for long?'

'For ten years in a personal capacity but I have been employed by the bank for most of my working life.' She smiled wanly.

'Mr Zaros and my father . . . were they old friends?'

'They had known each other for a great many years. His wife Eva was a Hungarian but she had many friends in Czechoslovakia. I believe she was a friend of your mother. She had returned to Budapest in 1956 during the revolution to try to get her mother out of the country. It was a very risky thing to do. The roads were blocked, the frontiers closed, the conditions were atrocious and she was expecting a baby.'

She bit her lip, distressed at the images that came back to her. 'They were trying to cross a stream holding on to a rope strung between two trees and using a fallen tree as a bridge. It was snowing and the current was flowing fast. Suddenly the tree under their feet started to move. Eva's mother lost her balance. Eva tried to help her and fell into the water. Someone pulled her out and ran for a doctor but it was too late. She had a miscarriage and died. I don't think Mr Zaros ever quite got over it. Perhaps that is what brought your father and him together.'

'Would you say that they were close?'

She nodded. But there had been disagreements, tensions between them from time to time. 'They were very rare,' she added hastily. 'I wouldn't want to suggest otherwise. But there was a serious breakdown in the relationship in 1968. Your father was in Prague. You must have been about two at the time.'

'Yes. Warren was Third Secretary at the embassy. The Soviets were scared by the pace of liberalisation in Czechoslovakia. They cracked down that summer. Half a million Red Army troops crossed the frontier. My mother was a Czech. Her brother was taken by the secret police. She went to try and find him. They were both shot. It was an execution.'

'How dreadful! Who gave the orders?'

'My father was determined to find out but he got nowhere. They took away his diplomatic immunity and put him under house arrest.'

'Mr Zaros was furious. He was desperately anxious to contact him.'

'It was not my father's fault. He was kept incommunicado until the crisis was over and the Soviets had their placemen back in power.'

'Mr Zaros may not have known that. He said that your father had not just let him down, he had betrayed a whole nation.'

186

'*He said that!* What can he have meant by it?'

She shook her head. 'I don't know. Later on, Poland came close to revolution. So did East Germany. After Latvia declared its independence it looked as if the Russians would march in and take over.' She shifted in her chair. 'I remember that Mr Zaros became very moody and difficult. It was not just the anxiety about the international situation. I felt that he was being put under pressure to become involved in some way.'

'To provide funds from the bank?'

'I assumed so, but it was very puzzling. The bank has never made large profits.'

'Fräulein Heideck, forgive me for asking a personal question. You never married?'

'I was married to my work.' That wan smile again. She dropped her eyes. 'But there was a time—'

'When you hoped Mr Zaros might remarry?'

She stiffened. 'You are very direct, Mr Rokeby.'

'I'm sorry. I don't mean to pry but—'

'Zoltán Zaros was not an easy man to get close to. We had a good working relationship. It never progressed beyond that. In all the years that I have been with him we only had one serious disagreement.'

She paused to collect herself before continuing. 'It is painful to recall. I told him I felt saddened . . . ' her lips tightened. 'No, it was more than that. I told him that after all the years that I had spent in his service it was humiliating not to be taken fully into his confidence.' A tinge of colour showed in her pale cheeks.

'What did he say?'

'He told me that if he didn't tell me everything about his business it was in order to protect me.'

'Did that satisfy you?'

'No,' she replied with warmth. 'It did not. After so many years of devoted service it grieved me.'

'But you thought about the explanation that he gave you?'

187

'I put two and two together. I knew that your father came to visit him several times a year but I never knew why. If they corresponded, the letters did not pass through me. If they spoke on the telephone, the calls were not made in the bank. I concluded that I was not to be told what lay behind the association.'

'How did my father make his appointments?'

She ran her fingers down her grey flannel skirt, smoothing away invisible creases. 'I will tell you even if it does not show me in a very good light. Mr Zaros used to place small, classified advertisements in some of the foreign newspapers. The invoices went to his home. I only found out when one was sent to the bank by mistake. I covered it up. He would have been angry if he had known.

'When your father visited the bank, he always came after office hours. Most of the staff had gone home. Usually there would be no more than four people still working on the premises. Mr Zaros, Mr Franz Strauben, the security guard and myself. I never met your father but we have spoken on the telephone. He always used a public call box. Mr Zaros let him in himself. They always went straight down to the vault where the safe deposit boxes are kept.'

'Presumably to check one of the boxes. Have you any idea what it contained?'

'None. But Strauben may have found out.' She stood up and walked with quick, nervous steps to the window. 'Mr Zaros has not been well for a number of years. He has worked very hard and his life has not been easy. He needed to lighten the burden. Strauben was taken on and after a trial period appointed general manager.' She reached into her handbag for a packet of cigarettes and then, with a wry glance at the notice on the wall, dropped them back once more.

'How did you and Strauben get on?'

'I never liked the man, never really trusted him. But he knew his business, I don't deny him that. He had trained in one of the big Swiss banks. He was very ambitious. He was a high flyer.'

'Did he give you any reason to distrust him or was it just a general feeling?'

Her pale eyes rolled up as she reflected for a moment. 'A woman's instinct, perhaps. He had a way of looking at Mr Zaros when he thought he wasn't being observed. I felt that he was worming his way into the organisation, building up a position of trust, watching for some opportunity when Mr Zaros would drop his guard. The chairman was old and ill. It was only a matter of time.'

'Could you not warn Zaros?'

Fräulein Heideck spread her hands in a despairing gesture. 'I tried several times but it was no use. He could be cruel when he chose. He said that if I didn't watch myself, I would turn into a typical middle-aged spinster. Jealous, carping, and disappointed.' With a little gasp she pushed the window wide open.

Scott jumped to his feet. 'Fräulein Heideck, you are unwell. All these questions. I'm sorry.'

'I shall be all right in a moment.' She tilted her head back and drank in the cold air. 'These last few days have been difficult.'

'Let me fetch you some water.'

'That would be kind . . . ' she murmured faintly.

When he came back, she had returned to her chair. She sipped the water slowly and when she spoke again it was in a stronger voice. 'Mr Zaros had a heart condition. I knew that he took pills for it but he took them surreptitiously. He would have been angry if he'd known that his secret had been discovered.

'But his condition deteriorated. He started getting palpitations and then from time to time he would have little turns. For a short period he was unconscious. He refused to take it seriously, passing it off as if it were no more than a catnap. He still worked the same hours but he became more of a figurehead. Then one day he had a bad turn and was unconscious for several minutes. Thank heavens he was not with a client. After that I managed to persuade him not to handle any more meetings.'

'Tell me, please, about the strongroom.'

'There are only two keys to the door. Mr Zaros and Mr Strauben each had one. The deposit boxes are made of reinforced steel and are stacked the length of the vault right up to the ceiling.'

'How do you get into them?'

'There are a number of dials on the front. You need a six figure combination to open them.'

'Do you think that Strauben stole the combination? Got into one of the boxes?'

Her voice sank to a whisper. 'I have no proof. I cannot be certain.'

'Please be frank with me, Fräulein.'

'Will you keep what I tell you to yourself? In a bank once confidence has been lost, it can be lost for ever . . . ' her voice tailed off miserably.

'I will try but I can make no promises.'

She stared at him for a long moment and then seemed to make up her mind. 'Then you will have to act as you feel you must. But remember this before you ruin us all. Zoltán Zaros is not a rich man's bank. It holds the savings of people that the chairman befriended, refugees whom he helped to escape from virtual enslavement. Many of them arrived here with little more than the clothes they stood up in. Imagine their lives. Prisoners first of the Germans, then of the Russians.'

Scott could afford her no respite. He had to know more. He poured her another glass of water. 'Please go on.'

'Mr Zaros began to have memory lapses. Information that he had previously kept in his head was now confided to his pocket diary. But it worried him. He talked about retirement. He toyed with the idea of selling but nothing came of it. Strauben pressed him to appoint him his successor. Mr Zaros prevaricated. He didn't want to hand over. Not yet. Then a little over a week ago, Strauben invited Mr Zaros to his house for supper. The manager has a large chalet close to the lake. Mr Zaros didn't want to go but he felt that he could not very well refuse.'

190

'Is Franz Strauben married?'

'Yes. He has a son at Grenoble university. The boy was not there that evening. After supper, his wife left the two men to their discussion. Something happened . . . ' she dabbed at her eyes with a handkerchief. 'When I think how Mr Zaros has been betrayed.'

Scott stretched across the table and took her hand. 'I know how painful this must be for you, Fräulein Heideck.'

She drank some more water. 'Mr Zaros had one of his . . . his fainting fits.'

'You hesitated. Do you suspect that there was more to it than that?'

She brushed the question aside. Her suspicions were her own business. 'The doctor was called. It took twenty minutes before he arrived. Strauben had ample time to look through the diary.'

'Where is the diary now?'

'I have it at home. That and . . . some other things that belong to Mr Zaros. I thought it safer. Mr Zaros was driven home and went straight to bed. His housekeeper was instructed to make sure that he rested the following day.' She shook her head and sighed. '*Rest!* Mr Zaros does not know the meaning of the word. The doctor might have saved his breath.

'The following morning Strauben was in very early. I wanted to speak to him but his office door was locked and he wasn't taking any calls. At ten o'clock, he came to my office. He apologised for not having been available earlier but said that something unexpected had happened which required his immediate attention.' Her lip curled disdainfully. 'He told me about Mr Zaros's little turn of the previous evening and said that he hoped he would follow the doctor's advice and have an easy day.'

'How did Strauben behave?'

'I didn't think about it at the time. I was so worried, so preoccupied but, yes, there was something. He was usually so calm, so controlled, but now that I think back, he was pumped up . . . there was a suppressed excitement . . . '

'What time did Mr Zaros come in?

'At midday. He complained that he had been given a strong sedative and had overslept. When he found out that Strauben had been in since six, he went straight down to the vault. He came back and I heard a door slam. I do not know what passed between them but I heard shouting. There must have been a terrible scene. Mr Zaros collapsed with a heart attack and was taken to hospital.'

'And Strauben brazened it out?'

'He became abusive. He said that he was not going to remain a minute longer in a place where he had been so insulted. He would resign at once. We would be hearing from his lawyers.'

The door opened and a young uniformed nurse bustled in. 'Do you both want to see Mr Zaros?' she asked. From her tone it was clear that she disapproved of such an arrangement.

'I will come in with Mr Rokeby,' said Fräulein Heideck. 'Then I will leave them together.'

'Very well. But he tires quickly. Mr Rokeby must only stay for a few minutes.'

Zoltán Zaros was propped up against the pillows, his pallid skin mottled with liver marks and almost transparent where it stretched over the bones. On the left side of his face the eyelid drooped and the cheek had sunk like a collapsed tent. Wires ran from pads on his chest to the ECG beside his bed.

His secretary took his hand gently in hers. 'Mr Warren's son is here to see you, Mr Zaros.'

One eye swivelled to look at the visitor. A tremor seemed to run through his whole body. His chest heaved and his mouth gaped as he tried to draw in air.

She hurried to the door. 'I'm afraid he may be having another attack. I must call for the nurse.'

Scott caught her arm. 'Please leave us alone for a few moments. If he doesn't calm down I will call for help at once.'

She hesitated. 'I cannot take any responsibility. If he—'

'You won't have to. Now, *please* . . . ' he closed the door behind her and drew up a chair beside the bed.

The old man huddled down into the bedclothes, the single eye blinking his agitation.

Scott took the photograph of his father from his wallet and held it up for him to see. 'I came to Europe to look for my father, Mr Zaros,' he said. 'Look, I have his photograph with me.'

Zaros attempted to raise his head, his lips trembled as they tried to frame a word, an eyelid fluttered, but the effort was too much for him and he sank back on the pillow.

Scott made a circle of the invalid's finger and thumb and placed his finger in between. 'Mr Zaros,' he said quietly, insistently, 'please listen to me. Warren Rokeby . . . was my father. If you can understand what I'm saying, squeeze my finger gently.' He felt a slight increase in pressure.

'Warren has had an accident – *a very bad accident*. You will never see him again.'

Zaros exhaled a long sigh. The little strength that remained to him seemed to drain from him and it was a long moment before he was able to convey that he understood.

Scott locked on to that one eye as if he could drill his meaning into the tottering brain. 'I know about the safe deposit box. I am going to see Franz Strauben but I must know what he stole.'

There was a knock on the door.

'*I need two more minutes,*' he called out. As further proof of his identity, he pulled his father's watch from his pocket.

The eye moved from Scott's face to the watch and back again. His mouth opened and closed like a dying carp. For a moment Scott feared that the strain had pushed him to the brink. He took Zaros's hands between his own. 'For Warren's sake,' he whispered, 'I must know. Was it money that Strauben stole?' There was no answering pressure.

'Did he steal something that could be sold for money? *A great deal of money?*' Zaros gripped Scott's finger with a strength that hardly seemed possible. Then relaxed.

Scott bent low over the bed and placed his mouth close to the old man's ear. 'Two final questions and then you must rest.' He breathed a prayer that the words would come out as he intended. Something told him there would never be another chance. 'My father was a diplomat, not a banker or a businessman. I have to know what was the link between you. *Was it the contents of that deposit box?*' Again that feverish grip.

Scott looked at him anxiously. The man's lips were trembling, his whole body was rigid with tension. 'Mr Zaros, I must know what is at stake. I don't mean a loss to the bank or its customers, distressing as that is. I mean great interests, national interests. *Have they been put at risk?*'

While Scott was speaking, the fingers of Zaros's hand spread and curled into an emaciated claw. With a supreme effort he snatched at Scott's watch. It was too much for him. His arm fell like a dead stick. His head slumped sideways and a thin trickle of saliva ran from the corner of his mouth.

Scott called out and the nurse hurried in. She looked at the patient and then at the screen.

'You have exhausted him,' she said harshly. 'You must go at once.'

Fräulein Heideck was waiting for him in the corridor outside. They took the lift to the ground floor and Scott walked with her to the entrance. 'Did you get what you wanted?' Her eyes were accusing.

'I'm afraid I've made him worse. I pressed him too hard.'

'It was wrong of you. But there is no time for that now.' She searched in her bag for a card and wrote Strauben's address on the back.

Scott gave her his business card. 'Please tell me about the Chalet Hirsch.'

'It looks out over the lake. You will see the stone eagles at the entrance to the drive.' She put a hand on his arm. 'Take care. He keeps a

194

vicious dog. And don't forget that there isn't an atom of proof against him. If you accuse him of theft, you could find yourself in a very difficult position.'

He watched her walk down the steps to the street, a lonely figure, her shoulders hunched against the wind. He could not wait to take another look at his father's watch. Zaros's behaviour when he caught sight of it had been so extraordinary.

He found a secluded corner in the reception room, took out his pocket knife and prised open the back of the casing. Inside was the inscription *JFK to WR*. This was followed by the single word *Vigilantia.* There were other letters and numbers which meant nothing to him. He would think about that later. He had to call his office.

Turcan and Hain were both out. Could they be reached? Apparently not. He didn't believe it. They had put him in the leper colony. All he needed was a bell to hang round his neck.

He called Budapest. Oszkar Varad was out. He tried Jerzy Torun in Warsaw. He was CEO of Pharmazin. A larger than life character, with a bushy black moustache, a huge jaw and hands like hams.

Torun went straight for his throat. '*Scott! Where the hell have you been?* I've been trying to reach you all afternoon. Is your company spying on me?'

'No. What makes you think that?'

'*Because I am not a complete fucking idiot!* That's why!'

'Calm down, Jerzy. Tell me what the—'

'I'm not going to calm down,' Torun yelled. 'If you want to know how I run my business come and ask me.'

'*Jerzy, that's bullshit!* You know I've always levelled with you.'

'Then explain this. Three men turned up at my office in a big black Mercedes. Belgian plates. Not a word of warning. Said they were with Descomptes.'

'The accountancy firm?'

'So you do know them!'

195

'Only that they are a big group with a head office in Brussels.'

'The cheeky sods wanted to go through our books.'

'Jerzy, they can't do that. They need a letter of authority.'

'They had one from Turcan! They waved it in my face!'

'Authority for what?'

'Are you telling me you don't know?'

'I swear I don't.'

'Authority to comb through our figures, to ask damnfool questions, to take photographs. Scott, if I don't get an explanation that satisfies me you can start looking for a new CEO. And remember, if I go, my team goes with me.'

'Jerzy, you're way over the top on this. I'm sure there's been some sort of mix-up.'

'I have grown a long nose over the years, my friend. I can smell a bad egg while the bird's still sitting on it. You have forty-eight hours – *not a minute more!*' He rang off.

31

ZURICH – LATE EVENING

Two men were finishing their meal in a restaurant in a quiet street off the Rennweg. They were in their early forties and both in uniform. They had graduated from Frunze Military Academy on the same day. Colonel Sergey Novorsk and Lt Colonel Yuri Rostov had served as platoon leaders in Afghanistan. The ignominious withdrawal from that disastrous campaign had run like an expanding fault line through the Soviet monolith until eventually it had brought the whole structure down in ruins. Their transfer to the GRU had been prompted by a realisation that their country had as many enemies within its borders as beyond them.

What wine they had drunk had done little to lighten their mood. Their conversation had followed a well-trodden path. The greed and corruption of those in high places. The time would come, they vowed, when retribution would catch up with those who enriched themselves by plundering the motherland.

They had no illusions that they faced an uphill battle. Russia was a kleptocracy, a lawless and divided country. The oligarchs were the real rulers in Russia. Like a pack of hyenas they gorged on the rotting carcass and grew fat.

'Meanwhile,' said Novorsk, 'our task, as soldiers, is to protect the country from its enemies. Which organisations, in your opinion, pose the greatest threat?'

'Militant groups from Georgia, the Baltic states, Poland, Ukraine and the central Asian republics.'

'Agreed, Yuri, but what is the worst that they can do? Load up a lorry with bombs and drive it into an international hotel or an embassy or a shopping mall? They choose soft targets. They kill a number of civilians, they take a few hostages and they knock the buildings about. It's tiresome, but for a global power like Russia it's a pinprick.'

'What are you trying to get me to say, Sergey? That I can see to the end of my nose but no further? Who is your source?'

'Zhanov.'

'I'm told he is a good man. He isn't wearing out the seat of his chair in an office. He is down in the street in the dirt and the dust, in the souks and the cafés, keeping his ears open.'

'I dismissed his reports as nonsense. Who were his contacts? Fantasists, hotheads, nihilists, dreamers? I was afraid to send them for evaluation. I thought that I would be sent on sick leave or even dismissed.'

'And the targets? Let me guess. They are right off the scale in terms of size and importance. The Federal Broadcasting Centre in Moscow. The international airports. Our urban underground system. Nuclear power stations, football stadiums and the like.'

'Correct. What is more, we are talking about very sophisticated planning. A structure of cells. Infiltrate one but it will not lead you to another. Infiltrate a dozen will not take you to the brains behind this.'

'Have they got a dirty bomb? If our FSB, the NSA and MI5 agree on anything, it is placing that at the top of the list."

'No. It's more dangerous even than that. The damage that a dirty bomb can do is, at some level, containable. I believe this is a gun. One that any hoodlum could use. The threat is proliferation and destruction on an almost unimaginable scale.'

'And the time frame?'

'Hours, perhaps. Days at the most.' From the street outside came the noise of running feet. Novorsk drained the dregs of his coffee and grimaced. 'Muhlder's rabble. That's the true voice of Germany, not the pap that we were fed today.'

Rostov bit off the end of a cigar. 'You make a mistake, my friend. They are not a rabble. They are very well organised. I believe that their aim is to discredit the police, demonstrate that they have lost control of crime, of illegal immigration and public order – and take over their job.'

'That is in Germany. What are they doing in Switzerland?'

'Immigration, particularly from the Balkans, is at a high level and growing. The Swiss don't trust the politicians to control it. Muhlder's message is that Direct Action is the only thing that works. Armed border police. A rough reception for gate-crashers and forced repatriation. His thugs are out on the streets to ram the message home.'

'I wish I knew who was bankrolling Muhlder. That operation doesn't run on air.'

His companion leaned over the table. 'Does the name Pieter Rohr mean anything to you?'

Colonel Novorsk nodded. He had heard it whispered.

'He will be at Sharpshooter. I will point him out to you. He carries a lot of weight with the young firebrands in the Bundeswehr.' From outside came the faint whine of a siren. Rostov cursed under his breath. 'The police are in for a busy night.'

'And if we are sensible, we will have an early one.' Novorsk left some notes on the table, reached for his cap and overcoat and the two men made for the door.

Scott sank the best part of a bottle of wine in a restaurant off the Kappelergasse. It curdled in his stomach. Turcan must be desperate. Descomptes would come up with some half-baked scheme, take their fees and blow. *The stupid, meddling SOB!* If he had set out to put the skids under Railton Europe he couldn't have made a better job of it.

As he left, a clock was striking eleven. He stood and listened. The jeering and chanting of Muhlder's supporters carried clearly on the crisp night air. Another sound, much closer. The tramp-tramp of booted feet. A humped shadow was moving along the wall like a boulder being rolled into the street. Then he saw them. There must have been twelve or more in the group. Shaven heads, hunched shoulders, hands hanging loose.

About twenty yards ahead a panel of yellow light spilled out as a door opened. Two men in the uniform of the Russian armed forces emerged, settling their peaked caps on their heads, buttoning their bulky frames into their greatcoats.

A single shout of '*Ausländer!*' instantly taken up by the others. Now they were running, hounds in full cry at the sight of their quarry. They narrowed the distance with bewildering speed, closed with the Russians, driving them back, sweeping Scott into the maul, one section splitting off, coming round behind them to complete the encirclement.

One man tried to grab Scott's arms while a third moved in, his lips curling back from his teeth as he lashed out. Scott half-parried the blow, feeling no pain as the metal studs skidded along his cheekbone. A Russian delivered a slicing chop to an exposed neck. The man went down with a curse. A face loomed up, the mouth and nose mottled with bright blood. A hiss of breath as he took a heavy blow under the heart, the blood bubbling from his nostrils as he crumpled.

Image succeeded image like snapshots shuffled by an unseen hand. A glimpse of a tattooed arm. A dagger design in livid reds and greens. Sunspots dancing on black leather. Hands grabbing a shaven head, pulling it down to a raised knee. A scream and the crack of splintering bone. Vapour rising from the struggling forms like a foul incense.

A Russian went down, three men clinging to him like hunting dogs on a bear. Scott caught his heel on the kerb and went over, a man following him down, forearm clamped against his throat, a hand rummaging in his pockets. Scott thrust his fingers into his eyes, rolling clear as the weight shifted.

He didn't hear the police siren. But their assailants broke off as sharply as if completing a drill movement. Hauling their casualties to their feet, they broke into a steady jog, the sound of their boots fading to a dull echo.

One of the Russians struggled dazedly to his feet and ran his hands over his pockets. 'The Makarov,' he muttered. 'It's gone.' An eye was closing and a trickle of blood ran from a scalp wound.

His companion hurried over to him. '*Your gun!* That's bad. Are you sure?'

'I'm sure.'

Scott felt for his pocket book. It was still there but his father's watch had gone. He cast around for it hopelessly.

'Have those bastards robbed you too?' The taller of the Russians looked at Scott with curiosity. He had spoken in German. His lips were broken, making his speech thick and slurred as if he'd been drinking.

'Nothing important.'

'Then we shall be on our way.' He jerked a thumb towards the flashing light at the top of the street. A van had stopped as if uncertain which turning to take. 'The police will only waste our time.' He lifted his hand in a half salute. 'Come, Yuri,' he said taking his companion's arm. 'The evening's entertainment is over.'

The van lifted its lights and accelerated towards Scott, braking fiercely as it reached him. The back doors were flung open and a German shepherd leaped out tugging its handler with it.

A police sergeant followed, the flashlight sweeping over him before moving to the houses behind them. 'We had a call from someone saying that there was a disturbance.'

Scott shrugged. 'A few guys horsing around.'

'Muhlder's men?'

'I reckon so.' The Russians were right. This was a waste of time. 'Was anyone hurt?'

'Just a scratch or two.' He raised a finger to his cheek where the blood was clotting.

'Did you lose anything?'

'An old watch, that's all.'

'Call at a police station and report it. Where are you staying tonight?'

'Near the station.'

'Avoid the Bahnhofplatz and get that cut seen to.'

From inside the van came a discordant banging and clanging as if a village band was holding a practice session.

Lights came on in the windows above their heads. '*Tell that woman to shut up!*' the sergeant shouted. 'The residents have had enough for one night.'

'*You tell your men to take their festering fingers off me!*'

Scott whirled round. He knew that voice. He followed the sergeant to the back of the van. All hair and teeth and flashing eyes like a wildcat in a cage, Julie Dixon was struggling between two burly gendarmes. '*Don't just stand there, Scott!*' she yelled. '*Get me out of here!*'

He turned to the sergeant. 'I know this girl. She works for a newspaper.'

'I don't give a toss who she works for. She's a trouble maker. We are holding her for her own protection. By rights we ought to charge her.'

'*You have no right to hold me!*' Julie cried. She wriggled and shoved but she was held fast.

Scott took the sergeant on one side. If she was released, he undertook to make sure that she went straight back to her hotel.

The sergeant hesitated. 'If she goes back to the rally and starts popping off again with her camera we'll be scraping her off the pavement.'

'I will make myself responsible for her.'

He gave Scott a long look. 'You do that.' He gestured to the policemen to let her go.

Julie scrambled out. 'Thanks for nothing,' she exclaimed. 'I have a good mind to—'

'*Save it, Julie!*' Scott grabbed her arm and dragged her away. He held her until the van had loaded up and rounded the corner.

Julie took a deep breath. 'I owe you one, Scott.' She turned round to look at him, staring at the long purple bruise under his eye. A handkerchief appeared from somewhere and she moistened it with her tongue and cleaned him up a little. 'What happened to your face?'

'One of Muhlder's buddies took a swing at it.'

'Any particular reason?'

'I forgot to ask.'

'I got some great shots of Muhlder. Then one of his rat-pack tried to take my camera. Things were just warming up when the police had to stick their noses in.'

'One of these days the cavalry won't make it in time.'

Her shoulders drooped. 'Scott, it's late and I'm knackered and you're starting to repeat yourself.'

'Where are you staying?'

She told him.

'I promised that policeman I would keep you out of trouble. Let's find a taxi and I'll see you back to your hotel.'

'No, you won't. I'm a big girl. I can look after myself.'

He watched her walk away, her breath hazing the darkness, her footsteps ringing on the cobblestones. Suddenly he was very tired. He had an early start in the morning. Fräulein Heideck's words came back to him. *Take care. Strauben keeps a vicious dog. You could find yourself in a very difficult position.*

32

BERLIN

Sonja Peetsch sat on the edge of the bath and rolled down her stockings. How many other women had sat there listening to Herman Stier pacing up and down the bedroom, slapping his boots with his riding whip?

She ran the taps, watching the water foam, snuffing at the fragrant scent of pine as she added the rich green essence. Her father had run out on her mother the day he learned she was pregnant. Set up house with a night club singer half his age. Sonja was only sixteen when her mother had died of cancer. She hadn't put up much of a struggle. She was worn out. Death had come as a relief.

She remembered kneeling in the rain in the regimented tawdriness of a suburban cemetery. She remembered how she had prayed. But not for her mother; she had prayed for herself. She wasn't going to be like her, one of life's victims, ground down by the struggle to keep a roof over her head and put food on the table. She was going to meet rich men, successful men. She had the face and the body to go with it. She was going to make them work for her.

Stier tapped on the bathroom door. 'Don't be in there all night, sweetheart.'

'I thought we had all night,' she replied sullenly.

He chuckled. 'So we have, but I don't want to waste a moment of it.'

'Are you undressed?'

'No, my pet. I want you to undress me.'

'I'm in the bath.' She ran her hands over her breasts trying to think herself into the mood. With the other men it had been different. She hadn't slept with them unless she fancied them. But that hadn't been difficult: power, influence and wealth were a big turn-on.

At seventeen she had gone to Frankfurt and got a job as a secretary with a company in corporate entertaining. Within six months she had persuaded the management to put her on the sales team. Soon she was pulling in more clients than the others put together. She was given a free hand. She could work when and where she pleased, provided she brought in the business.

She hustled her way into a smart set. Even between the sheets the men talked about nothing but business but that didn't worry her. Sharing her bed was business. Businessmen were always trying to go one better than the competition. If they wanted a stately home for an important presentation, a box at an exclusive race meeting, a chartered yacht for a cruise, she could fix it. Go to Sonja, people said. She can fix anything.

She flew in private jets from one fashionable resort to another, stayed in wonderful villas, frequented casinos and glamorous night spots. She was having a ball and her employers weren't complaining. They were getting their money's worth.

Then she had done something rash. She had become impatient. The pay and the perks were good but she wanted money, serious money, before the bloom went off her cheeks, before her body went from a surfer's paradise to an old bedspring.

She had met a rich oil man. During the course of their fling he had written her some very indiscreet letters. His wife found out and began divorce proceedings. He telephoned Sonja asking her to burn the letters or send them back.

She had laughed. 'Burn them? You must be joking, lover boy. Those letters are my pension. Buy them back or they go straight to your wife. Half a million dollars might seem expensive but a settlement will cost you twice that.'

The sucker had gone crawling to his wife. Confessed everything. She agreed to give him one more chance but she wanted to see the girl punished. He called Sonja and told her that he had recorded her threats and intended to hand the tape to the police. She wept down the phone, pleaded with him, but he had been implacable.

'I am going to teach you a lesson, you blackmailing bitch. I hope they send you to prison.'

Word got round, invitations dried up, her earnings collapsed and she was fired. She considered fleeing abroad but the money from selling her dresses wouldn't take her very far. Her nerves were in shreds. Every day she returned to her apartment expecting to find the police waiting for her.

Then she had a call from a man who said that he might be able to help her. They had met in the car park of an autobahn service station. He drove the latest Mercedes fastback saloon and they talked in the car.

His name was Pieter Rohr. He had heard about her 'difficulties'. He told her he had influence with the German business community. He might be able to persuade the man to drop the matter.

What did he want out of it, she asked. In her world nothing came without a price tag.

'A little assistance from you, Sonja.' He spoke in the harsh, guttural accent of the Cape Dutch. He wanted her to join the staff of one of the government departments. It was a short-term assignment but it would mean going to Berlin. 'You will live in a luxurious apartment just off the Kurfürstendamm. You will receive a generous salary and a nice bonus at the end.'

'Why should a government department employ me? What have I to offer them?'

Rohr chuckled. It was a horrible sound, like an airlock in a water pipe. 'Let us worry about that. Submit your application and it will be accepted. The work is simple. Nothing you cannot handle.'

She wouldn't do anything that would harm her country, she told him.

Her scruples did her credit, he said. He and his colleagues were patriots like herself. They were concerned that a senior officer at the Ministry of Defence was a security risk. 'A man with a questionable personal life should not hold such a sensitive post.'

'Why don't you go to his superiors?'

'Because without proof we cannot act. Accusations would just serve to put him on his guard.'

'You want me to go to bed with him? That's what you mean, isn't it?'

'We want you to get close to him, gain his trust.'

'Do I have any choice?'

'Frankly, no. Not unless you are prepared to go to prison. You would find that very disagreeable, believe me. Some of the inmates have the most primitive ways of making a new arrival feel welcome.'

She shuddered. She was trapped. But the moment she saw her chance, she would do a runner.

He turned in his seat and looked into her eyes. 'I know what you are thinking, Sonja. Why not play along with old Pieter until he has got you off the hook? Then take off.' She flinched as he ran the sharp edge of a thumbnail down her cheek. 'I dislike being double-crossed. Remember that, unless you want to be reminded every time you look in the mirror.'

'You . . . you wouldn't,' she stammered.

'Not if you do as you are told. Get close to Stier. Make him happy and wait for instructions.'

Make the director happy. She stepped out of the bath and wrapping herself in a large towel, patted herself dry. She slipped into a white satin nightdress and ran her hands down over the rich curves of her hips. If the director wasn't happy with all this, he must be very hard to please. She performed a little twirl before the mirror and opened the door.

Herman Stier was leaning back in an armchair blowing lazy smoke rings at the ceiling. He was still wearing his army tunic, tight-cut breeches and boots. The riding switch lay across knees. His briefcase was beside the chair. Even when he was in bed, it was rarely out of his sight.

He flicked a shred of tobacco off his moustache as he looked her up and down. 'I shall never know what witchcraft you women get up to in the bathroom that takes such an eternity.'

Sonja shrugged. 'Apparently you thought it worth waiting for.'

'I will tell you later whether it was or not.' He stretched his feet towards her. 'Come here and pull my boots off.'

She strode over to him and stared down at the imperious blue eyes, the disdainful curl of the lip. His jaw went up a notch and his breath came a little faster.

Her throat constricted and her voice was shrill with anger. 'There are some things that I might do for you but pull your boots off – *never!*'

'Is that so?' he drawled. He seemed unruffled by her refusal. It was almost as if he was waiting for an excuse to do something that he had a mind to do anyway. Moving quickly for a big man, he seized the switch with one hand and grabbed her by the arm with the other. He flung her face down over the edge of the bed. His arm rose and fell. Once. Twice. With force and precision.

'*You bastard!*' Sonja screamed. Tears of pain and humiliation welled in her eyes. She struggled to rise but he held her down effortlessly.

He threw the whip aside with a laugh. 'Admit it, Sonja, you asked for that. I am not used to being kept waiting and I don't like being cheeked. If my horse plays me up, it gets the same. Two sharp cuts behind the saddle. After that we get along fine.' He tugged her nightdress up over her rump. Two livid weals ran at diagonals across her buttocks.

Sonja moaned. They felt like red hot wires burning into her flesh.

'Crossed lances!' Stier exclaimed with satisfaction. 'Now you are a true daughter of the regiment.' He lifted her in his arms and placed her on the bed. Kicking off his boots and tossing his clothes over a chair he threw himself down beside her. He kissed her hungrily, licking the moisture from her lips while his hands found the hem of her nightdress and rolled it up over her body.

She drew back from him. 'You go too quickly. I'm not in the mood for it after that whipping.'

'Then get in the mood for it.' He pulled the nightdress over her head. 'The Russian peasants had an interesting custom in the old days. The night before a girl got married, her mother used to give her a few brisk strokes of the birch. It warmed her blood, took the chill off that cold Slav temperament. It wouldn't do to disappoint the bridegroom on his wedding night.'

'I'm not a frigid peasant girl,' Sonja retorted.

'Well, now is your chance to prove it.' His head went down and he cropped at her breasts like a horse let loose in spring grass after a long winter.

She flailed at him with her small fists, 'You are crushing me,' she cried. 'Hurting me . . . '

Stier grinned at her, baring his strong white teeth, his breath hot in her face, his eyes glittering with the fierce joy of conquest, 'Go on . . . fight me . . . I love it. It's like breaking a young filly . . . feeling her under you . . . bucking . . . rearing . . . twisting . . . giving her the spur . . . showing her who is master.'

She turned her head away so that he would not see the loathing in her eyes. One day, she promised herself, she would bring him low and exult in it.

Stier rolled to her side, his body slippery with perspiration, his chest heaving as he gulped air into his lungs.
She had struck a bargain, she told herself. She couldn't complain when the bill came in. She composed her features and found him again, moulded herself to him. 'You were wonderful, Herman,' she murmured. 'You are made like Hercules, so huge, so powerful. I never knew it could be like that.'

33

THE CHALET HIRSCH

Ulla Cranz was in position an hour before dawn. The sky was overcast, the air as cold and damp as a crypt. She covered the trail bike with brushwood and left it up in the trees. Slipping across the lane, she climbed over a gate into a field which sloped gently down to the grounds of the chalet. The earth was frozen hard and cropped close where cattle had grazed.

She moved cautiously, using the night glasses where the ground dipped and the mist lay thickest. Ahead, she could make out a post and rail fence. Stout timber rails with wire mesh at the base. It looked easy. Too easy. She ran her glasses along the thorn hedge to her left, examining it inch by inch. She tensed, her eyes narrowing. Where it made an angle with the fence something jarred. *A straight edge among the confusion of bare twigs.*

She crawled along the base of the hedge until she could stretch out her hands and touch the end post. Sliding down a zip in her bodysuit her fingers closed round the flashlight. Shuttering the beam with her fingers, she examined it. It was clean. Now for the hedge. There it was buried deep among the thorn branches.

The sensor was about four feet in height, cone-shaped and camouflaged in tan and olive. A rotating head with a hooded window on top. She had no way of knowing its range. Anything between twenty and forty yards. Her lips twitched. For an amateur, it wasn't a bad effort. She burrowed into the hedge, squeezing between the sensor and the post, keeping under the beam. She could feel the sweat trickling down her neck and running down the inside of her arms. No margin here for miscalculation.

She followed the line of the hedge until she judged it safe to rise to a crouching position and listen. No sound but the drips off the leaves and the lapping of water along the shore. It was no longer completely dark and the surface of the lake had a faint metallic sheen. On the far side, pinpricks of light showed where for some a new day was beginning.

She moved on again. A tall cypress hedge loomed up in front. The flashlight picked up the dull metallic gleam. Above her head the camera housing with its hidden eye gazed across the ground she had covered, its tracking system idle, waiting for the signal that never came.

She skirted the tennis court avoiding the stone chippings round the edge, keeping to the grass. From a corner of a garden shed, she scanned the expanse of lawn between her and the chalet. Four rose beds divided by a gravel path that led to the french windows. She exchanged her boots for a pair of buckskins, lacing them so tight they fitted like a second skin, and pushed her fingers into a pair of metal mesh gloves.

The light was strengthening every moment, the outlines of the roof taking shape, the security arcs under the eaves a pale nimbus in the gloom. She checked her watch. She had been well briefed. In a few minutes, Strauben would open his bedroom door, go downstairs and let the dog out. A large dog. *A dangerous dog.*

He would go to the kitchen and make himself the cup of steaming chocolate that his wife usually brought him in bed. Then he would return to his room to shave and dress. At eight o'clock, the maid and the gardener would bicycle up from the village bringing the daily newspapers and fresh croissants for his breakfast.

Ulla followed a path between pollarded nut trees that led to a flight of steps cut in a grassy bank. At the top was a swimming pool with a ranch-style building on three sides. The pool was covered by a heavy plastic sheet secured by stout cords that ran to rings at the edge of the stone-paved surround. She unfastened the two cords that secured the end of it. The pool was full, the water very cold. She unhooked the blackjack from her belt and ran her fingers over it, feeling for the lead inside its leather sheath.

Scott shaved carefully and changed the plaster on his cheek. His body was stiff and seemed to have acquired some new bruises in the night. He hadn't slept well. The man in the next room had brought a woman back with him and there were little gasps and cries until the early hours when they seemed to have discovered a more conventional use for the bed. Shortly after five he was woken by the garbage truck and the clang of metal bins being emptied.

He breakfasted and left the hotel at seven. By half-past he was clear of the city. The morning was dull and grey, the lake as smooth as satin. To get to the Chalet Hirsch, would take him about an hour, he estimated, using the back roads. Every few seconds his eyes lifted to the rear mirror. It was getting to be a habit.

Franz Strauben felt for the keys under his pillow. His fingers closed round them and went to the light switch on his bedside table. He drew back the duvet and swung his legs out of bed. The dog was restless. Gabi had gone to Grenoble to see their son Paul. The Doberman was probably unsettled by the break in routine. It emerged from behind the curtains and padded over to the bed.

It whined fretfully. He pushed it away. 'Why can't you stay in your basket, Schock, instead of disturbing me?' He went to the window and drew back the curtains. It was one of those winter days when the sun never showed itself. It suited his mood. It was as if he and nature were in collusion.

He must find another way of getting a message to Canton in Geneva. The botanical gardens had been a mistake. Too much cover. Too easy for someone to follow him without being seen. He put on his red silk dressing gown, pushing the keys deep into the pocket and went downstairs. Schock trotted into the sitting room and snuffed at the base of the french windows, his paws fretting at the woodwork.

'*Stop that!*' he said sharply. Pulling his dressing gown tight round him, he opened the doors. He shivered. The mist was damp, the air chilling. 'Go on, Schock,' he urged. 'Do your business and be quick about it.'

The dog bounded down the steps and darted across the lawn in the direction of the pool. His master watched it for a moment and then closed the doors and went into the kitchen.

When Adele arrived she would bring fresh croissants in a napkin inside her bicycle pannier. Croissants with cherry jam and a café crême the way only she knew how to make it. Patrice, the gardener, would potter about in the cold, raking up the last of the leaves. Like most rich men, for that was now his view of himself, he took pleasure in having a modest retinue of servants to attend to his comforts but he did not want them living in his house, prying into things that were none of their business. He rubbed his hands together as he watched the milk warming in the saucepan. He couldn't remember a moment in his life when he looked forward to the future with a keener sense of anticipation.

Ulla waited, rocking gently on the balls of her feet, perfectly balanced, listening for the light brushing of the dog's paws in the dew. A heavy dog, a dog moving fast, a dog that could kill. As it came over the rise it put in a short stride, gathered itself and leaped for her throat. She threw herself to one side. Quick as she was, she wasn't quick enough. The dog seemed to correct its line in mid-air, catching her a heavy blow on the shoulder, spinning her round.

It splashed down in the water midway between the edge of the pool and the rolled-back sheet. It paddled away from her to the cover, its paws scrabbling frantically at the edge, flecks of foam from its jaws spattering the surface as it tried to get a purchase. Ulla grabbed the cords and lifted the edge of the cover. There was a yelp as the dog realised its danger. With a snap of its powerful teeth it severed a cord like a knife cutting through spaghetti. Then a muffled howl as the cover was drawn over its head.

Ulla was curious. How would an intelligent animal react to this dilemma? It could take refuge in the darkness beneath the sheet until the air was exhausted or venture into the narrow channel of open water where its enemy was waiting. The dog's nose edged out from under the sheet. Lifting its head it gave a desperate howl for rescue. Ulla darted behind one of the pillars of the ranch-style building behind her.

'*Schock!*' Strauben hurried across the lawn. 'Where the hell are you?' He ran up the steps to the pool. He could see the hump made by the dog's head under the cover. '*Schock!*' he cried out again. How had it got under the cover? Why was one of the cords broken and the other trailing loose? He bent down to pick up the loose cord.

'Let me help you.' The voice came from behind him. She hit him hard on the back of the neck. He was only unconscious for half a minute but, when he came to, his pockets had been turned out, his wrists bound and he was being lowered into the pool. His feet flailed desperately as he struggled to tread water. As he opened his mouth to scream, a foot came down on his head. Ulla drew the cover over him and settled by the edge of the pool.

Two small tents formed where Strauben was pushing up with his fists. There came a dreadful gurgling sound. He raised the sheet a little. Two hands came out, stretching towards her in entreaty.

'*Let me out! . . . For God's sake!*' The words floated from under the cover in bubbles of terror.

Ulla bent down. 'I want to talk to you, my friend, and I haven't much time.'

'I'll do anything you want . . . *anything!*'

'I know you will.'

'Why . . . are you . . . doing this to me . . . ?'

'Because you are a very wicked man. You have stolen something that does not belong to you.'

'Help me out of here . . . and I will tell . . . '

'Tell me now where you have hidden it and you can stop paddling round and come inside for your breakfast.' She reached over and pushed the hump down into the water.

There came a muffled cry and the water seeping out from under the cover turned pink. The dog must have turned on his master. Ulla raised the cover a little. Strauben's lips were blue. Blood was streaming from a wound on his forearm. His hair had tapered to long black points against the chalky pallor of his neck.

'I believe you are ready to tell me something,' said Ulla softly.

Strauben gasped out the hiding place of the bonds, 'But they are no good to you . . . without the codes . . . ' he quavered. 'Only I know . . . who has the codes . . . '

'Tell me who has the codes if you want to live.'

'You promise . . . not to harm me?'

'Why should I want to harm you?' Ulla asked in mock astonishment.

Strauben moaned in an agony of indecision.

Ulla rested her hand on his head. 'Be quick, my friend. I am losing patience and you are hardly in a position to make terms.'

'Zoltán Zaros . . . must have . . . the codes,' Strauben gasped, 'but you will . . . have to hurry . . . he is a very sick man . . . he may not last many days.'

She smiled. 'Then you may see him before I do.' She clamped her hands on Strauben's head and, spreading her fingers wide, pushed him down, holding him under the water until the desperate threshing was stilled. Franz Strauben died with the knowledge that he had not told all he knew. With his last moment of consciousness it was his curse upon his murderer.

Scott turned down a narrow lane between a thickly wooded hill and fields that ran down to the lake. A row of poplars caught his eye. Where the lane curved, he could see the eagles on their stone columns. He slowed. There was a policeman on the gates. Beyond him he could see the back of an ambulance.

He wound down the window. 'What's happened here, officer?'

'An accident. The owner has been found drowned.' The jerk of his head said 'move on'.

He was too late. It was another dead end. His phone bleeped. Maxim Broz, managing director of Glycovik.

'Scott, what the hell are you people are up to?'

Scott took a deep breath. 'What's the trouble, Maxim?'

'Trouble? I haven't got trouble. You've got the trouble. I'm finished with you shysters. I'm resigning at close of business today and you can have that in writing.'

'Is this about Descomptes?'

'So you admit you instructed them?'

'I know nothing except what Jerzy Torun has told me. I'm going to Brussels tomorrow. I'm asking you, Maxim, as an old friend – hang on till then.'

A long pause. 'I'm not making any promises. Call me as soon as you get there.' He rang off.

Scott drove back to Zurich. Warren was dead. Now Strauben. Death came in many guises. It discarded its masks one by one. You left them where they fell and hurried on. But one day, one day quite soon perhaps, you would come across another. You would stop and stare and turn it over in your hands and recognise it as your own.

34

KK KEMIKAL

At first light, the massive doors of the hanger slid open and a forty-ton Yugoslav M84 main battle tank rolled out on to the concrete and made its way to the test ground. After the break-up of Yugoslavia, it was one of several that had been found in Croatia and bought cheaply from an agency dealing in surplus military equipment.

Pieter Rohr, Drucker, the gunner, and Schneider, the cameraman, drove behind it in a jeep. When they reached a large clearing in the forest, they stopped. Rohr radioed the tank driver to dismount and join them.

Rohr settled the KRG on Drucker's shoulder and loaded the kinetic round. 'The capacitor adds to the weight,' he said, 'but, against that, there is no ejection motor, no two-stage firing to worry about and no back blast. The guidance system and Mach 10 will do the rest. Fire when you are ready.'

The gunner took careful aim and squeezed the trigger. There was a 'Whoosh!' from the KRG and the air seemed to shake as if a high-speed express train had passed. A crimson circle no larger than a poppy appeared on the side of the cupola. There was a brilliant flash and the tank was bathed in a white radiance. As the cloud cleared, there was no sign of the tank. A thin plume of smoke rose up from where it had been standing.

Drucker scratched his head. 'If I hadn't seen it with my own eyes, I would not have believed it.'

But Rohr was not listening to him. He had heard the rumble of a plane and the sound was getting louder. '*Reload*!' he snapped as he raised the binoculars to his eyes. 'Overflying this area and the compound is strictly forbidden. The military know it, the airlines know it and the civilian aircraft authorities know it. It's a Beechcraft Kingair,' he muttered. 'Approaching from the south-east.'

'I see it, sir! It's at about five thousand feet.'

'*Take it out!*'

'Is that an order?'

'That's an order! And Schneider – keep filming!'

The air shook once more. A huge spark appeared where the aircraft had been and, as quickly, disappeared. A few seconds later, the tops of the trees swayed gently as if they had received a light dusting.

'Back to base,' said Rohr. 'I have a report to make.' The gunner and the driver offered to remain and clear up the debris.

'There will be very little debris,' said Rohr curtly. 'But if you find a few small pieces, put them though the compactor. I doubt whether there will be enough metal for a doorstop.'

Rohr had given the order on the spur of the moment and was apprehensive about Kraik's reaction. But Kraik was pleased. 'We are not ready to share our secrets,' he said. 'Give the gunner a bonus and make sure that the test range has no tales to tell. If the police search this area, we can close down till they have gone. Put the film in the safe.'

The BMW bike slowed and cruised up to the barrier at Perimeter Control. The guard stiffened, his eyes darting from his scanner to the rider. The man was carrying a pistol. He watched him closely as he removed his helmet. Then he relaxed a little. Knud Vossen, leader of Combat Group Rohm. He checked with the guardroom and handed him an entry card. The barrier swung up.

A long, straight asphalt road led to the inner compound, an area of several square miles protected by electrified fencing with intruder alarms and manned watchtowers at regular intervals. The heavy steel gates topped with razor wire provided the only point of access. Vossen swiped his card through and gunned his engine as they swung open. A twin, turbo-prop aircraft was taxiing on to the runway, the huge hangar doors closing behind it.

Beyond the small forest of aerials on the signals complex he could see the glass dome of Rohr's office. He had only seen him once and he was not looking forward to a second meeting. Rohr was made like a bear. It was said that he could kill a man by wrapping his huge arms round him, squeezing him until his lungs popped like balloons.

White-coated technicians were hurrying along the raised walkway between the laboratories and the pilot plant as he pulled up in front of the administration block and spoke into the grille. Access was by voice recognition; movement inside the building movement was controlled by touch memory panels on the door plates.

Rohr's guttural voice boomed out of a speaker beside him. 'Vossen! Take the lift to the top floor. Laubscher will meet you there. Do exactly as he says.'

Inside his black leathers Vossen felt the sweat trickling down his neck. He would be pleased to get out of this place. Over the years KKK had acquired a sinister reputation. People found snooping had been roughly handled. A reporter had developed a mysterious illness and died.

Few people could claim to having set eyes on Kraik, let alone having met him. His name was spoken only in whispers.

It was rumoured that he had made his first fortune in 1988 when the Russian harvest faltered, organising a cartel among corrupt merchants, cornering the grain supplies and reselling them when prices soared to famine levels. It was said that he had masterminded a similar operation the same year in Armenia after the earthquake disaster, buying up all the bulldozers and diggers available and ransoming them to the aid organisations at the height of the crisis.

Rohr paced up and down the floor of his office. Why hadn't Ulla reported?

A call from the armourer. 'I have the pistol that Vossen brought with him.'

'Examine it carefully and report to me later.' He pressed a button to admit Vossen.

The group leader was short and stocky with a powerful chest. A long thin scar ran from below his ear to the side of his chin. His head was bandaged. He stood rigidly to attention.

'What happened to your head?'

'Shrapnel. I'm lucky to be here at all. The army held an exercise near our base. They were using live rounds. Our ammunition is stored in a cave on the moor.'

'I know the place. Go on.'

'At three o'clock this morning someone tossed a grenade inside. I was checking on the sentry. He was one of my best men. He didn't stand a chance. How did the army find us?'

'Ludger Buhl was arrested in Hamburg. The army are interrogating him. He must have talked. Generalmajor Stier is behind this. Now tell me what happened in Zurich. Getting that pistol was good work, but the watch is another matter.'

'A passer-by got involved and Spickermann lost his head and robbed him. Sorry, Major.' He tugged down a zipper in his top and gave the watch to his chief.

'See that the man is punished. Without discipline, Vossen, a combat group is nothing but a rabble. Now go – and don't disappoint me again.' He returned the salute and dismissed him.

An encrypted message from Ulla was coming in from Zurich. Rohr ripped the sheet from the machine. As he decoded it, the words seemed to jump out at him. 'President JF Kennedy . . . DIDO . . . fifty million dollars in bearer bonds . . . am tracing the codes . . . let's talk about this.'

Kraik was already on the line. 'Ulla Cranz's orders were to deal with Strauben and bring the merchandise here – not to send messages.'

'Leave Ulla to me,' said Rohr thickly. 'I have handled her kind before.'

'No. We will do this my way. Without the codes the bonds may only be worth a few millions. She must bring us both. She has until midnight.'

'Are you saying we allow ourselves to be held to ransom!'

'I am giving you an order.'

'How much are you prepared to pay?'

'You can go to ten per cent of the face value.'

'Five million dollars!'

'I can add up.'

'She holds a pilot's licence. She will want a plane.'

'The details I leave to you. One last thing. The gold watch that Vossen handed in – give it to Snoeck. Tell him to examine it and report by midday tomorrow.'

'The watch is of no interest to us.'

'I didn't ask for your opinion. Do as I say. But first do a deal with Ulla Cranz.'

Rohr flicked a switch on the console. 'Ulla? What do you want?'

'Money. I am tired of living on crumbs. Ten million dollars and the bonds are yours.'

'We agreed a fee. It will be paid on delivery.'

'Don't jerk me around, Pieter. Those bonds are political dynamite.'

'They may be worth something to the Americans. But not to us.'

'The US Treasury would pay my price just to get them back.'

'Then go to them.'

'It's not my style, Pieter.' The tone wheedling now. 'I am only asking for a quick deal and a fair price.'

'Sorry. No codes, no cash.'

'I can get the codes.'

'When?'

'Give me till this evening. Shake hands on ten million and you will have the bonds and the codes by seven o'clock.

'Five million. That's my limit.'

'Paid in advance in US dollars to my account in Panama.'

'Half now. The rest on delivery.'

'You are a hard man, Pieter Rohr.'

'Meet me here at seven.'

'Forget it. You come to Zurich. I breathe easier here. It must be something to do with the mountain air.'

'OK. Our airstrip at seven.'

'We meet in the open away from the buildings. Come by yourself and bring the rest of the money.'

'If that's all—'

'It's not all. I've earned a holiday. I want a plane.'

'You can have the German Extra.'

'That will do. Have it fuelled and ready.' She rang off

35

THE WHITE HOUSE

The meeting had taken place in the John F. Kennedy Conference Room, generally known as the Situation Room. It had been chaired by the President. In attendance were the President's advisors. These included the Director of National Intelligence, members of NSA, the National and Homeland Security Advisors, the Whitehall Chief of Staff and the Secretaries of State, of Defense and of the Treasury.

The meeting had over-run its scheduled time. The President was late for his midday workout and it made him irritable. When the room emptied, he asked Mike Saxon and Coaker to stay behind.

'Information, disinformation and obfuscation, gentleman. That's all we heard this morning. We are up to our asses in alligators but no one has the guts to say so. What's the bottom line, Sam? What the hell have we gotten into? Give it to me straight.'

Coaker took a deep breath. 'We have been working on a rail gun for years, Mr President. International Arms Consortium got there first and we don't yet know who controls IAC. What we do know is that the KRG is man-portable and that the manufacturers claim that it is right off the scale in terms of its destructive power.'

'Why should we believe them?'

'A film of the test firing will be delivered here later today. Mike and I will be at the Sharpshooter Exhibition in Belgium when the prototype is being demonstrated. Then we will know for certain.'

'So, if it does what it says on the tin, we buy it up or we close the manufacturers down. Or both.'

'I believe that the German Army will be issued with the KRG, Mr President. No one else. We will have to pay millions in "protection" money to keep it out of the hands of terrorists – and that goes for the Brits, the other NATO countries, Russia and the rest. Only the French are getting special terms.'

'Who is making the KRG? What's to stop us putting the SOBs out of business?'

'The gun is being manufactured in France by Detonard. The company is a subsidiary of IAC. The French have put out a statement saying that if any action is taken against Detonard, there will be no control over the distribution of the gun. It could end up in the hands of terrorists in Iraq or Iran, Lebanon or Syria.'

The President turned to Saxon. 'Can we trust Germany with the KRG? After all, they have been a democracy for sixty years.'

'I question whether real democracy will ever take root in Germany, Mr President. The Germans do not want to take orders from some functionary in the Bundestag. They want to be ruled by Titans.'

'Tell me, Mike. Who are these Titans?'

'You read the report on Muhlder and Wetzlar, Mr President.'

'I did. I accept that Wolfgang Muhlder is a dangerous man, a rabble rouser with a big following and Jorg Wetzlar speaks for the former Ostis in the Bundeswehr, a large faction.'

'Not merely large, Mr President. Disaffected, resentful and dangerous too.'

'Are you seriously suggesting that we are threatened by an unholy alliance between these two – the army, equipped with the KRG, and the Extreme Right supported by a so-called Militia? Why, it's almost inconceivable! It would take a cataclysmic event . . . ' he put his hand to his head. 'Sam, do you go along with this?'

Coaker nodded. 'I do, Mr President. But, as you say, it would take a cataclysmic event – and a hell of a lot of money. A military coup doesn't run on air.'

The President's eyes narrowed and he looked from one to the other. 'Money,' he repeated. 'A hell of a lot of money. Are you two holding out on me? Is there something I should know? Something you have not told me?'

Coaker and Saxon left the building together. Saxon shook his head. 'We fouled up. We should have told the President about DIDO. I bitterly regret it. He gave us an opening. We should have jumped through it.'

'The President must know about DIDO.'

'You're putting out smoke, Sam. Don't play that game with me. If the President knows about DIDO it's only in the sense that he has the right to information about slush funds set up by his predecessors. He doesn't waste time on it. The money has already been spent or it has been misappropriated. It's so far in the back of his mind that it might as well not exist. We are the ones with the problem. Until we get those bonds back, we will be hot-rod racing with a drumful of nitroglycerin in the passenger seat.'

The two men parted without exchanging another word. Coaker waved to his driver and the car pulled up at the kerb. The vehicle had not gone a mile when Leah Stein called him. Pedlar aka Franz Strauben, was dead. Drowned in his swimming pool.

'What line are the police taking?'

'That it was an accident. Canton believes he was murdered.'

Coaker ground down on his cigar. Another killing. Another wisp of smoke above the rim of the volcano. 'Is anything missing from the chalet?'

'No sign of a break-in. His wife was away. She can't tell them anything.'

'What has Canton managed to find out about Pedlar?' He listened in silence. 'Is Zaros well enough to talk? It's vital that we find out what was stolen.'

'He had a relapse today. The hospital is not allowing visitors. Canton is trying again tomorrow.'

'It will have to do. Meanwhile get on to the Swiss police. We want a man posted on Zaros's door.'

'They will want an explanation. What shall I tell them?'

'Tell them he walks in his sleep.' Coaker snarled. 'Tell them what you like. But get it done.'

36

ZURICH HOSPITAL

Ulla Cranz left the Ducati in a quiet side street and walked the last two hundred yards to the hospital. It was just after midday. She hurried. She was wearing a light jersey and linen trousers and it was cold. She took the stairs to the fourth floor. In less than a couple of minutes, she had found an empty staff room with a row of clean blue tunics and trousers on a rack. In the lavatory, she put on these clothes over her own. One of the advantages of recent economies, she reflected, was that nurses' clothing was virtually indistinguishable from that of the cleaners and kitchen staff.

She checked in the mirror. Dark hair cut rather short. Pale olive skin. Brown eyes. Neat, competent. Ordinary. On the third floor, at the entrance to Ward C, she stopped at the door, looked through the large glass panel and found what she was looking for. A policeman in uniform on a chair outside one of the rooms. She sized him up quickly. An elderly man with a grey moustache and a swollen waist line, the type often found in the back office sucking a pencil and totting up parking fines.

There were, she judged, about a dozen private rooms in the ward. A woman came bustling out of one of them. Ulla opened the door for her.

'My husband is very hungry,' she said. 'He normally gets his lunch at twelve. Do you know how long it will be?'

Ulla smiled. 'I will go to the kitchen now,' she replied, 'and hurry things along. Please return to your husband and keep him company.'

Ulla took the service lift to the kitchen. They were short-handed, they said and were running thirty minutes late. Two girls had telephoned in and reported sick. She was told off for not wearing a security pass. She apologised. She had been in a rush that morning and had left it at home. They gave her a temporary one.

She went to the far end of the room where the trolleys were being loaded, took one and, together, with other members of the kitchen staff, wheeled it to the service lift. In Ward C, the nurse at the reception desk was busy. She looked up as Ulla entered and then returned to her papers. The policeman clambered to his feet as she approached. 'Mr Zaros has been leaving his food,' she said. 'I may be a little time with him.' She gave him a wink. 'Perhaps you would like to come in and help.'

'I don't think I had better—'

'I was just joking.'

He held the door open for her.

Ulla pushed the trolley in and left it by the window. Zaros opened a single eye. The green peaks on the ECG squeezed up closer. She searched the room. The bedside table. The drawer underneath. Nothing. The clothes in the wardrobe. The suitcase on top. Nothing.

She leaned over the bed. 'I have very little time, old man,' she whispered. 'Strauben is dead. I have the bonds. Before he died, he told me that you have the codes. I want them.' She yanked Zaros's head off the pillows and rummaged beneath them. 'Where have you hidden them?' She threw back the bedclothes. The invalid's chest creaked up and down like an ancient bellows.

She ripped open his pyjamas. 'You miserable old bag of bones. Have you got it on you somewhere? A little pocket diary, perhaps? *Say something!*' She inclined her head to listen, her lips opening like the mouth of a letter-box through which a dying man could post his soul to hell.

The old man's heart fluttered, his chest heaved up and in his scrawny throat his breath rattled like the last gasp of a worn-out pipe. Zoltán Zaros was dead.

Ulla moved to the window sill. She pushed aside a flower vase and skimmed through the cards. Only one was of use to her. It was from someone who signed herself 'Laure, your devoted secretary.'

On the table beside the bed she found a notepad with Laure Heideck's address. She checked her watch. It was almost half-past twelve. 'Mr Zaros doesn't look at all well,' she said to the policeman as she went out. 'You had better call a doctor.'

Scott telephoned Descomptes in Brussels and asked to speak to the senior partner. Edgar Labarre was out for the rest of the day. He rang off without leaving his name. He bought a New York paper and turned to the financial pages. A caption caught his eye: *Troubled Venture Capital Company Postpones Public Quote.* Railton's problems were making headlines. The company was haemorrhaging executives, most of them going to Fraser Outram. The bank was expected to call in its loans. Todd would be crowing.

His mobile telephone was ringing. It was Julie. 'Scott, I'm really gutted. Muhlder's rally was worth at least half a page. All I got was a lousy couple of columns.'

'Bad luck.'

'You sound a bit flat. What's wrong?'

'What isn't?' He wanted to wring somebody's neck but the neck was unavailable.

'No time to talk now. I'm off to Brussels. 'My paper wants me to cover Sharpshooter.'

'What the hell's that?'

She told him. 'The exhibition opens in three days.'

'You don't know anything about guns. Why did they pick you?'

'I won't be writing any technical stuff. What my editor wants is a write-up of some of the VIPs. Thumbnail sketches of companies making bombs and mines and guns. Interviews with the Merchants of Death.'

'That's not funny.'

'Sorry.'

He had to go to Brussels, he told her. 'I could give you a lift.'

'There has to be a catch in that somewhere.'

'We could stop on the way and have dinner. Stay overnight . . . '

'I told you there had to be a catch.'

'What do you say?'

'I say we split the bill and the fun finishes with the coffee.'

Fräulein Heideck lived in an old-fashioned apartment block in a quiet suburb of the city. Ulla's Ducati cruised silently into the service yard at the back. It was quite dark now and the rain had stopped. She removed the tool kit from the saddle bag, weighing it in her hand. The extra equipment made it feel heavy. She tried the rear door. Locked. She walked round to the front. There were few people about, but the home-going traffic was starting to build up.

A basement and five upper floors. Lights showing only in the basement and the second floor. The names of the residents were beside the buttons on the shiny brass panel by the door. How trusting people were. It never ceased to astonish her. Fräulein Heideck was in an apartment on the fourth floor.

She pushed the caretaker's bell and placed her ear close to the grille.

There was half a minute's silence before it crackled into life. 'Who is it?' The thin, reedy voice of an elderly woman.

'I have a parcel for Fräulein Heideck.'

'She's out. She usually gets back about six.'

'I can't wait. I have other deliveries to make.'

'I suppose I shall have to come up,' the woman grumbled.

'I shall only be a minute or two. I will leave it outside her door.'

'I shouldn't let you in. You read these stories in the newspapers.'

Ulla chuckled. 'But most of them are only stories. Stay down there and save your old legs.' *And not just your legs.*

'All right, but you must be quick.'

There was a click. She pushed through the door into the hall. A rack for letters. Pictures of mountain scenes on the walls. A worn blue carpet that led to an old-fashioned cage lift with a sliding gate. She took the lift to the fourth floor, waited half a minute, descended once more, reopened the front door and closed it again. She stood and listened. There was no sound from the caretaker's apartment. She padded up the stairs to a dimly lit half landing. There she settled down to wait.

Fräulein Heideck left the bank at half-past five. When she had worked for Mr Zaros it was often seven or even eight before she got away. But things were different now. The new manager had brought his own secretary with him. The girl was attractive in a rather flamboyant way, but casual about her work. She always seemed to be drinking coffee or gossiping on the telephone.

Some of the clients had complained that they weren't getting the service they were used to. Others had called to express anxiety about Strauben's sudden departure. The older ones would probably remain out of loyalty or inertia but the next generation could not be counted on to stay.

With a little sigh of dejection, she alighted from the bus. It had been a long winter and sometimes it seemed as if spring would never come. The wind was stirring the bare branches of the trees and the clouds were clearing. It would freeze again that night.

She rested her shopping on the top step and searched in her handbag for her keys. Another lonely evening. She would tidy the apartment, prepare her evening meal then watch a little television before going to bed. She dreamed of the day when she had enough savings to retire. She would like to find a small place in the south, perhaps close to the Italian border. People seemed friendlier there, they laughed more and spring came earlier in the year.

Inside the hall, she took off her headscarf and gloves and checked the rack on the wall for any post. Nothing for her. The lift creaked and squeaked its way up.

As she put her key into the lock, a hand clamped across her mouth stifling her scream. An arm drove her through the doorway and into the sitting room. She was pushed into a chair and gagged with her headscarf. She tried to twist round but her assailant kept behind her, one hand gripping her neck, the other rummaging in her handbag.

'You're hurting me. *Let me go!*' The words emerged as a strangled gasp.

Ulla snapped open the woman's purse. A few coins. A business card in the name of Scott Rokeby. She took it. 'Remove your raincoat,' she whispered, her breath was hot on the woman's cheek. 'And kick off your shoes.'

A muffled wail of terror came from her. 'Take anything you want,' she moaned, 'but please don't hurt me.'

The woman flicked her shoes away with her foot. 'I am going to loosen the scarf. If you shout for help, I will kill you.' She could smell the fear in her. Sour and damp. Overwhelming the tired fragrance of gentility and talcum powder.

The secretary held out her hands in an imploring gesture. 'Take my money . . . my rings . . .'

'That's not what I came for.' Ulla came round her chair.

Fräulein Heideck could see her now. Hard-eyed. Ruthless. A woman who would stop at nothing.

Ulla loosened the gag. 'Zaros gave you some things to hide. Where did you put them? I want them.'

'*I won't tell you!*' She wrapped her arms tight about her and glared her defiance.

Ulla pulled up a low table and began to unpack the contents of the tool bag, itemising each as if she was making an inventory. 'A stout length of cord . . . an earth clamp . . . '

Fräulein Heideck gazed in horror at the gloved fingers and the neat, methodical way with which she assembled these instruments of torture.

'An electrode holder . . . ' she continued in the same flat monotone. 'A small arc welding transformer which . . . '

Fräulein Heideck closed her eyes. 'You are just doing this to frighten me,' she said faintly. 'Promise me you won't use those awful things.'

Ulla thrust an electrode into the blunt nose of the holder. Her fingers were at the buttons of the woman's blouse.

'*No! Don't touch me!*' With a shriek she forced her way past her captor and ran to the kitchen. She tried to slam the door but Ulla was too quick and shoved her foot in the way. As she pushed her way inside, Fräulein Heideck cowered behind the kitchen table. 'If I get . . . what you want,' she quavered, 'you must promise not to hurt me.' Her eyes darted to the cuckoo clock high up on the wall.

Ulla pulled the wooden stepladder from the corner and placed it in position. It was old and rickety like everything in that place.

Slowly, laboriously, Fräulein Heideck climbed the steps and reached up to fumble behind the clock. Her fingers were trembling. It was difficult to reach.

'Let me help you.' Ulla put a hand on the ladder.

'*No! Leave me alone!* I have it. Let me come down by myself.'

'I shall.' Ulla drove her foot into the ladder sweeping it from under the woman. As she fell, her head cracked against the edge of the sink. Her legs gave a little twitch. Fräulein Heideck was dead.

Ulla ripped open the envelope. A pocketbook containing a diary, credit cards, a few Swiss francs. Something else – a gold watch carefully wrapped in tissue paper. She had seen a watch like that a few days earlier. But there was no time to think about that now. She pushed the envelope deep down into an inside pocket. In the sitting room, there was a small writing desk. She removed the address book from the top drawer, put the table back in its original position and repacked the tool bag before descending the stairs.

She left by the back door. The yard was lit by a single light, the Ducati in the shadow between two huge refuse bins. She bent down to open the saddle bag.

There were two of them. One came from her right. One from behind her left shoulder. The glint of knives. Ulla grabbed the transformer and swung it by its leads. Blood spurted from a splintered nose. With a choking cry the man reeled away.

The second was on her, slicing through her body belt, tugging it clear, turning to run. She hurled the transformer catching him a glancing blow on the shoulder. Not enough to stop him and he was haring for the gate, waving frantically at someone.

Ulla righted the bike and gunned for the entrance.

Rohr hesitated. His man was in his headlights. '*Get out of the way!*' he bawled, swerving round him and swinging the big Mercedes into the gateway.

Engine roaring, the Ducati raced for the closing gap. A crazy wobble, a screech of metal against brickwork, a tinkle of glass and it was through in a long arcing slide, accelerating away to a cacophony of horn-blowing.

'You disobeyed me, Pieter,' Kraik said softly. 'I told you to let Ulla have her money.'

'I got you the bonds. They were in the belt and they didn't cost you a cent.'

'Without the codes that may be all they're worth.'

'If she makes for the airstrip—' Rohr's phone bleeped. He listened and then covered the mouthpiece. 'It's Ulla. She has Zaros's diary and his watch. It's a half-hunter. She says she knows who has the other one.'

Rohr could hear Kraik speaking to Snoeck on another line. 'Tell me, Ulla, why should we be interested in an old watch?'

Ulla laughed. 'If you had looked inside it you would be interested. Give me twenty-four hours and I can give you the pair.'

'Your price?'

'It's still five million dollars – and no more dirty tricks.'

'Tell her it's a deal,' said Kraik. 'We have wasted enough time on this.' He was thinking about Snoeck's preliminary report on the watch. It had been given to Warren Rokeby by John F. Kennedy. Warren's son, Scott, must have got it from the police who recovered Warren's body. He was robbed of it in Zurich.

'Is Ulla bluffing?'

'No, Pieter. She believes that Scott Rokeby has the other watch. So she will go after him. If she was as clever as she thinks she is, she would know that we have it.'

'How would she know?'

'Never mind that now.'

'We can fix the plane. A call to Lutz and it won't get off the ground.'

'Let her take it. She won't be going far. Snoeck will work out exactly how much flying time to give her. Tell him I want to see him.' The syllables were vented like fumes of poisonous gas.

37

THE DRIVE TO BRUSSELS

Scott picked up Julie from the hotel at seven o'clock that evening and they joined the autobahn north of the city. A black Opel had stayed with them to Basel. He took another glance at the mirror.

'Stop fussing about your looks, Scott. You're stuck with them. The time to worry is when people start complaining.'

'There's a car behind—'

'These things happen when you're driving.'

'*You little airhead!* Do you have any idea how many times I have been—' he broke off. What was the point?

'No. I hoped you were going to tell me. If I sometimes seem flippant it's because mysteries irritate me.'

'I don't like them any more than you do.'

'You must remember I know next to nothing about you.'

He stole a look at her in the mirror. Serious-eyed, her lips compressed. This was a Julie he hadn't seen before. He told her about his work, his father's disappearance, the shock of finding out how he had died, the problems with the French authorities, then the disaster threatening Railton.

The broad sweep of the Rhine lay behind them and the black Opel left them as they crossed into Germany.

She wanted to know about the earlier years, about growing up in one Soviet-controlled country after another. 'You had no brothers or sisters. Weren't you lonely?'

'If I was, I got used to it.'

'Were you close to your parents?'

He had never known his mother, he told her. 'My father never talked about her. Everything I know about her I found out from his housekeeper and others.' If only Warren had been able to grieve over her, but her body was never found. And there were worse things even than death. Her brother's torn and bloody corpse was discovered in a cellar half-buried under piles of rubble. The fear that Erika too might have fallen into the hands of the dreaded State Security Service must have preyed on his mind.

'When she died, it must have been as if she had taken everything with her . . . laughter, music . . . my father wouldn't even have flowers in the house.'

'She left him a son.'

'It wasn't enough. My father and I were never close.' There was silence between them for some minutes and then Julie spoke again.

'That story I told you about clandestine night flights, remote airstrips— '

'I didn't believe a word of it.'

'I don't care whether you did or not. I didn't think that you could help me. I thought you would just get in my way.'

'And have you changed your mind about that?'

'No. Not yet. But I'm going to level with you.' She told Scott about her brother's work and his disappearance from the Fleetwood Institute and her row with the Vice-Chancellor. 'And now the police have him down as a fraudster who has stolen all the research papers to flog to the highest bidder. *It's grotesquely unfair!* David may be rather naïve but he is honest and loyal to the core.' She sighed. 'And I'm no closer to finding him than when I started.'

The phone bleeped. A woman's voice speaking in German, 'Is that Scott Rokeby?'

Scott slowed. 'Who wants to know?'

'My name is not important.'

237

'How did you get my number?'

'It doesn't matter. What matters is that we meet and talk.'

'What is there to talk about?'

'I saw your father before he died.'

'Before he was murdered. That's what you mean.' He braked savagely and swung the car into a lay-by.

'It was most unfortunate. It should never have happened.'

'Who was there?'

'I will tell you everything when we meet. You are in a car. I can hear the engine. Where are you going?'

'To Brussels. Not that it's any of your business.'

'It has become my business – and yours. There is a small airstrip that I use. It is just over the Belgian border. Make a note of the co-ordinates.'

Julie flicked on the light and ran her finger over the map.

'You see the large wood? Follow the small road to the northern edge. As you reach open fields you will see some derelict farm buildings.'

Julie pointed to her watch. 'About four hours' driving,' she whispered.

'You are not alone. Who is the woman with you?'

'A friend.'

'Expect me at first light. Don't be late.' There was a crackle and then silence.

'What's this about your father!' Julie exclaimed. 'Do you mean to say that it wasn't an accident?'

'Forget I said it, Julie'

'How can I?'

'Put it out of your mind. The French police still maintain that it was an accident.' He slipped the car into gear and pulled out on to the road.

Julie shook her head. 'You know nothing about this woman. Have you any idea what you're getting us into?'

'*You aren't getting into anything!* I'm going to find you a hotel for the night. Tomorrow you can take a train to Brussels.'

'*Sod that!* I'm coming with you.'

'You would just be a worry.'

'*Worry about yourself!* It could be a trap. That woman could have murdered your father. You could be the next on her list.'

'OK. But get this straight. I'm giving the orders. So do as you're told and cut out the smart-ass remarks.'

'Sometimes I get quite good ideas.'

'Ration them to one a day.'

An hour later they had grabbed a quick meal and Julie took the wheel while Scott dozed in the passenger seat. It was close to one in the morning before they were into Belgium. It was hard driving now. The roads were narrow and winding, climbing up hills, dipping down into ravines and they were tired and the weather was closing in.

Scott was awakened by the sound of rain drumming on the roof. He yawned. 'Where are we?'

'Not far from the RV.'

'Are you sure?'

'I said so, didn't I?' She pointed at a village sign and shoved the map at him. 'Check it yourself if you don't believe me.'

'I don't doubt you.' He squinted at the map.

Julie watched him out of the corner of her eye. 'Christ, you are irritating sometimes, Scott. Providentially you never married. You would drive a woman demented within a week.'

'A week is good going. I have never spent an hour in your company without someone trying to murder you or lock you up.'

Julie took a hand off the wheel to rub her eyes. 'Let's argue about it tomorrow. I've had enough for one day. I vote we stop and put our heads down for a few hours.'

They pulled off the road up a narrow track between old oak trees. Scott inclined the passenger seat. Julie moved into the back.

He heard her run down the zip on his bag. 'Feel free to ransack my wardrobe whenever you get the urge.'

Julie ignored the sarcasm. 'Thank you. I don't intend to freeze to death.' She found a jumper and eased it gingerly over her head.

Scott watched her in the mirror. 'What's the trouble? You are moving like an old woman of seventy.'

'My back is a bit stiff, that's all.'

'Do you want a rub down? I have got just the thing for you.'

'No.'

'It might help you sleep.'

'And again it might not. So peddle your snake oil somewhere else.' She folded her jacket and placing it under her head curled up on the seat. Within a few minutes she was asleep.

Scott looked down at her, the smudges of tiredness under her eyes, the dark lashes lying against her cheek, her forehead knitted with worry lines even in sleep. He still knew very little about her. What lay behind the brittleness, the flurry of banter and backchat that she seemed to use like a fencer to keep him a sword's length away? Only now that she was out of reach did he feel close to her.

They slept fitfully, waking from time to time to hear the distant rumble of thunder, the threshing of the trees and the ceaseless patter of the rain.

38

THE RENDEZVOUS

Julie was shaking him awake. 'What's wrong, Scott?' she cried.

He sat up with a start. 'What *is* the matter?'

'You were shouting in your sleep.'

'Was I?' He stared at her. 'I'm sorry. I must have been dreaming.'

He was cold and cramped. He took the flashlight and jogged up the track and back trying to get warm.

Julie searched her pockets for a comb. 'If there's one thing worse than getting up at this frigid hour it's watching some physical fitness freak shuttling up and down like a parrot on a curtain pole.'

'Could you pull something through your hair?'

'I have a comb somewhere.'

'Forget the comb. Nothing less than a chain harrow will do.'

'And you need a shave.' She rummaged in his bag and tossed his Remington to him. 'Try not to spray the clippings all over me.'

Five minutes later they were back on the road. The rain was unremitting, the road surfaces slippery and strewn with small branches. The trees were thinning out and as they rounded a bend they could see the farm buildings ahead of them.

'Drive past and keep the headlights on full.' She pointed to the scorched lines running across the field where oil or kerosene had been put down to make a primitive flare path. 'It's very crude. The smart operators use ground heat sources. They can't be seen.'

'There's no need to show off.'

'I'm telling you something you don't know. Look at those parallel skid marks on the grass. Those were made by wooden pallets. The plane comes in at about six foot off the ground, does a parachute drop and lifts off again. Try to learn something new every day, Scott, and in time you might become quite an interesting person.'

He didn't even smile. He had the night glasses to his eyes. 'How long a take-off run do these small planes need?'

'It depends on the plane. Two hundred yards could be enough for some of the little toys but four to five hundred yards is more like it.'

They tucked the Range Rover round the corner of a cowshed and made a quick recce. The farm buildings had broken windows and gaping holes in the roof. In the yard, dock leaves were growing through fissures in the concrete and the potholes brimmed with the night's rain.

In the east the sky was whitening. Julie shivered. 'Let's get under cover.' Beyond the car, they could make out the outline of a barn. It had been used as a makeshift hangar. Scott flashed the torch over the wheel marks in the soft ground. At the far end, bales of straw, mouldy with age, had been piled almost to the rusting corrugated roof to create a windbreak. He clambered up to the top. Julie followed and threw herself down beside him, stifling a violent sneeze as the dust rose in her nostrils.

Ulla blinked the perspiration out of her eyes. Altitude five thousand five hundred feet. How much longer to the airstrip? She felt terrible. First the nausea. It couldn't be food poisoning. She had only put down for a few minutes to make that telephone call and all she had eaten was a ham roll and gulped down a cup of coffee.

The muscle spasms began. Twitches round the mouth like a nervous tic. She turned the fresh air ducts on to her face. Pinched the skin on her cheeks. Waggled her head from side to side. Shrugged her shoulders. Twisted this way and that in her seat. Nothing worked. The sensations only got stronger.

That bastard Rohr was behind this. Something had been hidden in the cockpit. Something toxic. The fumes were killing her. With every breath she took, she was getting weaker. She had to get down. Reduce power. Lower the nose. She plunged into the cloud. Not far now. A few minutes' flying time. Surely she would see the end of the tree line when she broke through the cloud base.

As soon as she was on the ground she would be OK . . . deal with Rokeby and the woman . . . get the watch . . . torch the car . . . the police wouldn't waste much time over a burnt-out vehicle . . . some drug deal that went wrong . . . then she must find somewhere to hide up . . . make a plan . . . they wouldn't make a fool of Ulla Cranz twice . . .

She glanced at the fuel gauge . . . only twenty, twenty five kilos at most . . . she had been low when she left . . . violent spasms now in her arms . . . the muscles bunching and seizing as if they were wired up to the mains . . . trees below her . . . mist like a shroud . . . her limbs no longer part of her . . . jerking and shaking . . . the airframe bucking and pitching like a canoe in a rough sea . . . juddering . . . *close to a stall* . . . stick forward . . . freeing itself . . . back to the stall again . . . forward again . . . must get down . . . the tops of the trees close now . . . *keep wings level* . . . close throttle . . . select max revs on the propeller . . . carburettor heat on . . . turn fuel mix to rich . . . repeat . . . turn fuel mix to rich . . . cut the engine . . . branches brushing the underside of the fuselage . . . get a hand to . . . to the battery master switch . . . somehow . . . fingers jumping . . . like sausages in a pan . . . *watch that port wing!*

Beyond the roofs of the farm buildings, the woods were grey, drained of colour by the long hours of darkness. On the eastern horizon, dawn glimmered like the blade of a sword.

No sound but the tentative cheep of a waking bird and the rain dripping into the pools below.

Then they heard it. It was like the drone of a mosquito on a summer's evening. Julie trained the glasses on the black speck as it broke through the cloud.

The hum more distinct. 'She's coming in quite steeply,' Julie said breathlessly.

'Presumably she knows what she's doing. Can you see what she's flying?'

'A single seater . . . square wing tips . . . could be the German Extra.'

'She needs to bank . . . then level out . . . '

The rumble grew, the wings silvery as they caught the early morning light. Julie grabbed Scott's arm, 'What's she playing at? She hasn't altered line ... she has a wing down . . . she must pull up now . . .'

Scott grabbed the glasses from her. 'Two hundred feet . . . less. Pull up. Pull up! *Pull up!*'

Julie stared wide-eyed. 'I don't believe what I'm seeing.'

The aircraft dived into the trees and disappeared. Across the empty fields there came a faint sound like wood being split for kindling.

A moment of stunned silence. Then Scott found his voice. 'I'll drive. You grab the fire extinguisher from the back.' They slid down the bales and ran to the car.

He took the corner too fast and the car wobbled as the wheels churned in the wet verge. 'Can you see anything?'

'No sign of smoke.'

'How far into the wood do you reckon?'

'Three, perhaps four hundred yards at the most.'

He braked sharply. 'There's a track off to the right—'

'It's too soon.'

'It may be a long way before we see another.' He braked and swung down a broad, muddy lane.

Julie balanced the extinguisher between her legs and bent over the map. 'The planting changes. Soft wood here, hardwood in the middle. There's a dotted line between them.'

'No need to cover the waterfront,' said Scott testily. 'Just tell me where the track goes.'

'West for about a mile and then there's some sort of monument.'

Scott pointed through the windscreen. 'There's your monument. Where the tracks intersect, there's something moving . . . '

Julie tried to control the glasses. 'Slow down, Scott . . . we could break an axle in one of these holes.'

'I want a situation report not a driving lesson. What do you see?'

'Bikers. Four . . . five . . . six . . . all in black leathers . . . two of them coming this way.'

He slewed the car left-handed.

'*Watch out! You'll have us over!*' She snatched at a handhold as they wound in and out of the trees, bumping over roots, lurching into hollows in the ground, the wheels spinning in drifts of rotten leaves.

They slid to a halt under a clump of holly trees, turned off the engine, ran down the windows . . . and listened. The soft put-put of bike engines, throttled down, was strangely menacing. Then silence.

'We could be in trouble. I reckon there are two men on the ride. The rest are dragging the wood.'

'Are they looking for us or the plane?'

'Why don't you ask them?' Scott replied irritably.

'I might just do that.' Julie glowered at him, her cheeks pink with anger. 'Instead of skulking here like—'

Scott held up his hand. A new sound. Deeper in the wood. A faint ticking like a clock in a closed drawer. Then a creaking, splintering noise. Somewhere a branch had fallen.

They got out of the car and ran towards the sound. It was hard going, the brambles overgrown, the mist cutting visibility to a few yards. Then they saw it. The plane had come through the boughs of a large

245

beech tree at a steep angle, shearing off a wing and bending the other right back. The nose was buried in the ground, the propeller blades curled up like potato peelings. A wisp of smoke rose from the engine cowling.

Using bent and broken branches as footholds, they scrambled up to the cockpit. Julie took one look and slithered down to the ground.

A branch had come straight through the canopy stripping it of its bark, sharpening the white, sappy shaft to a spear point which had driven straight through the pilot's throat skewering her to the seat. She must have died instantly.

Scott took a deep breath, steeling himself to search the woman. He bent down, fumbling with zips sticky with gore. A mobile phone. A key ring. A few coins. The woman's eyes, glassy and protuberant above that blood-choked chasm seemed to follow his movements with a mute and baffled rage. *His watch!* Or one identical to it. He shoved it in his pocket.

Julie was leaning against the tree, the extinguisher unused at her feet. 'I can hear those . . . bikers,' she gasped between bouts of retching. 'They must be getting close.'

Behind the seat, he found a jacket. In the pockets, a passport issued in Berlin in the name of Ulla Cranz. A wallet containing Swiss francs in large denomination notes, a driver's licence. Credit cards. He put them back. His own business card with his mobile telephone number. Had she taken it out of Warren's wallet or was it the one he had given to Fräulein Heideck?

Another card with the address of a Brussels nightclub. A woman's name, Elena, scrawled in the corner. He removed both cards and an envelope that was already torn open. In it was a small leather diary with the letters ZZ embossed in gold. He pushed them into his pocket.

He ran his fingers under the seat. His fingers scraped against something metallic taped there. He tugged and a small, metal cylinder, perforated with holes, came free. He weighed it in his hand before dropping it into his pocket. He jumped down, landing awkwardly.

Julie raked her fingers through her hair. 'Scott, I've been thinking . . .'

'Think somewhere else. It's time to get the hell outta here.'

'You're being stupid. We don't know anything about those men. We don't know who they are or who they work for. Now is our chance to find out.'

'Use your head, Julie. Those bikers could give us a hard time.'

'We have a perfectly good reason for being here. We can say we were driving past when we saw the plane come down.'

They could see the bikers, like phantoms weaving in and out of the mist-shrouded trees.

He grabbed her arm. '*Do I have to drag you out of here!*'

They ran to the car. She drove faster than he would have dared, ignoring the branches flailing the windscreen screen and the brambles clawing at the bodywork. As they careered out of the trees, the two bikers were on the ride. Waiting for them.

'It's no good,' he shouted. '*Stop the car!* We're going to have to talk our way out of this.'

'*Like hell we are!*' Julie hunched down like a jockey approaching a big fence, set her jaw and put her foot on the floor.

They shot over a shallow ditch and headed straight for the two men.

'*Watch out!* You'll run them down!'

'*That's their look out!*' At the last moment she swung the wheel with one hand and with the other released the catch on her door and gave it a vicious shove.

A howled obscenity as man and machine went down.

'*Are you insane!* Do you want the whole pack on our tails!' Scott's wing mirror filled with the second man, the black-helmeted head bent over the handle-bars, the engine at full revs screaming like a buzz saw.

'*Hold tight!*' Julie cried. She stood on the brakes.

The mirror emptied. Scott turned to see the bike sideways on. It leaped the ditch, hit some hidden obstruction, the rear end bucking and sending the rider cartwheeling through the air to land hard among the trees.

They went into a long, sliding skid. 'Road coming up,' Scott muttered. 'Narrow gateway. High banks either side.'

'I'm not blind.'

'*Try not to kill us!*'

They caught the offside bank a glancing blow, snaked on the greasy surface but they were through.

'The front wing sounds like a panel-beating shop.'

'I can hear.'

They jinked through the lanes until they felt safe enough to pull in and lever the crumpled wing off the tyre. He walked round the car checking the bodywork. The hire company was not going to be very happy when they got it back.

They stopped again to buy a baguette and some slices of sausage at a village store and kept on driving.

They didn't talk. He felt tired. Drained. He must be getting old. It was cold in the car. He turned up the heater and closed his eyes. There was something else that he wanted to remember . . . something that was just out of reach . . . something important . . . but he couldn't quite . . .

39

CABINET OFFICE BRIEFING ROOMS, WHITEHALL

'I will wind up this morning's discussion,' the Prime Minister stated, 'with a brief summary and then update you on the reports coming in from Armenia.

'I called an emergency meeting of COBRA after we received a series of anonymous threats. MI5 and Special Branch are in no doubt that these were not sent by cranks. They demonstrated in-depth intelligence of the ways to circumvent security systems at London Heathrow and bring the airport to a halt. More disturbingly, they claimed that they would shortly be in possession of a weapon that is capable of turning our cities into a wasteland. "If you don't believe us," one message concluded, "take a look at what happened in Armenia."

'In western Armenia, the Russians have taken over a military airfield. The Secretary-General of NATO, you will recall, made a vigorous but unavailing protest because Russia is certain to use it as a base for their latest fighter planes.

'In the early hours of this morning, an explosion took place. This was reported in the local press and the radio as having been caused by an earthquake of 4.0 on the Richter Scale in a remote and lowly populated area of the country.

'The truth of the matter is that the runway was being extended. The site consisted of houses for the construction workers, offices for the project manager and hangers for the heavy plant. There were graders, crawlers, loaders, bull-dozers and excavators on the site.

'There was no crater after the explosion. There were no bodies, no rubble, no charred and twisted metal. There was a bare and level site and above it a dust cloud which took some hours to disperse. About fifty people are missing.

'On the face of it, we are threatened by a new weapon. It is as yet unidentified and is right off the scale in terms of destructive power. I echo the statements that I have heard around the table this morning when I say that this is a waking nightmare for our American allies and for all our partners in NATO. Nor do I exclude countries divided from us by ideology. The magnitude of the threat transcends those differences. It is of the first importance that we present a united front in making our response.

'Who is our common enemy? No one has claimed responsibility. Who has developed this weapon? Who is operating it? What lies behind this seemingly meaningless devastation? Finding the answers to these questions is not merely a priority, it is a prerequisite for survival.'

There came a sharp rap on the door and an aide entered. There was a buzz of talk around the table and the Prime Minister held up his hand for silence. 'I have just been informed that a package has been delivered by courier. It has been screened and opened. It contains a communication from International Arms Consortium, who are known to us, which needs to be addressed at once. With it there is a short film which will now be shown. The Cabinet Office has instructions to keep lines open twenty-four hours a day. The Chief of the Defence Staff and the heads of our security services are to report to me at 0800 hours every day until further notice. The meeting is over.'

40

A FARM, SOUTHERN BELGIUM

The Sauvin brothers had been in the field since first light, hoeing between what seemed interminable rows of cabbages. They were of the same stocky build, with the stolid, weatherbeaten features of those who wrest their living from the land. Lionel leaned the hoe against his shoulder and clamped his hands to the small of his back. 'This ache has been with me for so long it seems to have become part of me,' he grumbled.

'It's the damp and the cold,' replied Benoit. 'It gets into the bones.' He straightened to watch the vehicle approaching. Few cars passed that way. It had two wheels on the soft grassy verge and was sending up a shower of mud in its wake. 'Those idiots would do better to keep to the middle of the road. There's a deep ditch there.'

'And a bend coming up . . . ' Lionel shielded his eyes with his hand.

The car didn't slacken speed or alter line. All they could see of the occupants was the rounded humps of their shoulders. '*My God!*' shouted Benoit. 'Are they asleep? They will never make it.' Throwing down their hoes they started to run.

The front wheel leaped the drainage ditch but failed to get a purchase. The car lurched on to its side and skidded along the ditch as if stuck on a tramline. It jolted as it hit something and slid to a standstill, the upper wheels spinning in the air.

Benoit scrambled into the ditch, tugged open the door and reached across to turn off the engine. Driver and passenger were slumped against the far door.

Lionel peered past his brother. 'Anyone hurt?'

'I can't tell.' He released the catches on the safety-belts. 'Perhaps we should leave them and get help.' He put a hand to his head. 'I feel a bit dizzy . . . '

'Don't pass out on me, Benoit.'

'It must be the fumes from the engine . . . '

'Then let's get them out of there.'

Together they hauled the two to the top of the bank. The young woman was the first to come round. Her eyes opened and she struggled to her knees.

The man stared dazedly round him and then pushed himself into a sitting position. He took a few tottering steps towards his companion. 'Julie . . . are you OK?' A violent access of coughing seized him. His face turned scarlet and the tears streamed from his eyes.

Unable to utter as the waves of nausea overwhelmed her, she waved him away.

Scott ran his hands over his limbs, relieved to find himself still in one piece. He found the small canister that he had taken from the plane.

Lionel screwed up his face in a frown. 'Surely you are not thinking of driving the car? The engine must be giving off poisonous fumes. Next time you could be killed.'

'Or kill someone else,' said Benoit severely, stroking his fair, wispy moustache.

They would stop at the first garage, Scott told them, and get it checked out. Meanwhile they needed to be pulled out.

The brothers walked off a few yards for a conference and, after much vigorous gesticulation, Lionel trudged off to get the tractor.

Scott wedged the cylinder behind the tow-hook and secured it with a rag. A walk round the car revealed a cracked wing mirror and more scratches to the bodywork. If there was any serious damage they would soon find out.

He pulled Julie to her feet. 'Try to walk. You must get the circulation going.'

She closed her eyes. 'I can't. My legs feel as if they belong to someone else.'

Half-dragging, half-carrying her, he walked up and down the headland until a tinge of colour came back into her cheeks. She wanted to know how it had happened. He couldn't face an argument. He would tell her later.

The tractor rumbled back across the fields, a tow-line was attached and after a lot of argument, exhortation, spitting on hands and muttered curses from their rescuers they were back on the road.

Benoit shook his head as he folded the notes and stuffed them into his pocket. 'Foreigners. Crazy foreigners.' He picked up his hoe and went back to work.

The brakes had developed a tinny squeak. Otherwise the car drove all right. Scott felt cheerful enough to tell Julie about the cylinder.

'It was reckless, Scott. I wish you had buried it. It's a miracle we didn't end up like that woman.' Her mood was so sombre that he almost found himself wishing she had lost her temper. But if they could find out where the device came from, the risk would have been worth taking.

By midday they were on the outskirts of Brussels. Scott followed the signs to a large industrial estate. Polder SA, chemical analysts, occupied a long, low white building. Through the windows they could see technicians in white coats working in the laboratory.

Julie put a warning hand on his arm. 'Don't let's rush into this. How much do you know about this company?'

'Enough. One of our companies has given them some work.'

'Supposing they start asking awkward questions?'

'I shall remind them that they are being paid to answer questions – not ask them.' He retrieved the cylinder and holding it at arm's length turned it round slowly.

'No serial number. No identification marks. A few scratches on the base. That's all.'

She took it from him and raised it level with her eyes. She hardly seemed to breathe. It was as if life in her was suspended. The indentations were so faint they could have passed for scratches.

'Look . . . Scott,' she said, almost choking on the words. 'Am I imagining things . . . or is there a five-pointed star with a hole in the middle?'

He took the cylinder from her and examined the tiny insignia. 'What if there is? It means nothing.'

'But, don't you see? It means *everything*.' The tears were trickling down her cheeks. 'It means that my brother is alive.'

He shook his head.' I don't understand.'

'I will tell you later.' She bent down to pick up a stone and worked away at the marks until they were obliterated. Quite unexpectedly she kissed him.

'What was that for?' He put his hand to his cheek. It was wet where her face had been against his.

'For luck.'

Twenty minutes later he was back. 'They wanted me to leave it with them for a few days. I told them we had to have it back tomorrow.'

'I bet that will cost you.'

'You win your bet.' He didn't tell her that he didn't like the look of the manager, didn't trust him.

Julie was still walking on air. 'It couldn't be a coincidence. The pierced spur rowel was part of the coat of arms of the leader of one of the Cornish rebellions. When we were children, David and I used it as our secret sign.'

'Why didn't you tell me all this before?'

She closed her eyes. 'It was hard enough to go on hoping, praying, finding reasons for believing that David was still alive but at least I had only myself to convince. Now . . . ' She didn't finish.

When they got to their hotel there were two messages. A faxed letter signed by Railton Europe's chief executives insisting on urgent clarification of the parent company's intentions. Another from Descomptes. Eric Labarre and his partners had a full schedule of meetings all week and couldn't see him.

Scott telephoned the Zoltán Zaros Bank and asked for Fräulein Heideck. He fiddled with his business card as he waited, becoming more apprehensive with every moment.

'This is Herr Ritter's secretary, Mr Rokeby. Were you a personal friend of the Fräulein?'

'Has something happened to her?'

'A tragic accident. Yesterday evening. We telephoned her to tell her that the chairman had suffered a fatal heart attack. Getting no reply, we contacted the housekeeper who went up to her room. The Fräulein had used a stepladder in the kitchen and had fallen. The ladder must have been faulty.'

He listened, struggling to stay calm, to keep his voice steady as he framed a suitable reply. First his father. Then Strauben and Ulla Cranz. Now Zoltán Zaros and Fräulein Heideck. All dead. Like leaves fallen from a tree into slow-moving water, almost motionless at first and then nudged into the path of the current, eddying round and round, faster and faster in ever- tightening spirals before being sucked down into the vortex.

41

KK KEMIKAL

Kraik and Rohr went into the boardroom where Snoeck was waiting for them. The gold half-hunter was lying on the table..

'What have you been able to discover? asked Kraik

Snoeck carefully prised open the back. 'There is a engraving in ornate lettering – '*JFK to WR*. And the word *Vigilantia*.'

'We know about that,' said Kraik curtly. 'What do you make of the serial number inside?'

'CYB followed by ten digits. Some sort of code,' Snoeck muttered.

'Obviously. Continue.'

Snoeck took out a handkerchief and wiped the perspiration from his forehead. 'Many of the components are new. Behind the inner leaf, there is a miniature keyboard. The gear train and balanced wheel have been modified. They provide room for an antenna. The watch has a global positioning device and integrated circuitry. Map co-ordinates are shown on the small liquid crystal panel.

'If the battery becomes exhausted, fuel cells energised by body heat take over.' He turned the watch sideways on and pointed to the tiny pin-hole in the casing. There were a number of components that he had been unable to identify. 'The equipment has been continually upgraded. Beyond that—'

'You can tell us nothing.' He raised a finger as Snoeck turned to go.

'One moment. Have you any further need of Dixon? '

Snoeck shook his head.' We have pumped him dry and . . . ' he hesitated.

'There is something else?'

'He has become a security risk. We have found material in his locker that should not be there. He has been cautioned twice for going into restricted areas. Another thing, his health is deteriorating rapidly. My recommendation—'

'I did not ask for it. Return to your work. I want some privacy.'

Kraik beckoned to Rohr. 'Let us see whether we can make a little more progress, Pieter.' He withdrew five bonds from an inside pocket and unfurled them. 'Log in the number of the first bond.'

PROCEED flashed up on the panel.

'Log in the numbers of all five.'

FOR ACCESS TO DIDO – KEY IN ZZ CODE

Kraik's mouth stretched in a mirthless smile. '*So! We are locked out!* That fund could be worth a billion dollars by now and where is it? Without Zaros's watch, there is no way of getting to it.'

Rohr locked his huge hands together and yanked them violently apart. 'I should have caught Ulla! Torn her head off!'

'Instead you let Rokeby get to her. He and the girl have that watch.'

'My men can pick up Rokeby. Just give me—'

'*No! They had their chance.*'

Rohr blew out his cheeks. '*An hour or two, Kraik!* And I can deliver Scott Rokeby and the girl into your hands!'

'You were going to deliver Warren Rokeby into my hands. *Remember?* He owed me more than a death.' Kraik's eyes seared into Rohr's. 'When his car went over,' he whispered, 'are you sure that he was dead? Is it possible that he might have gone on living for a time? Still conscious?'

'There's no way of knowing,' Rohr replied brusquely. He was unsettled by the line of questioning. He had never seen Kraik in this mood.

'No way of knowing,' Kraik echoed. His head sank upon his chest. 'No way . . . of knowing.'

'*Kraik!*' said Rohr sharply. 'How can you concern yourself with such trivia at a time like this?'

Kraik started. '*Trivia!* Let me be the judge of that!'

'Surely we have bigger problems. The German police handed over Ludger Buhl to the army. He was threatened with a long prison sentence as a deserter. Generalmajor Stier interrogated him. Pumped him dry.

'Stier now has the location of the weapons caches stockpiled by the Combat Units. They are all in remote parts of Germany. I believe he plans to destroy these dumps under cover of declaring those places Restricted Areas and holding live firing exercises there. Without these weapons, the plans for a New German Militia are so much waste paper.'

'We know enough about Stier to ruin him. I leave that to you. I have other more important things to deal with. Rokeby—'

'But Warren Rokeby is *dead*! The son's business is *on the skids*! They are not worth the time it takes to say their names. *What can they mean to you?*'

A violent rictus contorted Kraik's features as though a high-voltage current had been passed through him. '*Never ask me that!* So long as you live, *never again ask me that*!'

42

KURFÜRSTENDAMM, BERLIN

Sonja Peetsch poured herself another Scotch. She hated this waiting, detested the apartment with its thick, white pile carpet, its shiny white leather sofas and white silk curtains. White, white everywhere. What were they trying to do? Bleach her grubby little life? It made her want to scream.

She started at the sound of a telephone. She must get herself together. Her nerves were all over the place.

'How are you, Sonja?'

Pieter Rohr. That horrible chuckle. She heard it in her dreams. 'A little nervous.' She dragged at the cigarette.

'There is nothing to be afraid of. Not if you do what you are told.'

'The telephone worries me. Sometimes I get the feeling that someone is listening.'

'Nonsense. The line has been checked. It is secure. Tell me about Herman Stier. What time does he usually visit?'

'He works late at the office. It is sometimes after ten at night when he comes here.'

'And in the morning?'

'He rises early. His briefcase is next to him on the bedside table. He shaves and dresses and then comes back and looks at me. I pretend to be fast asleep. He takes the briefcase into the sitting room.

'Once he left the door ajar. I got up very quietly and looked through the gap. He was sitting at the table. On it was a ledger As he turned the pages, I could see that it contained his bank statements. Beside it was an expensive leather-bound notebook. He was running his finger down the statements and then turning to the notebook and checking the entry there.'

'You did well. Stier is a careful man. He keeps meticulous records. I want you to photograph a few of those statements. Choose the ones where there are large amounts of money involved. Some of the entries will be cross-referenced to pages in the notebook. Photograph those pages too. You received the miniature camera?'

'I have it.'

'I will show you how to use it.'

'But the briefcase is always locked. Generalmajor Stier has a set of keys but they are attached to his belt. How do I—'

'You are a resourceful girl, Sonja. You will spot an opportunity. Run him a bubble bath. Tell him he looks tired. Suggest that he has a long, relaxing wallow in it.'

'Pieter, this is getting me down. I am frightened. The way he looks at me sometimes, I'm sure he suspects that I am spying on him. How long must I stay here?'

'What an ungrateful creature you are. He is a generous man. I believe he gives you jewellery.'

'He has given me one or two pieces but he forbids me to wear them.'

'He had no family money but he has become a rich man. In 1990, when East and West Germany were united, he was a major in the Quartermaster General's office of the Bundeswehr. The National Peoples Army had a lot of Russian equipment. Some of it was good stuff.

'My company would have paid a fair price for it but we didn't get the chance. Deals were done on the quiet and over several years. We believe that much of it went to the Middle East, sold off at very low prices. Herman Stier now has a town house and a nice estate in the country. All this on an army salary. It is a considerable achievement.'

'Are you saying that he is dishonest?'

'Until I have proof, I am simply making an observation.'

'I want to go home.'

'You have no home. Here, you have a smart apartment, a generous allowance. The Kurfürstendamm is very fashionable.'

'I am not free.'

'Freer than being locked in a cell. And you have your privacy. In prison you would have to share more than your toothbrush to keep those pretty looks.'

Sonja shuddered. 'Don't talk like that. I will do everything you tell me to do. I promise.'

'Live up to that promise. Now, tell me Stier's programme.'

'He is flying to NATO Strategic Command HQ tomorrow for a working lunch. In the afternoon he is going by helicopter to watch a demonstration. He has to be back at Teufelskopf, his hunting lodge, by six. At seven, his guests will be arriving for dinner. His staff car will collect him around midnight and take him to Schloss Falkenhayn.'

'Excellent, Sonja. You are an attractive girl and you have brains. Continue to please me and you could have a great future ahead of you. Disappoint me and you may have none at all.'

43

KK KEMIKAL – LABORATORY

Dixon arrived for work that morning but he was turned away by one of the guards. 'Haven't you heard?' the man sneered. 'Your work here is finished.'

'I won't accept that from you,' Dixon shouted, his nerves close to breaking point. 'I insist on seeing Snoeck.'

'Snoeck is too busy.' The guard brought his face close up to his. 'The word is, Dixon, that you are leaving us.'

'Then they are letting me go!' He leaned against the wall to steady himself. The prospect of going home was so unexpected that he felt quite light-headed.

'Letting you go.' the man chuckled. 'That's good.' He threw back his head and laughed. 'That's very good. Wait till the others hear that.'

The brief moment of euphoria vanished, leaving him sick to the stomach. There were rumours that a journalist had been caught hiding in a food truck trying to smuggle his way in. Nobody knew what had become of him but it was believed that he had been dressed in climbing gear, taken by helicopter and dropped down the side of a mountain.

Frightened and despondent, he climbed the stairs to the canteen. He was so tired. So desperately tired. Overwork and lack of sleep, the cold, insanitary conditions of his quarters and the poor food had all taken a toll of his health.

He had a pain in his chest and any great exertion gave him trouble with his breathing. But the physical privations were nothing compared with the daily torment of knowing that he had betrayed his vocation, his talent, everything in which he believed in the service of these criminals.

A hundred times he had cursed himself for his weakness, his cowardice. He should have stood up to them. Dared the devils to do their worst. At least he could have called himself a man.

He took a mug of coffee to a table by the window and gazed longingly at the dark green forest that stretched beyond the wire. They would never let him go. He knew too much. He had done what they wanted. He was disposable.

His thoughts turned to Julie. She must be looking for him. She would be worried sick. What would she do in his position? She was always braver and more resourceful than him. He had been given a job drilling holes in small metal canisters. He had asked what they were going to be used for but had been told to mind his own business. On one of them, he had etched a tiny symbol, a secret sign, that he and Julie had used as children. It was futile. About as much use as a marooned sailor putting a message inside a bottle and casting it into the sea.

How would Julie – how could anyone – get past the watchtowers and beyond that electrified fence? Night after night, exhausted but sleepless, listening to the tread of the guards up and down the stone-flagged passages, racking his brains till his head throbbed, he always came back to that fence.

He had made a habit of walking across the compound every evening at dusk. The guards were used to him by now. They would taunt him from their posts high up in the watchtowers, gesticulating to him to come closer. As he reached the wire, they would put on a dumb-show, agitating their arms and contorting their faces in a mime of agony. But they quickly tired of the game. The moment the searchlights came on, they would catch him in the crossbeams and drive him back to his quarters.

Was there some way of interrupting the electricity supply? The complex was powered by huge generators but sabotage was impossible.

They were too closely guarded. The fuse box seemed to be the weakest link in the system. It was in a passage that was only patrolled at night. Could the lock be forced and some device inserted which would ignite as the circuits switched over at dusk? Given a few seconds of darkness and confusion he might have a chance.

He had already failed once. He had got hold of some lead azide and hidden it in his locker. But Snoeck had found it. It had earned him a fortnight's solitary confinement on half rations. After that he had been watched even more closely.

The door opened and two technicians came into the canteen. One had a camera hanging by a shoulder strap and a small black leather case in his hand. He left the case on a table and pointed to the camera. 'Look at this, Haan. A Canon with a zoom lens. Quality stuff.'

'Another snooper?'

He nodded. 'They caught him trying to get a shot of the inside of a hangar. Roughed him up and took his gear.' The two men were in a hurry. A truck had to be equipped with monitoring equipment. They ate their snack at the counter, swallowed their coffee and left.

They had forgotten the case. Dixon's heart was hammering as if it would burst through his ribcage. There should be a flash attachment inside. He glanced round. Only two other tables were occupied. Nobody was watching him. His skin was breaking into a cold sweat as he slipped it into his pocket and pushed himself up from the table.

He had the glimmering of an idea. Everyone was busy with the final preparations for Sharpshooter. It was his last chance. But would it work? The thought of the high-voltage current surging back down that electrified fence sent a chill through him.

44

LES VAMPS, BRUSSELS

The night club was in a side street a few minutes' walk from the Grande Place. It was after eleven and freezing hard when Scott and Julie went down the steps to the entrance to be confronted by a burly man in a roll-neck jumper on the door. Scott gave him Ulla Cranz's card.

The man shook his head. The club was for members only. A note changed hands. They checked in their coats and followed the noise down a passage lined in faded plush into the interior.

The bar ran the whole length of the back of the room. A number of girls had paired off with customers. One, with fair hair that fell below her shoulders, was drooping on a barstool and hardly turned her head to look at them before going back to her glass. People at the tables were talking and drinking. In the corner a group of men in dark suits were engrossed in discussing business. Two women were dancing together under a slowly rotating globe that cast a scattering of coin-like silver spots round the walls. On the stage a pale, anaemic-looking girl in electric blue was shrilling an old Piaf number.

The woman snaking her way towards them through the haze of smoke had fluffy pink hair gathered up like candy floss. With her rouged cheeks, vermillion lipstick and skin-tight sequinned dress her age could only be guessed at.

She looked them over with a cold eye and frowned. 'I'm Rita. I don't think I have seen you here before.' She hesitated for a moment as if half minded to throw them out, before leading them to a table. 'Denise!' She snapped her fingers at a waitress and left them.

When Denise returned with the drinks, Scott asked her if she could point out Elena.

'*La Russe?*' Her eyes went to the girl they had seen by herself at the bar. 'Do you know her?'

A friend of a friend, Scott told her.

'I'll send her over but don't keep her long. Rita doesn't like it.'

The singer was cranking up for a high note. A man at a nearby table drained his glass and clambered to his feet. 'For fuck's sake, Rita,' he shouted, 'send your canary back to her cage. She's giving me a migraine.'

Elena came up to their table. A small oval face framed by long fair hair. Frightened eyes. She tugged nervously at her halter top. 'I can only stay a moment.'

Scott showed her the card that he had found on Cranz. 'There's no need to look so worried, Elena. I only want a few words about a friend of yours. Ulla Cranz.'

Reluctantly she took the card from him. 'Are you from the authorities? Or the police?'

'No. But I'm afraid I have some bad news. Ulla was in a small plane. She was piloting herself.'

'She's dead, isn't she?' said Elena dully.

'Her plane came down in some woods. She was killed instantly. There was nothing anyone could do. If she was a friend, I'm sorry.'

'We had a business relationship, that's all. She told me that she had pull with Rita. She promised she could get me out of this place.' She gave a little shrug, 'Anyway, like a fool I believed her.'

Julie took her hand. 'I don't understand. Why can't you just pack the job in?'

'*Pack it in!*' Elena squawked. Her hand flew to her mouth but no one seemed to have noticed. 'You don't walk out on Rita. Not if you owe her money.'

'You were broke. She lent you money . . . ' Scott prompted.

Elena sighed. 'Yes, it was the old scam and I fell for it. It cost me so much to get here that I was in debt up to my ears. Now I have to pay it off.' Her glossy mouth twisted in a rueful smile.

'Rita told me that there were two ways to do it. I could run round this dump carrying trays till four in the morning or find a rich idiot, fill him up with champagne and . . . ' she shrugged. 'Well, you know the rest.' She fingered the dark smudges under her eyes. 'I didn't get these sitting up all night reading theology.'

Scott canted his head at the men in the corner. 'What are they doing here? It doesn't look as if they came for the floor show.'

'Rita's friends. Often they stay till after three. Sometimes she takes them into the back office.'

Scott followed her eyes to a door to the right of the stage, half-concealed by a curtain. 'Did Ulla use Rita's office?'

'Who knows?' Her eyes darted round the room. 'Rita mustn't find me here. Forget that you saw me – and forget about Ulla.' She slipped away.

'I must take a look at that office,' Scott whispered.

'What shall I say if Rita asks where you are?'

'Say I am in the john; say anything you like but keep her talking.' He gave her an encouraging wink and made for the bar.

Julie buried her nose in her glass. One minute went by. Then two.

'Where is your friend?'

Startled, she looked up. It was Rita, hands on hips, her eyes black pebbles of suspicion.

'He won't be long. He isn't feeling very well.'

The eyes bored into her. 'I'm sorry to hear it.' She pointed to a chair. 'May I?' Shaking a cigarette into her hand, she sat down and lit up. 'You must forgive me for not being more welcoming . . . ' she was fishing for her name.

'I'm Julie.'

'We get very few strangers, Julie. Most of the people here have some sort of connection.' She blew a plume of smoke at the ceiling. 'I was wondering how you heard about the club.' She raised the heavily pencilled arches of her eyebrows.

Scott had heard about it, Julie replied rather lamely. This inquisition was unnerving. The room erupted in laughter and she turned gratefully in the direction of the stage.

A leggy blonde was being introduced, rather breathlessly, by a plump, perspiring man in a red bow tie. Dolly from Dortmund had long blonde pigtails tied up in scarlet bows to match her nipple tassels and shiny Lycra shorts. Three concentric rings had been painted on her belly to make a target.

A bashful young man recruited from the audience climbed up to the stage and was handed a toy pistol. He loaded it with a short wooden rod fitted with a rubber suction pad, raised a wavering arm and took aim. There was a roll of drums from the band and the missile shot out of the muzzle and stuck quivering in Dolly's ample cleavage. Cheers were mixed with boos and catcalls. The girl saluted the poor marksmanship with her backside.

Rita stubbed out her cigarette, dabbing at the ashtray with quick, nervous movements. 'I'm concerned about your friend.'

'Don't worry. It's probably just a stomach upset.'

'All the same that can be very unpleasant.' She half rose from the table. 'I keep some tablets in my office. Don't you think I should—'

Panic stricken, Julie grabbed her arm. '*Rita! Don't go yet!* There's something I must talk to you about.'

'Ah.' Rita tapped the end of her nose. 'Auntie Rita could smell something wasn't quite right.' She sat down again. 'What haven't you told me?'

Julie's eyes dropped to the table. 'I have made a mess of things. I got into trouble with the police. I was fined and had my passport confiscated until I paid up. I'm flat broke.'

'Won't your parents help?'

'I have no parents.'

'I'm not Santa Claus, my dear. What about your friend? Can't he lend you enough to get you by?'

'Scott? He's just a pick-up. I've only known him for an hour or two.'

'At least you can cadge a bed for the night.' Though from what she knew of men, the girl would get more sleep dossing down on a railway line. 'Did he suggest you came here?'

Julie nodded. 'He heard that girls can get casual work.'

'Sometimes. It depends on the girl. Can you sing?'

'Like a crow with a sore throat.'

Rita looked her up and down. 'You have nice breasts. Pull up your skirt. Let's have a look at your legs.'

Julie could feel the blood flooding her cheeks as she drew up her skirt.

Rita stared at the flaming cheeks and chuckled. 'Anyone can tell you don't strip for a living.' Dolly was coming off to whistles and catcalls. Rita took Julie's arm and pulled her to her feet.

'You can't say that Auntie Rita didn't give you a chance.'

Julie gaped at her. 'You don't mean you want me to go up there?'

'Why not? You won't pay many bills sitting on your bottom.'

'Strip off in front of all those people?'

'They won't bite you.' She nudged her towards the stage.

'How much will you pay me?'

'We'll talk money later. First, let's see what you've got.' Another little shove.

'But what about my friend? What on earth will he think when he sees me up there?'

'He will think what they all think. *Come on!*'

Rita marched her across the floor and up the steps. With a wave of her hand she silenced the band and grabbed the microphone. 'Ladies and gentlemen! When you think of England, what pictures come into your mind ? Buckingham Palace? Piccadilly Circus? Double-decker buses? Tonight Julie is going to show you that there are a lot of other attractions from across the Channel.'

'Is Julie going to show us the channel tunnel?' someone shouted to ribald laughter. The businessmen looked up for a moment before returning to their discussion.

Rita clicked her fingers at red bow-tie who was lounging against the piano. 'Felip! Bring on the chaise-longue. Let's see if we can do this with a little style.'

A few moments later, Felip reappeared through the back curtains, wheeling the chaise-longue. It had seen better times. Wisps of horse hair protruded from gashes in the pink velvet upholstery and one of the castors was missing. He manoeuvred it into position and swatted at the dust with a napkin.

Rita steered Julie to the middle of the stage. 'Loosen up,' she growled under her breath. 'Give the punters a big smile.' She lowered her mouth to the microphone. 'I want a round of applause for Julie from England.' The band came in quickly to cover the feeble handclaps.

As Julie stood there, the room seemed to swim out of focus. The upturned faces looked like rows of unwashed dishes. Through the blood beating in her ears she was dimly aware that the band was playing an old Abba tune. Somebody whistled. She had to move. Do something. *Anything.*

Removing her jacket, she strutted to the chaise-longue and hung it round the shoulders of the backrest. She kicked off her shoes and undid the top button of her blouse. Her fingers toyed with a wisp of horsehair. There was a stir of interest. Bereft of inspiration, she undid another button. The audience was becoming restive. Somebody started a slow handclap.

Red bow tie sidled past the band, picked up a drumstick and thrust it into the angle between the base and the headrest. There was a roar from the tables and her nervousness began to evaporate.

She opened her blouse but kept it on. Her back was not a pretty sight. She unclipped her bra and dangled it over the jutting prong. Up and down it went, the loose end twining round it, teasing it like a finger. Released, the rosy cups slid along its length and nestled at the base. There was a shriek of laughter, quickly suppressed and the room fell silent.

The fear had vanished, its place usurped by a giddy sense of power. She was flaunting herself and relishing it. Sticking out her tongue at the grown-ups with the same mixed feelings of shame and exhilaration of a child taking a hammer to the nursery crockery.

She raced her zip up and down and wiggled out of her skirt, trailing it from her fingers for a moment before letting it fall. Her stockings followed. The chaise-longue rocked as she climbed on to it and advanced stealthily on hands and knees. A long sigh came from her rapt audience. Feet shuffled on the floor and bodies shifted restlessly in chairs.

The drummer's stick seemed to quiver with apprehension as the polished flanks and jouncing buttocks clad in their skimpy knickers bore down on it. Her lips parted, her hands stretched out . . . There came a screech of splintering wood! The front of the couch dipped. Her behind bucked into the air. She snatched at the stick. It came away in her hands and she fell backwards. A frantic see-saw movement ensued before the long-suffering couch toppled over and decanted her on to the floor to a pandemonium of cheering, whistling and stamping of feet.

Flicking tears of rage and mortification from her eyes, she grabbed her clothes and ran through the hubbub to the temporary refuge of the ladies.' Scrambling into her skirt she dashed cold water on her scalding cheeks. She could hear Rita at the microphone.

There came a light tap at the pane. It was Scott. 'What are you hanging about for?' he hissed.

'*Hanging about!* That's good coming from you! If you knew what I have gone through in the last few minutes!' Her voice spiralled close to hysteria. She clambered on to a wicker basket and squirmed through the narrow aperture.

'Why didn't you keep watch instead of horsing around bare-assed in front of all those people?'

'Why? *You dare to ask me why?*' Dishevelled, streaked with grime and almost incoherent with fury she slid untidily into his arms.

'Christ, you look a mess!' he said as he lowered her to the ground.

She had to bite her lips to avoid crying out for she had scraped her back squeezing through the window. 'Did you find out anything?' she gasped as they climbed into a taxi.

'Rita's desk was locked but I got into one of the filing cabinets. She's running some sort of immigration racket.'

'That doesn't get us much further.' She turned away so that he shouldn't see her face.

He took her hand. 'Julie, there was photo on the wall. A group of people standing in front of a Learjet. Some of them were in business suits. There were a few policemen in uniform. Rita was there with some of her girls handing round drinks. Ulla was there.'

'Are you sure it was her?' The images from the cockpit came flooding back.

He was sure. The aircraft had the logo of KK Kemikal on the side. The name meant nothing to her.

'KKK is a big set up. It operates all over the world.'

'Have you any idea where the photo was taken?'

'No. But there was a car there with a Belgian number plate. I don't mind betting it is somewhere in Belgium.'

He hadn't told her the whole truth about that photograph. He didn't want to frighten her. Some of KKK's guards had been in the picture. He had been in some tough places but he had never set eyes on a more villainous-looking bunch. Only now was he beginning to get some inkling of what they were up against.

45

BRUSSELS

Early the next morning, Scott and Julie snatched a quick breakfast together. She popped a pill into her mouth and drained the rest of her orange juice.

'What's that dope you are on?'

'I bruised my back.'

'All in the line of duty.' He finished his coffee.

'*Scott Rokeby!* I saved your hide last night.'

'I'm not ungrateful. I merely ask whether it was necessary to create such mayhem. *Pas trop de zèle* – not too much enthusiasm – was one of my father's sayings. Talleyrand, I believe.'

'Now who's showing off?'

'Just balancing the books.'

'Scott, that photo – we *must* find out where it was taken.'

'KKK have an office in Brussels. I telephoned them asking for a list of all their branches. They prevaricated. Told me to write in.'

'What reason did they give?'

'Security. Government work. Defence contracts.'

'Where do we go from here?'

'I'm going to Descomptes. I suggest you go to the Registrar of Companies and do a company search on KKK.'

'I have got several interviews lined up. Three directors of big companies exhibiting at Sharpshooter, a minister in the Belgian Defence Department, a technical expert on—'

'Then we both have a busy day ahead of us. Let's meet back at the hotel at seven and compare notes.'

She chewed on her lip. 'Scott, I may need the Range Rover tonight.'

'You're not going, Julie.'

'Scott. I'm going if I have to crawl there.'

'Crawl where?'

'That's what I intend to find out.' She grabbed her bag, ran into the road and waved down a taxi.

Descomptes was situated in a modern office block in the heart of the business quarter. Scott was there the moment the doors opened. He exchanged a few words with the receptionist and skimmed through the papers on the table in the lobby. A big rise in the share prices of defence companies had made headlines. Over the page a caption jumped out at him. *Fraser Outram in talks with troubled venture capitalist company.* The girl coughed discreetly. Edgar Labarre was pushing through the swing doors.

Scott followed him into the lift. Mid-forties. Grey hair, grey eyes, grey suit. Even the steel-rimmed spectacles were grey.

Labarre pressed the button for the seventh floor.

Scott smiled. 'Same for me.'

Labarre returned the smile. 'Who are you coming to see?'

'You.'

The smile vanished and reappeared as if it had been glued back into place. 'Mr Rokeby?'

'That's right.'

'You are a director of Railton Ross?'

'Right again.'

'Didn't you get my message?' The doors slid open. 'I'm not sure I should be talking to you at all but I may be able to offer you a provisional appointment for next week. Telephone my secretary. She makes all my arrangements.' He stepped out, wheeled left, waved to a colleague and lengthened his stride.

Scott kept pace with him. 'Let's go and talk to your secretary. She seems to be in charge here. Perhaps she can make some alteration to her plans for the day.'

Two minutes later Scott was sitting on the large button-back Chesterfield in Labarre's office. He gestured at the mahogany partner's desk and the oil paintings on the walls. 'Business seems to be pretty good.'

Labarre sat stiffly on the edge of his upright chair. He examined Scott's business card, holding it between finger and thumb as if he had found it on the washroom floor. 'Your behaviour, Mr Rokeby, is outrageous. I don't know what passes for manners where you come from but it is not acceptable here.'

'I don't take lessons in manners from people who turn up at my companies without notice demanding to go through their books and questioning their employees.' He was struggling to keep his temper.

'Permit me to correct that statement.' Labarre picked up a pencil and sharpened it to a stiletto point. 'They are not your companies. They are controlled by the majority shareholders. Our instructions come from Jeff Turcan, the chief executive, and have the approval of the board. I have a copy of the company minute in my files.'

'That minute was not approved by me. At no time was I consulted.' These bloodless statisticians with their calculators and their spreadsheets. 'Have you any idea how long it took me to build up the trust, the loyalty and the friendship of the people in those companies? To convince them that we were not just another hard-nosed Yankee outfit that was going to work them like pit ponies and sell their hide for shoe leather?'

'I had my instructions.'

'*Instructions!* If you and your team of licensed snoopers had set out to foul up the works you couldn't have made a better job of it.'

'I take great exception to that remark,' Labarre retorted. He ran a finger round the inside of his collar. 'We do not snoop. We obtain information efficiently and with the minimum disruption.'

'Minimum disruption! *That's rich!* The managers of all those companies are on the point of walking out.'

Labarre's eyes dropped to the accounts in front of him. 'We accountants always get the blame when the axe falls but the truth is that the damage is usually done before we are called in. Railton has run out of money. Either it raises the cash it needs or it goes under.'

'How many companies does Turcan intend to sell? Two? Four? All of them?'

Labarre spread his hands. 'I don't know. It is a decision for the board. Our recommendation will be emailed to Mr Turcan this afternoon.'

'You put me in an impossible position. I have to have some indication. Something to fight with.'

Labarre shook his head. 'I'm sorry. The report is confidential.'

'Can you hold it for twenty-four hours?' Scott pleaded. 'I must have more time.'

'It can't be done. We are working to a deadline. We didn't set the parameters.'

Scott exploded. '*Railton Europe is falling apart!* I have sunk half my life into that business and you talk to me about parameters!'

Labarre picked up the telephone and spoke to his secretary. 'Ask Gilles Hullin if he can spare us a few minutes. And bring us some coffee.'

Gilles Hullin was in his late thirties. His dark hair receding at the front and flopping over the top of his ears reminded Scott of the black cap placed on a judge's head before passing sentence of death. Hullin shook hands briskly and took a chair beside his partner. His eyes ran over Scott and then returned to Labarre like a dog's to its master.

Thirty minutes later, Scott had won no concessions. Hullin looked over his horn-rimmed glasses and placed his fingertips together. 'Railton's position is critical. With every hour it becomes worse. To delay the report would be most irresponsible. I almost said reckless. I find it disturbing that Mr Rokeby should attempt to justify it.' He glanced at Labarre and received a concurring nod.

Scott took a deep breath. These men were stretching him on the rack. 'How often must I repeat it? The only thing that will persuade the managers to stay is a categorical assurance from the board that no action will be taken without consulting them. Give me twenty-four hours and I believe I can persuade Turcan to do things my way. Otherwise . . . ' He was silent. It was better left unsaid.

'Otherwise?' Hullin pressed him.

Scott raised his eyebrows. *You really want this?* 'Otherwise Varad, Torun, Broz and the others will clear their desks and call their lawyers. They have a strong case for constructive dismissal.'

'You wouldn't by any chance have put that idea into their heads?' asked Hullin with something like a sneer. 'The old poison-pill ploy? It's been done.'

'If I wanted to play that game, why should I be here fighting to get that report stalled?'

'To cover your back.' Hullin's voice was as silky as the tie round his neck.

Scott stood up. 'I seem to have wasted my time here.' He threw his papers into his briefcase. 'But before I go, I give you fair warning. I know those guys. They won't simply go home and work their way through a case of vodka, though they could do that later. They might set about making a few improvements to the factory layout. Have you ever seen a million dollars' worth of equipment after it's been dropped from a hoist? I have. You might call that sabotage but everyone would swear blind in court that it was an accident. A US company wouldn't stand a chance.'

The two men goggled at him like fish in a tank. '*But . . . but that's . . . barbaric!*' Hullin stuttered when he found his voice.

Scott shrugged. 'You have read your history. Those guys play hardball.'

'If we hold that report, it's our head that's on the block,' insisted Labarre. But his eyes had lost their sharp focus. His brain was busy with its calculations.

'If you send it tonight and your advice is what I think it is, Turcan will have a basket case on his hands. *Then it will be you that has the problems.*'

'What do you mean?' Hullin's pallid face was shiny with perspiration.

'Turcan will sue you for professional negligence. Forget your fees. You will find yourselves on the end of a writ that will make your eyes water.'

'But it wouldn't be our fault,' Labarre protested.

'Save that for your defence attorney.'

Labarre got wearily to his feet. His hand went to his forehead. 'Do you intend to tell your colleagues what you have told us?'

'Of course. I will contact them at once.'

Labarre's shoulders drooped. 'We will hold the report for twenty-four hours. Our recommendations will include a warning against reaching any decision without giving full weight to the impact on employee loyalties.'

'And the implications of wide differences in culture.' Hullin put in his ten cent's worth.

Ten minutes later Labarre's secretary was dispatched to the chemist to buy a packet of headache pills. 'And Pauline . . . '

'Yes, Monsieur Labarre . . . '

'The strongest they have.'

In the taxi, Scott pulled out the watch and looked at it again. It was almost identical to Warren's hunter except that it was attached to a short gold chain with a bar. The glass front was almost unmarked. His father's had been scratched from rubbing against coins and keys.

Lecointe was a small firm in the old quarter of the city. A selection of antique watches was on display in the window, each on a blue velvet mount and lit by spotlights. He had to wait some moments before a young man came to the door and admitted him.

'If you will kindly step into the back office, Monsieur Lecointe is expecting you.'

Calvin Lecointe had a fresh, pink complexion but his waistline had given ground to advancing years. He gave his visitor a sharp, appraising look before taking the watch and putting the lens to his eye. 'Eighteen carat, red gold,' he murmured.' Geneva . . . about 1840 . . . a very nice piece.' Delicately, he prised open the back. A pause. 'Would it be indiscreet to enquire how this came into your possession?'

Scott explained that it had belonged to a relation. It seemed easier.

'There is an inscription – '*JFK to ZZ. Vigilantia'*. Your relation seems to have had some distinguished connections. He raised his head. 'Might I ask what profession he followed?'

'He was a banker. Is that relevant?'

'It could be.' Lecointe's tone was ironical. 'An unusual provenance can increase the value.' He continued his examination. 'Alterations have been made over a period of years. A serial number has been added.' He lifted the inner leaf. 'There are several letters and digits on the small liquid crystal read-out, but I can tell you,' he added dryly, 'you will find them of little assistance in checking the time of day.'

His head bent lower. 'There is what appears to be a miniature antenna . . . ' He straightened.

'Mr Rokeby, I have been in this business for over forty years but I must confess that this is quite outside my experience. If you are prepared to leave it with us for a few days . . . '

Scott shook his head. He was grateful for the offer but he couldn't wait.

Lecointe took a silk handkerchief from his pocket, carefully polished the surfaces of the watch and returned it with a little bow. He came to the door with him and Scott could sense his curious eyes following him as he joined the flow of passers-by and was lost in the bustle of the metropolis.

46

DOWNTOWN NEW YORK

Jeff Turcan had arranged to meet his brother outside the Pierre Hotel at exactly quarter-past twelve. Todd was late and Jeff had been rubbing his hands and stamping his feet for almost ten minutes when the taxi pulled into the kerbside. He felt a twinge of resentment as the commissionaire stepped forward and opened the door. He would have to tip the man and he wasn't in the giving mood.

Todd moved across the seat to make way for him. 'You won't mind, I'm sure, if I have a look in a shop window on the way. It's Gail's birthday next week and I would like to buy her something nice.'

Jeff stood with his brother outside the fashionable jewellers, his arms wrapped tightly about him against the knifing wind while Todd, snug in his heavy cashmere overcoat, dilated on the rival merits of Cartier, Rolex and Patek Philippe.

At last he turned away. 'Jeff, you should wear an overcoat on a day like this. If I had known how cold it was I would have kept the taxi.'

Jeff puffed along, trying to keep up with his brother. The restaurant was off Lexington Avenue, less than a block away, but he was badly out of condition. He must try to get to the fitness club as soon as all this was over. Cut down on the bourbon and the smoking. Despite the cold, he was relieved when Todd stopped to buy a paper and he could catch his breath.

Todd glanced at the latest prices. 'Dow Jones down again. And what the hell's going on in Eurobonds. You can't give them away.'

Stepping out of the leaden day into an ambiance of rosy marble and glossy green palms, red plush banquettes and golden lamplight was like finding a jewel in an ashcan.

Jeff sucked his teeth as he stared at the menu. This was one of those places where oxygen masks should drop from the ceiling as the diners looked at the prices. Even the starters were a hundred dollars. He shot a sideways glance at his brother. Todd was testing the waiter on the sauces. When the wine list came he would go through the same routine.

'Try the honey lacquered duck,' Todd suggested. 'You won't regret it.'

'Anything you say.' There was a void in his stomach that nothing would fill, not the honey lacquered duck, the ginger crème brûlée, nor the fine cognac that rounded off his meal.

Todd poured himself a glass of Evian. 'What time is your board meeting?'

'Three o'clock.'

'Will Rokeby be there?'

'No. Not after stirring up a frigging hornets' nest.'

Todd smiled. 'Nobody likes being stung.'

'Mal and I are the ones who are pulling the stings out of our asses,' said Jeff resentfully. 'First you poach all our best people. Then you pick us up for peanuts.'

'That wasn't the word my bankers used.' Todd's jaw jutted belligerently. 'We did our figures on the assumption that Railton Europe would be liquidated. Now we are going to have to keep it. That could stretch us to the limit.'

'I was hoping for a merger – a partnership of equals – not a garage sale.'

'Look on the bright side. You and Mal still have a job. The way the market is going, there will soon be a lot of good men walking the streets.'

'Two-thirds of our old salary and a one-year contract. It takes some swallowing.'

'It's more than Rokeby's got.'

Jeff shook his head. 'That guy is the kiss of death.'

'With him gone, the Food and Drug Administration will come into line and you can start mending your fences on the Hill.' He took a cigar from the box and tucked it into his breast pocket. 'This board meeting – will it come to a vote?'

'I called Scott to ask if he was going to use his proxy. He put the phone down on me.'

'From what I know of him, he won't go quietly.'

'Let him come at us. He won't find it so easy.'

Todd grinned. 'Now you are beginning to sound a bit more like the old Jeff. OK, it's going to be a tough twelve months but we can crack it.'

'Given the will is there.'

'And the leadership.' He locked eyes with his brother. 'You know what I want from you, Jeff. No speeches. No long reports. No explanations or excuses. No memos flying round like confetti. Just make this work.'

Jeff drained the last of his coffee. 'Look, Todd,' he said quietly, 'there has been friction between Karen and me recently . . . and that's putting mildly. I've been under a lot of strain. I don't suppose I've been easy to live with. But I still had a business, a certain status. A woman will make allowances if she can see better times ahead.'

'You will get some shares, Jeff. You are still a young man. You can rebuild.'

His brother shook his head. 'Karen isn't the patient type. She won't like moving to a smaller house. New friends. New neighbours. If there had been children, it might have anchored her. I would have felt more confident that we could get the other side of this. As it is . . . I don't know how she will take it . . . or whether she will.'

'As bad as that?' Todd rubbed his jaw.

'As bad as that. We all like to feel that things are moving forward. Getting better. Marriage is no different. When the signals stick on red, people have been known to get off the train.'

'Would it help,' Todd measured his words as he reflected, 'if Karen reckoned there was something nice to hang on for?'

'It sure would.'

'How would she feel about a move to the West Coast?'

Jeff rocked forward in his chair. 'You mean it?'

'We need an office in LA. Next year we could be ready for it.'

'Are you tossing me a bone?'

His brother spread his hands. 'I'm making you an offer, Jeff, a generous one.'

It was so long since Jeff had smiled he had almost forgotten how.

'You need a CEO?' The words came out in a croak.

'I know just the guy. But he's got a tough twelve months ahead of him and he's got to prove he can deliver.' He called for the check.

47

TEUFELSKOPF, GERMANY

The sentry checked the passes, saluted smartly and waved the cars through the ornate wrought-iron gates. Flaming torches, like a fiery snake, wound through the park to the half-timbered hunting lodge at the head of the drive. From the heads of the flagpoles, the German tricolour and the Stier house flag, a black boar's head on a gold ground, snapped in the breeze. Behind the lodge, the dark trees climbed to a jagged ridge silhouetted against the scudding clouds.

The frosty air carried the pungent smell of wood smoke. Feet crunched across thick gravel. Yellow light spilled from a door bringing with it the strains of a regimental band. Two oak refectory tables set for dinner and laden with regimental silver ran the length of a panelled hall hung with antlers and other trophies of the chase. Guests were handing their great coats to orderlies or warming their hands before the huge hearth with its carved boar's head set in the capstone. From the next room, Stier's booming voice could be heard greeting the last of his guests.

'Welcome, Stefan! Have a glass of Krug. The eighty-nine. My spies tell me that is your favourite year.'

Brigadegeneral Stefan von Preuss acknowledged the compliment with a small inclination of his shiny, bald head. 'My dear Herman, your intelligence always was first-class.' Raising his glass to his host, he looked around the room where some forty officers in dress uniform were assembled.

'What makes you smile, Stefan?'

'Forgive me, but the wearing of medals at a private dinner. Is it not a little unusual?'

'You must indulge an old man's whim. Sometimes these young firebrands need a gentle reminder that we too have seen some soldiering.'

Brigadegeneral von Stollen, a tall, spare figure with a long duelling scar, came up to them smiling broadly. 'It is heartening to see so many of the old and bold here tonight?'

Stier chuckled. 'Very true, Hendrik, but we shall not have things all our own way.' He pointed to the group of younger officers gathered round the fireplace. 'The Kriegsakademie will see to that.'

'The War College,' von Stollen raised his hands in mock surrender. 'I trust they have left their panzers back at the barracks.'

'What is certain is that they have brought their appetites with them.' Herman Stier called for silence and clinked his signet ring against the side of his glass. 'Gentlemen. It has been reported to me that we are all present. As usual there is a senior and a junior table. At this stage of the evening, officers who prove incapable of telling one from the other can expect no leniency.' He waited for the laughter to subside before concluding. 'There is a rumour that a magnificent wild boar has been seen in these parts. Let us take our places in the great hall and see if the chef has managed to catch him.'

A haze of cigar smoke and brandy hung in the air. An orderly threw a log on the fire, sending a cloud of golden sparks up the chimney. In the gallery, the band was playing the Panzerlied. The young officers were singing softly or tapping their feet on the stone-flagged floor.

As the Tank Song came to an end, Stier snapped his fingers at an orderly. 'Send some beer to the band, corporal, with my compliments and a couple of jugs to the other table while you are about it.'

The younger officers were so quiet tonight they might have been in church. What had got into them? They were usually so rowdy and boisterous, bawling out the songs, banging their glasses on the table.

Rudeness, of course, was different. Last year there had been some unpleasantness. A glass of wine had been thrown at a general. Unpleasant accusations made. The affair had been hushed up but it left a nasty taste in the mouth.

General Gronstedt broke in on his thoughts. 'You have some fine pieces, Herman.' He gestured to the silver on the table.

'Salvage, Gustav, bought at sales to keep them out of the clutches of those blood-sucking dealers. It is all that was left of those fine old regiments. The rest? Consigned to oblivion by our political masters. In the First World War, my grandfather fought with the Grand Ducal Hessian Life Guards. Those were great days for soldiering. What do our modern conscripts know of the old traditions of pride and honour, of duty and sacrifice.' He laughed harshly to mask the bitterness.

Gronstedt nodded complacently. He had the soft pink cheeks and webbing of red veins that came with too much good living. 'It is tragic, Herman. Those regiments were part of a splendid heritage. Our forefathers must be turning in their graves.'

Stier nodded abstractedly. His eyes travelled back to the other table. He had heard the word *Grossmacht*. Quickly suppressed. The old dream of making Germany a world power again. Young men never changed. How sad that one day they would have to grow up and become like the rest of them. Middle-aged, venal, perhaps even a little absurd.

An orderly bent his head to give him a message. Wetzlar had requested permission to propose an extra toast.

Jorg Wetzlar, commander of an airborne infantry regiment was the youngest lieutenant-colonel in the army. His following among the ambitious younger element in the forces bordered on the fanatical. Their eyes met. Irony, contempt, impatience on a tight rein, written in every line of those austere features. Stier nodded resignedly. The orderlies left. The band stopped playing and the room fell silent.

Wetzlar sprang to his feet. 'At times like this,' he began in strong, ringing tones, 'when so much in our national life is dark and confused, which of us has not looked back to earlier days, glorious days when Germany came within an ace of building an empire that stretched from the shores of the Atlantic to the Urals?

'Which of us has not dreamed of the day when the Fatherland once more assumes the mantle of greatness? Which of us would not gladly lay down his life in the knowledge that he has brought that day closer, that his name will be inscribed in the pantheon with those of Rommel and Guderian, the great panzer commanders, with von Kleist the genius of the Caucusus campaign, with Kesselring the brilliant defender of Italy against impossible odds and with von Rundstedt, perhaps the greatest general of them all?'

Wetzlar's voice sank to a whisper but not a syllable was lost among that gathering. 'There are moments in a soldier's life, my friends, when Destiny steps down from her marble plinth, seizes the torch that bears the eternal flame, holds it aloft and cries, *"This is the path! To follow it you have but to dare!"'*

There were anxious looks from the officers at the junior table. One plucked at Wetzlar's sleeve but he shook his arm free and raised his glass high.

'Gentlemen,' his voice rang out in the stillness, 'I ask you to charge your glasses and salute the immortals. The toast is *"Heldengedenktag!"'*

For a moment nobody moved. A toast to Heroes' Memorial Day was bad form. It conjured up images of secret reunions in castle cellars, activists with swastika armbands, the swearing of oaths and singing of marching songs proscribed for over half a century. The senior officers clambered to their feet, some of them too drunk to know or care what they were drinking to. Others remembering the trouble of the previous year were anxious to avoid dissension.

Stier eyed the junior table over the rim of his glass. Wetzlar's supporters were Ostis. Newly enlisted officers in the National Peoples Army at the time of reunification, many of them denied the promotion that was their due because of their past, burning resentment etched into their features. Now they jumped to their feet, raised their glasses and roared out, '*Heldengedenktag!*' coupled with the name of '*Wetzlar*!'

Stier glanced at his watch. It was a quarter to twelve. Traditionally, at this stage of the evening, he and his contemporaries left the younger men to their songs and drinking. He led the way to the door.

A few minutes later, his Mercedes staff car swept down the drive. With a sigh he sank back into the comforting upholstery. The evening had unsettled him. He prided himself that he could detect a shift in the wind quicker than most. Those rabble-rousers were up to something. He would take careful soundings at Sharpshooter in the morning. Men like Wetzlar were dangerous. A year or two cooling their heels in the Balkans on peace-keeping duties would bring them to their senses.

As for the Old Guard, veterans like himself, they must feather their own nests because no one else would do it for them. In the past fifteen years, he had salted away a small fortune. It was in numbered accounts in half a dozen tax havens, safe from prying eyes.

To his astonishment, his car was stopped at the gates.

The sentry stepped forward and saluted.

'What is the meaning of this,' demanded Stier. 'Do you know who I am?'

'Yes, Generalmajor.'

'Then, let me pass. I am on my way to Schloss Falkenhayn. I will be spending the night there.'

'We have orders to provide an escort. Two outriders will accompany you there.'

Stier looked in his mirror. Two policemen on motorbikes had taken up position behind him. 'I do not need an escort.'

'I have my orders, sir.'

'From whom?'

'From my superiors, sir.'

'Why are the outriders not in army uniform?'

The sentry could not tell him.

'Very well,' said Stier. 'But you have not heard the last of this. *Driver!*'

The sentry had to jump back as the General's driver gunned the engine and the big car roared out of the gates.

48

THE ARDENNES

Julie threw her briefcase into the back of the car. She had emailed the article to her paper. 'The Press Office at NATO HQ was very helpful. They had profiles on most of the big beasts who will be at Sharpshooter. You can't cram three days work into one. It is skimped and it shows but it will have to do.'

As they drove out of the hotel garage, the snow was falling and a sulphurous sky promised more on the way. An Opel joined them as they crossed the Brussels ring road.

'What did you find out about KKK?' asked Scott.

'I got nowhere with a company search. It's exempted from making returns. I checked through my database but there were many private airstrips and the company could have operated out of any of them. I called a contact at the Aero Club. All he could remember was that a KKK security man had roughed up one of their members for making an unauthorised landing in a Restricted Area.

'He wanted him to take the company to court but the man was too frightened. He wasn't even prepared to provide details of where he had landed.' She asked Scott about his visit to Polder. 'Did they know where the cylinder came from?'

'If they did, they weren't telling. What's more, they refused to return it.'

'*They can't do that!*'

'Apparently they can under the public health regulations. They said it was not empty and what remained was highly toxic.'

Julie pulled a large-scale map from the glove pocket and spread it across her knees. 'I had no idea the Ardennes forest was so enormous. It starts in France and stretches across Luxembourg and south-east Belgium into Germany.'

'It's rough country. Several thousand square miles of dense forest, marshes, mountains, caves and rivers'

'KKK could be almost anywhere.'

'So we have to narrow it down. Look at the eastern end of the forest. There is a section close to the Belgian borders with Luxembourg and Germany outlined in red. It's a Restricted Area.'

'For the military?'

'Maybe that is what KKK would like us to think.'

They skirted Namur and after they crossed the River Meuse, the Opel turned off. Julie took the wheel. She was worried. She was booked into the Falkenhayn that evening. 'A lot of the press will be there. My editor will be furious if I don't show up. They won't know where the hell I am.'

'It would be nice if one of us still had a job tomorrow,' said Scott gloomily.

She glanced at him. 'Are you serious?'

'Railton is being taken over by Fraser Outram. It's run by Jeff Turcan's brother. The good news is that they will keep the European side. But that doesn't help me. I'm out.'

'After all you've done for them!' She thumped the dashboard angrily. 'Go for him! Get your lawyers on to it! *Go for the whole lousy bunch!'*

He should have felt angry. It was strange but at that moment he didn't feel anything. Only a sort of numbness as if a limb had been amputated.

'There's something else, Scott, isn't there? Something you haven't told me?'

There was. Mary Seton had telephoned him. Chet Carling, the lawyer who looked after his father's affairs, had called her. The American Consulate had informed him that Warren had been killed in a car accident. They had given him no explanation for the delay, beyond saying that the police were still investigating. The information was to be treated in the strictest confidence.

'Carling told Mary that my father had left a letter to be given to me in the event of his death. I called him and asked him to put it in his office safe.'

'Why? You should have got him to read it or email it to you. It could explain everything.'

'Perhaps it does.'

'Scott, you aren't making sense.'

'I don't want to talk about it, Julie. I have a bad feeling about that letter . . . that's all.' Years ago, when he was hardly more than a child and his father was in one of those black depressions, Scott had gone to Mary Seton in tears convinced that he was in some way to blame. She had told him about the time when Warren was very ill with a raging fever.

In his tormented imagination, Warren was back at the legation in Budapest in command of the Marine Guard. A man with his wife and child had come to the gate of the compound. The boy had hair which glittered like frost and eyes which seemed to burn like live coals. The father had cursed him, called on the Fates to punish him, before he and his family were dragged off to prison.

In Scott's distress, perhaps it had helped to know that there were some things beyond the powers of a small boy to alter. In the past bleak days, he had found his mind casting round like a lost hound until it came back to the story of that curse. A hundred times he had told himself it was absurd. After all it was almost fifty years ago. Had his father been living in its shadow all those years? Was it something that his death did not finish? Had Warren written to him to warn him that he had come into a dark inheritance?

The road unravelled like a yellow ribbon in the headlights. A lorry went by in a whoosh of noise and slush. The wind snatched at a flurry of snow and whirled it away into the darkness.

They were on small roads now, driving through forest broken in places by snow-smothered clearings or desolate stretches of bog covered with rusty, wind-bent grass. Once they caught a glimpse of an abandoned farmhouse, its windows broken and sightless.

Julie glanced down at the notebook on Scott's knee. 'What do you need that for?'

'I wrote some figures in it.'

'A map reference? Why aren't you levelling with me?'

'It's just a hunch.'

'Then share it with me!'

Scott opened the back of the watch and held it under the interior light. 'The read-out hasn't changed.' He told her about his visit to Calvin Lecointe and the inscription they had found inside. 'Zaros's watch and my father's, the one that was grabbed off me by one of Muhlder's thugs in Zurich, are probably identical. I believe they both have a global positioning system. They talk to each other.'

Julie braked sharply and pulled up. She took the map from him and checked their position against the reference. Looking up, she pointed to a bright haze above the tree line. 'We are on the edge of that Restricted Zone. *Admit it!* That's where your father's watch is.' She glared at him accusingly.

'Then tell me how it got there,' he retorted angrily.

'It was probably stolen to order.'

'It was a street mugging. I just happened to be in the wrong place at the wrong time.'

'I don't believe it.' She switched off the lights and wound down the window. 'I think that whoever has your father's watch knows exactly where we are. We could be driving straight into a trap!'

'OK. So, now you know why I didn't want you to come.'

'Well, I'm here. Get used to the idea.'

'Then do what I tell you! Pull off the road and let's get the car under cover.'

They swung down a narrow ride and pulled in tight under the trees. They stripped some of the smaller branches for camouflage and checked their equipment. Flashlight. Night glasses. Wire-cutters.

Scott caught Julie's eyes on him.

He shrugged. 'OK. It's very amateurish but it's the best we can do'

They followed the line of the track, keeping just inside the trees. It was freezing hard, the air like splinters of ice in their nostrils. The haze ahead of them grew brighter with every step. They rounded the bend and crouched down in the cover of the overhanging branches.

Scott pulled the night glasses from his pocket. The barrier was less than a hundred yards away, a guard stamping his feet outside the hut, the barrel of a gun projecting from the line of his body.

'It's quite a set-up,' he whispered. 'Radio masts, satellite domes, aircraft hangars.' He passed her the glasses.

Julie took a deep breath. 'It's strange, but suddenly David seems very close.'

'Celtic intuition?'

'Please don't sneer.'

'I wasn't.'

Beyond the wire, a jeep came out of the glare and screeched to a halt in front of the hut. The driver jumped out and spoke to the guard. They ducked down instinctively, for the two men seemed to be staring straight at them. Then something caught the men's attention and they turned away.

They aimed for a point where the fence made a right angle turn and ran south along the line of watchtowers. It was slow going, the snow up to their knees in places, the branches plucking at their clothes at every step.

Julie caught his arm. 'This is hopeless. At this rate it will take us all night.'

Scott froze in mid-stride. She followed his eyes to where a glint of reflected light showed just inside the tree line. They traced the mast upwards, lost it among the foliage. Found it again. The sinister black hood seemed to be looking straight down at them. It moved, panning away forty-five degrees. Then stopped again. They held their breath.

It was fifteen seconds before it moved on. They stood motionless, shoulders hunched, huddled into their hoods, breathing the exhalations of their lungs, feeling their limbs grow stiff, their blood run sluggishly, closing their minds to the fear that they had already been seen. Then, choosing their moment, they crept deeper into the trees.

It took them almost an hour to reach the edge of the treeline close to the corner of the fence. Through the branches they could see a Sikorsky warming up in front of the hangars. A wisp of smoke drifted upwards from one of the buildings. From somewhere came the jangle of an alarm. Searchlights were sweeping the line of trees that ran along the western perimeter.

Scott's eyes followed the beams. 'My guess is that someone's made a break for it.'

'Do you think . . . that David's . . . got away?' She was almost incoherent, choking on the words.

He put his arms round her, held her until she was calmer. 'Don't get your hopes up, Julie. It's a very long shot.' He was wasting his breath. Julie had that feverish look he had seen before.

'*Scott!* Something tells me that it *is* David! We *must* find him before those devils do.' She took a step forward. A rabbit bolted from a clump of brushwood, crossed the track and ran straight into the fence. There was a brilliant blue flash. It leaped into the air and fell backwards into the snow, its legs quivering. A final convulsive twitch and it lay still.

'There goes your first casualty.' He had spoken more harshly than he meant but it had shaken him.

She stared at him white-faced. '*That's an awful thing to say!*'

He pulled her down as the edge of a beam leaked through the branches, washing everything in silver. The engine note of the helicopter rose to a shrill whine, drowning every other sound. It lifted off and headed out over the watchtowers.

He canted his head after it. 'If your brother got out, that's the way he went.'

She squeezed his hand. 'You think he got away. I know you do.' Her eyes were shining.

They worked their way left-handed, keeping under cover. The trees were not so thick now and they could only move in the dark intervals. It was snowing again. From behind them came the murmur of voices. Then an order being shouted. The yelp of a dog.

They crept into the shadow of a tree trunk as the beam swept back again. Julie felt Scott tense. As the twilight returned, he ran to where a contour in the snow had caught a sliver of light. Crouching down, he shuttered the torch with his fingers and examined the footprints in the pale pink glow.

'There's something odd about these.' The left foot had made deep grooves as if it was bearing the whole weight of the body. The right had scuffed the surface hardly breaking the crust.

Julie snatched the flashlight from him. 'It is David, isn't it?' She gave a little cry. 'And he's hurt!' She followed the trail for a few yards, keeping the torch low, then scuttled on again, pushing her way through low branches. She bent down. Her hand went to her throat and she tore the collar open and gulped in the freezing air. At the base of a tree trunk was a small depression where someone had stopped for a few moments to rest. Round it the snow was spotted with drops of blood.

The helicopter came flailing in low over the top of the trees. It made a wide arc to their left and began making methodical sweeps parallel with the line of the fence. Julie was kneeling in the snow, her breathing harsh and painful, her lips moving soundlessly. Scott took her arm and pulled her to her feet. They ran across a small clearing and cast about trying to pick up the trail but fresh-fallen snow had removed all traces of it.

The helicopter was close now, its ugly snout probing the darkness like a pig rooting for food. Julie pointed to a dead pine leaning against its neighbour. They scrambled into the hole at the base, wedging themselves under the ledge of earth and torn-up roots. It was coming in again, very low, a shadow against the winnowing snow. The tree creaked and groaned, lumps of earth pattered down on their heads and the snow crashed about them. As the beat of its engine faded, they crawled out. Julie stubbed her toe on something and went down. 'Watch out for that root!' she hissed.

'*Don't move!*' he brushed away the loose earth and stones round her feet. 'That's no root. It's some sort of cable. We better get out of here.'

Behind them, pinpoints of light were bobbing among the pines like fireflies. A stick snapped under a boot. A dog whimpered. With every step, the drifts were getting deeper. They struggled on to the edge of the trees and crawled under some low branches. Ahead of them was a firebreak some thirty yards wide. Beyond it nothing but the forest and the slanting snow, dashes of white on black as if an invisible hand were working over a huge canvas. Through the night glasses, the compacted surface of the track shone like polished jade. A movement caught his eye. There were men posted in the trees.

To their left, they could hear the rumble of a vehicle. At the far end of the firebreak, two pale yellow moons rounded the corner. The moons grew larger. A jeep rattled towards them, bouncing in and out of the rutted track, and slewed to a halt about twenty yards short of their hiding place. Two men in the back sat motionless, nursing their rifles between their knees. The driver climbed out and stamped his boots on the ground. He was a big man. Beside him the jeep looked like a toy.

He planted his feet astride and cupped his hands to his mouth.

'*Dixon!*' he bellowed, 'We know you're in there and we know you're hurt. You've lost a lot of blood. Give yourself up. You haven't got a chance.' He hitched at his gun belt.

Julie gave a little gasp and rammed her fist into her mouth to stop herself crying out.

'*Dixon!*' he shouted again. 'We have picked up your sister. If you don't come out I shall hand her over to my guards. *Don't make me do that, Dixon!*' He pushed up the peak of his cap and his eyes swept along the edge of the trees. 'I will give you exactly ten seconds . . . ' he started counting. 'One . . . two . . . '

There was a cry from somewhere.

'Three . . . four . . . '

'Wait!'

'*That was David!*' Julie dragged herself out of cover. '*David!*' she screamed.

'*Are you crazy!*' Scott threw himself on her, thrust her face down into the snow.

'Five . . . six . . . '

'*I'm coming out!*' Dixon stumbled from the cover of the trees. His movements were stiff and disjointed, one arm hoisted, clutching at the air as if to pull himself along, the other hauling a dragging leg by a blood-soaked rag.

Julie pushed herself to her knees. She wanted to shout a warning but her throat was contracting like the onset of paralysis. As the shot hit him, it seemed to spin him round. Through her blurred vision, David seemed to be running to meet her, his arm raised, his mouth open as if shouting a greeting; the crimson rose on his chest blossoming until there was nothing else in the whole world but that prodigal outpouring of life and her own despairing cry calling his name.

49

SCHLOSS FALKENHAYN

Schloss Falkenhayn was situated just inside Germany's border with Belgium and a short drive from the permanent exhibition site where Sharpshooter would open the next morning. The ancient fortress had been badly damaged in the last months of the Second World War and remained semi-derelict until it was purchased by a business consortium and rebuilt as a hotel and conference centre.

Use by members of the general public was discouraged. Once or twice a year, a small number of accredited journalists was added to a guest list made up of government officials, senior members of the armed forces and businessmen with close links to the Bundestag.

A drive of almost a mile through parkland led to a gatehouse where passes were inspected and vehicles checked before visitors were permitted to proceed under the stone archway and across the moated bridge. Here they would get their first uninterrupted view of the fortress with its towers and battlements before entering the galleried hall with its massive hearth and walls lined with Flemish tapestries.

The reception rooms were lavishly appointed in Biedermeier-style furniture, gilt-framed mirrors and oil paintings. There was a particularly fine Winterhalter in the drawing room. The accommodation on the four upper floors varied in standard from comfortable bedrooms to luxurious VIP suites.

It was well past midnight. Liam Maes, defence correspondent of Belgium's *De Standaard*, looked up at the long case clock as it chimed the half-hour. He was a slightly built man with a fair moustache and pale, restless eyes. Leaning back in his chair, he stretched his legs. 'I assume the same old hacks are here for Sharpshooter?'

Glen Holtz of the *New York Times* ran his fingers over a bluish jaw. 'Not Bailey. I'm told he smashed himself up skiing. The *Courier* is sending a girl. I haven't seen her yet.'

'What about Werner Mach from *Die Welt*?'

'His paper called him halfway through dinner. Apparently they are running a centre page exposé of a high-ranking German general who has been caught with his hand in the till.'

'Raoul Vasset from *Le Monde* is around somewhere.'

'The last time I saw that randy little Frenchman, he was in the bar chatting up Anna Giarda from the *Corriere*. I couldn't help wondering if their minds were solely occupied with defence matters.'

'Hers was,' replied Holtz and they both laughed. The smile left his face. 'Germany is in a very strange mood.'

Maes rattled the ice round in his glass. 'Pre-election nerves. That's all.'

'But no wavering from Muhlder. To hear him talk you would think he was already Chancellor.'

'Beer hall bombast. He won't get anywhere.'

'People said the same about Hitler.' Holtz drew on his cigarette and the lines on his forehead deepened. 'On the way here I drove through one of the garrison towns and stopped at a bar for a beer and a sandwich. The town was so quiet. The troops were all in barracks, the shops virtually empty. Then half a dozen bikers in black leathers came down the street, riding line abreast as if they owned the place.'

'No sign of the police?'

'They seem to have gone to ground. There was an old man at the next table. What was going on, I asked. Where was everybody? He fixed me with a sort of Messianic stare and raised his glass. His hand was trembling.'

'Too much German gin.'

'I wish I could believe that. He said he hadn't felt that way since the day he joined the Hitler Youth. I tell you, my friend, something is in the wind.'

His companion shook his head. 'Germany is important but it's still a side-show. There's a much bigger story out there. How close is your paper to the national intelligence agencies, to their agents in the field, in the streets, in the mosques, in the refugee camps, at prayer meetings?'

'Not as close as we would like. We have our contacts – NASA, GCHQ, NATO, the Russian Federal Security Service and others.

'Those organisations have one thing in common. They are scared to hell and back. There is a desperate shortage of hard intelligence but enough to indicate that dissident groups have been planning destruction on a scale that we haven't seen since the big bombing raids in the Second World War. They are reconnoitring major strategic targets – airports, power stations, railway and motorway hubs, telecommunications systems.'

'What have they got? Explosives? Nerve gas? It isn't that easy to bring a country to a full stop?'

'You heard about the airport extension in West Armenia. There's a rumour doing the rounds that the devastation was caused by a revolutionary new gun. The story is that it's a rail gun for use as an infantry weapon.'

'I don't believe it's possible.'

'We will soon know. The prototype is being demonstrated at Sharpshooter.'

'Even if does everything claimed for it, it will never be used. It will be like the hydrogen bomb. The nuclear countries will buy it up and lock it away.'

'I wish I could believe that. I wish like hell I could believe that.'

Glen Holtz turned and looked round the room. 'Pavel Gribov has disappeared.'

Maes fished in his pockets for his cigarettes. 'He had to take a call from *Izvestia*. That was twenty minutes ago.' A flame ran from his thumb as he snapped the lighter and lit up. 'There is a flap on in Russia. Does the name DIDO mean anything to you? And I don't mean the Queen of Carthage.'

Holtz raised his eyebrows. 'Those rumours that JFK set up a secret fund – all in bearer bonds – at the height of the Cold War. They've been doing the rounds for years.'

'Well, pin your ears back. The latest rumour is that the Russians have copies of the bonds.'

The drone of a helicopter came to them, the sound growing in volume and setting the glass pendants tinkling in the chandelier above them.

Pavel Gribov burst into the room. 'I must get back to Berlin at once,' he said. He had been drinking and his speech was slurred. 'Our military attaché has received some extraordinary documents. Anonymously. He flew straight to Moscow. They are being examined by our Federal Security Council. All our ambassadors have been recalled for consultation. This could mean war.'

Maes nudged back the curtain and watched Pavel stride out of the castle. The helicopter touched down as lightly as a dragonfly on a lily pad, picked him up and clattered away into the darkness. 'Europe is sitting on a powder keg,' he muttered. 'Just one spark . . . that's all it takes . . . and this could be it.'

50

KK KEMIKAL

The cell was as cold as a tomb. Concrete floor and walls. The only source of light a grubby ceiling bulb covered with wire mesh. A thin trickle of blood ran from the corner of Scott's mouth. He pointed to the only object inside the room, a rectangular stone block against the wall. 'Is that a bed or a sofa?'

Julie gazed at it blankly. 'I don't know anything any more. All I know is that David is dead and it was my fault.'

'It wasn't. They would have—' he checked himself abruptly.

'Shot him anyway?' she turned on him, her eyes wild with misery. 'We shall never know! Not now!'

He grabbed her by the shoulders. 'Hold on, Julie! We're not finished yet.'

She pushed him away and shuffling across the floor to the heavy steel door stood with her forehead pressed against it, her eyes tight closed. 'David was going to give himself up. Until I shouted. Then he saw me. He was running towards me when they shot him.'

'It wasn't like that, Julie!'

'It *was* like that!' She banged her head against the cold metal. 'I can't get it out of my mind. A man called Rohr killed him. Pieter Rohr.'

'Made like a mountain gorilla?'

'That's the one.'

'I blame myself. If I had put the watch in the bank, none of this—'

'It wasn't the watch. I called to David. If only I had kept quiet, he might have stood a chance!' Her fists pounded on the door until the cell rang with the sound.

A guard hammered back, cursing them in an unintelligible tongue. Julie slid down the wall and sat on the floor, her head between her hands.

From outside came the throaty roar of a big engine, then the screech of a tracked vehicle turning. Scott went to the tiny, barred window. A big tank was climbing up a ramp on to a transporter. He turned. The tramp-tramp of boots was coming down the passage. A key rattled in the lock. A guard thrust open the door. 'Hold out hands!' he ordered in a harsh, guttural voice that was just recognisable as English.

They hesitated. '*Do it!*' he yelled. Two more guards appeared in the doorway. He snapped the cuffs about their wrists.

The guards escorted them down a long corridor to a lift that took them up several floors to the amphitheatre. The room was in semi-darkness. In the beam of the projector they could make out rows of tiered seats and a scattering of people in white coats who might have been medical or laboratory staff. The guards pushed them down into seats right at the back and stood on either side of them.

Scott felt a sudden chill. The hairs rose on the back of his neck. It was as if a panel behind him had been silently slid aside and someone was staring at him. As he turned his head, he caught a glimpse of a man's face. It seemed to slip out of focus and withdraw into the shadows.

A tall man with sallow features was standing at the lectern. He had looked up for a moment as they entered and continued without pausing. 'The developments of the past few hours have provided us with an exceptional opportunity to move our research forward in an area which is of great importance to our work.' He pressed a button on the lectern.

On the screen beside him the torso of a man appeared. His lower limbs, blackened and charred, looked like the remains of a log fire.

'Pain,' said Snoeck, 'is inseparable from the human condition but scientists, even the most eminent,' he gave a self-deprecating cough, 'know surprisingly little about it. The subject in this photograph was anaesthetised and the lower half of his body exposed to very high temperatures for a period of almost an hour.'

'*You devils!*' Julie cried out. 'You abducted my brother and forced him to work on that poison.'

'*Silence!*' the guard bawled. He slapped her across the mouth with the back of his hand.

'*Leave her alone!*' Scott yelled. He struggled to his feet but two guards forced him down into the chair and held him while the third ran a band of adhesive tape across his mouth.

Snoeck ignored the interruption. 'The subject was a man in his sixties. He was terminally ill. A substantial sum of money was paid to his relatives.' He pressed a button again. An anatomical diagram showing the human body in cross section appeared on the screen. He pointed in turn to each of the layers in turn. Epidermis, corium, fat, fascia, muscle and finally bone.

'Pain receptors,' he continued, 'in the skin and other tissues are excited by mechanical, chemical or, in this case, thermal stimuli. That the subject experienced no pain for a period of over forty minutes demonstrates the remarkable properties of the new drug.' His eyes shone with excitement. 'I have high hopes that tomorrow's experiment will yield important new data.

'One last point. The drug will be in a liquid form but it can be readily converted into powder or gas. As a gas, it has considerable potential in the field of crowd control. The Combat Units are pressing hard to be allowed to use it in advance of licensing as part of the programme of field trials required by the regulatory authorities.'

He crossed the platform to the window, peered through the venetian blind and gave a little nod of satisfaction before returning to the lectern. A graphic of a tank interior flashed up on the screen. 'Most of you will have heard of our new gun. The KRG will be making its debut at Sharpshooter. Up against the KRG will be a main battle tank protected by armour that is a generation ahead of its time. For the purposes of our research, the tank will be equipped with monitoring equipment so that the effects of extreme temperatures on organs and tissue can be relayed to the command vehicle.'

The lights went up. While Snoeck took questions, a member of the medical staff was laying out on a table hypodermic syringes, swabs and a phial containing a clear liquid. It was exactly one-thirty in the morning.

51

THE *COURIER*

Duggie Bains was asleep in his terraced house in Spitalfields, in London's East End, when the night editor called him.

'Give me that again, Vince.' The hail was beating against the window, making it difficult to hear. He listened for ten seconds, then cut him short. 'I want Chris and Jock in my office in thirty minutes. And you had better pull in the senior leader writer.' With his foot he prodded the recumbent form beside him into wakefulness.

'*Duggie!*' the girl wailed, blinking at him through her tousled yellow mane. '*It's the middle of the night for fuck's sake.*'

'I'm sorry, Gail, but I haven't time to explain. Make some coffee while I get some clothes on. I want it black and hot – and then I want you out of here.'

The table in Bains' office was strewn with papers and empty mugs. The meeting was two hours old and nothing had happened to improve his temper. He went to the window and his fingers crackled down the slats of the venetian blind. 'Julie never showed up at the Schloss Falkenhayn. The *New York Times*, *Die Welt*, *Le Monde* and the rest were all there. She's made us look like a bunch of tossers.'

'We have the photos and the profiles of some of the main players.'

'I know, Chris,' Bains snapped, 'but we need someone on the spot. Things are moving so fast. What sticks in my craw is that until our man gets out there we shall have to feed off the wires.'

The eyes of the four men ran down the screens. The German Press Agency carried a report of the suicide of Generalmajor Herman Stier. His secretary, Sonja Peetsch, had admitted photographing his bank statements and sending them to the editor of *Die Welt* but had claimed that she was only doing her duty as a patriot.

Russia's Security Council was studying a set of documents which, it said, emanated from the White House and posed the gravest threat to peace in decades.

'Look at this!' hissed Bain. *Breaking news*: *The defence secretaries of the NATO countries together with Russia, Israel, Iran, China, India, Pakistan and Korea have cancelled all engagements at short notice to watch a demonstration of a new infantry weapon at Sharpshooter. The exhibition is to be formally opened at 0900 hours by Daan Brouckmans, the Belgian Minister of Defence.*

In Russia there are reports of ground troops massing on the Polish border.

52

THE DRIVE TO SHARPSHOOTER

Julie awoke with a scream that only she could have heard. A tape ran across her mouth. Her wrists and ankles were bound tight, the length of cord between them making it impossible to stretch her legs. She felt giddy with nausea although whether from the drug or the rocking of the truck she couldn't tell.

Using her elbows and feet she slithered across the floor until she made contact with something hard. A box of some kind. Laboriously she manoeuvred herself into a sitting position and laid her cheek against the wall of her prison. Metal boxes. Boxes with lifting handles. Boxes piled one on top of the other. She tilted back her head and sniffed. The odour of some thick, heavy material above her.

Something close to her shifted. She froze, her heart hammering. Someone breathing. Scott? But supposing it wasn't. The clatter of nailed boot studs on the wooden floor. The cover was thrown back. A rush of cold air on her face. A blinding light in her eyes. The torch swept over her and darted away. *Scott!* Tied up like her. Walled in by ammunition boxes.

'Visscher!' Someone called out from the cab.

Their guard turned his head. In the half-light Julie could see the lips drawn back to expose stained and broken teeth, the beard running round the line of the jaw like a black scar.

The truck was slowing. The cover was thrown over them again but it was done hurriedly. Julie could still see Scott slumped against the gun-metal glimmer of the boxes. The driver shifted gear and they came to a stop.

A window was being wound down. Someone speaking French. Asking for documents. The rustle of paper. The screech of a tracked vehicle close by.

Visscher's name called again. Booted feet coming down the road along the side of the truck. The guard grumbling as he moved to the tailgate and dropped to the ground.

Scott had managed to sit up. He tapped with his heels on the floor to get Julie's attention. He was rolling over on to his back . . . rocking his body to and fro like a cradle . . . his boots tapping the metal with each forward movement. *Idiot that she was!* Why hadn't she thought of that? She swivelled about and tried the same trick. Rocked back . . . too far . . . just a clumsy half somersault. Grinding her teeth with frustration she tried again. This time she made contact but she couldn't put any force into it.

The driver revved the engine impatiently. The sound of returning feet. The man at the checkpoint had seen enough. A tap on the side of the cab. Their guard climbed aboard once more. The truck moved forward again. Julie could see Scott's eyes. He was thinking what she was. That a chance had gone. That there might not be another.

Kraik and Rohr were being driven to Sharpshooter in the company's armoured command vehicle. It was fitted out with banks of television screens and communication equipment. The television showed a huge crowd packed into Berlin's Potsdamer Platz, waiting for Wolfgang Muhlder. There came a great cheer as his motorcade could be seen approaching.

The black Mercedes, pennants flying, was accompanied by outriders from the Siegfried Combat Group who had the honour of providing the escort. Muhlder leaped out before the vehicle stopped and walked through the throng, shaking hands and waving to his supporters.

His white open-neck shirt and suede jacket made a startling contrast with the heavy coats and mufflers of the throng. It was as if he alone were impervious to the bitter cold. As he climbed up to the platform to another barrage of flashbulbs, the combat group formed a square round him facing the crowd.

Muhlder stretched his arms wide in an appeal for silence and a hush fell over his audience.

'*Kameraden!*' he cried, 'We Ostis have been very patient. Year after year, we have stood by and watched while non-Germans in their millions poured across our frontiers taking our jobs, our housing, filching the very bread from the mouths of those least able to defend themselves.'

This was greeted with a roar from the crowd and the chanting began: 'Muhlder! Muhlder! Muhlder!'

Muhlder paused for a moment and his eyes seemed to stare into their very souls. '*Kameraden!* When the wall came down, they told us that everything would be different. The poverty, the squalid tenement blocks, the polluted lakes, the dying forests, the wasteland of concrete and rusting iron that was our inheritance. All would all be swept away.' He lowered his head and glared at them. With his massive shoulders and bunched fists he looked like a fighting bull on the point of charging. '*Kameraden!*' he bellowed. '*They lied to us!*'

'Muhlder! Muhlder! Muhlder!' rumbled across the Platz like thunder.

'*Kameraden!* The time for talking is past. *The time has come to act.*'

Kraik gestured to Rohr to turn off the programme. 'What are you doing about Dixon? I don't want any loose ends.'

'There won't be. When I reported him missing, I said that we have had problems with snoopers and that Dixon was worried about agents of Russian Intelligence. I used the Makarov. When they find his body, they will find a Russian bullet in it.'

'Excellent. Now what can you tell me about the formation of the new Militia.'

'Tonight,' replied Rohr, 'there will be widespread disturbances and destruction of property among immigrant communities. The German Federal Police Force is already overstretched. They will have to ask for help. The Combat Units will be in the areas affected at first light and will restore order. Muhlder has booked air time on all the main TV channels. He will announce that, in response to the emergency, these units will form the new German People's Militia. They will have the task of imposing discipline throughout the country and policing the borders.'

Kraik went to a safe in the corner of the cabin. He took out two half-hunter watches. Opening one of these, he went to the miniature keyboard on the inner leaf and logged in a series of numerals and letters. In the readout panel, the figure of $1,075, 436, 289 flashed up.

'A little over a billion dollars,' murmured Kraik. 'The DIDO fund is held by a consortium of Swiss banks. It has been competently invested over the years. I have decided to allow Wetzlar and Muhlder to draw on it up to a total of five hundred million dollars. At twelve noon today, I will make the first transfer.

'Stier is dead and discredited. Wetzlar will use the man's disgrace to purge the senior ranks of the army of anyone who opposes him. He will replace them with his own men and equip the Bundeswehr with the KRG gun. Copies of the DIDO bonds are now in the hands of the Russians.

'Their Defence Minister has stated that Russian has given up control of 700,000 square miles of territory of which more than half has gone to the NATO bloc. He claims that the DIDO fund will be used to finance the installation of missile sites in Poland, Turkey and Ukraine. This, he warns, could lead to war.'

'The Americans could say that the fund has been stolen.'

'They wouldn't dare. It would make them a laughing stock.'

'The Russians are bluffing. Sabre rattling.'

'Hardly that. They are mobilising thirty divisions. Ground troops will be on their western frontiers by nightfall.'

'Kraik! *You have overplayed your hand!*'

314

'I think not. All the pieces are falling into place. Muhlder needs the backing of the army and he needs money. By twelve noon today, he will have both. He will call for the Bundestag to postpone the elections. Before the day ends, he will be Chancellor at the head of an emergency government.'

'You have promised the KRG to Wetzlar but it is only a prototype. Detonard will need millions to manufacture it.'

'They will have all the money they want. When the US, the Russians, NATO and the others have seen what the gun can do, they will pay us billions of dollars to keep the weapon out of the hands of their enemies.'

'When will elections be held?'

'There will be no more elections. Germany will be ruled by a military junta. Wetzlar regards the reverses at the end of the Second World War as just unfinished business. Germany will regain her lost empire.'

'What about the Russians?'

'Have you ever seen a pack of wolves pull down a bear? I have. The Russians have many enemies. The Chechens, the Uzbeks, the Tajiks and others. They may be small in size but, acting in unison, they are very dangerous. The threat that their fighters will be armed with the KRG will be enough to keep the Russian bear on its chain.'

'And the United States?'

'The country has grown weary of being the world's policeman. Foreign adventures have sapped its strength. The US will retreat to Fortress America and pull up the drawbridge. Germany will be the next global superpower. In 1940 they had the best army in the world. But for the follies of their leaders, nothing could have stood in their way.'

'You are trying to turn the clock back sixty years. *It cannot be done!*'

'It *is* being done. The Germans will be masters of every foot of soil between the Urals and the shores of the Atlantic. That is my will. That is their destiny.'

The vehicle slowed. Kraik moved to the window and stared out across the ranges to the line of national flags. In his mind, he was standing at his father's side during the chaos of that night almost fifty years before. The night that he and his family, in their desperation, had come knocking on the door of sanctuary only to be turned away and condemned to the living death of the Soviet gulags. The night that his father had denounced his betrayer. The night that his son had bound himself by the same oath and vowed to hunt down the Rokeby family and destroy them.

How far he, Kraik, had travelled since that that night. A Titan among pygmies. That is how history would view him. Kraik, the man who set a torch to the ragged jigsaw pieces of the old world and wrote his name in letters of fire across the new.

53

SHARPSHOOTER

The day had dawned cold and grey. The flags on the long line of poles hung listlessly in the still air. The mist rising from the fields would take hours to clear, while the frost like a thin coating of salt would be there all day. Even before it was fully light, traffic was heavy on the approach roads. Security vetting was tight and queues of visitors were already beginning to form.

Blue haze hung in the air where armoured vehicles were rumbling off trailers and moving to hangars in fenced compounds. On the outside stands, sales staff could be seen racking brochures and engineers checking telephone lines. An Apache helicopter was being unsheeted and manoeuvred into position. In the hospitality tents, tables and chairs were being set out, bottles unpacked and glasses given a final polish.

Visitors, some in uniform, were climbing the broad flight of steps that led to the main entrance and passing through to the reception area. In the packed atrium, people were standing in groups, discussing the latest news. A leading politician calling for Wolfgang Muhlder's rally in Berlin to be cancelled had been assaulted and taken to hospital.

Stewards had to call repeatedly for silence before they moved to their seats. Daan Brouckmans, the Belgian Minister of Defence was in earnest conversation with his German opposite number. An aide whispered in his ear and he came to the stand. The square jaw cracked open in a genial smile but his eyes were troubled.

'I am not here to make a political speech, ladies and gentleman,' he began, 'but to welcome you to Sharpshooter, an exhibition which has acquired the well-merited reputation of being the showcase of the international defence industry. Whatever your field, government, military or commercial, whatever your interest, weapons and munitions, intelligence and command systems or police and security equipment, here at Sharpshooter you will find the latest and the best.'

He paused to clear his throat before continuing. 'This exhibition takes place against a background of unrest in Germany and levels of tension in Europe not seen for decades. In the testing days that lie ahead I ask our friends in the media to show restraint in their reporting of the present difficulties.

'The German Defence Minister has asked me to use this platform to state what should need no reminder, that the modern Bundeswehr is under the political control of a democratically elected government. Far from posing a threat, her armed forces are dedicated to preserving peace and freedom.'

His eyes swept round the room before dropping to the papers in his hand. In a few words he thanked the exhibitors for their support and the organisers and staff for their hard work under exceptionally trying circumstances. 'I conclude by wishing all our visitors an enjoyable and successful exhibition.'

Several members of the audience jumped to their feet with raised hands but the Minister pleaded a busy schedule and aides hurried him away. Sharpshooter was officially open.

Giant marquees were crammed with exhibitors' stands selling every type of military equipment, intelligence and surveillance systems. Mike Saxon and Sam Coaker distanced themselves from their technical staff and found a deserted corner of a tent.

Saxon leafed through the index at the back of the catalogue. 'The International Arms Consortium is not on the list.'

'IAC don't work like that,' replied Coaker. 'They are so big they would need a marquee to themselves but they keep a very low profile.

The parent company KKK are brokers in industrial chemicals. That operation provides a useful smokescreen. Detonard, their subsidiary, has a stand here. They will make the KRG. If the prototype does what they claim—'

'We will hang our heads in shame.'

'OK, Mike. We should have got there first. So we must deal with the fall-out. First, the Russians.'

'They will back down. After today, it won't be difficult to persuade them that the main threat does not come from the USA but from their own backyard.'

'What about the President?'

'We can expect to be roasted over a slow fire. The Treasury is reserving billions of dollars to keep the rail gun out of the hands of terrorists. If we could say that we have brought the DIDO fund back home, it would be our get-out-of-jail card. Have you heard from Leah Stein?'

'Yes. She spoke to Canton this morning. Swiss banks are tight-lipped as clams but he has discovered that the trustees have lost control of DIDO.'

'*Hell!* Does he know the identity of the new owners?'

'No.' Sam Coaker looked at his watch. 'Eleven o'clock. It's time we moved to the range. I hope that bloody gun blows up and takes KKK, IAC and Detonard with it!'

Rohr hadn't walked twenty paces before he was stopped by a young man in service dress. He saluted and introduced himself as Captain Neame. 'ADC to General Sir Horace Milne . . . '

' . . . Commander Permanent Joint HQ Northwood.' Rohr finished the recital for him. He looked the young man up and down. His hair was too long. Why did the Household Brigade turn out officers who looked more like male models than soldiers?

319

'Absolutely.' Neame was disconcerted by this mountain of a man. 'Sir Horace is right behind me,' he continued, rather flustered. 'There is an urgent matter that he wishes to discuss. Is there somewhere we can talk privately?'

'No. I'm pressed for time.'

General Milne was bearing down on them. He was a short, thick-set man with a brisk, no-nonsense manner. 'Pieter Rohr . . . ' he thrust out his hand. 'I can see you're busy so I shall be brief. I will be at the demo of this new gun of yours. So will our top technical chaps. If it does one half of what you fellows claim—'

'I am confident that it will do exactly what we claim. I presume that you have seen the film?'

'I have, as have my colleagues at the MOD. If recent reports can be believed, so have a ragbag of disaffected hotheads that I would not trust with a box of matches let alone a supergun.'

'I cannot comment on that.'

The general's eyes narrowed. 'Is it true that the KRG could revolutionise warfare?'

Rohr shrugged. 'You will be attending the demonstration. You must make up your own mind.' He glanced at his watch. 'Now, if you will excuse me . . . '

'Hang on a moment, Pieter Rohr.' The General rubbed the back of his neck to mask his irritation. This wasn't the way he liked to negotiate. Lunch at his club or over a round of golf at the Royal Berkshire was the way to do these things. Life had taught him that if you couldn't browbeat a man into seeing things your way you could usually flatter him. 'We would like to keep this new toy of yours in the family, if you take my meaning.'

Rohr turned back to him, frowning. 'I'm not sure that I understand you, General.'

Bloody mercenary. Of course Rohr knew what he was getting at. 'I think you do,' he retorted, fighting to control his temper. 'If pariah states or terrorist groups got hold of the KRG, it could make a nonsense of the Allies' entire defence strategy.'

Rohr spread his hands. 'We have invited sealed bids from selected parties. That includes the United Kingdom. The envelopes will be opened by my chairman at twelve noon. Beyond that, I can tell you nothing.'

'It is extortion! Protection money!'

'I did not say that.'

'Well, I did. My understanding is that we will not be offered the KRG. We will be railroaded into paying huge sums to keep it out of the hands of terrorist organisations.'

'You will find that it is a good investment.'

'What guarantee have we that the gun will not end up with these fanatics? It has been reported to me that representatives of these groups are here today. From Somalia, Pakistan, Iraq, Afghanistan, Syria, Lebanon, West Africa, Colombia . . . '

'It would surprise me if they were not.'

'So the UK can go to hell in a handcart for all you care?'

'In a word. Yes.'

The General flushed with anger. 'I advise you to tread carefully. We are not wholly without influence.'

Rohr snapped his fingers. 'That is how I rate UK influence. You Brits dropped out of the big league fifty years ago and you are still on the slide. The Gulf War was your last shout. Without the US you couldn't even keep your trousers up.' He turned on his heel and strode off up the hall.

General Milne, quite cool again now, rubbed his chin thoughtfully. He had given the man fair warning. Rohr should reflect that the British, whatever their shortcomings, sometimes meant rather more than they said. He and his colleagues would be wise to co-operate. Or else. But 'or else' wasn't his department.

54

INTO THE TANK

The cover was thrown back and a pair of arms reached down and pulled Julie up off the floor. She was carried to the tailboard, handed to another and dumped on the ground. She was so cold and cramped, she wondered that the blood was still running in her veins. The glint of a knife. Her heart turned over. Then a tug at her wrists and ankles and the sound of a blade ripping through cord. Her hands were still bound but the relief of having the use of her legs again! She hobbled forward. The hangar smelt of oil and rubber and machinery.

The tank looked huge. On the rear deck there was a man standing impassively. Waiting for her. She was lifted up and half-dragged, half-carried to the turret. As she was lowered into the hatch, she caught a glimpse of Scott. He was on the ground with two men bent over him.

A pair of hands seized her and let her slide inch by inch into the dimly lit interior. The man divided her legs with his body, pressing her back against the turret wall, the sour smell of him rising like steam from his damp vest.

'My name is Zdrarko,' he chuckled. 'Everyone know Zdrarko.'

A gust of air against her cheek. The loader's hatch had been opened. With a muttered curse, he pushed her from him. A knife appeared in his hand. He turned her round and slashed through the cords. She heard a clink of steel. A handcuff with a length of chain attached was snapped on her right wrist.

Zdrarko pointed at a small space on the turret floor to the left of the breech block. '*Down there!*' He fixed her with his black eyes until she was in position, paying out the chain, swinging the free end in a warning not to give him any trouble. The sound of booted feet on the metal deck. Zdrarko turned and grabbed a pair of ankles as they came down through the commander's hatch. Scott had come to join her.

Rohr watched the KRG being sheeted up in the back of the jeep. Snoeck took the wheel. Beside him was Drucker, the gunner. 'I should have liked to make the presentation,' Snoeck complained. 'I was in charge of the final trials.'

'I want a slick, professional job,' replied Rohr curtly. 'Crespel is the man to do it. Controlling the tank remotely is of the first importance. You know exactly what to do. Park beside the weapons pit. Make sure that the radio is operating on the top line and that Drucker has got everything he needs. Kraik and I will follow in the command vehicle. Report to me every five minutes.'

A few moments later both vehicles were on the range, lurching and bumping on the rough ground. Somewhere behind him, Rohr could hear the throaty roar of the tank starting out for the demonstration area. A red flag was being run up the pole.

Zdrarko had shut the twin hatches above Scott's and Julie's heads and left them chained together. There was a rumble from the engine, a screech of tracks on the concrete and they were pulling out of the hangar.

Scott ripped the tape from his mouth. '*Give me more chain!*' he yelled. He clambered up on to the commander's seat. If he could lift one of the hatches they might have a chance. But it was hopeless. Heaving with all his strength they did not shift at all. He peered through the periscope-like instrument in front of him. The tank was following a wide concrete road lined with fir trees. Suddenly it stopped. They were at the entrance to the ranges.

'The driver is getting out,' he muttered 'Walking away.' The engine revved. They were off again. He stared at Julie. '*What the hell is going on?*'

Julie was searching the bins round the turret wall. 'The systems must be remote controlled in some way.'

'You mean that a radio is driving this thing?'

'I reckon so.' Her voice was barely steady.

'Then it's time we started digging ourselves out of this tin can.' He jumped down to the turret floor. 'First we need to find some tools.'

Julie slammed the last bin shut. 'There aren't any.'

'Not even a pair of pliers?'

'A grease-gun. That's all.'

'Are you saying we can't even get at the wiring?'

'What with? Our teeth?'

'So what do we do! *Sit here and fry!*' In his frustration he yanked at the chain that ran from his wrist to hers.

'Don't do that! *It hurts!*'

'If you think that hurts, stick around here and find out what —'

'Belt, up Scott!' Julie took a deep breath. 'We may not have much time, so listen. I've been in one of these things years ago.'

Scott groaned. 'Back in the steam age. How do you think that can help?'

'The systems will have been updated but the basics haven't changed. A tank still comes in two big chunks – the hull and the turret. The driver sits in the hull. The rest of the crew – commander, gunner and loader – are in the turret. The floor is just a big turntable so that the gun,' she pointed at the massive gun cradle that separated them, 'can be aimed in any direction.'

'What about the ammo bins? Are they all part of this merry-go-round?'

She nodded. 'But the wall behind is part of the hull. It doesn't move with the turret.' She pulled at an electrode pad at the base of her neck. A red light flickered on a metal box attached to the wall by two steel brackets. It was probably a relay unit. What was happening to them was just data, peaks and troughs to some twisted bastard gloating over a screen.

'And those?' He jerked a thumb at the red buttons beside him.

'Smoke grenades.'

'They won't help us get out.' The tank was slowing. Scott raised his eyes to the scope again. A jeep towing a trailer was making its way towards them.

Julie was on hands and knees examining the front of the turret wall.

'There must be some way we can get to the driver's compartment. I ... do not ... understand.' She growled her frustration. 'This was how I did it last time. The driver got out of the hatch in front and I crawled through.'

'That was last time,' said Scott brusquely. The massive breech block was in the way. They were sealed in.

55

THE FIRING RANGES

The observers leaving the buses were made up of politicians, civil servants, businessmen, scientists, high-ranking officers and weapons systems experts. Most of them were in heavy coats, some in cloth caps and anoraks. The uniforms of armed services of twenty-four countries were represented.

They walked to a rise in the ground that provided a view of about a mile over the heath. Rohr in his combat fatigues was waiting for them. At his side stood a tall man with steel grey hair brushed back without a parting. In his dark suit with the broad chalk stripe, he made a striking contrast with his companion.

Pieter Rohr was well known to many of them. He greeted them in a few words before introducing the recently appointed Vice President of Detonard. 'My colleague, Laurent Crespel, will be giving a brief presentation on the KRG before the demonstration.' For those not familiar with his career he outlined the senior appointments that Crespel had held in the defence industry.

'Before I hand over to him, I must remind everyone here that it is not permitted to take photographs or to use recording equipment. I make no apology for excluding a few of our guests whose ingenuity was not quite equal to that of our scanning equipment.'

Rohr expressed regret that at this early stage it was not possible to release a detailed specification of the KRG. 'World-wide patent applications covering certain areas of the weapon's capability have been registered only recently so you will understand the need for reticence.' He concluded on a lighter note. 'At the end of the demonstration there will be an opportunity for you to ask your questions . . . and for me to decide whether to answer them.' There was no laughter. He gestured to Crespel to take over.

'What you are going to see,' Crespel began, 'is a man-portable, shoulder-fired infantry weapon capable of destroying a main battle tank and its crew with a single projectile. The tank is at the leading edge technically. It is equipped with explosive reactive armour to provide additional protection against a kinetic energy missile and to reduce penetration capability.

'The KRG has a sophisticated guidance and control system and an underslung battery. This is the weapon that experts told us was still several decades away. Others claimed that it belongs to the realm of science fiction. What is certain is that if our parent company had not had the vision and resources to step in and provide the funding when Detonard ran out of money we should not be standing here today.'

In a few words, he sketched in the history of the KRG explaining that the extraordinary power was made possible by a giant leap in battery technology and in the development of a new alloy capable of dissipating the frictional heat caused by the high muzzle velocity. He then invited his audience to gather round the screen mounted on the side the truck.

Crespel clicked a button on his remote control and the speakers crackled into life. 'This short film that you are about to watch was made at our research establishment under the direction of their head of department, Ulrich Snoeck.'

The screen filled with a diagram of a metal box in cross section, first showing the thick walls and then a close-up view. 'The mice inside the scale model,' the commentary continued, 'do not have the same enhanced protection as the tank but the walls consist of the same high-strength plastics bonded into the composite armour. What you are going to watch first is the result of a Barrett rifle with a standard muzzle velocity fired at point-blank range.' An AP bullet could be seen in slow motion trailing airwaves and ricocheting harmlessly off the armour.

'Now for a kinetic round.' The camera panned to a short length of tubular steel held in a vice. Wires ran from it to a console. A hand could be seen flicking a switch . . . then the bullet appeared in flight . . . its nose changing shape . . . the moment of impact . . . metal pouring from the hole like molten lava from the mouth of a volcano . . . the shapes of the mice against a dazzling brilliance . . . then the screen went blank.

For some moments there complete silence. 'We lost a lot of cameras filming that,' Crespel laughed to break the tension.

'Not to mention the mice,' somebody joked.

There was a babble of excited comment but many remained silent, their expressions grim. Crespel folded his heavy black-rimmed glasses. 'If you train your binoculars on to the flagpole with the red flag, you will see a weapons pit. The KRG gunner is in position and Ulrich Snoeck is in the jeep with the radio equipment.'

Heads were turning the other way. From behind and to their right came the rumble of a heavy tank on the move. Crespel concluded his briefing on the tank's design and performance. He finishing by saying, 'For firepower, mobility and survivability this tank would be a world beater. But the KRG, as we shall demonstrate, will make it and its kind as obsolete as the old cavalry charger.'

In the exhibition brochure, there was a description of the scope of the demonstration:

The tank will be driverless and will be controlled by radio. It will follow an oval course moving between fixed waypoints. On the first lap it will maintain a speed of approximately 30 mph (48 kph).

The main armament is a 125mm gun. This will be traversed to different positions during the demonstration. As the tank comes past for the first time, this gun will be aimed directly at the observers. In the weapons' pit, the gunner will be firing at it with a semi-automatic rifle using red tracer at a range of 800 yards (731 metres). This will provide a useful demonstration of the effectiveness of the laser sight when locked on to a moving target.

The tank will be in dead ground for a short period at the end of the first lap. On the second, the speed will be cut by half to give observers the opportunity to watch the tank at the moment it is hit by the KRG projectile.

The tank came into view, the roar of its engine carrying clearly in the still, cold air. A pale gleam of sunshine glinted off the grey-green camouflaged surfaces before the clouds closed over again. It stopped. A vehicle towing a trailer appeared from a belt of pine trees and drew up alongside. Two men got out and could be seen unloading a sheep from the trailer.

Crespel broke in on the thoughts of many of those watching. 'We all regret the necessity of using live animals to simulate the crew but there is no realistic alternative. War is a serious business. A dead crew is a crew that will not fight again.'

The sheep was led by a rope to the tank, lifted on to the deck, lowered inside and the hatch cover closed once more.

For a few minutes, Rohr fielded questions on the KRG. No, the company was not prepared to discuss pricing or licensing. No, a full specification would not be made available until all the patents were in place. Yes, he did realise that the world was a dangerous place. If it were not, men like him would be out of work. No, he was not prepared to discuss politics.

'When can we inspect the tank?' The questioner in a tweed cap and anorak had a broad Scots accent and was chewing on a pipe stem.

'I do not know what you expect to find,' replied Rohr, 'but, after a few minutes to allow the dust cloud to clear, you will be permitted to move to the site where the tank was engaged by the KRG.'

Rohr spoke into his mobile. The tank moved forward again, a spurt of blue smoke coming from its exhaust as it picked up speed. Drucker lowered his eye to the laser sight.

56

UNDER FIRE

As the tank moved forward, the sheep darted from its hiding place under the breech block almost knocking Julie off her feet. It cowered against the wall of the hull, its flanks heaving with fear.

'The poor creature is terrified!'

'That's one smart sheep for you,' Scott grunted as he peered through the scope. They were following a muddy track between low scrub and gorse. Some two hundred yards ahead it dipped but reappeared again at the top of the next rise. '*What the hell!*' The gun was traversing and a whole new panorama was coming into view.

'For God's sake, Scott! What can you see?'

'Buildings, tents . . . '

'How far away?'

'About half a mile.' A muzzle flash. Just a bright spark . . . then a red parabola arcing towards them.

'Tracer! *Get down!*' The bullets bounced off the armour like hailstones on a tin roof.

'*Scott!*' Something ricocheted round the walls like a demented hornet and fell spinning to the turret floor. She bent down to pick up the spent shell.

'*Don't touch it!* It must be red hot!'

'The breech is wide open!'

'*Then close it!* That bullet must have come straight down the barrel.'

Julie wrestled with the handle. '*I can't move it!*'

'Shove something up it!'

Her fingers scrabbled round the turret wall. A steel box came away from its mounting.

'There's only this . . . ' She struggled with it. 'It won't fit. It's too big.'

'Forget it, Julie.' The firing had stopped. The turret was on the move again. Scott glued his eyes to the scope. He could make out a truck . . . a group of spectators . . . a mound of sandbags . . . all sliding out of vision. Low bushes. Patches of gorse. 'They won't fire now. There's too much cover.'

'Scott . . . ' Julie's hand was over her heart. She was struggling to control her breathing. 'They are just . . . playing . . . with us. Who is there who hates us enough to do this to us?'

'Kraik.'

'You don't even know what he looks like.'

'I have seen his face. I would know it again if I saw it.'

'We are not going to see it, Scott. We are going to die. Or did that slip your mind!'

'*Calm down, Julie!* Nothing will happen yet. Not till . . . '

'Not till when?'

'Not till we are on the second lap.'

'Then what?' Her laugh was on the edge of hysteria.

'I don't know. But it gives us a little time.'

'Time for what?'

'*How should I know!*' He bawled at her. 'Time to say our prayers.'

She shrugged. 'OK. Someone had to say it.' She slumped over the gun cradle, her head in her hands.

The tank ran down a steep incline, the gun dipped. Out of the corner of his eye he saw the block swing up.

'*Julie!*'

She jerked her head clear as the hunk of machined steel cantilevered to within inches of the turret roof.

'*Are you insane?*' he raged at her. 'Get away from that thing before it takes your head off!'

White-faced she stared at him. 'What happened?'

'When the gun goes down . . . '

'The breech block swings up,' she whispered, her eyes screwed shut. 'I'd forgotten.' She picked up the metal box again and turned it round in her hands. 'If only I could wedge this under the chain . . . ' Her eyes turned to him.

'*That tiny box!*' It was some ten inches square and made of thin gauge steel. Just a boiling vessel. He turned away so that she wouldn't see his face. In her eyes there was a glimmer of something like hope. 'Try it. It might just work.'

'It *has* to work!' She placed the box on top of the breech block and stretched the chain over it.

His eyes went back to the scope. 'Another gully coming up! *Keep the chain taut!*'

They plunged down into the gully. The block heaved up . There was a screech of tearing metal.

'That *must* have broken it!' cried Julie. The box was crushed flat. Julie swept it on to the floor and wrenched at the chain. The links were cracked and bent but they still held. With a howl of frustration she savaged them against the edge of the block.

'*Stop that, Julie! It's futile!*'

'What isn't!' She clawed at the wires and electrode pads. 'If I'm going to die I'm not going to let some bug-eyed boffin watch me doing it.'

'Leave them alone! Let Snoeck think it's all going to plan.'

'And isn't it?' They were going to die. But nobody deserved to die like this. A moment of unimaginable agony. A moment that must feel like all eternity. And then extinction. The turret was turning again. Her eyes swept round it. A small gap was opening up between the gun cradle and the turret wall. 'Scott!' she shouted. 'I remember now. There's only one way to get through to the driver's hatch. When the gun is over the rear deck.'

'But it's moving too fast. *There isn't time!*'

'So we slow it down. Give me all the chain you can spare.'

Scott jumped down beside her. Julie grabbed a handful of chain and wrapped part of it round an ammunition bin. 'Now! We need something on the hull wall. *That relay unit!*'

'It's not strong enough.'

'There's nothing else. It will have to do.'

Scott ran the chain along the top of the box. '*It won't hold!* There's not enough clearance at the back!'

'Wedge it with this.' She threw the oilcan to him.

He hammered the links down and sprang back from a shower of sparks. 'It's slowing!' The gap behind the gun cradle widened. *Clunk!* The turret jerked round as the wall brackets bent under the strain.

She crouched down like a terrier at the mouth of a rabbit hole.

Clunk! The links in the chain were stretching, small fissures appearing in the tortured metal. 'Julie! *It won't hold!*' Mistime it and she would be caught in a huge meat grinder.

She darted through the gap dragging the spare chain after her. Scott shut his eyes. *Clunk! . . . Clunk!*

A sleeve tore away but she was through. 'Scott! *I made it!*'

Clunk! . . . Clunk! Clunk! A bracket snapped. The turret juddered round, picking up speed. Taking him further and further away from her.

'Come back, Julie! *For Christ's sake!*' If the chain held, it would pull her back through the gap. But there was no gap. It had closed again. The chain snaked tight as the slack was taken up. It hummed like an overstretched piano wire. He heard her scream. A loose length of chain whipped across the floor as the weakened links severed.

'*Julie!*' All he could hear was a low moaning.

'Julie! *Speak to me!* Are you hurt!'

Julie's eyes were screwed shut, her face contorted with pain, her voice just a croak. 'If you call . . . being slowly dismembered being hurt . . . I won't argue with you.'

He almost laughed his relief. 'Thank God. A split second longer—'

'We're wasting time. Tell me what to do.'

'Try . . . everything . . . foot brakes . . . '

'They . . . don't work . . . '

'What about the gears?'

'There aren't any. It's all automatic.'

'Try reverse.'

'I tried. No use.'

'There must be a master switch.'

'I have tried everything.' He could hear her gasps of breath. 'Nothing . . . nothing . . . nothing works.'

'Is there a driver's manual?'

'No. But there's an exhibition brochure. The demo is timed to end at 11.45. It's 11.30 already.'

'What are they firing at us?'

'First a high-powered rifle. Then the KRG rail gun. Man-portable . . . shoulder-fired . . . muzzle velocity . . . do you want to know what it can do?'

'*No!* Try the handbrake!'

The tank slewed and slowed.

'That's it! *Pull harder!*'

They were in a right-hand curve. Straightening out again. Lap two had begun. With a shudder the turret stopped rotating. Spindly pine trees gave way to low clumps of scrub, then open ground. The flagpoles came into view again . . . then buses and a camouflaged truck with antenna masts on the roof . . . then a long line of observers.

They were crawling along . . . sitting ducks . . . he had got it all wrong . . . a small movement behind the sandbags . . . was it imagination or could he see a helmeted head? Surely, it was shifting position . . . the eye was lowered to the sight . . . the stock nestled into the shoulder . . . the finger tightening . . .

He lashed out at the panel. No reaction. The buttons stared back at him like rows of mutinous eyes. In a paroxysm of rage and fear he drove his fist at the red buttons beside him.

A WHOOSH from outside. '*Smoke!*' he yelled as the canisters spiralled into the air, the particles falling like rain, billowing into white clouds.

57

DEADLINE

'*Hold your fire! Await further orders!*' Rohr lowered his binoculars and hurried to the command truck.

Kraik rose from the table. The DIDO bonds and the two gold half-hunter watches were beside him. 'I have just spoken to Muhlder and Wetzlar. They insisted on a reassurance that the transfers from the DIDO fund would be made at exactly twelve noon today. That is in seventeen minutes. I have given them that undertaking. There must be no slippage.'

Rohr trained his binoculars on the smoke. 'The problem is that there is very little wind and a belt of trees is stopping it from dispersing.' He held up his hand. 'Snoeck is reporting. He says that Rokeby and Dixon have immobilised the tank. They must have freed themselves.'

'They must be dealt with at once. The smoke will provide excellent cover for what has to be done.'

'There is some rough ground to cover. Let me take the motorbike. I can deal with those two and be back inside ten minutes. Drucker can take his shot. You will meet your deadline.'

'*No!* We cannot risk another hold up. You and I will take the command vehicle. Tell Crespel to explain that a radio wave caused the smoke dischargers to malfunction and that there will be a very short delay while we disconnect them. '

'Drucker will want fresh orders.'

'He is to wait until we are on our way back. When he judges that we are at least one hundred yards from the tank and he has a clear target, he is to fire.'

They lurched across the rough ground, bumping in and out of vehicle tracks, the acrid smell of the phosphorus in their nostrils. Rohr braked hard as they reached the edge of the smoke. He checked his watch. Fourteen minutes to the deadline. He jumped out, ripped the mirror off the wing and plunged into the smoke.

Scott could see the huge figure of Rohr lumbering towards them. In one hand he held a pistol, in the other something else that gave off a dull glimmer. He was moving with astonishing speed for such a big man.

Scott scrambled down to the turret floor. 'Julie, release the handbrake!' he shouted.

'The brake is off.'

'Then they've stopped us. We're stuck here!'

'Scott, listen! I've got my hatch open.'

'Can you get out!'

'I . . . think . . . so. Can you . . . get in here?'

'Not a chance.' The turret was stationary. The breech block sealed him in as effectively as a safe door.

Boot studs on the metalwork above him. Rohr was up on the rear deck.

'Julie, get out quietly and make a run for it. Try to get help.'

'What about you?'

'I'll be all right.'

'*Scott! You haven't a hope in hell!*'

'For God's sake, Julie! *Just do it!*'

The rasp of metal overhead. Rohr was using a tool on one of the hatch covers.

Where could he hide! *There was nowhere!* Nothing that would conceal him for more than a few seconds. The chain clanked against something. He wrapped it round his arm keeping a short length in his hand.

His eyes were on the two hatches. *The loader's hatch was opening.* He climbed up on to the commander's seat. His heart was going like a trip hammer. He could hear the man breathing, the stud of a boot scraping on steel as he changed position.

A mirror came through the hatch. 'Didn't expect that, did you?' Rohr chuckled.

Scott swung the chain. Missed. Rohr snatched off a shot. It pinged round the inside of the cupola. Above the rumble of the engine there was a shout from outside. *Julie!* In the mirror Scott saw Rohr's head snap round. The cover was slammed shut. A rattle as it was secured.

Scott threw himself against the hatch but it was hopeless. He was trapped in this iron igloo. He jammed his eyes to the scope. Julie was standing in front of the tank staring back at him through the swirling smoke. Suddenly she straightened as if she had seen what she expected. Her body braced itself, her lips parted, her eyes seemed enormous.

'*Run, Julie!*' Scott screamed. Rohr was moving towards her along the side of the turret. From the front he had a clear shot. Her face had taken on a deathly pallor as if she had already departed for another element. Only now did she turn to run. She hardly seemed to be moving, stalled like a sprinter who tears a hamstring at the start.

Rohr raised his arms. Took careful aim. Scott shut his eyes, flailing out, slashing blindly at the instruments round him. Rohr fired once. Twice. There was a thump of smoke mortars and a howl.

Rohr was writhing on the ground, his face scorched and blackened. A single canister had caught him from behind at point-blank range. He clutched at his injured shoulder as he attempted to get up but collapsed. Kraik gave him no more than a glance.

A patter of feet on the steel deck. Scott peered through the grimy rectangle of glass. Through the swirling smoke, the figure of a man in black, his tunic buttoned to his chin. A man with a pistol in his hand. The eyes in the snake-like head shuttling between the two hatches, a tongue flickering between the thin reptilian lips.
Scott waited hardly daring to breathe. *The clink of metal on metal above his head*. The hatch cover . . . rising . . . slowly . . . cautiously. With a

violent heave, Scott threw up the hatch knocking Kraik off balance and sending the pistol skidding across the deck.

Kraik staggered to his feet. His eyes darted to the gun and then back to the open hatch. Scott lunged for his foot . . . grabbed his ankle . . . got the chain round it . . . tugged with all his strength. Kraik fell with a choking gasp as the breath was driven from his body. Scott hauled himself out and flung himself on the man like a savage animal. Pinioning his arms, he hurled him headfirst down through the opening. He threw himself on the cover but Kraik had got his hands underneath. With a strength that seemed beyond anything human he held it open as, inch by inch, Scott forced it down, slowly squeezing out the daylight until only Kraik's eyes were visible, glowing like the fires of hell beneath the dark rim of the world.

58

HOME RUN

Scott caught up with Julie just before she broke clear of the smoke, which was thinning fast.

'How did you get out?' she gasped.

'Kraik turned up with a can-opener.' He pointed to the command truck. They ran to it. He took the wheel, gunned the engine and they leaped forward, churning up the track and leaving a cloud of dust behind them.

'When I heard those shots I thought Rohr had finished you off.'

'So why didn't you run for it instead of pulling that kamikaze stunt?'

'There was still a chance.'

'It was crazy. Rohr had you stone cold.'

'It saved your life, didn't it?'

'If you insist on arguing the point, I saved— '

'*Scott!*' she screamed. There was a brilliant flash from across the range.

They skidded to a halt under some trees and looked back at the tank. From the top of the turret a shaft of blinding white light blazed upwards turning day into dusk. Something whistled overhead and scythed through the firs sending branches crashing to the ground.

'*What the hell was that!*'

'One of the hatch covers.' A movement caught his eye. The unmistakable figure of Rohr limping out of the smoke. 'That guy has got some explaining to do. The same goes for Snoeck.'

341

Rohr had broken into a lumbering run.

'The police will have a job to catch him. In a few minutes he'll be deep in the woods.'

Two big helicopters were coming in low over the trees. Then the sound of a police siren.

Scott left his seat and went to the rear of the truck. The radio was crackling. On the TV screen, the German Chancellor was speaking in front of the Bundestag. There had been an attempted coup. It had failed. Wolfgang Muhlder had been arrested. Obersleutnant Jorg Wetzlar had shot himself. The combat groups were being rounded up by the army. Elections had been postponed but would be held at a date to be decided.

'I think we've been spotted," said Scott. 'Things could get very busy here in a few moments. On the table there were two gold watches, five bearer bonds and a notepad. He put them in his pocket. 'Let's leave the truck here and take the bike. Bring the map with you.'

Through the trees, they could see police cars with flashing lights racing up the main approach road.

They ran the bike down a ramp at the back of the truck.

'Where am I meant to go?' asked Julie.

'Behind me. *So hang on tight!*' They cut along a fire break and kept to the lanes until they had put ten miles between themselves and the ranges.

'Where are we going?'

'Switzerland. We can be there in time for dinner if you keep quiet and let me concentrate on driving this thing.'

59

EPILOGUE

Scott and Julie had a late dinner in Basel. They discussed their next move and disagreed about everything except the importance of agreeing about something. They telephoned the American Ambassador in Bern. He listened to what they had to say and it was close to midnight when they were sitting in his office.

His Excellency listened some more and telephoned Bradley Vaughan, the Secretary of the US Treasury.

'Brad, I have two visitors with me. Scott Rokeby, an American citizen, and Julie Dixon, who comes from Cornwall in the UK.'

'I know about them?'

'I'm impressed. But do you know that they can put their hands on rather more than a billion dollars of ready money?'

'It's our money. Treasury money.'

'They don't dispute that it's your money, Brad, but they feel that they deserve a fair reward for recovering American property. Judging by what they tell me, the opposition didn't always see their things their way.'

'They should transfer the funds at once. Then we will talk about a possible reward. I don't have the authority—'

'Brad! Stop horsing round! They are standing up . . . putting on their coats . . . '

'Two and a half per cent! That's generous. It's as far as we can go.'

'It won't wash, Brad. They insist on ten. Anything less and they will be out of that door!'

'*Five per cent!* I have already exceeded my authority. Have I got a deal?'

He had, but there were conditions. Scott and Julie had to sign a letter undertaking not to divulge the terms agreed. The American State Department, at Scott's insistence, contacted the French authorities who confirmed that Warren Rokeby's body would be released without further delay and flown back to the US.

After the transfer was completed, Scott was allowed to keep his father's watch. Zoltán Zaros's timepiece was given to his niece.

Within a few minutes of the KRG firing at the tank, the Belgian authorities designated the area as a crime scene. It was cordoned off and observers were not permitted to go there. According to an official communiqué, the KRG had proved a failure. The tank had only been partly destroyed. Most of the damage, it stated, was caused by the explosive reactive armour and not by the projectile.

The KRG never went into production. Detonard was put into administration. A clean sweep was made of the former senior management of KKK and IAC. The new directors were eminent men of undoubted integrity drawn from public life. The two companies were soon making substantial losses.

Ulrich Snoeck and several of the guards at KKK were given prison sentences. The prototype of the KRG disappeared and there were rumours that the Americans had it. All the drawings and the patent applications for the rail gun went missing. It was believed that Pieter Rohr had them. There were reported sightings of him in Brazil and Argentina but none were confirmed.

Fraser Outram were reluctant holders of the European pharmaceutical companies and Scott Rokeby had little difficulty in purchasing a controlling interest in them and taking them under his wing once more. Julie set up the David Dixon Foundation to continue the work of her brother into developing new sources of energy for the benefit of mankind.

Jorg Wetzlar left a recording of his last moments. Attempts were made to suppress it but it was leaked and a right-wing tabloid published a transcript:

A breath of wind is stirring the German tricolour. My eyes are fixed upon it as my lips close round the muzzle of my pistol. Somewhere, I can hear the sound of a river in spate, the dark river that bears all true sons of Germany to their Valhalla. Beyond its further shore there will be other sunsets, other dawns. One day the bands will play again, the flags will fly and the drums will beat to the rhythm of a million marching feet. One day—

Meet the Author, Charles Owen

I was born in 1935. When the Second World War broke out a few years later, I was shipped off from a Devonshire hill farm to Australia. My father, who had been wounded in the First World War, was then in MI5. He believed that the Germans might invade and probably wanted my mother, sister and myself out of the way.

In 1942, we were returning to England when we were torpedoed by a German submarine in the North Atlantic. The ship was sent to the bottom but after taking to the waves in a lifeboat we were all rescued by the US Navy.

Aged 12, I went to Eton. Top hats were being phased out. They were routinely maltreated until the boys wearing them looked like something out of the music hall. But if the school was slowly changing, the house where I boarded lacked all mod cons and was later pulled down.

In 1956, in my first term at Cambridge and despite the objections of the Foreign Office, I set off for Budapest in the hope of helping the Hungarians in their revolution against the Soviets. My involvement made little difference to the outcome of that tragic affair but the experience provided the inspiration for *The Dido Decrypt.*

I did my National Service with a cavalry regiment in Germany. Our job was to discourage the Soviet forces from crossing the Rhine. As a tank commander, it was wise to keep well in with your driver. If he was cross with you, he would give you a bumpy ride that would loosen every tooth in your head.

Battlefield simulation exercises could be hazardous. I remember a particular incident. A squadron commander, a veteran of WW2, ordered tank commanders to close their hatches and then sprayed the Centurion tanks with machine-gun fire. The tanks were travelling at top speed but one of the troop leaders had left the breech of his 20-pounder gun open. A bullet came straight down the muzzle and buzzed round the inside of the turret like a demented hornet. It was very fortunate that there were no casualties.

A spell in stock-broking and merchant banking persuaded me that I was better at making things than making money and there followed many productive years as the export director of an engineering company. We were contractors to the Ministry of Defence and there was a lot of travelling to the Middle East. The work was absorbing, exacting and, sometimes, frightening.

In 2000, for the *Daily Telegraph*, I began writing up the stories of the surviving men and women who had been awarded the Victoria Cross or the George Cross. That led to writing the obituaries of those who had had adventurous and distinguished careers in the British Army. To date, several hundred of these can be read on the internet.

In the course of reading private papers and unpublished memoirs that have passed through my hands, I became fascinated by the exciting and often perilous careers of servicemen and women who were involved in clandestine warfare: spies and counter-spies, secret agents and members of the Special Operations Executive who were parachuted into enemy-occupied countries to train and arm the Resistance. A book relating the fictional exploits of a captain in the Intelligence Corps will be published next year.

Acknowledgements

My foremost debt is to Pierre, my brother-in-law, who helped with every aspect of this book. I drew unsparingly on his knowledge, guidance and seemingly limitless patience and I am enormously grateful.

Rosie heroically volunteered to give the manuscript a thorough vetting. My son, James, a successful author, has many demands on his time but was never too busy to come to my rescue with sound advice.

Georgie and Edward kept the home fires burning – no easy task in winter on the Lancashire-Cumbria border – and provided invaluable moral and logistical support.